Wastin

Wasting Time

Sarah Harris

FOURTH ESTATE • *London*

First published in Great Britain in 1998 by
Fourth Estate Limited
6 Salem Road
London W2 4BU

1 3 5 7 9 10 8 6 4 2

A catalogue record for this book is available from
the British Library.

ISBN 1–85702–786–8

Typeset in Sabon by
Avon Dataset Ltd, Bidford on Avon B50 4JH

Printed and bound in Great Britain by
Biddles Ltd, Guildford and King's Lynn

For David

With thanks to Clare Roberts, Katie Owen, Kate Goodhart
and Joanna Prior

Chapter One

Someone had been shot, that much was certain. Ellen recalled the shooting, the screaming crowd of black faces. Her soup had boiled over, creaming the hob as the announcement came. It had panicked her; she had wiped up the mess, the pieces of mushroom, and in the panic she hadn't listened out for his name, the name of the dead African, shot that Thursday. Oh, Ellen had underlined it all right, underlined the man's name in *The Economist* the following day along with the European Union's agricultural spokesman, Franz Fischler, the motor-racing champion Damon Hill, and Kakharman Khozhamberdi, the leader of the Xinjiang separatist movement in China. But then, Ellen Abrahams had to remember so many names. It was too much to expect her to think of every black African premier as they died, one after the other, on the television.

Low, dull sounds garbled their way from the adjacent office through to the room where Ellen sat, her skirt hugging her like clingfilm, her low-cut jacket sticking to her cleavage. Leaving the African answer blank, Ellen continued her test, writing the names Joao Baptista de Matos, Rerngchai Marakanond, and Joacham Bitterlich, as sheer tights pasted, sweatily, to her legs. She liked writing the long names, littered with consonants, on to the test form, the names she remembered from her folder, which was fat with white paper inside her bag. They had all been written down and filed away in the folder and in her memory, where fact upon fact dried with the ink and the passing of time.

Ellen Abrahams had facts at her fingertips: information on geo-political, domestic and general events; lists of names and places and presidents; columns of coups and capitals and constituencies; tables of world trouble spots, gross national products and temperatures. She knew everything, or thought she did, that sunny afternoon in April 1996, as bright colours bled through the window, and an Irish personnel officer, Aileen Knowles, interrupted the test to ask if Ellen was ready to be interviewed for the *FastNews* producer's job.

She led Ellen out of the white cell and into the noise of the office next door. They walked along, passing door after identical grey door, talking small. The personnel officer soothed the cold corridors with her soft Dublin accent, while Ellen's voice exploded along with comments about the heatwave and the beef scare.

'This place is such a maze. I always get lost,' said Aileen, while Ellen's stomach jumped to the tune of some new contraceptives, swallowed that morning along with half a bottle of beer and some wet strands of chicken breast.

Three men in suits faced Ellen. To the left of the panel sat Elliot Banding, *FastNews* deputy editor, long and thin, darting a little tongue out at intervals to lick the tight mouth, which sneered. To the right of Elliot sat Simon Nuttall – the other deputy editor – his face fixed like a runner's before the firing of the starting gun. He was a man whose career had frozen over close to his thirty-fifth birthday, despite the drip-drip of ambition and the dried-up, demonic wife who had given him two demanding daughters, his first job in television and a recurring stomach ulcer. Both men – Nuttall and Banding – knew that Ellen's interview was a vehicle for their competition and that at least one of them would be weeded out by the process.

The editor of *FastNews*, Dan Berkovsky, was sitting one moment, and standing the next, scratching his bottom, as well as the floating strands of hair thrown around his head, as Ellen sat opposite him, mentally chanting the name of the Chief Secretary to the Treasury in a kind of personal mantra. He stared at Ellen's breasts as she answered Aileen's first question about upward career paths. Elliot's tongue darted out wetly in preparation for his own set of questions, which began with one on the proposed timetable for rail privatisation.

Berkovsky scratched the pits of his arms and watched the girl as she answered Elliot's questions as if reciting a recipe. He remembered her curriculum vitae, which had all the right ingredients: a decent girls' public school; an Oxbridge degree; experience with *FastNews*' main television competitor, *Direct*

Live. And he felt something like disappointment pulling at the roots of his teeth. Dan Berkovsky wanted someone common. He wanted a producer with the grit of a working- or lower-middle-class background: someone who would have come to the interview unarmed and disarming, without a degree, a designer suit, or a fashionable allergy to dairy products.

He wanted someone informed and worldly. This producer would know where the Kurile Islands were, or where Tony Blair spent his summer holidays. She would know when and why the Labour Party chose Michael Foot as its leader, and not Denis Healey. He would understand the exchange rate mechanism and the pattern of earthquakes; the inner workings of the IRA and the former Soviet *nomenklatura.* This producer would be able to talk to Foreign Office officials and fishermen; council leaders and dinner ladies; scientists and secretaries. This producer would have creative chromosomes and would know, instinctively, how to direct the camera; how to shoot pictures for the small screen. This one would trim landscapes to fit inside the television; this one would chop up action, filmically. This one would never cross the line between funny and frivolous. This producer would never, ever betray the magic circle of television, and tell of its trickery.

This mythical producer would have legs that travelled for miles, or bones carved perfectly inside spotless complexions. She would be unusually blonde or he would be fair, because Berkovsky liked to be surrounded by golden trophies, pouring yellowing white sunlight everywhere, like wet labradors or champagne. After all, television was a glamorous business.

But there, in front of him, was Ellen Abrahams. She looked as if someone had manufactured her, according to the instructions, for a TV production line. Stamped *Ordinary*, she came complete with requisite symmetrical face, ultra-bright teeth, and real, short hair which, with frequent brushing, can appear almost straight. There was the regulation public-schoolgirl puppy fat; the trademark healthy skin and (as is standard on the brunette model, these days) matt-red lipstick, painted on to perfection.

Berkovsky looked at Ellen's familiar face, thinking of the thousands of girls he had known, sliced from the same schools and sent to him as they reached maturity, to impress him, and men like him, in positions of influence. He looked at her mouth, as it spilled predictable answers, and he was sick and tired of listening to her speak, and to thousands of women like her.

'Why do you want to work on *FastNews*?' asked Aileen.

'I like the variety,' said Ellen, recalling one programme where they had sandwiched an item on Why People Aren't Going to Musicals Any More in between films about Zaire and Bosnia. Flitting about like that must be fun, she thought. One moment theatre and the next, war.

'What would you do if Boris Yeltsin died?' asked Simon Nuttall, who spoke Russian fluently and as often as he could.

'Well, an obit, definitely. And then six minutes on his successors. A discussion after that. Galina Staravoitova down the line from Moscow,' said Ellen, as Simon glanced over at Dan, with affection.

'Do you think *FastNews* should do anything on Wimbledon this year?' asked Elliot Banding, aware that Simon had the advantage point.

'Racquets getting smaller. Balls getting bigger. Should that be the case? I'd interview Greg Rusedski,' said Ellen, as Elliot glanced over at Dan, with envy.

Aileen was glad that she had never heard of Galina Staravoitova or Greg Rusedski. But then she had time to read tabloid newspapers as well as for the odd facial at her local, sneering salon. And she was the only one present drinking coffee, sipping with pleasure, while everyone else thirsted for something stronger, like alcohol, or appreciation.

'If Yasser Arafat was shot down in a plane tonight, Stephen Dorrell resigned from the Cabinet and the European Union passed a motion forcing Britain to accept a single currency, what would be your running order for *FastNews*?'

Ellen found opinion difficult now. Having mastered the interview process, she was aware that there was no such thing as a right answer; just a wrong way of answering the question. 'Yasser Arafat first.'

'Why?' asked Nuttall.

'I don't think that the Prime Minister would agree with you there,' said Berkovsky. 'Anyway, we do too much on the Middle East,' he said dismissively. 'People aren't interested.'

'Well, they're a hell of a lot more interested in war than in Brussels or Westminster. We put too much store by what happens in the House of Commons. We should be covering events in the real world instead,' Ellen said, with dimly remembered feeling.

Dan Berkovsky felt excited. He scratched his right hip as Simon Nuttall and Elliot Banding exchanged schoolboy smiles. Ellen Abrahams, in her starter for ten, had answered the bonus question correctly, and Aileen, who sensed the mood change, half expected the wall to open up, delivering Ellen a bow-wrapped Ford Fiesta, complete with emergency airbag and interior locking facilities.

'We're going to be running a series called "Women In Power, Women of Achievement", Ellen,' Dan said, leaning forward in his chair. 'Each producer will pick one woman to profile. An inspirational woman, one who has perhaps touched their lives. A woman who has changed the way they think, perhaps. These films will be important, partly because for once the producer will have the luxury of time; I'll expect them to be made over a long period. But principally because I'm going to choose the best one – the one with the most guts, the most passion – to enter for the TV Prime Awards. And, as you know, win that and next time around *you'll* be interviewing *me.*'

He smiled. She smiled. (They always spoke of passion.)

'So, which woman would *you* choose?'

She was off-target, weight-wise today. Ellen tended to gain weight with nerves, boredom, hunger, tragedy, happiness, and the daily grind of living. She tended to lose weight with life, happiness, tragedy, hunger, apathy and nervous energy. She was fat or thin depending on the day, the year, or the career stage, the diet, the diuretics, the number of calories consumed, the scales, the puking or the lying. Today she was heavy in her smart, maroon outfit, looking for room to spread inside the suit, bought expensively in a designer showroom, as a shop assistant complimented her, on a commission basis only, and persuaded her to buy thin, spiky shoes that were biting spitefully into her feet.

'It would have to be the MP, Lou Matherbay,' she said.

The trouble was that Ellen didn't admire people any more. She had left all that behind with pop stars, posters, and pubescence. Did they expect her to hang on to all that starry-eyed stuff, knowing them – the politicians and the serious celebrities – as she did? Did they want her to talk about these people with reverence, or affection? If anything, Lou Matherbay irritated Ellen, banging on as she did, even at her age, about 'putting the ideas back into political life'. The name had come to Ellen out of the many in her mind, and in newspaper print. Frankly, it was the only appropriate answer, given that, just a month ago, Lou Matherbay had crossed the floor of the House, to join the Pluralist Party.

Matherbay hadn't made the move to find a safer seat. (With the Pluralists as the minority, third party, there was no such thing as a safe seat, only the cushioned constituency pews of rural areas.) She hadn't made the move to raise her profile. (Lou had one of the most recognisable faces in the House.) So, naturally, there had been talk, taking up space in newspaper comment pages and political TV discussion shows (like *FastNews*) that, with a Pluralist leadership contest just six months away, Lou might just have joined the party, in order, one day soon, to lead it.

For that reason, the move had been newsworthy. Lou Matherbay, now the grande dame of mavericks in British politics, had once been a leader among women. 'Women in lipstick unite,' she had said, more than a decade ago. 'Your playground has conspired against you.' But it wasn't simply her feminism, her beauty, or her trail-blazing style. Matherbay had once taken all of the world's treasured institutions (Royalty and Democracy) holding them up to the light. 'Look,' she had said. 'Smash the fakes.'

'Lou Matherbay. Would-be Pluralist leader,' said Ellen.

'Oh *yes*,' said Dan, breathing out. 'Very inspired. Might breathe new life into the Pluralists. She's always been a role model for young women. A fighter. Televisual. But only if she *does* declare herself. Otherwise, there'd always be the "why bother" factor.'

'Oh, she'll declare herself all right,' said Ellen.

She heard a familiar victory then, a strange, silent applause from the four facing her, and realised that they were applauding not her answer, but her ability, in an uncertain world, to be certain.

Elliot Banding's bleeper went off. 'Sorry,' he said. 'Shall I read this outside?' he asked Berkovsky, flicking his fingers towards the door.

'No, give Ellen an idea of what it's really like working for *FastNews*,' said Dan, grinning to one side of his mouth. 'An idea of the long hours, the low pay, the ungrateful bosses . . .'

Simon Nuttall leaned back in his chair, peering at Banding's bleeper. 'Damn, shooting in Birmingham. I'd better go, hadn't I, Dan?'

'What would you do during a shooting, Ellen?' asked Berkovsky, ignoring Nuttall.

'Oh, I don't know. Duck, perhaps?' she said, with cynicism, to Aileen's smile, and Dan's smirk.

'Get a crew off to Birmingham, Elliot. Make sure there're at least two good producers out there. We'll try and do something down here, something vox-poppy. Mind you, need some Birmingham voices. And a piece on the gun laws. A couple of experts, some psychologists. OK, Elliot. You'd better go.' Nuttall was confused. Did sending Elliot out there mean he was unfashionable or a useful accessory here, with Berkovsky? Twisting the chunky ring on his finger, Simon decided to sulk.

Meanwhile, Elliot was almost wetting his underpants at the door. He found news events erotic; substitutes for frightening, sexual women. 'Let me know as soon as you can how many dead there are,' Berkovsky told him, and Banding longed to say: 'Roger, boss. Will report back as soon as I can.'

As for Ellen, she was as good as employed, even offering to help out in their emergency. 'I was *Direct Live*'s producer on the ground for the Brighton shooting, so I have lots of good contacts,' she said. But they let her go, 'for now'.

When she was out of sight of the *FastNews* building, Ellen went shopping. She placed on the newsagent's counter a Mars bar, a Caramac, a packet of low-fat cheese and onion crisps, a bag of Maltesers and a Twix. She said to the sour-eyed newsagent: 'I'm babysitting tonight, so this should keep them quiet.' And the woman, whose own weakness was for dry white wine, smiled politely and thought of her twenty-two inch waist. Ellen thought, walking to the tube: *I'd beat her in the O level department, anyway.*

Miriam Abrahams had spent her husband's hardware fortune on Ellen's exclusive, English education. As a result, Ellen had ten O levels (grade A); three A levels (grade A); and a BA from Cambridge, to which she had later added, at the cost of ten pounds, a master's degree. Ellen had an impressive curriculum vitae which listed modern American literature and square dancing among her pursuits. (Although she had never danced a square in her life, she made sure she knew enough of the steps to get by in an interview.) Now, however, she knew that a curriculum vitae was of little use. What really mattered, of course, was *who one knew*. But luckily for Ellen Abrahams, she knew everyone.

On the tube home, she was the only passenger eating. Ellen liked the anonymity of low, closed carriages. She was the only one ripping open the Maltesers and scooping them into her mouth at Finchley Road; unwrapping the Caramac and the Twix and munching them between Wembley Park and Preston Road. She was the only one pulling apart a bag of crisps as the tube pulled up at Northwick Park. By the time Ellen arrived at Harrow-on-the-Hill, she felt sick to the stomach. But at least she had eaten dinner.

She passed Ranjit Singh's newsagent on the way home and went inside to brag a little and to buy an *Evening Standard*. Mrs Singh stood behind the counter, her sari bandaged around her folds of fat, where a waist once was. Ellen wished that it was a Sunday, and that Ranjit was there to impress. Each Sunday, Ellen walked to Ranjit Singh's shop to buy a toppling tower of newsprint and to share, if just for a moment, her achievements and a slice of that day's news.

'Ah, it is the one,' he would say to Ellen, as she walked in, hiding her pyjamas under her long black coat. 'It is the one who buys *all* the papers,' he would tell his other customers or, if the shop was empty, his own four walls. 'You want them all this Sunday, do you?' he would ask, winking badly.

'Yes please, Ranjit,' Ellen would say.

'You even want the *People* and the *News of the World*?'

'Yes, Ranjit.'

'And the *Observer* and the *Sunday Telegraph*?'

'Yes please.'

'Not these two? The *Sunday Express* and the *Mail on Sunday*?'

'Absolutely.'

'She does!' he would say, with pride, to anyone who might be able to hear his words. 'She wants them all! So clever! Such a success! Such an educated girl.'

Last Sunday, Ranjit had pointed to an article about failed small businesses, saying: 'Look at this. Look at this. It is terrible. Your people and my people, we come over here, we work very hard, we make something of ourselves. These people,' he had said, pointing at the door, 'they do not understand what is going on in the world. They do not want to find out.' Ellen had nodded, squeezing the bulk of paper into a striped sheath of a bag and ignoring the tear at the corner, as the *Sunday Times* made itself comfortable. But she had to admit that, as a Jewish girl, she felt terribly British.

Ellen walked home to her closed, sectioned-off world, all made safe by the power of positive thought and newly-installed burglar alarms. She lived out her life in a very small section of London's *A–Z*. She mapped out her days in secure terrain. Life happened in the home, because the video recorder was set well in advance and she had her dishwasher, her friends and a portable TV.

Home was a whole house, bought at a snip for £98,000, and within walking distance of Harrow-on-the-Hill tube station. It had a tiny garden, plus swing. Nobody else lived there, apart from Ellen. There were three bedrooms upstairs, an updated kitchen with space for another washing machine, a bathroom with low-level flush WC and an entrance hall with terracotta flooring. It had its own separate garage for her Fiat Uno, jutting out on to the driveway, which wasn't quite sweeping (perhaps just swept, joked the estate agent, Jeffrey Bell of Top Estates Limited, who now, incidentally, was Ellen's fiancé).

Wiping her stereo clean of dust, Ellen switched it on. She had an uncanny knack of hitting the top news headline whenever she turned on the radio. Sometimes, Ellen felt as if it was her only regular piece of good fortune. 'Two people have been shot dead and twelve injured,' sang the clear tones of Josh Berry, the successful twenty-six-year-old who had been to all the right places, 'after a man ran around a Birmingham shopping arcade

9

today, shooting at random.' Berry's voice drifted around the house as Ellen returned a pink-backed book from the red section of her bookshelf to the pink section, so that she would feel more comfortable.

'Our reporter, Fiona Stade, is live at the Pleasure Shopping Centre in Birmingham now. Fiona, how are people reacting there?'

'I heard shooting and then I saw this man running. It was terrible. I hid behind the cold meats section in the supermarket. I had been buying our tea,' said a woman in the radio report, thick with a Birmingham accent.

'Isn't it awful? This place has always been so safe and nice.'

'I think I know someone who's been shot. Just now. I think it was . . .'

'Great vox-pops,' thought Ellen, polishing her extractor fan.

She walked around the house, rotating objects to right angles. Jeffrey was fine as fiancés went, particularly as he didn't live with Ellen, but he had a habit of moving things around. Finding some brown hairs in the bath, she showered them through the plug hole.

She was always cleaning but always having to clean. Dust collected in cupboards, behind her books, or on her kitchen counter. Dirt lined Ellen's shelves. If Jeffrey stayed the night, he would shave at her spotless sinks. And he would sit on her plumped-up cushions, lose her remote control, use her lime-green pot, which was for display purposes only, and put it back next to the yellow-lined crockery. *Is it so much to ask?* thought Ellen, emptying the ever-full dishwasher. *That her house should look like those* Through the Keyhole *on TV.*

Chapter Two

Myra Felt saved everything, from tin cans to whales. She collected campaigns, and banners, and badges and rosettes. She found causes that had been lost for years. She founded pressure groups and letter-writing meetings, sub-policy groups and debating societies. If there was a corner, she would fight it; if there was an opinion, she would divide it; and if there was a motion, she would second it. In short, she found ends indiscriminately, and marched to them, all the time eating organic food and smoking Cartier cigarettes.

But Myra was now twenty-six, and in need of an income to keep her in voguish clothes, thick, bitty orange juice and tall bottles of virgin olive oil stuffed with leaves. If she didn't stop beating on about the poor or the homeless, she would be joining them, because conversations about the Rowntree Trust and incomes policy would not buy her underwear or political magazines, old radios from Camden market, or pewter teasets from Portobello Road.

So she sat, like a package, inside the Pluralist Party's whips' office, which was itself a bigger package, inside the House of Commons. A month ago, before she saw the job advert for a parliamentary press officer for Britain's third party, she might have refused blood from a Pluralist donor, checking the label for impurities. But that had been before Lou Matherbay had become a Pluralist.

For Myra Felt, the idea that Matherbay had thrown in her lot with the Pluralist Party was enough to make the Commons' third party irresistible. When Myra had seen the Pluralists' advert, seeking a press officer, it had been as if Lou herself was inviting Myra to take part in her life, personally and politically. So now she sat, waiting to be interviewed and in need of nicotine as well as (of course) this position.

A fax machine emptied its fill of memos on to Myra's right

shoulder, as she fiddled with a drying wart on a long, skinny finger. Someone called Sara Cinnamon sat at another desk, drinking red wine from a frosted glass and flicking through *Hansard*. The leaping and whooping sounds of young men drifted down from the room upstairs. Myra tried to sink into the sofa to look comfortable and in place as she picked at her naturally blonde hair, bought a week ago from the chemists – *Naturally Blonde* – along with half-a-dozen flapjacks and some unperfumed soap.

But Myra did not blend into backgrounds. She stuck out, all over the place, with bones everywhere, colliding in a rush to point through the thin material of her clothes. Hers was a living, breathing, energetic face, with dirty, ropey, long curls bungee-jumping around it, and eyes that cracked like car windows, in grey and in blue. Those features might have been ugly in another time, and another place, but stolen for Myra's face, they were joyful and alive.

It was hard work keeping up with Myra's face as it stretched about, like Lycra, as she thought. And as she was led into the interview room, Myra was vaguely aware of being surrounded by brown trousers taken in at the flares; rainbow-coloured ties loosely knotted at the neck; pastel pink and blue shirts, striped pale. She felt like an unwelcome guest at some seventies glam-rock reunion. Whoever coloured the politicians beautiful during the 1980s hadn't thought to make over the Pluralist Party.

'Sixteen,' she said finally. 'No, fifteen,' said the Treasury spokesman, smugly. 'I'm afraid we only have fifteen MPs here. But if you're offering us another . . .?' And Myra smiled, as if she was amused. But she was thinking: Why place so much emphasis on *fact*?

'So, with what area of Pluralist policy do you disagree?' asked Raymond Hines, the party's deputy leader, who believed that voting was best left to those who had studied comparative political institutions at degree level. '*Vox populi est vox diaboli*,' he had said last week, commenting on Lou Matherbay's change of political allegiance.

'I'm not sure we *need* Matherbay's support,' he had said. 'We can't take people into this party on the basis of *popularity*.'

'The voice of the people might be diabolical, but it's almost always right,' Billy Todd had said later to Larry Beat in the tea-room. 'We need Red Lou. She adds a bit of colour to the party, some shine.'

'She adds that fading film-star look, I'll give you that,' laughed Beat.

'Although I'm not sure Hines'll have noticed *what* Lou looks like. That man spends far too much of his time on constitutional papers. I mean, he's just worried that Lou may stand against him. And I can tell you Billy, if Lou *does,* I for one won't be on Hines's leadership campaign team. Raymond's starting to forget the reason he's in politics.'

Billy Todd had wiped the whisky from his adolescent moustache. 'Yes – to get us elected, goddammit,' he had said.

Myra, who would have found it more difficult to talk about those areas of Pluralist policy with which she agreed, glanced at her heroine – Lou Matherbay – for support, and threw up the E word. The room fragmented at that: the dreaded 'Europe'. MPs shifted their seats around, leaning left or right, and creating blocs of chairs. 'I didn't know we *had* a policy on Europe,' said Billy Todd, his accent all educated Edinburgh.

Outside this tiny room, Myra would have talked on, about Europe, in ways she had only heard from Matherbay. She would have discussed enlargement, expansively. She would have talked about tearing down boundaries, to create a brotherhood of man. She would have argued against a more assertive European Union, aggressively. But this was the House of Commons, and not some pub annexe, where she could smoke urgently, all the time bending coasters and spouting forth, while drinking neat vodka. This was a dirty, airless room in the House of Commons, oppressive with history and dry humour.

'Which personalities would you promote, particularly, in the party?' asked Larry Beat. 'Would it be Ray Hines or Lou or . . . ?'

'All of you,' said Myra. 'From what I've seen, I think you all have really strong personalities.'

Lou Matherbay laughed, loudly, from the back of the room, as Myra allowed herself a proper look at the politician and she was amazed to see her in full focus, as if she was Lou Matherbay's elder sister, and not Lou herself. Fame had played its tricks on this well-known woman's face, projecting the cheekbones and softening the orange nest of hair. The formerly beautiful face which, when introduced to politics, had been an adolescent boy's dream – all soft skin stretched around bones – now shrank back into a blanket of fine lines, as if in hiding from all the attention. Myra was faint at the thought of Matherbay's presence at her own interrogation.

Once Myra's eyes adjusted to the sight of Matherbay, however, the hollow cheeks and the startling, red hair gained prominence over the crushed skin. As she answered a question about Westminster's lobby system, Myra began to feel more comfortable in her presence. Because Lou smiled at Myra, and with her whole face.

Fortunately, the red-wine woman – Sara Cinnamon – interrupted her interview. Myra had begun to get carried away, using the word *member* far too often. But she had done well in disguising her true, subversive nature. She had not mentioned her membership of the Anarchy Alliance, Liberty, Greenpeace, the Anti-Gun lobby and the Socialist Workers Party. Although she was one of life's joiners, and forever taking out new credit cards, she did not like her membership, or her allegiance, to be taken for granted. She had, during one confusing period, sabotaged a hunt one week and taken part in one the next. But then Myra Felt's fixations could not be confused with any firmly held beliefs. She was passionate about everything, from bagel slicers to world peace.

'Yes?' Larry Beat had asked, as Sara had opened the door, then had closed it to fit just her head. 'Sorry to bother everyone,' she had said, in a happy sing-song voice. 'But there's been a shooting in Birmingham. Everyone's jumping up and down, and it's very exciting.'

'Thank you, Sara,' said the Agricultural Affairs spokesman. 'One last question, however. What do you think, Myra, you can do for me?'

'Oh, so much,' she said, at the edge of her seat. 'You should be on *Farming Today* every day, talking about the environment and animals and intensive farming methods.'

'Well, that just about covers everything,' said Lou, ambiguously, smiling over Myra's head.

*

The House of Commons was more familiar to her now that she was almost a Pluralist, and part of a mainstream political party. When Myra had entered the Palace of Westminster, she had felt very anti-establishment. But now, as she left the building, all Myra could see were MPs, so important an hour or so ago, littering the corridors like schoolboys bored after morning assembly. Former Cabinet Ministers laughed on the telephone. Well-known television commentators queued up for the chance to chat with some better-known MPs. Taking the wrong turning, Myra found Tony Benn at the photocopier and watched enthralled, for several minutes, as he pressed the same button over and over again, choking up sheet after sheet of paper. Pregnant with the expectant pride of new membership, Myra's exit was taller, straighter-backed, more British than her entrance.

After her interview, Myra went shopping. She was always buying things: rose-coloured foot balm; peppermint back brush; sun-dried tomatoes; *French For Beginners*; Burke's *Reflections on the Revolutions in France* in its original print; *How to Stop Shopping*; products that bulged out of her toilet cabinet, her bookshelf, or that hid on the floor, underneath a more immediate passion.

However, despite Myra's purchasing power, she did not seem to end up owning anything. There was no sign of a mortgage for a place she could call her own. There was never a hint of a pension or a car. Yet she had built up at home a mountain of products which said something pertinent about her preferences. There was that shampoo, whose cover girl stroked her hair in a stream. There was the Cartier cigarette habit; the brown worm fibre cereal; the chocolate-smelling cocoa butter. Unwittingly, Myra had spent her money on developing safe, consumer boundaries, to protect her in a city where people recognised themselves in others, not with smiles or casual conversation, but through the comparison of their consumer durables.

Her own consumer durables stood the test of comparison very well. Aside, obviously, from Marion, friends copied her. She found her dresses turning up in their wardrobes. In flea markets, they would wait for her opinion before buying. Once, she had worn purple lipstick and had found that became quite the thing. She used stained-glass windows as tea-trays where, for others, they were strictly ornamental.

She had tried so hard to adopt eccentricities, they were beginning to grow into characteristics. The almost religious marching for political causes, the certainly sleazy sit-ins – they would be ludicrous in anybody else's life, but for Myra, who tried everything once, they fitted perfectly alongside the antique gramophone and the red feather boa.

'Can I try this on?' she asked a shop assistant in a sportswear shop, holding up a violet leotard. 'Yes, if you keep your knickers on,' said the assistant. All this and valuable relationship advice too, thought Myra, smiling, as she disappeared into a changing-room-cum-discotheque, complete with flashing lights, clothes rails, and nearly-naked dancing women.

She looked at herself in every mirrored direction, finding only that the angle did not exist to flatter her in a leotard. Her breasts near inverted at the shock of wearing sports gear. Her legs knocked at the knees, funny bones laughing at her reflection. She was a leftover attraction from vaudeville comedy. Myra changed back into her loose, patterned skirt and lacy, doll-sized top. 'I wish,' she thought, looking enviously at a woman in the corner, laced through with muscles, and tried to remember her advantages. That she might not look good in a gym but she would in a flowered, poppied field with the light shining just so.

The more, let's say, rural Members of Parliament were sitting with Sara Cinnamon, discussing the day's candidates for the job of parliamentary press officer for the Pluralist Party. Such a position could not be filled by anybody. It could be filled comfortably by that man in the suit, John Hockton-Gray, with a good background, but nobody could remember the man, merely the suit.

Ray Hines wanted Timothy Crockton, the one who had read his paper on the Single Transferrable Vote and how to get it transferred, but Ray knew that he did not win battles of this nature – not when it boiled down to personality. Billy Todd liked Julia Macdonald, because of the legs, covered in tartan tights; and the politics, dripping with Scottish nationalism. But the conversation did not stay long at Julia Macdonald, or Timothy

Crockton or John Hockton-Gray. It fluttered about, landing prettily on Myra Felt every so often, whom none of them preferred. Sara said that there was no agreement on any of the candidates, apart from Myra Felt. And Billy Todd returned, sulkily, to his pet topic of Julia. Ray Hines argued that he was scared of Ms Macdonald and Larry Beat agreed about her ferocity, suggesting that it might not go down well with the punters in the press corps. And back the conversation would go, to 'dizzy' Myra Felt, brought there neatly by Sara Cinammon. And when it came time for Larry Beat to be at a strategy meeting, for Ray Hines to be in the Chamber, for Billy Todd to be at a restaurant, and for Lou Matherbay to be in a television studio, the conversation concluded with the appointment of Myra Felt, whom none, apart from the unelected member present, preferred.

'Och, it's a shame about young Julia,' said Billy Todd, on his way out.

'You just liked those legs,' Larry Beat said.

'I must say, I didn't notice any legs,' said Ray Hines, creasing his eyebrows.

'And *that*, my boy, is why you *may* not win the leadership,' said Billy Todd, who wanted to be one of the people.

How terrible thought Myra, sitting at home watching *Direct Live*'s coverage of the shooting. *How completely terrible.* It was showing bloodied bodies, lying on the streets, some covered up, some not. Women were in tears, talking on the television about their daily routines, shot to bits by this man, Graeme Somebody, who was being cared for by the community.

Myra had been in Birmingham just last month, for a meeting of the Anti-Vivisection Society. She had shopped at the Pleasure Centre; smoked into a cup of coffee at the Pleasure Dome; handed out leaflets about cruelty against animals at the centre's statue of a smiling salesman.

The telephone rang, yet again, and Myra wondered if it might be the branch head of her local anti-gun lobby. She had been trying to shrug off that particular cause for some time now, as it seemed to attract only young men who shopped at special shops for thick, dark blue jeans, turned up at the ankle. Like the trainers that they wore, these men looked and smelled as if they had been locked up for too long inside dark cupboards. She picked up the receiver, which was sticky with soup stock.

'Myra Felt?'

'Yes?' said Myra, hoping it was one of the dark, sneering men from the Socialist Workers Party, who talked in loud voices about society coming together.

'Larry Beat speaking. We met today. You came to the interview for a parliamentary press officer?'

'Yes?'

'Well, we'd very much like to offer you the job, if you'd still like to take it.'

Yes, oh yes. As close to ecstacy as anyone like Myra Felt could possibly be, with anyone like Larry Beat MP.

Chapter Three .

Susan Lyttle sat on the Southport–London coach, reading Balzac's *Eugenie Grandet*, as *Sleepless in Seattle* came down at her from one of the tiny televisions hooked from the ceiling like life-support machines. If the coach arrived on schedule at Victoria Station, she would be several hours too early for her interview. Then Aunt Cyn would win ten pounds from Aunt Jane, in one of several of their bets about Susan's trip to London.

'I bet it will rain,' Aunt Jane had said that morning, as Susan had tried on short-sleeved shirts. 'I bet you a fiver it won't,' Aunt Cyn had said. 'I don't think this Mr Matlock chap will take to Susan,' she had said. 'Oh, of course he will,' Aunt Jane had replied. 'Bet you twenty,' said the other aunt, holding out a precisely manicured hand.

Aunt Cyn liked a bet and saw no reason why her niece's journey through life should be less interesting than Aintree during the Grand National. 'My life's over,' she would say. 'Why won't you let me take a gamble on yours?'

Through the coach window, London came in, shaped like picture postcards: of red buses, and tall, proud townhouses, glowing Nash cream, with different-coloured people pressing together on the streets. Susan saw lovers everywhere, and felt very neat, and very English, in an EM Forster kind of way.

She could have sat on that coach much longer, leafing through London, without commitment. But the coach groaned to its stop, and the other passengers collected their bags from the shelves above them, and left without so much as a backward glance. Susan felt vaguely betrayed, because she had thought, impossibly, that they were in this together.

Her excuse to be in the capital fell apart as soon as she saw the crowds of people, all with reasons of family, or friends, or livelihoods, moving about with purpose. She stood with an Underground map that Aunt Jane had marked for her, punctuating Susan's route from Victoria to Tottenham Court Road with arrows and exclamation marks. She felt smaller than she had six months ago, when she had taken a stand against her aunts and applied for jobs outside of Southport. 'You won't like it there,' Aunt Cyn had said. 'Things happen to people in London,' Aunt Jane had added.

But it seemed, despite its size, as if nothing could happen to Susan in London. Londoners did not smile, or stop, or speak, unless they were talking through Tannoys, or to officials. If there was an incident, Susan felt sure that it would be accidental and followed by apologies. Newspaper headlines did not scream of life here in the capital, where people marched smartly and stiffly, as if to their deaths. Susan found that she too was marching along, clutching her clasp handbag and the clanking plastic bag, which contained a box of cream cakes and two bottles of Dandelion and Burdock. And she found the right coloured line, and the correct train, and the exact carriage, which had to be in the centre in case, in Aunt Jane's words, 'there is a terrible tube crash'. So she sat, as if taking part in society, confronting a line of people sitting opposite and her own fear of life outside Seabank Road, Southport.

The dark tunnels guided Susan along the Underground, affectedly bored, as if they had better things to do with their time. The heat enveloped everyone tucked inside the train, scenting them with sun-tan oil and sweet, fizzy drinks. All the world sat opposite her: Asian, Eurasian, African, Caucasian. And Susan, who had lived her adult life in Southport, sat, scared by the black-skinned man opposite, whose muscles leaked sweat; she was surprised by the hot, pink lady, fanning herself with a paperback, because she sat beside the black man without any obvious fear.

Despite her long journey, Susan looked as if she had stepped out of a children's-clothes catalogue rather than a stuffy, hot coach when she arrived at Dutton's three hours and three cafés later for her interview. She was the sort of girl whose clothes could not crease, or smell of anything other than pink fabric conditioner. She had sprayed perfume over her blouse that morning, but she still smelled of fresh cotton sheets, soaked in meadow flowers, as she waited in the reception area at Dutton's.

Susan Lyttle's pale brown, bobbed hair glowed blonde in places where it could barely be used to advantage. She had spent her life, so far, with her parents; inside Seabank Road with her aunts; at school; in a shoe shop; at secretarial college; and in the library, so her skin, which might be peach or apple, if it had been subjected to the right temperatures, was actually unripe apricot.

There was no reason why this secretarial job shouldn't be hers, and why this young woman shouldn't hear the words 'delighted', 'offer' and 'accept', as opposed to 'regret', 'decision' and 'high standard'. Because, although she was the proud owner of one hundred and twenty-one rejection letters, all on headed notepaper, from employers as diverse as the Meat and Livestock Commission, the Ipswich Theatre Company and the European Bank for Reconstruction and Development, Susan had been highly trained at Southport's Secretarial College and had a clutch of GCSEs and three A levels, including one grade A in English literature.

She ached for a fix of literature now, a dollop of some dreamlike other world, where things happen, in abundance. She knew, however, that always having one's head in a book shut out life, and with it the possibility that something might happen. So she kept away from *Eugenie Grandet* for now, and her final few pages with that gentle, fictional friend. She waited, instead, for a real-life receptionist to call out her name and transport her to a new life, away from the library.

Her tan court shoes sponged into the soft carpet, as men and women came in and out of the building, absorbing the artificial light, as well as comments which floated to and from Kelly and Karen on reception.

'You were drunk last night.'

'Put it this way, I wasn't in a fit state to operate heavy industrial machinery.'

Karen had travelled around India, living for months in a tent near Jodhpur. She had slept on buses, and with men from different cultures. Kelly had been called quiet and dull. But, on reception, Kelly was the vivacious one. She liked her view; sitting inside a semi-circle, with her fat legs hidden behind the counter and her shoes kicked off. Karen, who felt locked inside this spaceship of a reception and loathed the scenery, talked in whispers and could only connect coldly, via the switchboard.

Sitting away from the semi-circle, Susan fancied that these two women were fixed in stone, immutable inside offices the world over, and that this world was impenetrable to someone like herself, who took pleasure in owning a one-day Underground travel pass and sometimes had a problem passing words.

Fortunately, this problem only struck infrequently – but on important occasions. Her mouth gave way now, for example, as she faced Mr H Matlock in a white World of Leather swivel chair. The mouth collapsed and the words did not come. It was the same for Susan on school speech days, supermarket trips and encounters with the opposite sex. She had a voice, but sometimes it just didn't deliver.

At home, Susan had practised for her interview with her aunts. 'The thing to do is to growl, sexily,' Aunt Cyn had said.

Aunt Jane: 'No, she just wants to speak nicely.'

Aunt Cyn: 'This Mr Matlock's a man, isn't he?'

Aunt Jane: 'Don't scare Susan, Cyn. You know that . . .'

Aunt Cyn: 'All I'm saying is, she's got sex on her side and she should use it.'

Sex was a difficult subject for Susan Lyttle. She was twenty-three, yet her body still surprised her in the bath. Just a few years ago, tiny, budding breasts had given up growing and flopped down, as dry, thick hair grew on dark places around her body, reminding her, several years after puberty, that she was a woman.

Susan Lyttle nodded at each of Hugh Matlock's questions. 'Hugh Matlock, hello,' he had said, shaking her shaking hand on meeting. 'Would you like a cup of tea?' Susan nodded, so a young girl on work experience had been called for. Two or three questions in and the girl had returned with a teetering tray. Susan accepted a cup, and sipped at the cold, coloured, milky water, nodding and smiling for England, as Hugh did all the speaking.

'Did you like working in the shoe shop?'

'The shoes are a family business, is that right?'

'You'll like Dutton's then, Susan. Family firm, this. Still several Duttons. And I'm married to one. Hilary Dutton, the third daughter.'

'Glad you didn't go to university, Susan. Your predecessor did. Thought she was too good to get me tea and do my typing. Looks like you could have done, though. Good exam results, these.' Hugh tried to imagine the young girl naked. It made him feel less nervous.

Her stomach swimming with all the tea she had drunk in the last two hours, Susan suddenly found a flood of strangled words. 'They needed help in the shoe shop, so I didn't go on to take a degree and I . . .'

'Don't worry, my dear. You're better off taking your exams at the university of life, believe me. You know, Susan, I don't mind telling you, I've seen a number of women for this job, *a number of* women. But you seem right, somehow. I don't feel that you're going to start a revolution here in the office, burning calendars or whatnot.'

As she walked out through reception, there was a man, with golden curls, green eyes, and several different women, who looked curiously at Susan Lyttle. 'Are you coming to join us?' he called out. '*God*, I hope so. We need some gorgeous women about the place.' And Susan, enchanted by this Thomas Hardy Angel, fancied it as fate that they should meet in this romantic way. She carried his image out of reception with her, along with her clasp handbag and the bottles of Dandelion and Burdock, now covered in the cream of her cakes.

Secretly, Susan loved everyone, from the man who sought her out at the shoe shop to buy black leather lace-ups to the man with angry young spots who sat for hours in the library's Health and Beauty section reading medical directories. She thought that if only they knew how hard she could love them, they would love her back with equal enthusiasm. If only they knew how good she was, at love, they would be the Prejudice to her Pride, or the Beautiful to her Damned.

'I couldn't swap these black shoes for brown, could I? Only I've come a long way,' the man with the auburn hair had said. He had come a long way just to say it to Susan and she had looked out for him after that. She had looked out for him and loved him, as Lily Dale had loved her Apollo in Trollope's *The Small House at Allington*. 'I'll get them from out back,' she had said to him, unthinkably finding the right words. His feet figured in her life, after that. Those long, knobbly feet, with sprouts of hair on the toes, that she had measured, attentively. They were a manly size, with skittle-shaped toes. She would look down, one day, to find those manly feet there again and then they would be together, for ever. They would lie next to her own near-filleted feet.

'He's worn the black ones in. You shouldn't have let him swap them for brown,' Aunt Cyn had said. But how could Aunt Cyn, from an entirely different generation, understand love in the 1990s?

'Do you come here often?' the man in the library had said to her, as she had walked past him on her way to Romantic Fiction. 'Do you come here often?' he had asked her, in her dreams – on the beach, as the sun set or on the beach, as the sun rose. He had been with her through long smelly days in the shoe shop. He had given her hope as she had read Thackeray's *Vanity Fair;* hope that a woman like herself, who, at twenty-three still ran about for fun, rather than in an exercise class, could possibly be as seductive as the wicked Becky Sharp. But the words would not come out to meet the library man.

'We need some gorgeous women about the place,' the Angel had said, in reception. Susan had walked out on Kelly's words, 'Putting you through', carrying him with her through the double doors, around Oxford Circus, and deep down underground to the tube station. The Angel floated past the ticket machine, sat opposite her on the tube and beside her on the coach, leaning his head on hers, gently, as she slept, asking her whether marriage was entirely out of the question, and licking cream from the cleavage of her meringues.

'Did I win my bet, then?' asked Aunt Cyn, as Susan came down the coach steps at Southport. 'Did Mr Matlock not like you?'

'I'm sure he loved her, just as we do,' said Aunt Jane, who had found the time to slice just half of the eggs and tomatoes necessary for an egg and tomato salad. 'Oh, you didn't eat the cakes. And you didn't drink any fizz pop. You should have drunk, Susan. It's such a hot day.'

'Look at the line of my tan, Susan,' said Aunt Cyn, flaring her nostrils, to reveal the plastic surgeon's scar. 'One afternoon in the sun and I'm golden brown,' she said to Susan, leading her to their car, as she lifted up her skirt. 'Lovely, don't you think?'

'So, this Mr Matlock?' said Aunt Jane, twisting the key in the ignition.

'Well, I see you haven't brought him back with you. I suppose we really will be eating cakes and drinking fizz when *Susan* brings back a boyfriend . . .' said Aunt Cyn.

'What does Susan need with a boyfriend?'

Smoothing back her blonde-grey bob, Aunt Cyn said: 'She's twenty-three, Jane. Nine years older than when I . . . Oh, if only Susan had inherited *my* family's good looks instead of her father's. To think she could have looked like Margaret, with that mane of red hair . . . Mind you, Margaret was not the cleverest. A *good woman*, yes, but when brains were handed out, she was out serving meals on wheels . . .'

'Aunt Cyn. Do not talk about my . . .'

'Sorry, sorry. Forgot I can't talk about your precious mother.'

'Aunt Cyn, I . . .'

Aunt Jane panicked at the wheel. 'Now, now,' she said. 'This is such an exciting day. Remember what to say, when you start to feel angry – Aunt Jane. You say: *Aunt Jane . . .*'

'My mother was beautiful . . .'

'Your mother had sex for *pleasure.*'

'You say Aunt Jane. *Aunt Jane.* Please.'

Tears dripped from Aunt Jane's nostrils as she drove. Aunt Cyn took Susan's arm and said quietly: 'My sister was a *good woman* – may God preserve us from good women. But, despite her looks, she didn't have two beans to rub together. So, take my advice, Susan. Don't be a good woman. They only ever attract poor men.'

Susan had a whole floor to herself in the house in Seabank Road. Three beds – one large, one medium, and one small – occupied her bedroom. She slept in the large, four-poster bed, with the slithery red cover, the eiderdown with pretentions to duvet-dom, the hot-water bottles slung around the bed like cuddly toys. Piles of second-hand books rose from the floor, next to the real synthetic-fur animals, which Aunt Jane sewed together in her spare time.

She sat on her four-poster, reading a book about a man who

shot an Arab on the beach, for pleasure. And she imagined her Angel shooting someone in the chest and the stomach. He would escape to her, to Susan Lyttle, and she would touch his chest and his flat stomach. And then they would have sex, or he would refuse to have sex, as he was so cynical. They would have tea instead, or he would refuse to have tea, as he was so cerebral. But they would almost certainly kiss, just as he was dragged away to face his fate.

'Susan. Tea!' called Aunt Jane, up the stairs. Susan went down to meet her fate, which, traditionally, would come in the form of fried fish, and egg and tomato salad, sliced to meet the rectangle of an oven dish.

'Aunt Cyn, I would like you to meet the Angel,' she would say, floating into the room beside the man with golden curls, who had enough presence of mind to compliment her aunt on the way she had kept her looks.

'Why, hell-o,' Aunt Cyn would say, taking out the best cutlery and falling in love with Susan's Angel. 'You are so beautiful,' he would say to Aunt Cyn, grabbing her by the hand and rushing her off to a lifetime spent at grand hotels, where the two of them would drink tea and eat *petit fours* before dinner.

Even Susan's dreams were starting to end unhappily. Propping Albert Camus' *The Outsider* up against the pickle jar, Susan stared sullenly at her Aunt Cyn, and wondered if she would ever escape Seabank Road and its regular salad suppers.

Chapter Four

Myra Felt believed that the world could be divided into those people who liked smelly cheeses, and those people who didn't.

Ellen Abrahams believed that the world could be divided into those people who divided up the world and those people who didn't.

Jeffrey Bell, Ellen Abrahams' fiancé, had bought Ellen a tube of toothpaste, wrapped in red ribbon, which now sat in the airing cupboard. 'I use yours all the time,' he had said, appearing with it.

Ellen had thought that, like all romantic gestures, it was of little real value to the recipient. Because Ellen's bathroom was, quite clearly, green-and-white checked, and not blue-and-white striped, like the tube of toothpaste. 'Oh, Jeffrey. Bit twee isn't it?' she had said. 'Wrapping *toothpaste?*'

'Ellen, telephone for you,' yelled Jeffrey, as she folded her winter jumpers away, inside the generous storage space in her bedroom. 'Oh no, pretend I'm out,' she yelled, frantically folding jumpers. 'I'm too *busy*. Pretend . . .'

'Hello . . . Helen, hi . . . you haven't . . . oh dear . . . that's awful . . . well, I'm sure it is . . . I can't believe he would . . . and you were so perfect tog . . . well, of course, except for him . . . that is terrible . . . Look, I can't . . . The bastard . . . Listen, I have so much to do . . . Hmm . . . I really have to go . . . Of course . . . so much to . . . Bye . . . yes, absolutely . . . Bye.'

'So how was Helen?' asked Jeffrey, coming into the bedroom and sitting on a pile of Ellen's freshly ironed underwear. 'Has that man left her again?'

'Yes, he keeps coming and going,' she said, taking the pile of underwear from underneath Jeffrey, finding creases, and tossing the lot into the ironing basket. 'But I think they'll always be together, at intervals. Do you *have* to sit on my ironing?'

'I thought they were your knickers,' said Jeffrey.

Ellen Abrahams had four basic meat-and-two-veg-type friends. The rest of them, the floaters, the good-timers and the bad-timers, the ones who filled up the Vs and the Ws in her address book: they were all luxury items. At various points, Ellen had asked herself: Do I really *need* that person in my life? The answer, invariably, was No.

Before Ellen decided on a dropping policy, people cluttered up her life. They picked away at her time or festered, like sores, on the end of a telephone, blistering on about Ellen as she had been at school, at Cambridge, or at journalism college. And Ellen, who shed layers of herself like skins, each time she moved from one situation to another, wiped out the ghosts of Ellen's past. She stopped returning telephone calls. She left her answering machine on all the time. But she still had her staple friends: Bridie, Elizabeth, Helen and Lucy. They stayed at the back of her life, propping her up with their insecurities.

'*Elizabeth? . . . You've just been made what . . . redundant? . . . God, I didn't think that happened to . . . that's terrible . . . But listen . . . yes, awful . . . But I've got so much to do . . . I don't think I can . . . Yes, of course . . . Well, I don't know what I'd do . . . So much to d . . . Elizabeth, I have to . . . Bye . . .*'

Ellen wondered at her friends' lives, as they moved from one major crisis to another with the speed and control of Linford Christie, while her own life fell out of synch at the first mention of chocolate. Jeffrey's giant bar of Galaxy lay in Ellen's fridge and she was doing her best to keep away from the kitchen, until he returned from a client visit. 'Take it away,' she would say. 'Come back with something less threatening, like strawberries or salad.'

'*Bloody hell, Bridie . . . that big? . . . well, what can you do? . . . They can't just take away your . . . all your . . . I hope you don't mind, but . . . how will you live without any credit cards? . . . Listen, I have to g . . . I have to go . . . yes, completely . . . So much to do, you see . . . Bye . . .*'

Money burned holes in Ellen's pockets, her pound-handies, her current accounts. As Ellen couldn't stand shopping, she couldn't get rid of it. It was such a waste of time. ('D'you think I should buy this, Ellen?' 'Oooh, d'you like this hat?') She preferred to make lists. That way, she wouldn't end up with two of anything, or be forced to alter her shade of nail varnish. (I can't believe you carry the serial number around, for *lipstick*, Lucy had said. But Lucy never bothered with make-up.)

'Lucy...How are?... *She's been attacked again?... Your mum's boyfriend?... Well, call the police... No, don't do that, call the police... I said, call the police... She can't let him back in... You can't move back in with her... Look, I really can't talk... Well, I have so much to do... No, Darren dumped her... no, don't come round now, we'll arrange something properly... Well, what about my brother?... No, I can't.*'

Ellen's friends, who could leave half a meal on their plates; who could switch careers midway; who could serve honeydew melon on pink china – surely they envied her for her meticulousness, her mortgage and her mix-and-match wardrobe?

Wet teabags were deflating, like fallen parachutes, on to Myra Felt's kitchen counter: the inevitable fall-out after a meeting of the Camden Residents Against Crime Association, particularly if there was a new member, as there had been that morning. Che Silcott had kindly offered the services of his new girlfriend, Celine, in the partisan fight against mindless violence in the Camden and King's Cross areas and the girl had asked Myra if there were any biscuits.

'Well, why not help yourself to my biscuits? After all, you've already got my boyfriend,' Myra grumbled, finding a packet of Chocolate Rich Teas behind swirls of dead pasta in her cupboard. Celine took seven of them and spent the rest of the meeting scraping and sucking the chocolate from each biscuit with her teeth. She then stuck the skinny, soggy remains, one by one, on top of the television.

As February turned into March, Myra was recruited to CRACA (after a night of passion with Che). 'Don't feel you have to,' he said. 'But it's really a very important part of *me* and I do want to share all of my life with you. Besides, as you *live* in Camden, you'll get a lot out of CRACA meetings.'

Myra had met Che that pouring morning at yet another anti-animal-apartheid rally. He had stood, slightly apart from the core of the action, holding an empty Tesco carrier upside down and rolling his head almost on to his shoulder so that, presumably, he could see the stage. His skin was fashionably thick with grain and his plaited hair had matted beyond colour. Myra looked at his feet, wrapped in paisley socks-cum-shoes and black with muck. And there, on the ground, beside the sock-shoes, was a very dead supermarket chicken, covered in clingfilm, labelled and sitting on a blue polystyrene plate.

'You've dropped your chicken,' Myra whispered to him.

'I'm sorry?' he said, looking at Myra with distaste, as if she had interrupted his thoughts to ask him if he might marry her. 'If I were you, I wouldn't leave it lying around. People might get the wrong idea,' she said, worried by his confusion. 'They might think you like eating *dead animals*,' he heard her say, as he saw his quick-roasting chicken on the floor.

He looked like Pippi Longstocking on speed, with his Rasta plaits flying and drying around his head. Myra found him attractive. 'Oh my good God,' he said, kicking the chicken away. 'I could have been killed. They would have killed me.'

Having saved his life, Myra abandoned her marching friends to buy Che coffee. 'Animals aren't really my bag,' Che said, drinking cappuccino with Myra in a Camden franchise of a chain of exclusive cafés. 'I'm more of a crime person. Myra squeezed her bag between her legs. 'I fight crime, in a non-establishment way,' he said, pushing Myra's bag away with his feet and rubbing his leg against hers. 'Like a vigilante, you know?' And as the leather of his sock-shoes scratched against her recently waxed and stinging leg, Myra thought: No pain, no gain; and formally fell in love.

Myra hoped that, at last, she had found her revolutionary guru; the man who would save her from standing still. She wanted Che, who was thick with jumpers and stubble, to be her philosopher king. She wanted him to be her Plato, her Socrates, her Proudhon, or her St Augustine. She wanted him to come to her, hiding the fresh blood of his battle wounds, perhaps wearing the Confederates' American Civil War uniform. (She found that particularly attractive.) She wanted him to spend the night with her, stopping off at her apartment along the road to revolution.

But the road to revolution was long and littered with dull CRACA meetings, where Che would talk of the need for non-violent action. He spent the night with Myra, and every night after that, growing fat on her pasta and rich on her overdraft. He grew complacent and critical, setting Myra's video recorder to record a Chinese cookery programme at three o'clock, each and every morning, and complaining about the size of her breasts. 'The truth is I'd like to make obscene amounts of money,' he told her once, watching a Lottery winner on the television waving his big cheque around. 'I might start a cult or something.'

'Do you ever think of cleaning up this dump?' he asked her on another occasion, throwing roaches on to the floor as he watched *Friends*. 'I know you pretend to like animals, but do you *have* to live like one?'

And yet it was Che who had ended the relationship, rather than Myra.

'You're too homely for me,' he told her one day in the kitchen, as he opened a tin of Baxter's Cream of Red Pepper soup. 'I don't believe in staying in one place. I'm a wanderer,' he said, waving the tin-opener in the air, as it clawed tightly to the top of the tin. 'You're not committed to the work of CRACA. You're very young, very needy and . . . damn,' he said, burning his finger as he lit a match to light her gas oven.

Myra cried: pathetic little dribbles ran down her cheeks, drying around her chin. 'I'm more radical than you think,' she said, as Che ate her soup from her pan and watched her television.

'It's more a state of mind,' he said, finishing the soup and placing the hot pan on the table. 'Your mouth might say Class Struggle but your mind is saying Laura Ashley.'

'I could wander with you,' Myra called, from her bathroom. She reeled out a mess of tissues, to wipe her face dry of tears and pink veins. 'I went Interrailing around Europe *twice*. And I'm a good traveller. I'm always the one with the toilet roll and I don't need a hairdryer. My hair naturally curls,' she said quietly, looking in the mirror and wondering if she had the strength to be one half of a couple again. She still had her TV, a credit card, a rented flat, a live-in landlady, countless friends, a university degree and a good assortment of second-hand china. She had taste. If anything, she had too much taste. And, although she lacked experience, she more than made up for it in motivation.

Myra slouched on the toilet seat, smoking. Taking a bottle of shampoo from the wire cradle hanging above the bath, she read: 'B5 enriching moisture shampoo, for hair with that special salon bounce'. The front door clicked as Che left, and Myra realised she would never see him again, or at least not until the next CRACA meeting.

Susan did not pack many of her possessions. There was the shawl, bought after *Madame Bovary*; the pink lightbulbs; the watercolours. She packed her books, of course, and her wooden blue memory box, as well as her clothes, all of which had escaped the brush of any particular fashion era. And she filled a plastic drawstring washbag with useful things like sponges, toothbrushes and dried-out flannels.

Most things dried out, eventually, at the house in Seabank Road. Even Aunt Cyn, whose beautiful, younger image hung in the hallway, crumbled with the building that held her. Furniture flaked if a stranger stayed too long. Paint peeled from broad, brown bannisters. Floorboards creaked and the cellar swirled with black dust. Crocheted squares, knitted to conceal fraying chairs or hung to hide the modesty of stripped paper on the walls, were now in need of cover themselves. And the real open fire in the drawing-room spat coal at the house cats as they clawed and chewed at the carpet.

The house was decaying, but it was huge and there was always somewhere to hide. As a young girl, Susan would slip into Aunt Cyn's room on the first floor to finger her gold jewellery or dab eau de parfum on her legs and behind her ears. Muslin, silk and lace battled to drape from tall, slender cupboards, which stank of old scent. Pink lightbulbs studded the mirror and sent candystriped beacons over bottles and baubles and banknotes. Fivers and tenners floated, forgotten, on the table beside stale and drooping restaurant menus. A gold-painted bed stood in the centre, posted from four corners and draped with all manner of material, in a shrine to Aunt Cyn's sexuality.

Susan sat for hours in this room, imagining herself to be Aunt Cyn, trying on the white leather gloves that shrank to her fingers and the wide-brimmed hats that spoke of F Scott Fitzgerald and

Henry James. She borrowed bits here and there; little bits of Aunt Cyn's life that, presumably, she wouldn't miss. She unscrewed two lightbulbs once and took them back to her room. She cut squares of muslin and silk and lace and sneaked them out in her pocket. Gold brooches, soft leather belts and love letters all found their way into Susan's room.

Aunt Cyn's room was a square of magic inside a decrepit mash of a house that Susan was beginning to loathe. But, despite wanting desperately to be out of it, she could not imagine the house without her. It would surely fall down on her leaving, crushing its occupants as they served one another cream cakes, or roast potatoes for Sunday lunch, or as they switched the television on in the evenings, always to ITV. She would leave them commenting on adverts or variety shows and, as she left, they would disappear with the magic acts, which they watched constantly, in amazement that such things could happen before their very eyes.

'Now this will change your mind,' said Aunt Jane, handing Susan a piece of ginger cake, topped with cream. 'Oh, thank you,' said Susan, scraping off the cream with her spoon and leaving it on the side of the plate.

'I've been thinking, Susan . . .'

'Yes?'

'I've been thinking about your move.'

'I know.'

'And I wondered if it would help if you had another floor here. I mean, if you were to take the top two floors, like in a proper flat, and we could do it out . . .'

'No.'

'We could do it out in a young, modern way with all sorts . . .'

'No, Aunt Jane.'

'And you could manage the shoe shop *by yourself*.'

'Aunt Jane . . .'

'Please.'

'I'm sorry,' said Susan, looking out of her window at the shop opposite, which dangled plastic windmills and spades and buckets and balls from its front. 'It's all sorted out. I've got the flat and the job at Dutton's and *everything*.'

'How often will you come back?' asked Aunt Jane, wiping

the mucus from her nose with an extraordinarily large hand-kerchief. Susan tried to think of a reply worthy of fiction, as Aunt Cyn walked into the room, stepped over Susan's clothes and sat on the bed next to her sister.

'Well, isn't this cosy?' she said, staring straight at the pink lightbulb. 'All this family atmosphere and not a stretch mark in sight.'

Ellen Abrahams filed her *FastNews* acceptance letter in a box file marked 'Professional'. She was listening to a radio report about some Sri Lankan Tamil Tigers, concerned about the conversation she had just had with her mother-in-law-to-be.

Frankie Bell was the only woman, ever, who could find dirt in Ellen's house. But then she would go searching. Jeffrey's mother was fond of Ellen, but only in the same barbed way she had been fond of Jeffrey's school teachers. Because Girlfriends and School Teachers criticised her son, but at least they *talked* about him. And she liked to talk about Jeffrey too. He was (as Frankie joked) as much a part of her as her womb had been. And both had come out of her body at about the same time. Boom, boom.

Ellen was ever anxious to impress Frankie. Frankie had, undoubtedly, ever impressed Ellen. She admired Frankie's house in Hendon; its prettily papered rooms. She liked Frankie's scarves tied neatly at her neck with a pin. She adored Frankie's hair, which never fell out of shape; the polished nature of her mahogany dresser; Frankie's garden, trimmed within an inch of its life.

Ellen would have liked to have been a child, growing strong inside Frankie's house; peeling padded, floral toilet tissue in the bathroom; helping herself to a brightly coloured yoghurt; finding the cutlery set whole, in the right cabinet, and matching the expensive crockery.

Frankie liked, however, to edit Ellen's life. 'You might want to cut out the fatty foods,' she would tell her, staring at her stomach, or: 'Don't push this job section of your life. There'll be children to consider soon enough, believe me.'

'You're a stenographer, aren't you?' Frankie's elderly mother had once asked Ellen. 'I told you, Mother, she's a typist,' said

Frankie, with mock patience. 'I'm a television producer,' Ellen had hissed urgently, to the grandmother's confusion. 'Yes, I didn't understand what it meant either,' Frankie had said, giggling loudly, behind her hands. 'I think it's a fancy word for an *administrator*.'

But her son, her boy. 'My son's a property negotiator. Very upmarket sort of deals. Ellen's done very well out of my Jeffrey. Her bit of pocket money will help, I'm sure, but Jeffrey, between you, me and the gatepost, is doing *exceptionally well* . It won't be long before he can afford a five-bedroomed house in the centre of Hendon, *believe you me*.'

Frankie had phoned Ellen a) to insult her with the subtlety of a television quiz-show host talking to a contestant and b) to ask her where they should put Ellen's own mother, who was suffering from early Alzheimer's, at the wedding reception.

'She won't *say* anything, will she?' Frankie Bell had asked, cradling a mobile telephone to her ear and spraying hairspray around her flick-back Farrah Fawcett hairstyle. 'I mean, we've never discussed your mother, and her little problem . . .'

'I wouldn't worry about *that*, Frankie,' Ellen had started to say.

'You see, I'm just not sure about her sitting at the top table. I mean we all know what Miriam was like, when she had her *faculties*. I mean, *I* – out of anyone – *knows* Miriam. When she ran the Kenton Jewish Ladies Guild . . . Well, she called it running it. When anything went wrong, it was over to us in Hendon. Frankie, you'll arrange it. In that *appallingly loud* voice. What I'm trying to say is, she's hardly an advert, is she? And since Barry died, all those years ago, she's been perfectly . . . Well, all I'm saying is, I don't know what the Hendon *community* will say if Miriam, you know, *sits there*.'

'Actually, I'm not sure I want her there at all, Frankie,' Ellen had said conspiratorially. 'I mean, I have very little to do with Mum now.'

'Well, I don't think we can get rid of her *entirely*,' Ellen's contingency mother had said, suddenly concerned, and passing her small, bald husband in the hallway.

'You going to have some hair with that hairspray?' Mr Bell

asked his wife, grabbing the telephone. 'Hello, Ellen,' he said loudly, at his wife and into the telephone receiver. 'And if you don't mind, at the price of these calls, *goodbye*, Ellen.'

Jeffrey had not returned from his house-viewing, so the chocolate still lay, attractively, in the fridge. Frankie Bell's telephone call had interrupted Ellen's day, which was supposed to go: *13.30: File* FastNews *acceptance letter; 1335: Black coffee and slice of watermelon; 1345: Read the* Guardian; *1430: Write to bank; 1445: Ring re: reception venue; 1500: Read the* Daily Telegraph; *1530: Exercise video; 1615: Book wedding lilacs; 1630: Ring re: bridesmaids' outfits.*

Mr Muscle and Mr Sheen had washed and sprayed every orifice and object in Ellen's house. Even the *Daily Telegraph*'s front-page trailer – The day Mr Major met Mr Adams by accident – glittered with wax polish. Cushions had been shaken and carpets vacuumed. The scent of artificial mixed flowers hung around a corrugated plug in the dining-room. Windows squeaked and counters defied advertising copy-writers to come up with new superlatives. Even the toilet reeked of citric acid.

Ellen, too, had been scrubbed clean. She now smelled fresh, of expensive sports deodorant. The waves in her newly washed, brown hair were almost under control. She wore white pumps, a white shirt and a white leather-strapped watch – all gleaming as if they had been sterilised in disinfectant.

But it was 1400 and Ellen had not yet read a newspaper. The chocolate still lay in the fridge. And the doorbell rang, as Ellen peeled the final hint of green from her last apple. It was Helen. And what was worse, it was Helen in leggings.

'Sorry,' she said, hugging Ellen. 'I know you're busy but I had to come round. Jeffrey's not here, is he?'

'No, you're OK. I sent him out for an airing,' said Ellen, despairing as Helen sat on the couch and squashed a firm, fleshy cushion. She looked at her watch. 'I don't think I've got *long*, Helen. I mean, I have to start reading up about Lou Matherbay, you know?'

Jeffrey's description of Helen went as follows: 'She has a Cotswolds face – very neat and pretty – but her clothes are in need of some modernisation and the overall good impression is

36

brought down by one or two ugly features, such as her fat legs and biggish ears.'

Helen's description of Helen: 'Hideously unattractive with elephantine ears.'

Helen was dropping crumbs of chocolate on to Ellen's clean carpet. Ellen was eating the crumbs. 'I thought he was deformed, at first,' said Helen. 'And then he told me he had been circumcised, which, of course, explained why he wouldn't eat the prawn sushi from Pret à Manger. At the time, I thought he was being generous, or romantic, feeding them to me, but then he tells me it's some sort of religious allergy and that, just as I can't eat olives without my spots breaking out, or my ears growing, Solly breaks out in his grandfather's voice if he so much as *looks* at shellfish.'

Ellen stared at the stack of newspapers on the table. Helen was now punctuating her speech with snotty sobs wiped, greasily, on to the empty chocolate wrapper. 'And he (sob) had such a (sob) lovely (sob) voice. Oh Ellen . . .' she said. 'Do you think we could go for a walk outside his house?'

When Jeffrey returned, to face his empty chocolate wrapper, Ellen's couch was full. Helen, Elizabeth and Lucy sat with a lisping Bridie on the three-seater. Ellen was on the floor reading Martin Kettle's column in the *Guardian*. The sofa women were competing over the size of their respective agonies.

'Well, I don't see how you can compare being made redundant to my losing Solly. Jobs are easy to find, but a man . . . !'

'Excuse *me*, but I think being told you're just not up to it by your boss is pretty awful actually, not to mention . . .'

'At least you can afford to live on what your father gives you,' said Bridie.

'Who cares about work if the pay is so damned lousy, you get so overdrawn that your bloody credit cards are taken away?'

'I think it's worse to be told you're not up to it by a man than a boss. A boss . . .'

'You can all fall back on your families. Just who can I rely on, with a mother who . . . ?'

'You can rely on Ellen, obviously,' said Jeffrey, who had come in on Lucy's lament. 'How can you read through this racket, Ellie?' he asked his fiancée, who was still lying on the floor, consuming facts. Jeffrey's mobile phone rang.

'Please don't *call* me that,' said Ellen, blushing furiously.

'I just can't believe that my career is *over*,' said Elizabeth, ignoring Jeffrey, who had started to talk loudly about cyclical fashions in selling property. Having met Frankie Bell, Elizabeth sympathised with Jeffrey over what was obviously a hereditary illness – mobile-phone ear.

'Well, at least you get regular sex,' Helen said.

'Oh, not *that* again,' groaned Jeffrey, whose telephone swelling had gone down. He found it difficult being around women, in the plural. 'Pur-lease. I'm sick of hearing about women's periods. There's always women in this house, talking about their bloody periods. Ellen, I'm off home. If you need me, phone me there, or bleep me. I'm turning this thing off,' he said, closing his mobile phone and leaving the house, forgetting his briefcase.

Ellen continued to read the newspaper. 'Yeah, OK,' she said.

'Oh, I can just see that,' said Lucy, who had graduated straight from a mild addiction to cigarettes, six years ago, to a full-blown sugary-snack habit. Affecting a girlish accent and with her mouth full of candy cigarettes, she said: 'Sorry to bother you, Mrs Bell, but it's sweet little Ellen here, and I need your son to come over and shag me, *now.*'

'I do concede that it's difficult finding a decent man in London. I mean, I out of anyone concede that. But, all I'm saying is, being made redundant, feeling redundant, is terrible for one's self-esteem,' Elizabeth said.

Four of the sweet cigarettes hung out of Lucy's mouth. 'I was made redundant ju—'

'That was during the recession. How do you think it feels during boom time and there are no comforting magazine articles about people who are much worse off than oneself and committing suicide all over the place?'

'Shall we open Jeffrey's briefcase? We could find out about some juicy affair that he's having,' said Bridie, who wanted some attention. She fingered the case combination.

'Oh, but I *know* what he's up to,' said Ellen, looking up from an article about business etiquette in the *Daily Telegraph*. 'He's been in and out of almost every woman's house in North-West London, measuring them up, screwing them for every penny. Never a dull day inside Jeffrey's briefcase.'

'Ellen,' asked Helen, her eyes dripping panda sensitivity. 'Any chance of a lift home?'

Myra felt that she had come through her wilderness years. Her flat in Camden was stuck, however, in a barren urban wasteland, the small block held up, surprisingly, by the rubble that surrounded it. She had rented it in a hurry, thinking she could do something with the kitchen or the bedroom; make it 30s-style or 40s or 70s. At the time, Myra had liked the impermanence of the place; the fact that it looked as if it was about to be pulled down.

The Flatmate, unfortunately, came with the flat: the Flatmate's concerned frown; the labelled milk; the yellow Post-it notes: Could you NOT leave the gas on when you go out. It will cause a FIRE!!!

Flatmate looked pinched all over. She worked in a newspaper cuttings library and had a great deal of responsibility. Every day she had to mark sections of the newspaper: Europe; Crime; Neil Kinnock. Sometimes it was hard to categorise, and then she consulted the Chief Librarian. Somebody else, with less influence, would cut out the articles marked neatly by Flatmate. And in the afternoons, she had to file the cuttings in different files; and sometimes these were placed in the wrong file, which meant miserable conversations in the evening. Myra would become panicked. She found Flatmate's responsibility very stressful.

But now she was on her own, heating a bowl of stuck corn-flakes on the gas ring in order to burn them clean. Half a cigarette, twisted and wasted, smoked away happily in the ashtray. The flat stank of slippery, homemade tomato sauce, of pesto and cold tea. Members of CRACA always drank an awful lot of tea, leaving their dregs in mugs for somebody else to clear up.

Sometimes it was hard to tell the stained red of her carpet from the stains Myra made when she dropped red wine on to the floor in her bedroom or pounded pasta into the pile on clumsier, slippier, busier days. Myra collected rubbish, swarming with city dust, in the same way she collected other items. Her bookshelves, for example, were caving in under the philosophical weight of Machiavelli, Rousseau, Hobbes, Locke, Marx and Aquinas. Her dressing-table, piled high with assorted, coloured cosmetics, looked like an old-fashioned chemist's, and her raggedy clothes fell from cupboards, over chairs, desk-top and her bed. Every one of Myra's surfaces begged for air as she suffocated them, daily, with piles of fresh rubbish.

The telephone kept ringing, bringing people's voices into the flat; voices which Myra barely recognised. Everything about Myra was extravagant or emotional and, consequently, she had a legion of soul-mates: apparently thousands of friends, picked up at various institutions like school or university, collected at political gatherings, bus-stops or in cafés. They all stayed, simply because Myra did not have the heart to throw anything away.

Despite the numerous entries in Myra's address book, only Marion – a childhood friend – thought of her as more than a temporary diversion. And, curiously, Marion, unlike Myra, had been stuck, like glue, in her own character, for years. Passions for alternative music, rock parties and her own, rather dirty, bed had grown up in Marion, and were now fixed, whereas Myra simply plastered on 'phases', tiring of her life each September, at the start of the academic year, and switching to a yet more advanced personality.

She decided to keep the bowl, with the three cornflakes dug into the design at the bottom, and placed it at the back of the cupboard marked with a blue sticky label reading: MYRA FELT'S CUPBOARD, which Flatmate had kindly stuck up. Wandering into the living-room, where Che's new girlfriend had left her dribble of tea-soaked biscuits, Myra switched the television on at a soap opera and immediately felt the pain of one of the characters, who had just discovered that not only was he HIV positive, but his father had died in a prison accident. Celine's biscuits were a painful reminder of Myra's singular state. Looking at them made her cry, while the telephone rang and voices spilled from an answering machine which was already full up to bursting.

'*Myra, it's Marion here. Don't you dare work for the Pluralists – bunch of boring bastards! No one's that desperate for a suit. Call me back. – I'm at Sid's squat, but we're going on to Terry's later.'*

'Myra, it's Kasha here. I'm at Eva's and we're all going on to Terry's. You should come . . .'

'Myra, it's Terry here. You coming round? We're going to this new club night at O'Kelly's . . .'

Sitting on CG Jung's *Flying Saucers*, which was sitting on Vincent Wright's *The Government and Politics of France*, which was sitting on a hard-backed raffia chair, Myra dabbed her wet face with the spine of Aristotle's *The Politics* pulping the tip, slightly, before going to fetch a towel. She did not want Flatmate, who would be returning soon, to see her upset. Myra's hormonal surges would be easy fodder to a woman who found threads of grated carrot tucked under the carpet and placed them on the kitchen counter, with the words: 'Don't Let This Happen Again!' Myra Felt was cursed with pre- and post- and mid-menstrual emotion. Her tears were a witches' brew of oestrogen, testosterone and progesterone. They dripped like magic, each time Myra was dumped.

Myra blamed the fact that she was so often dumped on her parents. If, in childhood, she had been abused, or abandoned, Myra might not have suffered so terribly in adulthood. Roger and Penny Felt were clearly unsuitable as role models for Myra, *viz* her most interesting childhood memory being the arrival of a video recorder (albeit with remote control).

Her parents had been bored by suburban childhoods themselves and, sadly – as is so often the case – had bored their own three children in turn. When Myra had confronted her father about this, Roger Felt had, for possibly the first time ever, looked up from his newspaper. 'You know, Myra,' he had said. 'You probably think that your mum and I are suffering from False Memory Syndrome. But the truth is, we have been abused, systematically, throughout your childhood, by our middle daughter.

They had passed on all their defective genes to Myra. Her firmly married sisters had inherited the prize-wining character-istics. Myra had to make do with a distorted D chromosome, which made her drink too much at parties, buy unnecessary things from department stores, and take pleasure in the sound

41

of her own opinions. She liked to have political arguments. Her passion lent her power, at least for the duration of the argument. And, yes, she had been known to change her mind. But Myra called that 'spiritual growth'.

Marion, however, called it 'political prostitution', remembering Myra in a former guise. ('You can't go on a hunt, Myra, just because Luke says it's *romantic*. It goes against everything you believe in.') Yet, for the duration of the argument, all the world's statistics and diagrams and scientific experiments could not budge Myra from a new belief system. She had that much integrity, anyway.

Myra heard the door shut, slyly. Flatmate had returned. 'There's a smell of burning here, Myra,' she shouted from the kitchen. 'There's a distinct smell of burning.'

'Just toast,' said Myra, hoping that Flatmate would not follow the smell to her cupboard and the blackened cornflakes bowl. 'And don't worry about the mess. That'll be cleared up as soon as . . .'

'But I do worry,' said Flatmate. 'I *do* worry, Myra. The whole place smells of prostitutes.' Myra blinked at the comparison, surveying the kitchen and its inkpools of black tea squirting through cracks in teapots. Flatmate moaned on, grinding her own small day into even smaller lumps of useless information, for Myra to dispose of as she wished. 'Then Kevin dropped the sugar into the filing cabinet. And that was it – I just had hysterics. By the way, Toni, Lynne and a woman called Sonia from something called the Anti-Movement called yesterday. Oh, and Julia Potter too,' she said. 'Where do you *go* every night? I'm beginning to feel like your personal message machine.' She threw away Myra's rubbish, shaking her head at each sign of dirt.

Myra would have to be a Pluralist. She would be starting as press officer next week and had been swotting up on the difference between a Private Notice Question and an Early Day Motion. For all her university degrees and emphatic opinions, Myra did not know much about the mechanics of political life.

'Oh, and Binnie from Save The Mammal invited you to her . . .' said Flatmate, plucking a (possibly pubic) hair from the floor and carrying it away from her nose to the dustbin. 'And someone called *Grog* popped round while I was in my *towel*. I was so embarrassed. I mean, where did he find *that name?*'

Myra lit a cigarette and placed the dead match back in the box. If she was to be a proper Pluralist, she ought to start thinking more conservatively. Men like Che would have to go, she thought, then she realised, sadly, that Che had already gone, by choice. Perhaps all her friends would have to go too. Particularly Marion, who was not so much unemployed as anti-employment. Marion despised those she labelled as 'suits'. 'They don't realise,' she would say. 'Offices are *a jail sentence.*'

Flatmate's voice rattled in her ears and Myra wondered, vaguely, whether she ought to read the Pluralist policy documents sent to her in the post, with a now familiar yellow sticky on the top pamphlet. It read: *Myra. Would you be for Lou Matherbay, should she stand, or Ray Hines in the leadership battle? If you read these, you'll see how little Hines stands for. Hope to welcome you on board. Yours, Sara Cinnamon.*

She hoped that Sara Cinnamon would not take up Flatmate's role during office hours, sticking notes on anything fixed to the ground. The thought of working in an office, without it being voluntary or 'for experience only', terrified her. She would have to be useful, constantly.

Myra tossed her cigarette butt out of the window, and continued to contemplate employment.

That day, Susan Lyttle wore black; in mourning both for Seabank Road and for Maggie Tulliver, who had died that morning. 'Black?' her Aunt Cyn said, squeezing lemon juice over the Saturday salad. 'A man magnet, I don't think.'

They were all about to leave. Susan sat in the drawing-room, with her suitcase packed beside her, staring at the open fire, which toasted banana skins black. *The Mill on the Floss* lay closed on the wobbly bridge table near the fire, but its heroine Maggie Tulliver's dark eyes jumped and pricked their way through the flames.

'Oh God, she's got that look again,' said Aunt Cyn.

'It's because she's leaving us today,' said Aunt Jane.

'I'll bet you it isn't.'

'Maggie's drowned,' said Susan.

Aunt Jane's eyes drained of everything mundane. Aunt Cyn took her own eyes from the particular.

Salads and cakes and television variety shows; prunes and loganberries and whole, roast potatoes; these were the delicacies visiting them daily and as all the young men vanished from their lives. They performed, hammily, the roles of wicked aunt and nice aunt, which kept them safely predictable. If they didn't, if they stepped out of character for a second, Aunt Jane would not know what Aunt Cyn would do, and Aunt Cyn would not know what Aunt Jane would say.

Susan performed a kind of cameo role with the Fry sisters. When she was alive, Cyn and Jane's sister – Margaret – had acted the same role, beautifully depressed by two characters so fixed they were almost caricatures. Susan's own temperament was fluid, dipping and diving with the fictional people she loved and loathed; her aunts, as a rule, accepted the swinging moods. But when Susan mentioned death, the Fry sisters considered the scale of her orphaned sadness, and then the Seabank stage collapsed.

Aunt Jane drove Susan to the coach station, stopping off at the supermarket to buy lemon squash and custard powder. Aunt Cyn sat in the back, sneering at the 'commoners' eating chips and carrying cans of lager to take on to parties. 'Why the little tarts think they're attractive to men, eating *saveloys*, I don't know,' she said, wanting desperately to show some affection to Susan. She managed, at last: 'At least Susan is a lady.'

Susan sighed wearily, staring through the gasping traffic at her Angel. His face followed her own, smiling those roly-poly lips and darting those raisin eyes into her; eyes which must have been black they were so dark, dripping into her own, from stationary buses, shop windows, signposts and street corners.

She felt sad until she remembered why: how Maggie had died that morning, and how alone Anne Brontë's Agnes Grey felt this afternoon. Susan, too, was lonely, as the small streets got bigger and then stopped at the coach station, while *Agnes Grey* fell to the floor. She was lonely, as Aunt Jane put her bags and her suitcase into the coach hold, adding one carrier of her own, containing childish food and noisy, sickly drinks for her niece. She was lonely, as Aunt Cyn stood, draped in toffee-coloured fur, away from Susan and Aunt Jane as they hugged, with genuine warmth. And she was lonelier still as Aunt Cyn surprised her at the coach entrance with a cold, hard envelope, thickly filled with banknotes so tatty they looked like old money.

Cynthia Fry was the girl in the song. She was the girl in the picture, painted some time ago, as a mark of respect for the beauty of that particular age. She was the girl in the song one could look at for ever, taking pleasure for oneself from that face. But the girl in the song came dear. She demanded chunks of gold and dollops of diamonds, to wear around her silhouette. She expected keys to expensive hotels, serving champagne in silver buckets and sycophancy on tap in the lobby. She wanted engravings marking, richly, her every possession. She liked yachts and yearned for fat, broad beds, coated in thick tapestry covers and stern, white sheets folded over, as in schoolbooks, by chorus-line chambermaids. She wanted milky cleanser and powdery rouge, furry drapes and stiff, slip-on slippers that fluffed and flowered, like powder puffs, on top.

Cynthia Fry lost her looks in the fire of time. Skin tugged backwards and hair burned silver. Long legs shortened with the pull of gravity, pale arms freckled dark brown, permanently, under expensive sun. She grieved at her loss with insensitive, unsupportive men, who came and went and then went altogether. When the young men went and the older men came, and as the older men left, Cynthia sank into Seabank Road. She lost her parents to heart trouble and cancer. She lost her sister and her brother-in-law through the window of a car. Small troubles visited her and her younger sister after that. But there was always the shoe shop, her vanity, her gambling and her trinkets. She had Jane, and sometimes she even had Susan.

Aunt Jane watched her niece through the small coach window. Susan was reading; turning the book's pages quickly and rhythmically, oblivious to other passengers still boarding the coach. And as she stared, Jane Fry felt a strong strain of pain in her stomach and her legs. She speculated over this agony, wondering whether it compared to childbirth. 'Susan,' she called, through the thick window glass. 'Remember to wash the salad before you eat it, in London.'

Jane Fry had almost been married, on several occasions, pulling out each time, before it became a family embarrassment. The Fry name was worth preserving. It stretched back – as a matter of record – to 1066. Jane Fry had traced the family tree, spending hours in local museums and libraries and with well-known genealogists, looking for her Fry roots. As a spinster, she had had time to kill. Her dead Lyttle sister was to blame for that.

When Margaret was born, plain Jane was twenty and starting to settle into her face. But all the prettiness in the world, inherited or paid for, could not have saved her from having to bring up the fiery, flame-haired Margaret, as Mummy barked orders from Seabank Road's Queen bedquarters. She was a spoiled, stinking child, smelling and clean, clean and then smelling. Jane bathed and hated her into adulthood, while her crippled mother and dying father hung about their house, bored and leaving the washing up for others, like guests waiting for the cab home. Grown, Margaret Fry had turned glamorous, resembling, strangely, Lou Matherbay – the woman who had made politics beautiful. But while Lou had used her beauty to shake up political Britain, Margaret had used *hers* to find a Lyttle husband.

Jane had half expected, at Susan's christening, to be asked just as soon as she had cleared away the cheese straws and caviar canapes) to take on this girl-child of Margaret and Peter Lyttle's. Seven years later, and unexpectedly, she had been expected to do just that. When Susan arrived, sullenly, at the house in Seabank Road, Jane looked at her with relief. Because she looked like a Lyttle – like Peter – and not Margaret, who had stolen her opportunities, screaming in the drawing-room, the cellar and the larder, bringing the house to a halt with her good looks, soiled nappies and sour-smelling food.

But Susan was shy, like Jane. She drifted in and out of fiction. She wandered into Jane's life, long after the men had left, and as a girl, rather than as a baby. Jane could mother Susan without compunction. She could adore her, compulsively.

Then, of course, there was Susan's money, that had come with Susan. The Fry sisters could dip into the trust fund to pay for her upbringing, which had been expensive. Sometimes Jane felt that they had dipped into Susan's fund too often. But Margaret and Peter hadn't left a great deal, she would think, guiltily. And the shoe shop, of course, was partly Susan's.

As *Agnes Grey* closed with Susan's eyes, she thought of the Angel and his words to her: 'Will you come here again?' His hair had dyed yet more golden with her attention, curling furiously. His mouth now pouted, of course. They would be together, in Claverley Grove, Finchley Central; lying in the middle of squalor, as in *The Room At The Top,* only together.

Aunt Cyn had, surprisingly, sorted out the bedsit, ringing old friends and estate agents and old friends whose children were estate agents. It had all been a show off, of course – to prove to her sister and to Susan that if she wanted something she could still get it, quickly, just by being Cynthia Fry.

Susan thought it would be a little paradise; in the middle of civilisation and with the paint still pink, or blue, or white and beautiful, as in *Howards End* or *The Vicar of Bulhampton*. She thought it would be a tiny country cottage, dropped like an apple into a pail of toffee, in London. She thought her life would be like paradise, surrounded by people with interests, rather than habits. It would be peopled with the men and women of *Tender is the Night* or *A Proper Marriage;* people who came and went, and did not stay, stuck and sitting, for ever.

'Lunge, two three four; jump, two three four. Lunge, two three four; jump, two three four.'

A scrawny woman star-jumped to all four corners of the television. She was Essex woman, without the sex. 'And, good, well done,' she said indiscriminately, at any *Video Shape and Dance* viewer. Ellen Abrahams, she of the flesh folding all over, was bending her body as far as it would bend, jumping and then lunging. She was remarkably good at the stretching exercises at the end of the tape, when the dyed-blonde face said: 'Circle those fingers . . . and *good,*' but, having caught up with exercise videos a decade too late, Ellen did not, quite frankly, have the energy level required.

Falling on to the couch, ironed an hour ago, on a very low heat, Ellen grabbed at a cushion for support. She wasn't fit to take her pulse, as the video lady had suggested, and lay breathless on the sofa for some time, like an eighty-year-old asthmatic with a thirty-a-day cigarette habit.

Ejecting Essex woman in mid-flow, Ellen groaned at her schedule. She had eaten her way through more than her fair share of the fridge but she *had* finished Michael Heseltine's biography and had begun the Lou Matherbay tome as well. She hadn't skipped the final chapter, either – Looking To The Future – despite her decision, made some time ago, that political predictions were, truly, none of her concern.

Heaving herself from the sofa, Ellen switched on the radio. She hated being out of touch for more than a minute, once cutting a holiday in the Scottish Highlands short so that she could return to the more 'civilised' world of news bulletins. As she had told Jeffrey, mountains popping with purple heather were all very well in their place; but *she* liked to breathe in a bit more than fresh air. Seriously, she needed a regular injection of news. Without it, she felt as if she was missing out on life.

She listened to a report on the on-going war in Chechnya. It lasted for two minutes, before switching to an update on the weather. She noted down the name of a global-warming expert in her personal address book, before climbing the stairs to her stark bedroom.

She needed a treat and it came with a glimpse at her wedding dress, filed away in the white-clothes section of her wardrobe. She had had the dress altered early, despite the shop assistant's shrill suggestion that: 'Most brides prefer to wait until *just* before their wedding day to have the dress altered. Until then, Lord knows *what* will happen to the waistline.' But Ellen would starve into a size-ten dress. 'Look, I'm a paying customer. *Please* take it in,' Ellen had said in the changing room, as assertive as any woman could be without being able to breathe out.

'But it's too tight now. I don't understand,' the assistant had said. 'Can't you just wait for a *couple* of months?'

'No,' Ellen had said. She liked to be early. She sat in airport departure lounges for hours, rummaging through boxes in The Body Shop (with no intention of buying anything), waiting for her check-in call. She got dressed for an evening assignation in the low hours of the afternoon, just in *case*. (Her father had died, prematurely, after a second heart attack.) Her hair was washed before it was dirty. (Her mother had become senile in her *fifties*.) Ellen's legs were waxed well before summer. She was engaged to be married long before it was strictly necessary.

Six months before her wedding was due to take place, Ellen's slim bridal dress was pressed into the wardrobe. Ellen slunk down on to the floor, to be near the silk hem, and allowed herself, for a minute, not to think about her failure with Frankie or *FastNews* or wedding-day schedules. But the sounds of news analysis on the radio, a style Ellen had learned by rote, drifted through to the bedroom. The broadcaster's words developed into meaning. A bomb had gone off in the centre of London.

Ellen pressed her nose against her silk dress and wondered how many businesses had been bombed. She held the edge of the dress as she had a piece of rag when weaning herself from Mum: tightly and with control. Her thoughts folded over in non-sequiturs, as in a game of Consequences. How many dead? How many wedding invitations? Could her Lou Matherbay film win a TV Prime award? How many injured? How many calories in a crumb of chocolate?

'Early evidence suggests that the bomb was probably the work of terrorists,' the radio reporter said. 'Well, obviously,' muttered Ellen. 'It's not going to be somebody's shopping dumped in a dustbin, now is it?'

In 1994, Ellen had met the radio reporter at a skills weekend. They had worked on a project together and he had been all fingers and thumbs, asking her to help him find bits of discarded tape. 'What are you doing here, if you don't know what you're doing?' Ellen had asked. 'But I thought I was here to learn,' he had said, grabbing at spaghetti-like twirls of tape in the dustbin. 'But I'm not here to teach you,' she had grumbled. In retrospect, of course, she had been right to react like that. After all, he had almost *ruined* her project with the loss of that tape.

'The bomb went off a short time ago in the heart of . . .' said the reporter, and Ellen's thoughts overlapped, uncontrollably. Really, she needed to make a list. She needed to make a list now.

Androgynous girls and hermaphrodite boys throbbed about in tight T-shirts, saying: 'Babe' or 'Eat Your Own Sperm'. Skinny hot-pants flared around the floor, gathering dust, as young people snorted, popped or drank their drugs at O'Kelly's club in

Brixton. They looked, the lot of them, as if they were out on day-release from the confines of *I-D* magazine.

Myra Felt stood out amongst them, in a long, satin, red skirt, a tiny white T-shirt, and a generous pasting of blue eyeshadow. She held a pile of cigarettes, carelessly, like lollipops and had transformed herself into all cute, gelled curls and Constance Carroll lip-gloss.

'So, you pleased you came?' asked Marion.

'Oh, yeah.'

'Only it's been a bit hard to prise you away from your political friends lately.'

'Look, I'm sorry, Marion. I'm not going to apologise just because I care about our *environment*. I mean, if I don't do something, who will?'

'D'you know, call me mad, but I think you'd find that life would go on, even if you didn't *march* all the time, or sit in trees, smoking dope.'

'I just don't want it to go on like this. Can't you understand? I *hate* . . .'

'Oh, no. This is a club. Just take a night off, for God's sake.'

Of all Myra's men, Marion had especially loathed Jack Temple. But then, he had been the one to transplant Myra from Marion's music scene to a definitively political one. Although Myra had been studying politics at the time, it had all been academic. Jack had been the one to lead her astray – away from Marion's fixed belief in lounging around – to one of active participation; in demonstrations, marches and *society*.

During the hottest month of 1991, Jack Temple had appeared at Myra's door, in her hall of residence, sporting a naked chest which swam with muscles, a fashionably floppy, blond fringe and a Labour Party red rose, which climbed from his trouser pocket. 'For me? Oh, you shouldn't have,' Myra had said, flirting outrageously.

'I'm sorry?' said Jack, who saw a pretty, spindly woman, with grubby, long blonde curls, staring at his crotch.

'The rose,' Myra said, laughing and pointing; and Jack laughed, looking beyond her at the plastercast Plato bust, sitting on the window ledge.

'Right,' he said, going straight on to explain to Myra the

principle behind the common ownership of the means of production, distribution and exchange; as well as the need to dispense with this principle in the run-up to an election.

'I don't believe in elections,' said Myra. 'I believe in passion changing politics. I mean, have you read any Matherbay? She said . . .'

Jack, of course, proceeded to change her mind. He talked to her of social underclasses, lost generations, and the minimum wage. He sat on her bed, preaching sexual equality. He reminded her that Lou Matherbay, despite her eccentric views, was a Labour MP. He pointed to her Plato bust calling the philosopher names, such as The Very First Socialist. But it was the offer of a pamphlet which Myra found persuasive. They had had to fetch it from his room in the postgraduate block. And Myra presumed that it would turn into something more permanent, like a relationship. (The Labour Party would have been proud of Jack Temple. For Myra's vote, he sacrificed three pamphlets; two guest passes to a fashionable nightclub; one denim jacket; some Class A drugs; an entree into all the right raves; and, eventually, his body.)

One month in, their romance ended, but for Myra – politically – it was just the beginning. He had opened her eyes to a world of alcohol, drugs and freely available attractive men. Superficially, she could see that there were poster campaigns, petitions, speechifying, and politicking. But, beyond that, Myra suspected there lay party invitations, club first-nighters, overnight sit-ins and men with radical, subversive urges. Of course, she didn't want to restrict herself to Labour, when there were other men to be exploited in alternative organisations.

The inevitable happened. Myra slowly degenerated from supporting her local Labour Party (in meeting places above shops and offices) to supporting the environment (in meeting places halfway up trees). Lured by the glamour and the glitz of fundraising dinners and riotous rallies, Myra ignored the seamier side of politics – the picketing; the leafleting; the lying. It was only a matter of time, and too late, before Marion saw her on the streets, muttering obscenities at City types, and selling copies of *Socialist Worker*.

Myra stood in the ladies' toilet, staring at the lines on her face in the smeared mirror. She was taking refuge, away from the music which jumped off beady bodies, and the posters which screamed abuse at taut, young things, dancing hard. Stretching out a wrinkle, Myra remembered her dirty, Pluralist secret. Although she had lied thus far, Marion was bound to catch her at it one day. She would discover her in a compromising position, and Myra would be forced to reveal her sordid double life, of Pluralist press officer by day, and underground political activist by night.

'But Lou Matherbay switched,' she would say, aware of Marion's contempt for the capricious MP. 'They're the party of the future, Matherbay said. And, in six months, they'll have a new leader. A new *style*.' But Marion looked at life head-on. She did not understand restlessness, ambition, or idolatry. Gurus, political or otherwise, had no hold on Marion, for whom life was more than clear. Marion, of course, had not suffered parental sarcasm. ('I don't suppose you'll ever find a *job*, will you, Myra?') Marion had not suffered successfully wedded sisters. ('Do you think, Myra, that you'll *ever* get married?') Marion had not suffered suburban living. ('It's just not what one *does*.') Then again, Marion, in both the professional and the personal, sought satisfaction. Myra, by contrast, looked for reassurance.

She would not confide in her friend about the Pluralists. Marion would be led to believe that nothing had changed. Least of all Myra Felt.

Susan's London tube journey – along the black line – was interrupted by a bomb going off elsewhere.

Aunt Cyn had told Susan to take a taxi from Victoria to Finchley Central. But at the taxi rank, a man who had stared at the wrong bloke's girl in a pub had been shouting for casualty, his bottom lip falling bloodily from his face. Scared, she had braved the Underground instead. But as the evening tube drunkenly belched its passengers along the tracks, even the image of Susan's Angel appeared frightened.

The sky was descending, like grey and hazy net curtains, when the train pulled in to Finchley Central – the first proper suburb north of London.

Tiny lights stared hopefully from windows. Susan dragged her luggage from the station, following the estate agent's map past dirty launderettes and desperate second-hand stores. Claverley Grove looked neat and tidy, compared to big Ballards Lane, which shunted the street to its side, as it got on with more important things, like buying, selling and pushing steamy traffic through London.

Susan was too tired to be disappointed in the house, which did, at least, have the grace to display a garden gate. She rang the top bell and a man appeared at the door, pressing together the fly of his jeans. 'Susan Lyttle?' he asked, as she stared at his trousers. 'Just been on the toilet,' the man said, by way of explanation. 'Now, hold on, that estate agent left me keys for you. Where the fuck did I put them?'

Susan froze to the floor as the man sprinted up the stairs, hair sprouting on his head, chest, chin, nose and upper lip. 'Here you go, then,' the Yeti man said, appearing again, with a large plastic label, holding two tiny keys. 'That one's for the front,' he said, pointing to one. 'And that one's for yours,' he said, dangling the other, upside down. 'See you around, I s'pose.'

Susan opened the door to a small square room, which gave birth to a bathroom, out back. A cooker, a fridge, a cupboard and a sink skulked in one corner as a sofa squatted, like a terrified hostage, in the other. Staring at the scene was, of course, a television.

Susan sat on the sofa. She longed to call Aunt Jane on the telephone, which was glued to the wall, like a pub condom machine. She longed to see Southport and its fairy lights, growing and glittering on the trees along Lord Street. The sofa lurched and Susan stood up, apologising. She felt oddly embarrassed and lifted one hard cushion a fraction, inspecting it, as Aunt Jane had told her to do with public-toilet seats.

As she inspected, the entire contraption sprang out, wondrously, into the distinctive shape of a bed. Susan was seven years old again and her rooms were magical, as in *Bedknobs and Broomsticks* or *The Phoenix and the Carpet*. She was at that age when gnomes and elves fed on wicked adults, and fairies slept in the living-room. She was at that age when, if one believed hard enough in psammeads, a sofa would transform

53

itself, willy-nilly, into a bed and a bed would, willy-nilly, switch back into a sofa.

Susan unpacked soft, Aunt Jane bedclothes to stretch around the sofabed. She ran the tap with grey, dull water, until it turned properly pale. She filled the hot-water bottle with boiled, leaded London water. And then she emptied her second bag, packed with novels. Piling book upon book, Susan surrounded herself with a wall of old paperbacks.

Sitting on her magical bed, she immersed herself in Jane Austen, forgetting about modern, trafficky Finchley Central and descending deep into Hertfordshire, circa 1810.

Chapter Five

Susie Lyttle hops about the school playground, in the severe heat. She is, of course, Laura in *Little House on the Prairie,* but she could just as easily be Darrell in *Malory Towers* or George in *The Famous Five*. Because Susie decides on the book of the day and adapts it for the playground. 'What shall we play, Susie?' 'What is it today, Susie?'

Susie's regulation pleated grey skirt flaps about, as she jumps around, like a rabbit on heat. 'Ma, can I have my lunchpail?' she yells at a taller girl, who has been cast, by Susie, as the mother. 'Pa, can you take me fishing?' she screams at a plainer girl, who has been cast, by Susie, as the father. 'You can have anything you want,' says the Ma figure.

Other girls seek Susie out in the playground. They want to pet her and pat her little, fair head. Boys roll marbles around, fighting for the largest, clearest one to present to Susie. The most attractive dinner lady in the school finds extra cubes of iced sponge or double shovels of chips on Fried Wednesday to give, secretly, to Susie. They fight over her, incessantly, while she simpers.

Susie has a snub, stub nose. Picture-book blonde hair sweeps like down against her back. She has tiny, pale feet which are perfect for plimsolls. She has round, brown, pea eyes. She has soft, rosehip skin. She has a baby-soap look. She won the Northern Region Miss Pears competition in 1977. Susie Lyttle has won spelling competitions, hangman tournaments and reading prizes. She is a literary genius, is Susie. 'I hear she reads like a grown-up,' says one rumour. 'Not a grown-up, a *writer*,' says another.

She plays the glockenspiel in the school orchestra, despite her musical dyslexia. She ruined last year's annual concert, tinkling notes out of sequence, and purely for pleasure, as parents blamed best friend Bayla, who shook her maracas, angrily, but on time.

Last year, Susie's class had learned the story of Joseph with Miss Turnstile – their teacher and, for many, their first love.

'I want all the fair children on this side of the room and all the dark children on the other,' Miss Turnstile had said. Brunettes ran to the left and blondes to the right of the room. 'Right. You lot,' said Miss Turnstile, pointing to the right, 'will play the good guys – Joseph and his family. And you lot,' she had said, pointing at the dark children, with evil in her eyes, 'will play the Egyptians. The *baddies*.'

'But, Miss Turnstile,' said Susie Lyttle, seeing best friend Bayla Gittel sobbing on the left. 'Joseph was Jewish and so is Bayla. Surely she should be on the *right*?'

'Susie Lyttle,' said Miss Turnstile, smiling. 'Stop bucking the system. It is there for a *reason*.'

Susie puts the commas in other children's work. They queue up to ask her to 'put the grammar in'. Many of them think she is magical, because she knows what to do when Miss Turnstile or Miss Robbins asks them to punctuate *now*. Sometimes, Susie adds full stops and speech marks. On special occasions, she puts in question marks. For special friends, she exclaims and she hyphenates. Bayla Gittel always has beautiful brackets.

It is a scorchingly hot day and some seven-year-old girls take their shirts off. One is humiliated by a cotton vest. Susie Lyttle is perfectly formed. But Bayla Gittel has a huge strawberry birthmark, staining her chest. Little people come to stare. Bayla is, of course, oblivious to the growing crowd of children. She is blind Mary in *Little House on the Prairie*, walking with her hands stretched out in front and her black eyes shut. As Bayla walks, half-naked and blindly, around the playground, whispers begin about Susie. She is wanted in Miss Clitheroe's office. She is wanted in the assembly hall. She is wanted at home.

'Susie Lyttle,' calls one child, bravely. 'I heard Miss Anderton tell Mr Pethick that you should be at home.'

'Yes,' says a smaller child, growing in confidence. 'I heard the nice dinner lady tell the ugly one that it was a damn shame and that you should be in the secretary's office.'

'It's true,' says a big-eared boy, with charm bells around his wrist. 'I heard Clinky Clitheroe tell Miss Anderton that she should tell you to come to the office . . .'

'I was there,' says the boy's sister, all teeth and thick, salmon-pink hair. 'Miss Anderton was saying: "Why should I be the one to tell her? It shouldn't be *me*." '

Susie Lyttle is excited. Not much happens at Salford Primary. Even the balloons, which her class had floated from the window – with messages attached for children in Nepal, or Africa, or the Falkland Islands – were found last week interfering with the pipes around the local library. The only black child at Salford Primary went missing from the register after just one week. When other children, from neighbouring schools, were sent home once after a meningitis scare, authority figures at Salford dismissed the bug as a severe case of 'rumour and influenza'.

But here is something. Susie can forget about the terrible tornado consuming the little church on the prairie. She can ignore the crowd of orphans descending on the Ingalls family home. She can dismiss the monster cockroaches eating their way through the Olsen merchandise store. Because Susie Lyttle is wanted in Miss Clitheroe's office.

'You're wanted in the headmistress's office,' says Miss Anderton, as the bell sounds the end of lunch break.

Children stare jealously as she marches proudly away. They go back to their cold classroom, to make toy gonks in Arts and Crafts, using squares of felt, and needles, already threaded by Mr Tolpuddle.

As for Susie, she sits in the secretary's office. She is put there by Miss Anderton, who seems embarrassed. She waits, with her shirt back on and smart, tucked into her grey skirt. The radio hums low, next to the manual typewriter, which is tall and clumsy on the secretary's desk, as Miss Anderton leaves. Susie feels important. It is as if she has been called in to save Salford Primary from the everyday.

Grown-up tunes on the radio tell it how it is. Bending and stretching her little legs, clicking her fingers to the music, Susie feels four again, and on her mother's lap, as the television plays to an adult audience. She feels privileged, and awed. There is a plate of plain biscuits on the secretary's table. There is half a packet of ten-penny tissues and a leather-strapped watch. There is a pile of thick, grown-up books, dull and lifeless. The secretary's chair is swivelling, empty, as if she has been called away in an emergency.

She goes to Miss Clitheroe's door, as if to knock, because she has initiative and she has been left there for some time now. Voices come through in adult echoes; leftover radio voices.

'... was a car...'

'... break her...'

'An Aunt, called Jane...'

Susie thinks, importantly, of her own Aunt Jane. She has an aunt called Jane; living in a holiday place, near funfairs and ice-creams and long stretches of hard, crumbly sand. 'And that was a tune by...' the radio man says. She is seven years old, so it is certainly a conversation about her own aunt, as no one else has an aunt called Jane.

Pressing her ear to the chipped door, Susie listens, hungrily, for more. 'Well, someone will... tell her... parents dying, both of them.'

'Yes, that was John Lennon there, singing about...' Susie hears, as she moves away from the door and closer to the radio. 'Now, for all you romantics out there, this one's for you.'

Susie is tired of adult pleasures. She hears voices, her own age, clipping through the secretary's half-open door. 'Smelly, stupid...' The office is now dull; the radio unexciting; the biscuits boring. She wants to see Bayla and Moira and her half-completed green gonk. She wants to practise blanket stitch. Miss Clitheroe's door is attractive. She presses up against it again, pulling up her ribbed white socks, which shimmer, brilliantly. 'Well, it's no use... Poor Susie Lyttle. Her parents are dead and she... has... be told.'

Surely the voices will emerge from that room, in a second. Surely they will come out and laugh and laugh; to see Susie standing there, cheekily, with her ear to the door. Miss Clitheroe will clasp Susie to her big bosom, calling her a monkey and wrapping her in fat. And she will tell her that her parents are dead.

Susie feels strangely sick. She feels as if she has eaten four sticks of toffee apple; one after the other, as at the first school fair, when she had brought Mother to shine beside short, fat mums. 'She looks like a *princess*,' Bayla had whispered. '*I think* you look like that politician, Lou-something,' Mrs Gittel had said.

'Lou Matherbay? Oh nooo,' Mother had said, so pleased that she had said yes after yes to stick after stick of toffee apple for Susie.

The door opens to Miss Clitheroe and her secretary, Sally-Ann. Sally-Ann looks embarrassed and rushes back to her swivelling chair, as if in an emergency. Barry Manilow sings on the radio.

'Why don't we sit down?' asks Miss Clitheroe, taking Susie Lyttle away from Barry Manilow's voice and Sally-Ann's benign smiles. Miss Clitheroe closes the door, carefully turning the knob, as if it is stiff and difficult. Her own office smells of thick carpet and cold, milky tea.

Susie Lyttle knows about death because her grandmother died last summer, from something called the 'see word'. Everyone, Susie knows, loves a dead person.

'She's gone to the heavens, Susie,' they had said, about Grandma Q. 'Don't worry, she'll be with God there.'

As if Susie had cared about that stinking, shrivelling woman who sat in bed, smelling of pee and shouting at Susie to be quiet. They had all been nice to Susie then, buying her a pound bag of penny sweets and putting her in front of television cartoons. 'Should I be upset?' Susie had felt like asking, as her mother had cried, painfully, and her Aunt Jane had tiptoed around, being helpful. 'What should I feel?'

Miss Clitheroe takes Susie's hands and she knows she will tell her about her parents' death. The hands feel fat and clammy against her own, and she wants her mother to take her hands instead. She wants Mother to tell her that she is dead. She wants Daddy to sit beside her, reading *The Hobbit* to Susie. He could interrupt the chapter to say: 'Susie baby, I'm sorry. But I'm dead.'

Miss Clitheroe is using the 'angel' word to Susie. But that is a word for Grandma Q, not Mother and Daddy. Susie looks at Miss Clitheroe and thinks of Enid Blyton's Mr Meddle, interfering in other people's lives to disastrous effect. Meddle, meddle, meddle. She wants to sew up her gonk for the display. She has had enough excitement and wants to return to play with her friends, as they shoot marbles or play swing roulette; running through the playground swing, as the swinger goes backwards and forwards. Last year, Richard Peddleton cracked his head open playing swing roulette, and after that the game was strictly forbidden. But it is all the craze again now.

'I want you to be very brave, Susie. Your Aunt Jane and your Aunt Cynthia have spoken to the school and everything's sorted out. You will live with them.'

'But I want to live at home,' says Susie, who is suddenly learning of the real situation. 'What about my box?'

'Your box?'

'What about my box and my books?'

'Well, you can take them with you to your aunts'.'

Susie knows that this situation will not last. She will be over it soon. It is like the time when Mother told Daddy she was leaving home and they could 'go stew'. It is like the time Daddy threw out part of Mother's newspaper clippings collection. 'You're obsessed with the woman,' he had said. 'I married *you*, not some man-hating bitch.' It is like the time she broke Joseph's stick in the end-of-term school production, or when Susie cracked Richard Peddleton's head open, with the school swing. Sooner or later, everything returns to normal.

Sally-Ann comes in with tea and a creamy cake. 'In shock, I think,' whispers Miss Clitheroe. 'I'll just leave the tray here. Poor little rabbit,' says Sally-Ann, winking furiously and putting the tray down on a pile of school reports.

'I'm not in shock,' says Susie. 'I want Mother.'

'My dear girl,' says Miss Clitheroe, crying like an adult, without making any noise. 'I'm not trained for this,' she says and sips at her cup of tea, as Susie feels helpless and thinks: '*Daddy would be able to deal with* her, *no trouble.*'

She remembers a photograph of Mother and Daddy, which sits by their bed, as if it was a private, grown-up object, and not to be played with by 'little hands'. Her mother is laughing with her blurred face, her blunt face-bones, her straight teeth. Mother's bright hair is in black-and-white, while Daddy looks down at her, wisely. It is as if he does not quite understand what the laughter is all about but that he loves her so much, he will tolerate her crazy behaviour.

'How did they die?' asks Susie.

'It was a car accid . . .'

'Can I go and sew my gonk?'

Susie Lyttle is talking about a gonk and thinking of the time when she lost the national Miss Pears competition. As the winners' names were announced, Mother smiled at Susie, laughing with the other losers' mothers. She stroked her hair, declaring Susie 'beautiful in my eyes, which is what counts'.

On the train journey back home, Susie's mother did not say a word. They walked towards the taxi rank, and she said: 'What bothers me, Susie, is that you didn't really *try* to win.'

Susie sits with Miss Clitheroe drinking warm orange squash and talking about green gonks, and she feels she has again missed the point. And that, sooner or later, she'll be made to feel unhappy, about something she is doing now.

'Is someone coming to get me?' she asks, biting her lip.

Eyes are growing from corridor floors and tall ceilings. Eyes are staring from children's faces and teachers' turned heads, as Susie walks, hand in hand with Sally-Ann Whittle, the school secretary. She is going to collect her gonk. Although, suddenly, that seems an odd thing to want to do; like something a character would do in a children's book written for grown-ups to smile at. She wishes she could be taken to a place where she can be left alone, to be small.

They are not kind, these eyes. They are not the eyes Susie normally sees around the school. These children stare, as they stared at the black child when she came to their school, for a week. They stare at Susie as they stared at Janet – the black girl – patting her fizzy head and putting their fingers between her inside-out lips. Susie tries to be *Harriet The Spy*, who wouldn't let stares like these bother her. But she has something else to contend with – Mother and Daddy are dead. Mother is dead.

Susie won't be able to apologise. She had planned to say sorry for the flower-bed mess, the trampled-on lilacs. 'I can't forgive you for this,' her mother had said at the school gates as she had left Susie, without saying goodbye. 'This is the final straw. You're just nothing but trouble,' she had said, leaving Susie for the last time, ever.

They arrive at Susie's classroom and Sally-Ann asks Susie to wait outside, so that she can go inside and talk to Mr Tolpuddle, who is taking Arts and Crafts. There are loud noises as Susie and Sally-Ann approach but, as Sally-Ann enters the room, the sounds cut out.

Susie waits outside, listening to a silence that is not like Class Two Alpha, which erupts at the first mention of Harvest Day, when children bring in food from home. Tears do come, as she thinks of the thick, quilted cakes that Mother gives her to bring in on Harvest Day. She thinks of Calum Smith, in her class, who last year brought in a short, square packet of plain, stale biscuits. They all laughed at him. 'Even the spastics' home won't want *these*,' Paul Gregory said, throwing the biscuits against the wall, smashing them to smithereens.

A small boy, with large glasses, passes a tearful Susie in the corridor. 'I know why you're crying,' he sings at her, delightedly. 'I know why you're crying . . .'

'Why?' snivels Susie, turning away.

'You're the one whose Mam and Dad are dead!' he says, triumphantly.

'Here you are,' says Sally-Ann, coming out of the classroom, to hand Susie her gonk and a pile of rough books, shredded from play fights. 'What are you doing here?' she asks the boy with glasses. 'Get to your class.' And to Susie: 'Come on, love. Let's go.'

In the car, on the way to her aunts' house, Susie sees her home. Squashed lilacs. But she doesn't say anything. She is just glad that it hasn't died with her parents who are dead. The ivy remains, covering the deep red brick of Susie's house, keeping it warm. The hot sun is still there, outside, where people lie and drink cold, sugared drinks. Susie's games, on the prairie, now seem far away and childish. 'I hope you're not going to go to see Cyn looking like *that*,' she hears Mother tell Daddy. 'You *know* how patronising she can be.'

Mother and Daddy will be there, at Aunt Jane's. They will carve up penny wafers from an economy block of ice-cream, wrapping each segment carefully. 'Don't let it drip,' Mother will say to Susie. 'I want a tuppenny,' she will tell them, for her troubles.

'Home James and don't spare the horses,' Susie wants to say, as the car pulls up at the house in Seabank Road, where the gate swings, badly. Her mother and father always say that when they come home, to Camphor Avenue, in the car. Once they even said: 'Home James' after that row in the car, when Mother and Daddy threw cheese at each other. Lumps of Brie and Cheddar and Stilton flew about, on to the windscreen and Daddy's face and Mother's hair. 'For God's sake, stop it,' Mother yelled. 'Why the hell did you pack cheese for a *picnic?*' Daddy screamed back at her.

There won't be any dinner parties any more, thinks Susie, as Sally-Ann makes a big fuss over Susie's clothes, which have mysteriously appeared in a large bag underneath the front seat of the car. She won't hear Mother and Daddy saying their goodbyes to the last guest, as she rushes down the stairs, to eat leftover salmon balls and prawns on tiny toasts at midnight.

The house at Seabank Road is not exciting and not filled with colouring books and fizzy drinks. It is tall, and painted only in parts. It is not a holiday place, after all, thinks Susie, walking up the path with Sally-Ann. It is a place where grown-ups go to die.

As Sally-Ann rings the bell, Susie thinks of the time Mother walked out of their house, with her suitcase packed. 'What shall I do with Susie?' Daddy asked. 'You can both go stew,' Mother said. 'Leave her with Jane, or something,' she said, looking hard at Susie. And then: 'Thank God we just had the one.'

Tiny footsteps annoy Susie, who hears them come to the door. It is Aunt Jane. 'Oh darling,' she says, at the doorstep, squeezing all life out of Susie with a hug.

'Is that Susie?' her other, meaner, aunt says, appearing kindly, beside Aunt Jane.

'My name's Susan,' the small girl says, her eyes elsewhere.

Chapter Six

London terrified her. The beautiful chalk houses had been an illusion, kept there as a façade for visitors. Those who were in on the secret had seen the dusty, towering blocks behind, the dwarfish, fat buildings, the thin and wispy high streets, selling rotting fruit and frozen pies. Susan Lyttle walked through London in chunks. South Kensington and Chelsea; Notting Hill and Ladbroke Grove; the City of London; King's Cross and Camden. The chaos of London would be Susan's; the deep, dark houses, old and cream, and the menacing council estates, caged in damp, patchy green.

'Please, Susan, please,' her Aunt Jane had begged her on the telephone. 'I worry about you. *Try* not to do anything danger-ous.' But how was Susan to live life like the women in the sanitary-towel adverts if she was unable to go outdoors?

In Bermondsey, she walked along Crucifix Lane, finding the black tunnel naturally enough like death at the end of regular, peaceful roads. She had not expected to emerge whole from the tunnel's terror. But she had escaped, catching the tube to Victoria. There, bursting with beggars, St James's Park approached.

Susan sat on a bench, passed by two women, one old, one young. The older woman, both familiar and famous, was, of course, her dead mother. Or, rather, her spitting image. She, surprisingly, had her newspaper face on and was attracting gasps, not just from Susan. (It's . . . D'you see . . . ! Her. . .!) The older woman was just yards in front of Susan who, naturally enough, followed her from behind, keeping close, jealously keeping track of the two designed women; the younger one a beautiful, skinny girl, a girl held up with feminine dress buttons and hard, masculine boots. The young girl chatted animatedly to Lou Matherbay. *Lou Matherbay.*

('Being my wife not enough for you?' Daddy had said.

'In case you haven't noticed, we're not in the fifties, Peter. Women are . . .'

'Lou again, is it? Bloody Red Lou Matherbay . . .')

Lou Bitch Bloody Matherbay. Susan shadowed the woman her mother had wanted to be, styling her setter-red hair big and lacquered to match Lou's, shopping for expensive clothes with Daddy's money. 'Well, if I'd married a man with any spunk!' she would say on Accounts Day as they pored over figures. 'A *successful* man would *want* a well-dressed wife.' Out with her scissors, cutting up newspapers in search of Lou pictures, Lou words.

'Oh Myra, I didn't realise we wanted the QEII Centre. It's at the other end,' Susan heard Lou say.

'Oh,' said the girl. 'Well, isn't there time?'

Myra, her head covered in long curls, talked incessantly. Carving pictures in the sky, she talked with her hands. Lou, meanwhile, moved in comparative silence, occasionally pausing to acknowledge her star quality and the pedestrians who silently shuffled, staring. The cars were stopping, not at traffic lights, but for the silhouette of Lou Matherbay.

The women, walking along Victoria Street, stopped for the young girl to fumble inside a large beige bag. 'They're here somewhere,' Myra said to Susan's mother, who was locked inside beige couture, as Susan stared in at the Army and Navy Store's half-dressed window display, pretending admiration for naked mannequins. 'Oh, thank God,' said Myra to Lou, taking out matches (from a messy pack of rice cakes) and striking red the end of her cigarette. 'My own opium,' she said, breathing deeply.

Matherbay smiled at Myra as she chatted on, walking up to an ill-fitting cathedral. Her face had faded, like the photographs of Mother. 'They're always beautiful, aren't they?' asked Myra. 'I love churches. It's as you said once. It's not religion that's important, so much as believing in *something* . . .'

Susan kept close as Myra found words and sentences and subjects to discuss with Lou, who kept silent, as if entertained. Susan's tongue tied drily. She watched Myra, who stood speaking at the cathedral, ignoring the shadow of the House of Commons behind it, as if it was an architectural embarrassment, concentrating, with sophistication, on the cathedral, and talking at it, while Susan's mother listened intently, absorbing the words.

Lou Matherbay placed her hand on Myra's shoulder. 'Myra, please don't panic. They'll all be naked people, dressed up.' Susan Lyttle lost them then, just as Lou touched Myra on the shoulder, lightly. She lost them on 'Myra' or perhaps 'dressed up'. Lou patted, affectionately, someone called Myra, who knew how to walk and talk, and how to look *London*, as Aunt Jane would say. ('Very sophisticated. Very London.')

For Susan, it was now a matter of buying cigarettes and curling tongs.

Delivering her to the claws of the Queen Elizabeth II Centre, Myra Felt stood, inflated, at the back of the room. She had had her first conversation with Lou Matherbay. They had had their first exchange of ideas. Myra had discussed with her, in no uncertain terms, religion, cigarettes and routes around London. Lou Matherbay, in return, had been polite. But she hadn't talked about 'putting the passion back into politics' or, indeed, anything remotely significant.

Myra stared around her at people, all with a purpose, engaged in conversation or coffee. She wanted rid of the mauve, muslin-feel dress and the Dr Martens boots, worn only to impress Matherbay. God, if only Myra had been less average, less *suburban*, talking to Lou for the first time might have been momentous. (Her ridiculous opium comment!) It could have been a meeting of minds.

'Are you with the Pluralists?' asked a woman, smiling sweetly, if artificially. She stared at Myra's flat chest, which read – closely, on a badge – *Press Officer, The Pluralists*. 'Myra Felt? We spoke on the phone. I'm Ellen Abrahams. From *FastNews*. Doing this profile of Matherbay.'

The *FastNews* woman was wearing the smartest of suits; the sheerest of tights. Her nails, Myra noticed, were manicured; her lipstick expertly applied. Clearly, she had nothing to hide; her hair had been cut short to reveal the neatest of faces, with features so tidy they must have come out of a packet. She had a tiny, pointed nose, straight, white teeth, and skin so clear, it glared.

'Oh yes, well she's here,' said Myra Felt, pulling her hair

around her face. She needed a cigarette; she needed to breathe proper, pub-like, smoke-ridden air.

'Oh, right,' said Ellen. 'But it's actually you I wanted to talk to. I wondered if you might be able to tell me whether Matherbay's going to be running for the leadership? I mean, it's sort of my film's *raison d'être*. So, if she *doesn't* . . .'

Myra was having trouble holding down a job, let alone a career. How then, she wondered, did Ellen have time to buff and polish her nails? Myra peered up at Ellen. 'I er . . . I don't know,' she said, honestly.

'Oh. The thing is, I'll need to talk to someone who *does*. Someone who *does* know a bit about her. So, d'you know a woman who does?' she asked, the artificial smile returning.

'But the leadership election's months away, isn't it?'

'Early October, I've heard,' said Ellen, the smile receding. 'I just wondered if Lou might have declared her hand, that's all. Because I'm going to need to shadow Matherbay properly, as soon as she's announced it. I mean, these films are important. It'll need to be different; I don't want the rubbish that everyone else has on her. I want something *out of the ordinary*. You'll need to help me, Myra. I mean, I want this film to be special. Between you and me, it could even be up for an award. If she stands, of course. Otherwise, there's no new beginning, is there? As leader, do you think she'll return to her old style of campaigning? My editor says . . .'

There was nothing uncertain inside this woman; nothing awkward or uncomfortable. Just an engagement ring flashing from the left hand, dipping light on her notebook.

'There's so much library material available. I mean, I'm spoilt for choice like that. But it's *now* I'll want. It's today . . .'

This woman was engaged to be married. Someone, somewhere loved her indefinitely. You didn't get a ring like that, a statement of such permanence, without spending *time* on your personal life. Myra, who spent almost all of her time thinking about men, yet was routinely single, was testimony to that. So how, Myra wondered, did Ellen find the time to sleep?

'At some point, of course, I'll want to interview Matherbay properly. I mean, I *will* want to film her at home, eventually. You know, the domestic Lou Matherbay. It's just that I can't spend that sort of camera money until I know for certain whether she's going to stand against Raymond Hines.'

She was the sort of woman Lou Matherbay could speak to. A washed, ironed, and dry-cleaned woman, tailored to fit a woman's shape, with hips to give birth through and breasts to make love to.

'Of course, with all Lou's involvement in the Abortion Amendment Bill, there probably won't be much time. That's why I need to know before any general announcement. I mean, as I said, this is a long-term project for me. It'll have to be fitted around anything else *FastNews* wants.'

What about Rwandan refugees? Myra felt like asking, child-ishly. *What about rabbit mutilation?* Why go on about some *Bill* passing through the House of Commons? That wasn't politics, it was procedure.

'I think Lou feels strongly about artificial wombs,' she said at last.

'Well, are you sure?'

'Actually, no,' admitted Myra.

Ellen lost patience then. One could tell, because her mouth twitched. 'Look, you'll have to understand,' she said. 'I'm not interested in your spin. I mean, I'm sorry. It's just that I want to go beyond all that. I need the *facts*. How many committees she's served on. How she feels about Labour's abortion amend-ment. Constituency local-election results, year-on-year . . .'

She could not truly cope with Ellen's strange language, the slang of a woman used to life, with all its precedents, looking above Myra's head, as if for someone more important or uplift-ing. 'So, you'll fax all that through, will you?' she asked.

Myra felt cold, locked outside Ellen's world, nodding. 'Oh yes. I mean, Lou Matherbay's *bound* to run for leader, I think. I mean, of course I don't *know*, but in my opinion . . .'

Ellen had spotted Lou Matherbay. 'Hell-*o*,' she said.

'I'm sorry. Have we met?' asked the politician.

'I'm from *FastNews*. We *must* have . . .' she said, assuming that by now she knew everybody.

'Well, I must say,' said Lou Matherbay, who had met many a woman like Ellen. 'You do look *terribly* familiar.'

Chapter Seven

It is a surprisingly hot day. Women are walking around, bulging pale flesh through last summer's fashions; furious with the early sun, which caught them unawares, disallowing time for diet sheets, exercise plans, bikini-line waxings. Men are down to their white shirts, pink sweat trembling through their shame at being caught with their heads down, contemplating work and unnatural wealth. But, through the crowds of people walking along Oxford Street, stripping off for Soho Square, there are the odd couple of thin brown ones, like strips of bark, welcoming the weather, washing in it, pouring still bottled water over their heads, drenching and exposing their chests through tops. These people are as seasonal a variable as sun hats.

It is London, April 1982. Around corners, across Regent Street, past Piccadilly Circus, along the road that leads nowhere, away from the pastel mass of stinking, hot humans, a twelve-year-old Myra walks, pale curls spilling out of the black rainhat. The elastic is gripping Myra's mouth, which is trying not to smile. Myra links one arm through her friend Marion's, ostensibly in friendship, although, truthfully, for support. They are both weighed down, as they walk through horrified stares and around collapsing laughter. They are weighed down by their raincoats, stretching, rubbery with winters, down to their swelling feet, encased in wellingtons. They are burning through the woollen gloves, the cashmere scarves, borrowed from sisters. Like torches, they carry umbrellas, used properly and formally just a week ago, useful then against the dripping rain, now depressed objects of derision. Marion walks slightly in front of Myra, who is being dragged, a little, by the hook of her friend's arm.

Marion and Myra are searching for Interest in their lives; wearing winter clothes for the heat; wearing summer clothes for the cold. It is all Interesting stuff. They are looking for

Interesting People, each with their favourites, as with liquorice sweets, boxed chocolates, and children in a classroom. Marion prefers clean, drawn faces, drug addicts, lilies of the valley, bending and white. Myra has a penchant for lines, deep around the eyes, crisp around the mouth, and beautiful eyes. Blue, blue eyes. But they share a sweet desire for cheekbones, sunken cheeks framed hard; cheekbones for themselves and cheekbones in others. Teeth torn out at the back to make room for the hollow, as in Marion; and cheeks sucked tight, clamped under teeth, as in Myra. The cheekbones, the eyes, and the winding shapes; the black Gothic, witchy clothes, the perfected layers of rags. They want their world, which seems more alive, more stretching, more chaotic than their own. It is untidy, and for Myra, who leads a tidy, neat life, trimmed at the edges, laced only with these days, where she looks for interest in others, it is more real than real life.

Life back home, in the Felt household, means Roger and Penny sitting, usually on the old worn sofa, which has turned to foamy fat, the green wool tiring of colour and fraying, tearing, about the wooden frame and foam stuffing. Closely comfortable and complaining, sewn together over the years, despite his temper and her voice, with the the thread of blame and sour criticism. They blame the Government, the Council or the Restaurant. They criticise radio presenters, television announcers or park-keepers. They complain about their taxes, untidy gardens in Ruislip Gardens, their daughters or their car. Yet they stay together, sometimes enjoyably, but mainly because their chairs are in a good position, close to the television but far enough apart from each other.

All life, for Myra's mother, is in Waitrose. Penny Felt can always find what she is missing there. There is some power to be had in zooming one's trolley around. Afterwards – relief – in a cup of coffee (and a wicked fruit slab) downstairs at Debenhams. Cordoned off, they enjoy a gossip – Sheila Hanrahan, Gillian Isleworth, Brenda Redbridge (if it isn't her day for the building society) – safe, behind ropes, discussing the children.

'How is Leslie?' ('And his skin problems?')

'Well, he's taking three O levels early. But it's difficult for him, being brighter than the rest. And Ruthie?' ('Such an ugly girl.')

'Oh, Ruthie's fine. Her ballet's a problem, starting to take up all her time. But Phil and I can't stop her dancing, can we? It would be like *removing her legs*. So, Sheila, what have your two been doing?' ('Still struggling, academically?')

'Well, the boys are starting to show interest in them, already. I mean, I know I should be delighted that they're so . . . But the phone's for *them*, all the time now. Never for poor old me!'

The four women laugh, like china bells. Somehow, these intimacies always leave them feeling further apart.

'So, Penny, how's *Myra's* new friend?' asked Brenda. 'The rather unusual one? Ruthie says she's strange. Very grown up. Still, if it doesn't *bother* you . . .'

Of course it bothers Penny. Marion has incense in the bedroom and candles in the loo. *Her* parents allow her to express herself, in red ink, all over the bathroom mirror; to pierce her left ear four times, and to fill the holes with golden crosses. *She* is allowed to dress in black, even in the summer.

'Look at her, Mummy,' says a child of Marion, now that they have removed the joke, taken off the mackintoshes, the wellingtons, the hats and the gloves. She is in a long, black skirt to her ankles, with a fur-collared lacy black camisole, buttoned with small velvet rounds. Myra is wearing a dusty red dress, studded with glass beads at the collar and at the waist; dusty because she had retrieved it from the dustbin. Her mother hates that dress, despite the fact that, when it had first been designed, it had been designed with mothers in mind.

Inside the public toilet, Marion turns her head upside down, backcombing the roots and spraying her straight, brown, matted mass of hair, for firm hold. Myra poisons her jam-tart lips with a blood-red lipstick, layering it on thickly, pouting and adding more, stretching the corners and filling them with cracks of colour. Powdering their faces white, like clownish ghosts, they emerge to face a woman, holding hands with her son, who stares. 'Mummy, it's a prostitute,' he says.

Myra and Marion are intimate with London's armpits: little, bitty roads that cobble *à la* Dickens; tumbling houses tucked behind monuments; wayward routes to alternative art houses; a wall, laid out along Piccadilly, behind a permanent jumble sale offering pine boxes and macramé to grateful tourists, addicted to the authentic. Their own wall, fitted inside an elderly and expensive bit of London, unsold and hidden, looking down on olde cheese shops, big, round slabs of yellowing goo in the window, and gentlemen's outfitters, balding and hairy heads, blushing with the sun. They know where David Bowie drank pitch-black coffee when he was Davy Jones. They know where Mick Jagger slept, on which side of which bed, at the London School of Economics. They once ordered a slice of the same chocolate cake eaten by the guitarist in The Psychedelic Furs as he sat with his newspaper in yet another corner of the city. The knowledge and the tastes and the discoveries creep them closer to a real life, lived out, obviously, by beautiful, interesting people with mined cheeks and doped eyes. They know a little London, and they hope that London might know them a little, too.

'Look, we don't want to nose in,' says Gillian Isleworth. 'But did you know, Penny, that Myra, and that friend, Marion, kind of let themselves loose around London . . .'
'Run *wild* around London,' says Sheila Hanrahan.

In Ruislip Gardens, excitement comes in Bank holiday day trips, cocooned in the car, with whingeing sisters and flasks of flat, supermarket cola. Itchy name tags, sewn inside shirts, miserably confirm that Myra is a Felt, and there merely to uphold the family name.
Roger and Penny know what is *right*. They knows of a thousand and one ways to protect the Felt name from embarrassment. 'Don't do that, Myra. They say it isn't good for you,' Penny says to her, for example. 'Your mother's right,' says Roger. 'It'll make spots grow on your tongue.'
Myra imagines the *They* of *They say* to be a group of people sitting above the Wimpy bar in the high street, deciding, with a vote, that Myra Felt should not, for example, read the *NME* in public.
'Did you know that we live in a stereotype, Mum?' Myra asked, last week. 'Marion says that if writers want to describe

72

how *boring* life is in suburbia, they always use Ruislip.'

'Well, that's all right then,' Penny said, reaching for the Basildon Bond. (She always found security in the blue, lined paper.) 'Because we live in Ruislip *Gardens*.'

'I don't mind if Myra wants to go to Oxford Street occasionally. It's important, at that age, to live a little,' says Penny, picking out the raisins from her fruit slab.

'It's not London. It's just that sometimes . . .' Brenda starts to say. She looks helplessly around. 'Well, I don't see why I should be the one to tell Penny. Just because Ruthie told *me*.'

'Sometimes,' finishes Gillian. 'She follows strange men.'

'He's interesting,' says Myra, of a man with black, flapping hair and a broad, floury face.

'Is he interesting enough to follow?' asks Marion, who disapproves of his flabby arms.

'Definitely,' says Myra, who likes the cabbagy hair, stale with hairspray. 'Let's do it.'

And so they follow the Interesting Person into Foyle's bookshop, as he studies the current affairs section, from A to Z, without lifting a book. Myra, bored, picks up *The Female Eunuch* and folds back the cover to read its introduction. 'Please don't destroy the books,' says a customer, muttering into the fourth button down of his white shirt as if it were microphoned. 'I'm sorry,' says Marion, guiding her friend away. 'For God's sake, Myra, watch him.'

They note down his every movement. By recording his every action, they give them a significance. Just as Marion writes: 'He has gone back from Z to M, as if looking for something in particular,' the Interesting Person lifts a book from the shelf marked M and folds it into his trouser pocket.

'He's stealing it,' whispers Myra to Marion, in orgasm.

'He's stolen a book,' says Marion, in disbelief. 'Oh Myra. We've got him. We've found him. He's heavenly. Definitely the most Interesting Person we've ever followed.'

The Interesting Person is heading towards Leicester Square, book in pocket, kept on a long leash by Myra and Marion, who trail him, as he teases them unknowingly, stopping and then starting. 'Write it down, write it down,' says Marion to Myra, who now has their notebook, as he stops to stare at a long, polished chicken hanging by its legs. 'He is interested in chickens,' writes Myra. The man goes to another restaurant window, this time to peer at a pig's head, glazed with bronze. Myra adds: 'and other dead animals.'

They lose him at Charing Cross Road, as intellectuals jostle Myra and Marion in a push to get into second-hand bookshops, famous for their obscurity.

'We've lost him,' says Marion.

'It's a metaphor,' says Myra.

'Literally,' jokes Marion.

Despite approaching, with dragging feet, their thirteenth year, they haven't had time to kiss men or boys. But Myra has dreamt of kissing, without telling Marion. Easier than she imagined, a hazy image now, of the comic one in *Fame*, kissing her on her mouth as she stood at a bus-stop, eating sweets. 'But, no,' she said to him, vaguely aware of the sensation of surrender as he pressed his lips, neatly fitting, to hers. Initially his lips had felt soft; she had tasted lemon sherbets, but he kept his mouth on hers, stuck tight like toffee, for the duration of the dream, and she woke tasting envelopes, and screaming: 'Get off. Get off me.'

They have practised kissing, Myra on a Franz Hals print of *The Laughing Cavalier*, Marion on a plaster bust of Edmund Kean, which stands, seductively, on a pillar in her hallway.

'I ought to phone home,' says Myra. 'They won't let me out of the house again otherwise.'

'No way, Myra, he's there,' screams Marion at Myra, as the Interesting Person walks past the window of their shop, momentarily pictured behind mannequins.

They are on track again, shadowing the Interesting Person, as he walks into a shop marked out by its second-hand, fashionable clothes. 'I hope he isn't interested in shopping,' says Marion, who likes her Interesting People in clothes that are breathed on naturally, breezily; not hunted out and bought, looked for and taken away, in plastic carrier bags, with the receipt stapled to the rim for all to read.

'Oh, I don't know,' says Myra, who wants to buy all of the

clothes, hanging in rigid lines, around the shop; the different shades of black T-shirts; the grey jackets; the plimsolls lined up in pairs, as if ready for a gym lesson. She leafs through a rail of jeans, looking for two legs as long and slim as hers. 'It's getting late, Marion. Oughtn't we . . . ?'

'No. He's going,' says Marion, pursuing her prey.

They walk, the three of them, along Drury Lane, past the theatre with its painted posters in red and in black. Myra is concerned about her mother, seeing the worry clinging to her face. ('But I don't understand why you can't just go to the local shops. Or wear pretty colours. Why you can't just be normal, like other people's children?')

Myra does not tell Marion of her concerns. Marion glides, has vintage tastes, smells of the stage and dysfunctional, unclean families. She rarely has a parent in the home, or clean, dull clothes; her mother and father are actors; her neckbone stands out at a fashionable angle. She has big breasts, Wicked Witch red shoes, antique handbags bought at shops where Myra browses. Her life is lived, it seems to Myra, *en pointe*, as Myra sags, breathlessly, at the back.

'Look, I don't want to say anything out of turn,' says Brenda Redbridge. 'But Ruthie thinks that this *Marion*'s on drugs.'

'Pippa's at an age when she wants to read teenage magazines,' says Sheila. 'So I do have some inkling what you're going through. But I would never allow her to . . .'

'Ruthie isn't allowed on a *tube* without my say so.'

He is going into Holborn tube station, sucked down into the Underground system, while Myra and Marion buy tickets and despair at losing him. But there he is, at the bottom, studying a bra advert, so they are able to overtake him, only to find that he had turned right to the Piccadilly line, instead of left to the Central line. 'I told you he'd take the blue line, Myra,' says Marion. 'He's hardly the type to go to Bond Street.'

Marion and Myra are good at Underground maps; they know parts of London that few would wish to reach. On days when Interesting People elude them, they travel to the end of the lines: to Morden, via Bank; to Upminster; to Heathrow, pushing each other in trollies reserved for the traveller; to Cockfosters; to Ealing Broadway.

He does look different, this Interesting Person, waiting for the tube to arrive, taking out Lou Matherbay's *Breaking the Barricades* from his pocket, unbending it, reading the first page as they wait, carrying it in his left hand as the train arrives. 'Note that down, Myra,' says Marion. 'The left hand,' writes Myra. 'Ringless.' They sit with him in the carriage, as he turns from the first to the last page of the book, with bloated mothers, about to burst with children, trying desperately to control the ones that they have. 'Write about them, Myra,' says Marion. 'They might be significant.'

The train stops at Russell Square, and Interesting Person climbs off, as do Myra and Marion. It is just the three of them, waiting for the lift to take them upwards, two of them snickering, in the style of generations of girls like themselves. He stands, peering at them, pondering them, which Myra and Marion find irresistible.

He turns around, and turns around, as Myra and Marion half-walk and half-collapse with the heat of the situation and its humour. He looks at them, and looks at them, half-walking, half-turning, half-smiling, as he walks. He stops, as if waiting for the two girls, both beautifully blushing, to pass him by. But they, too, stop because the situation is now, indeed, interesting.

'What I don't understand is, why follow people?'
'Ever since she *deliberately* fell out with Ruthie . . .'
'Well, she's fallen in with a very bad apple now.'
'This friend sounds like a terrible influence.'

'There's no need to follow me,' he says. 'You can walk with me, you know.'

It is the first sound he has made, and the first sound Myra and Marion are hearing, from Interesting Person. 'He's heavenly, definitely,' whispers Marion, and Myra walks forward, anxious for Interest to walk with her, glowing all around her, like the breakfast-cereal commercial. 'Come on, Myra,' she says.

'Do you do this all the time?' he asks them, as if they are used to grown, interesting men talking to them; as if Myra and

Marion aren't melting to the pavement, melting with the heat, like wax candles; melting with self-consciousness and the over-weight carrier bags, melting with the moment.

Only that morning, Myra had sat with her sisters, fighting over free gifts inside Shreddies, in a clean, square house, and racing to dress as Dad twittered about the rats in his company and Mum poured milk into a jug and sugar into a bowl.

'Yes,' says Marion, synchronising with Myra's 'No'.

'Why were you following me, particularly?' he asks, sharing his glances between the girls. 'What was so interesting about me?'

'Well, firstly, you're a drug addict,' says Marion.

'And you have cheekbones,' says Myra.

'You have an interesting life.'

'Lived interestingly.'

'There's nothing interesting about my life,' the man says, laughing. 'You've picked the wrong man. And I'm *definitely* not a drug addict.'

'D'you want to come in for a coffee or something?' asks the man, who studies politics and lives in Russell Square; who breakfasts in Soho and finds Myra and Marion 'eccentric, but entertaining'.

'Yes please,' says Marion, and Myra follows.

The corridors and the grey stone steps inside smell of urine and windy, cold air, welcome against the outside heat. The bannisters are painted rock hard, as in hospitals; a support for Myra, who wobbles with excitement and deliverance from everything humdrum and ordinary.

Unlocking an inner door, the man welcomes them into his tiny flat, carelessly painted white and furnished for one. Another man sits at a table, twisting the dial of a radio and smoking two cigarettes at once. He is dressed in black, half his yellow hair shaped to fit inside a black beret, which sits, planted, on his beautiful head.

'Al-ex-ander,' he drawls, out of the movies. 'What a pleasant surprise. Where have you been? Babysitting?' he asks, indicating Marion and Myra.

'They followed me home. It was the least I could do, to invite them in.'

'What the *fuck* are you following Alexander for, dearios? When you could have followed *me*. I've just been to the supermarket.'

'We would have, I'm sure, had you been outside,' says Myra, falling in love again, on one leg.

'Well, what did you get then?' says Alexander, going over to a weighted carrier bag which sits next to the radio, on the table. 'This is Ben, by the way,' he says, flicking his knuckles at Ben, who says: 'Benjamin to them.'

Alexander picks out a carton of milk from the carrier. 'Is this it, Ben? You just got milk. Bloody hell, couldn't you have got any biscuits?'

'Couldn't stretch to biscuits. But I did get some of this,' he said, taking out a little plastic bag, filled with white powder. 'Went to Barney's.'

'But I'm hungry,' says Alexander, going out, to his only other room. Benjamin lined up some powder on the table.

'They *are* drug addicts,' whispers Marion, excitedly, to Myra.

'Is that pot?' asks Myra of Benjamin.

'You've worried me now,' says Penny. 'I mean, Myra's always been restless. Not like Fiona and Jacqueline. They just get on with their lives.'

'Middle child,' says Gillian, confidently. 'Desperate for the attention.'

'But she's always defying us. She tells us she goes to the Wimpy. Take today, I only gave her money for a banana sundae and a whipped hot chocolate.'

'You mean she's out today? Oh, *Penny.*'

'Oh, *Penny.*'

'Take a seat,' says Ben to the girls, as Alexander returns and lights the gas for a whistling kettle, which he shakes for the sound of water before dropping it to the flame.

'Where shall we sit?' asks Myra as Marion sits, cross-legged, on the floor, throwing her bulky carrier bag next to the wall. Myra joins her.

'Coffee or tea?' asks Alexander, all motherly now.

The girls cry 'Coffee' as Benjamin switches the radio on, to the sounds of Big Ben chiming. 'Fuck, it's the news already,' he says, to Alexander, who leans, hopelessly, on the kitchen counter.

'Britain has declared war on Argentina . . . further reinforcements are expected to reach the Falkland Islands . . .' says the radio to the four of them, who sit around it, staring at it, as if it were television without the pictures. 'Fuck me,' says Benjamin.

'I don't believe it,' says Myra and Marion, who have never, properly, heard the news before.

'The Tory bastards,' says Alexander, glumly.

'It'll mean World War Three,' Benjamin says, to the sound of the kettle whistling, flames rising around it, on the gas. 'It's just what Matherbay said – the next world war will start with the Falkland Islands. The Argies'll be dropping bombs on London soon, just you wait.' Myra shivers.

'What are your politics?' Alexander asks Myra, looking straight at her.

'Well, I don't think I have any,' says Myra. 'But I quite fancy David Owen.'

'Fuck that,' says Alexander, his eyes firing. 'The only one worth listening to is Lou Matherbay.'

'The only one worth *fucking*, you mean,' drawls Benjamin.

'But isn't she a bra-burning bitch?' asks Myra, quoting Roger Felt.

'And you believe that?' asks Alexander. He flicks through *Breaking The Barricades*. 'Here, listen to what she says about women . . .'

Myra listens greedily, liking it better than drug addiction.

'The truth is,' says Brenda Redbridge, opening her soft, pink leather handbag. 'If anything *does* happen, Penny. (I'll pay for this, by the way.) Not that I want to scare you, but there'll be no going back.'

'One wrong experience is all it takes.'

'She'll never be the same jokey, light-hearted little Myra,' says Sheila Hanrahan, fighting with Brenda over the bill. 'You paid for it last time. Let me pay.'

'The bad . . .' says Gillian, handing the waitress a tenner.

'*Gillian*. We wanted to pay.'

'The *bad* will have happened.'

The girls are on a train, which is taking them home. 'I think that was a turning point,' says Marion, tearing open a stick of beef, pressing the plastic, forcing the beef to reveal itself.

'Weren't they beautiful and heavenly?' asks Myra, biting open a packet of ginger biscuits, sold in pairs.

'They were hallucinations,' says Marion, chewing the beef stick. 'They appeared from nowhere, like hallucinations.'

'We'll call them the Hallucinations,' Myra says, crumbling a biscuit in half with her hands.

'Benjamin Hallucination and Alexander Hallucination,' agrees Marion.

The tube finds home territory, as always, filling up with child's-eye houses, leaving no space unturfed, or built upon, or scattered with plastic, theme pubs (for entertainment's sake). Ruislip Gardens, where, just to stand out, one needs planning permission.

Myra sneaks a look inside her bag at Lou Matherbay's *Breaking the Barricades*, a present from Alexander.

'Doesn't everything feel different?' asks Marion.

'It's the end of an era,' says Myra.

Chapter Eight

He had blond hair, curling like Cupid's, or a choirboy's, and green eyes, dotted black. His skin was hard, and male. Sleeping, he looked sweetly soft. As he breathed, he inflated the duvet around his stomach, rhythmically, and Myra lay there, mesmerised by a man's life, in her bed.

She was profoundly, disastrously, hopelessly in love with him. As his muscles twitched, irritatedly, she sighed. As he breathed in, her stomach curdled. She hugged her spindly knees to her bony chest, wrapped herself in a dressing-gown, and went to make real, dark coffee. 'I am in *love* again . . .' she sang to the radio host.

Charles Pickford, had, of all the places and of all the parties in all of London, chosen to be at the same event as Myra Felt. Not only that, but he had chosen to be in the same room. He had chosen her room out of several teeming with live and lithe ladies, belching smoke and laughter freely into the hall. He had then chosen to drop the butterfly of his earring on to the carpet, next to Myra, forcing her to join in the hunt with Charles, Ken and Jerry.

He had asked *her* to help him, Ken and Jerry look for the butterfly despite the fact that several women stood around, bored and unaccompanied, whereas Myra was busy, talking to a very interesting zoologist. 'Sorry to bother you, but I don't suppose you're standing on my butterfly?' he had asked, leaning seductively towards Myra. As she moved from her spot, he said: 'You wouldn't help me look for it, would you? There's something about you. I just know that you'll find it?'

Charles's eyes bounced with green. His face was oval, sharp-chinned and cheeky. His breath smelt beery and his friends were leering. 'What the hell,' thought Myra. 'The zoologist is married.'

Myra liked the moment of attraction. She adored it when a

man noticed her and approached her, his eyes dilating and his colour diluting. If anything in reality correlated with the movies – the sort of movies Myra went to see – then this was it; this moment when sex appeal worked its spell over Myra.

The man could be fair, or he could be dark. He could be round or he could be long. He could be stupid or he could be an *intellectual*. His mother could play a large part in his life or his friends could. His drug of choice could be cocaine or it could be the sounds of a rugby changing room. Myra would not mind because the man had, for that moment, chosen her and the being chosen was so delicious to Myra that she could almost taste it.

She agreed, charmingly, to his request and hunted for the butterfly with such a display of Miss Marple it was nudging embarrassment. When he went to get her a drink from the kitchen (because Myra's beer dregs had been polluted with cigarette ends), she knew that this was her test as, had she not waited, he could have taken it that she, for one, did not think him text-book handsome. And she *had* waited for him because she, for one, did not care if he was text-book handsome.

Myra was unlikely to become a VIP, fêted and admired, cosseted and desired, at G7 functions or BritPop award ceremonies. She wanted this moment where, for one moment, she was a very important person. So, with her full-length, grey patterned dress which made women dismiss her with an E for effort and certain men long for a night with her, Myra seized her moment.

It was a long moment, as they poured beer and vodka down their throats and discussed whether it was right to fine parents for bringing their children late to school. They talked about whether it was proper for single parents to parent, and whether, in the future, there would be such a concept as a parent. As Ken and Jerry floated away from them, Myra and Charles discussed marriage, birth defects and divorce. They argued about state versus private education, the minimum age of consent, and girls' names.

At some point in the evening, they discovered they were on the cusp of Pisces, together. They both liked the names Dilys and Fabergé. They realised their shared ability to crack knuckles and the ability of bending elbows forward, just before breaking

point. He laughed at her jokes, which were always self-depre-
catory, and they drank, became drunk, and still they drank.

He was a management trainee with Dutton's, but would have
liked to have had the nerve to take up photography *full-time*.
She told him of her longing for curves. And he had said, seductively: 'Rugged the breast that beauty cannot tame. Forget *tits*.
You, Myra, have a great bod.'

They chose fifty-six Desert-Island Discs, six Room 101s and
twelve examples of British Comedy At Its Best between them.
By the end of the evening, they knew more about each other
than Elizabeth did Darcy, Scarlett did Rhett, or Vera did Jack.
Romance, be served.

There she was now, percolating coffee, single-handedly. She
had pressed two slices of bread into the toaster. If she had had
eggs in her fridge, she would have experimented – thrown them
in a frying pan with a dash of olive oil. Hell, if she owned any
sausages or mushrooms she would have flung them in the frying
pan too, gone the whole way, sautéed potatoes, hashed her own
hash browns, halved her own grapefruits, found maraschino
cherries and squashed them in the centre. She would be pinnied
now, if she owned a pinafore, baking bread if her oven worked
properly, churning butter if she could only find a churn.

'Lo,' he said, walking into her kitchen, dressed.

'Hi. D'you want coffee?' she asked.

'Got to go actually. I'm playing footie this afternoon.'

'Oh, right. Where?'

'Regent's Park.'

'Right near me.'

'Right.'

In retrospect, Myra was certain she must have said more than
that. They must have talked as he went towards the door,
treading over her junk mail, as he opened the door, as he walked
down the path, as he opened the gate, stiffly. There must have
been some mention of a telephone there, a ring, a sometime
ring. She couldn't remember if he had talked about telephoning,
but she sat by her telephone, typically, anyway, waiting for it to
ring, and waiting for it to be him.

His oval face had become increasingly cheekboned. His eyes
were blue now and his lashes darker. On Monday, he grew three

inches in her estimation. On Tuesday, he developed huge, rippling chest muscles. On Wednesday he was the spitting image of a young Ryan O'Neal.

On Thursday, as he talked to her on the telephone, he was an ugly version of Rory Bremner. But they were dating by then, in an American sense. By Friday, he was her boyfriend and by Saturday, her man. There was no doubt about it, she was in a relationship. Myra did realise, while in the delicatessen, that she spent more time choosing cheese than she spent choosing men. But then, with cheese, there was so much more choice and it was all spread out on the counter.

Charles Pickford had photographed her. 'You're lovely,' he had said, shading her properly. He had shown Myra her own image, dressed in grubby red and skinny cream; framed in half-light. He had scribbled at the top: *As much beauty as could die.* And she had squealed, staring at the camera's lies – the spilling curls, the false curves. 'Thank you,' she had said, as if her image was in his gift.

He had met her friends – Lisa, Lennie, Sandra, Kate, Marion, Dill – in appropriate, expertly planned chance circumstances. He had met other of her friends – Sell, Tyrone, Kasha, Tim, Paula, Neil – people that Myra had arranged in advance around her home. 'How many friends do you *have?*' he had asked her after a party which had followed a Make-Che-Jealous CRACA meeting. It was only then – or when he had met Jackie, Monica, Jenny and Eva – that Myra felt she had more than fulfilled her good girlfriend potential. She had, after that, allowed herself to spend more time with him alone, photographing each other with Charles Pickford's flash camera or comparing alcohol content in bottles of cheap off-licence wine.

('Very nice,' her friends had said. The women, even Marion, had flirted with him. The men had discussed football and sexual innuendo in children's programmes. 'Seaman Staines. I mean!')

Reaching 'I love you' had been almost effortless on Myra's part. He had said it so quickly, inside yet another quote, as they had eaten in the cheapest Chinese restaurant in London. 'You made me love you, you know,' he had half-sung. 'I didn't want to do it.'

Half an hour later, however, Myra had had to ask him again. 'So you love me, do you, Charles?'

'You know I do,' he had said, fumbling for fairly small change. Myra had worked her way through the address book, telling sceptical friends about Myra and Charles, Charles and Myra. 'It didn't sound ridiculous in context,' she had insisted. 'You know, honestly, I made him love me.'

'Yes, of course,' Marion had said, apparently with some sarcasm. She considered love a germ that one showered off. 'And then *all your clothes fell off* . . .'

Charles and Myra were inside yet another eaterie, eating. 'You'll like this place,' said Charles, who seemed a little distant. 'The crêpes are good.'

'Which one would I like the most?' asked Myra, who usually forgot to eat. (Breakfast, lunch and dinner merged into one small snack, at three a.m.)

'I don't know. Honey and lemon?' he suggested irritably, scratching his testicles. She smoked over the other customers.

'The special,' ordered Myra, as Charles looked everywhere but at Myra. 'And for you, sir?' the waitress asked, trying to interest Charles in her breasts. 'Oh, the same,' said Charles. 'Whatever . . .'

'So what do you think?' she asked.

'About what?' he replied, suddenly bored.

'I was saying about Lou Matherbay. *Apparently*, Sara is manoeuvring to make her stand in October. Ray Hines is furious. He thinks, as deputy, he's the natural next leader. But there's talk of new blood, sweeping clean. After the by-election, in Peyarth . . .'

'Listen, Myra . . .'

The waitress appeared at the side of the couple as they closed in on each other. 'Oh sorry,' she said, waving a bill-pad aggressively. 'Hope I'm not interrupting anything.'

'No,' he said, his eyes coming to life. 'Of course you aren't.'

'The special's off, I'm afraid,' she said. 'Sorry.'

'God, and on our wedding anniversary too,' said Myra, comically.

'Myra, *please*,' he said, moving away from her, as the waitress left with their new order. 'You are so . . . so . . . so silly,' he said, surprisingly finding the right word. 'Why the *fuck* did you say it was our *anniversary*? I can't make you out,' he said. 'I don't understand you. And I don't think it's working out. You're *strange*. I don't think *we're* working out. I brought you here to . . .'

'To dump me?' asked Myra unhappily.

Myra and Charles sat, she playing macramé with the paper napkin, he stiff-still and suddenly more attractive. 'Why?' she asked, uselessly. But he had run out of beautiful phrases, just when Myra needed words. She had never had a proper explanation from men in general, an explanation for her failure with them. No matter how neatly Myra matched her life to theirs, forgetting her own world for the duration of the relationship, she did not seem to end up with anything approaching emotionally long-term.

Charles Pickford mumbled something about commitment as a large heart-shaped crêpe was delivered to their table covered repulsively in nuts, honey, coconut and chocolate. 'Happy anniversary,' said the waitress, leaving the couple-no-more to tuck in – Charles stabbing at one side of the heart with his fork and knife, Myra licking spoonfuls of neat honey, scraped off the soggy crêpe.

'If you want to get in touch with me you can go through my lawyer,' said Myra, standing at the exit to Crêpe City. But he did not seem interested, not in the irony of the situation, her humour or, indeed, in Myra Felt.

Chapter Nine

If Meryl rows with Mary and Elaine and Karla have a fight, Elaine may have to be with Meryl, leaving Mary to partner Ellen. Or Ellen may end up with Meryl, who, incidentally, looks like a Chinese wrestler, stout and strong with a stretched, broad head. Or she could partner Lydia, who tours the edge of the changing room, looking for her left plimsoll.

'Find your partners please, girls. We'll be jumping through hoops today,' says Miss Lafferty, Physical Education Instructor, inside the large assembly hall.

There might be a chance of either Janice or Julia. Julia, however, may partner Lisa, leaving Lorna bereft and, possibly, hopefully, with Ellen. Plumpish Kathryn is looking for a partner, as is Tabitha, who walks with a limp. Ellen stands to be noticed, skinny frame erect; the pin of her kittenish, semi-pornographic pleated skirt pricking her right leg. The girls go off in two by two, hurrah, hurrah . . .

'Come on. Come on. I said, find a partner. Josie, Julia, Candice, Ellen . . .'

Josie, Julia and Candice stand in the corner, their bodies creasing with laughter, shaking with it. 'But Miss,' they say, reading from a newspaper. 'It says here, young girls shouldn't *need* to take part in physical activity . . .'

'Whaaat?' asks Miss Lafferty, her legs crossed, foundation pastried on, lipstick shiny and blue eyes bright with intent, thinking about that tart who stole her fiancé. 'It's what it says here,' says Candice Turk, fiercely (feared throughout the school, from caretaker to cat). 'In Miriam Abrahams' *diary*.'

'What *are* you talking about?' asks Corinne Lafferty, dry body rising to stand, as a thirteen-year-old Ellen stiffens. A button is hanging from her shirt by a thread. The line of Corinne's mouth forces to a smile. 'What are you reading from?'

'The diary. By Miriam Abrahams,' reads Candice, her perfect

face blonde and symmetrical. 'In the *Kenton Gazette*. Miriam says here: "Why do young girls need physical activity? Take my Eileen, little stick of a thing. She *hates* all that running, all that jumping." '

It is cold in there, in the assembly hall. It is cold for a stick-like Ellen, a rapidly maturing Ellen Abrahams, who creeps, for camouflage, against the wooden frames which climb the wall, stickily. She is trapped by the high green-glass windows, the double doors – thick and slow – and the slithering, crusting pipes on the floor.

'Miss Lafferty?' asks Candice Turk, eyes innocent. 'Might Miriam be Ellen Abrahams' mother?'

'Is that true?' Miss Lafferty asks Ellen, who vanishes into a background of brown wooden stripes, breathing assembly-hall air. Corinne Lafferty snatches the newspaper from Candice's clutches, peering at the diary photograph. 'Well, there is a likeness,' she says, to the girls' chuckles. 'All that *hair*, perhaps.'

As the laughter comes close, Ellen pushes a hand through her long, curly, brown hair for support. It has felt dry lately, fanning around her head, all the oil sucked away. The assembly-hall atmosphere is dry, taken over with sounds. Miss Lafferty says: 'So, Ellen, your mother thinks physical education is bad for you? Is that right?'

'She's not talking about me. That girl's *Eileen*,' says Ellen quietly. 'And anyway, that woman *is not my mother*,' Ellen says, to schoolgirls, standing around her in an arc.

She thinks of Mum. She thinks of Miriam blowing through boutiques on Saturday afternoons, filling them with that sheer heavy weight of noise, and leopard-skin blouses, popping open over huge *Carry On* film breasts; popping open in public places. She thinks of Miriam, playing intimacy by numbers.

1) 'Mind if I browse? We won't take up room. We're only little.'

2) 'Ohhh, now these are what I call clothes! Have you owned it long?'

3) 'Is there a discount for being a columnist with the *Kenton Gazette*?'

4) 'Just joking around!'

5) 'Well, my columns are *entertaining* and *informative*. Like the BBC.'

6) 'What do you think of this hat? Oooh, you're just being nice.'

7) 'You know, this is a nice shop. Like my husband's shop on the high street.'

8) 'I'm getting this hat. This hat is Miriam Abrahams!'

9) 'You don't know Hardware Barry's? Ellie, she doesn't . . .'

10) 'Yes, round the back of Dutton's. Come and visit. We'll give you a discount, won't we, Ellie? D'you know, I feel like we're old friends.'

And only when Mum has a ten per cent discount on her hat, as well as a close friend in Angela Copthorne of Styles By Angela, does she pay for anything, spilling her handbag on to the floor to reveal dirt collecting on handkerchiefs, a lining cracking with lipstick, two huge pairs of underpants.

Insanity is hereditary. You get it from your kids screamed the sticker on the windscreen of their Honda Civic as, six months ago, Miriam and Ellen sold rubbish from the boot of their car. 'Get your knick-knacks here,' yelled Mum at the Kenton car-boot sale. 'The Abrahams are giving it away. Ten Enid Blytons a pound!'

'Oliver Smith,' said a middle-aged man, approaching Miriam. 'You know, you're taking away my customers. So, either my approach is wrong. Or *you're* better looking.'

'I must be better looking then,' Miriam said, spluttering with laughter. 'Because I don't have *an approach*. Miriam Aberahams. And who, *are you?*'

'Oliver Smith. I edit the *Kenton Gazette*,' he said. 'Do you know it?' he asked.

'Know it?' she yelled. 'I get it every week!'

As Ellen packed up, Oliver offered Miriam a column in his newspaper. 'I'm taking a chance, I know that,' he said. 'But there aren't enough characters in this world,' he said. 'Or in Kenton. And you certainly know how to tell a story.'

Mum knows how to tell a story and how to sell white, cracked china pigs; one-armed dolls; Ellen's old *Look-In* annuals; the knitted bits of nothing; the gardening encyclopaedia, with the sign on it saying: *In mint condition.* She knows how to sell an

Etch-A-Sketch that doesn't sketch, a four-year-old diary (with the whole of April missing); an *Operation* game, minus its plastic organs.

'I want you to meet someone!' she yelled last year, at JFK airport in New York. Running through the crowds, in an insane yellow trouser-suit and tall heels, she screamed: 'Franklin, meet the Abrahams. Ellie, Darren and Barry. *This* is Franklin.'

An African-American man, presumably an old friend, ran up behind Miriam, a grinning soulmate, pressing their hands into his, as the Abrahams smiled, *en masse*. The family empathised with Franklin over his diabetes, the premature birth of his daughter, and his timeshare losses in Miami. They found out, some time later, that Franklin was their taxi driver, waiting to take them to the Upper West Side.

Miss Lafferty tucks the newspaper inside her tracksuit trousers. 'OK, enough fun,' she says, as if it is fun. 'I want balls through hoops.'

And there they go marching two by two, hurrah, hurrah.

Candice Turk jumps through the hoop. Hurrah, hurrah.

But look at Ms Abrahams, all alone, jumping a hoop made just for one.

It's. Not. Much. Fun. On your own.

Hurrah. Hurrah.

Interrupting, an adult head pokes through the green door-glass, smiling. 'Sorry to bother everyone,' it says. 'It's only *me*. Miriam Abrahams,' the face beams, from a different world. Teenage girls squeal and scream at the sight, turning to each other and laughing hard. 'It's *Miriam Abrahams*,' mocks Candice.

As the head, attached no doubt to a body, comes inside the gym, Ellen is doomed to visibility, leaning on the five-foot wooden beam, kicking her heel, pulling the loose strand on her gym top, until it drags to a satisfying length.

'*Miriam Abrahams*,' says the woman again, paw forward to shake Corinne's delicate, pink-painted nails on hands not made for this world. She shakes her own mess of lacquered brown hair, red with cheap dye, and a stripe of grey loose like a feather around the head. She is wearing the animal-print top, squeezed around freckled, sunbed-tanned breasts to hang low, around tight leggings. Around her waist is a clinking-clanking gold-chain belt, loose and useless.

'Oh yes, Miriam Abrahams,' confirms Corinne Lafferty. 'From the *Kenton Gazette*?' she mocks.

'I'm famous?' screams the woman, her foundation orange against her neck. 'Oh, you mustn't!' she says, spraying laughter. '*Corinne*, you mustn't. Or there'll be an accident.'

And, for Ellen, the moment freezes. Mum, vulgar in the synagogue and in crowded shopping centres, invading Ellen's reality. She is stuck there, this huge, low-cut woman, stuck standing, shouting at fêtes: 'I got it. I won the *raffle*.' Loose with words, pouring over Ellen's father, as he tries, despite her size and his heart trouble, to restrain his wife. 'Barry. Let me *go*,' she says, dancing. 'I won the fruit basket.' 'No,' said Barry, trying to shrug off his East End accent. 'Your ticket's pink, look.'

'Oh, Corinne, *anyway*,' says Miriam, releasing the PE teacher. 'I hope you don't mind my interrupting but my daughter *won't eat lunch*. I've seen doctors – they say she's too thin. My own Mum thinks I'm starving her. And I don't know what to . . . Where is she?'

She produces a huge lunch box, to laughter. She looks around for Ellen, who is blushing red, behind a beam. 'Ellie. *There* you are!'

'I'm not *hungry*,' says Ellen, feeling pain, the pain of the moment.

'I thought she wasn't your mother, Ellen,' whispers Mary Tucker, giggling close.

'Go *away*,' snarls Ellen.

Miriam approaches, lifting the lid on a lunch box to reveal thick white sandwiches; bars of chocolate; slices of salami; a potato latke; a large bag of Jelly Babies. 'God, Ellie. Anyone would think I'm poisoning you,' she says, sitting, legs either side of the beam, facing her daughter. 'Here, there's egg and onion sandwiches . . .' Miriam rubbishes through the lunch box, announcing item by item. She sits, blouse-splitting with every breath, on the beam. 'Don't give me this, Ellie, like you do at home. All I ask is that you *eat*.'

In Ellen's home, cupboards jam with spreads and breads. Out-of-date cereals push for space around jars of honey and bars of chocolate. Sweets lie everywhere, over fried everything. Big pots of stew sit beside ladles of lokshen, as they pile on to Ellen's plate. Kneidlach fight kreplach inside soggy ('I never follow recipes!') lemon meringue pie. In Ellen's home, breakfast is bound up with battles, supper consumed by argument.

Now, Miriam asks: 'What can you do with young girls?' of Corinne Lafferty, who has never known. 'My daughter refuses my food.'

'Still,' Miriam says, standing up, pulling down her top, to cover every swelling. 'I've done my best. Barry says I should let her starve. But how could a mother do that? Tell me that?'

'*Please*, Mum,' hisses Ellen. '*Go home.*'

A button falls from Ellen's chest to the floor. Lydia chucks a stray ball at Miriam as she leaves, larger than life, turning at the assembly door. 'Oh well. I'll see you, Corinne, at *Open Evening*. We'll have a chat about Ellie's little problem then.' Ellen crushes the button underfoot, as Mum leaves with the parting shot: 'And Ellie,' she says. 'You'd better bring that box back empty. Or it won't be me you'll have to deal with. It'll be *Barry*.'

Without a parent present, the room seems empty. Young girls rush at the daughter, led by Candice. 'You need to eat, *Ellie*,' they say. 'If you want to be fat, like Mummy.' Candice Turk shoves bits of bread into Ellen's mouth. Laura Renton unwraps chocolate, pushing it into Ellen's mouth, inside her pale, drawn face. And Sophie Wright hops about, ever the spectator, pouring with laughter, as her friends fill Ellen's face with food.

'Come on. Come on, girls. I said, *girls*,' says Corinne Lafferty, tired of Abrahams entertainment. 'We've had enough interruption. I want balls in hoops.'

In the showers, girls throw cupfuls of soapy water over Ellen, as she pulls on her socks, bent and knickerless; as she towels the water away, defiant in the private knowledge that there will be tears in the water she will be wiping off with the fluffy yellow towel Mum bought specially that week, after she begged and pleaded to be rid of the yellowing white one.

Teachers roam St Mark's School for Girls in shadows, unable to be found as Gillian Cooper shuts her mouth tight and tens of girls roar with laughter, at her brace. Teachers roam, unseen, as Jennifer Bryony hides behind a toilet door, crouching, with stiff pain in her left shoulder, as a hundred girls swarm the school, looking for Jennifer Bryony, who has written to a magazine problem page about menstruation.

'Your mother's a *tramp*,' whispers Candice Turk, pulling at the stitch where a button had been. 'Your house was a mess that time I came round. And look at you. I mean, doesn't she know how to sew?'

Ellen screws gym clothes into her bag. Despite the rigid rules about homework, she will not write the composition tonight. She will not translate the French about the mince and mincing Xavier. She will not draw the human heart. She is using pain.

'You might be unhappy now,' says Dad. 'But pain's good, see? I've 'ad so many times when things aren't going my way. And I could give up but I don't. I've had 'em all laughin' at me. *Laughin*'s easy. But I use what I feel, to spur me on, see? Without pain, I wouldn't know the value of *anything*. Pain,' as Dad explains, 'is *useful*.'

Ellen hangs on to hers now.

Barry Abrahams is in the business of hardware, and bettering himself. 'I left the East End with a bag of nails and an idea,' he says. 'And I've built up six shops from nothing,' he says. 'Six shops,' he says. 'From *nothing*. My wife can have what she wants. New curtains, an extension. My children can have what they want. Hi-fis, an education. OK, I've had a little heart attack. But my children will inherit six hardware shops. From *nothing*.'

Last year, Ellen came home with a silver year cup.

'I'm so proud of you,' yelled Mum.

'Second in the *whole year*,' Dad said.

'I'm so proud of you,' yelled Mum.

'We'll celebrate next year,' said Dad, 'When you come in *first*.'

Wrapped warmly in unclaimed fifth-former coats, cheaply perfumed, she is hiding in the cloakroom. Checking the streets are free of the sounds of children, she runs for a bus. On the bus, stray voices leap at her.

'So, my boss says to me, no. And I say, yes. And he says, no. And I say, well I'm leaving . . .' 'So you've left your job?' 'Well, I had to make the decision some time.'

And Ellen looks at these two women, with places to go, and with decisions to make. She thinks of her home: a dilapidated semi, rotting outside, kept filthy inside with Miriam's outbursts, Miriam's overnight hobbies; the china dolls, the half-eaten, browning bananas in the fruit bowl, the so-called antiques (newly bought), the pots of dry, forgotten stew.

('Don't touch, Ellen. Don't move my *things* . . .'

'Candice is coming round. I want things to look neat, that's all.'

'Don't touch. This way, I know where everything *is*.')

The women on Ellen's bus talk about their lives. 'So, are you moving out of that dump?' one woman asks the other. 'Next month,' says the other, as Ellen thinks of her life, taken over by grown men and women, by Miriam and Barry, by Miss Lafferty and Mr Porter. Her life, mapped out before her, by amateurs. Her school uniform, soiled with a schoolgirl stink. Her crumbling home drawing up, through the bus window.

Only five more years, thought Ellen. *And then I'm free . . .*

Chapter Ten

FastNews had been replaced that day by a Giving Birth Season Special and Ellen had been given the day off. Finishing a Lou Matherbay biography at three a.m. she had barely slept, but she needed, of course, to make the most of her time.

So she sat, at her bay window in Harrow-on-the-Hill, exhaustedly reading the newspapers. She discovered that the Social Democrat José Francisco Pena Gomez was declaring himself 'virtual President' of the Dominican Republic, and that the man from number twelve had reversed into the lady from number seven's garden railings. Ellen leafed through her notebook, found D for Dominican Republic, crossed out Joaquin Balaguer next to President and wrote José Francisco Pena Gomez.

'I know it was you. I know it was you,' the lady from number seven was saying to the man from number twelve. 'You drove straight into my posts.'

Ellen had, stupidly, arranged to have lunch in West Hampstead with her brother Darren and Lucy. There just isn't the time any more, she thought, unfolding an envelope of newspaper cuttings, headed *Lou Matherbay*. 'The Belgrano campaign . . . 72.6% . . . highest House profile . . . two children, one at Harvard, one on drugs . . .' she muttered, scribbling in her notebook.

The Women In Power, Women Of Achievement series had started without her. Films about Margaret Thatcher and Madonna had been shown, to wide appreciation, last week. Yet Berkovsky had told her: 'I don't want you to start filming, Ellen, until Lou announces she's standing for leader. Otherwise, she's old hat, isn't she? Just some blip on the political landscape. A *maverick*.'

She had long dreamt of receiving a TV Prime award. 'I'd just like to thank all those who thought I'd never make it,' she would say. 'Candice Turk, Miss Lafferty, Mr Porter, Dad . . .' *Dad?*

Other producers were, however, ahead of her in the race. For those special shots, tracks had been hired, dollies paid for. A camera had been booked, 'for filming down a mine shaft'. One producer was in training for his portrait of Liz McColgan; the film entitled: 'The loneliness of a long-distance runner'. Ellen had overheard another say: 'I'm sorry, I don't care how much it costs. If I'm going to be filming Diana eating toast, I'll need a mini-crane.'

'I could profile another woman,' Ellen had tentatively suggested.

'But the whole point is that you care about Lou Matherbay,' said Berkovsky. 'I thought, from what you said in your interview, that she was important to you. Give it time. There's no hurry.'

'Arrested in 1982 . . . three husbands . . . vs hunting, fishing, men's toilets . . .'

She dressed for lunch, with half an eye on a televised summit, watching Yeltsin, Kohl and Clinton – big and broad – line up to be photographed. The three big men jockeyed for position and joked for the cameras whilst the heads of smaller, less influential nations stood, embarrassed, at the back, and the Japanese Prime Minister slipped through the larger men to the front, smiling.

TO DO:

Nails cleaned out: Yes.

Newspapers read: Yes.

Apple pie defrosted: Yes.

Lipstick on: *No.*

Whitehall official said today that spending on mental health-care needs to be doubled. Blaming both central government and . . .

Not wanting to have lunch on an empty stomach, Ellen made herself a guilty Stilton sandwich. Food, for Ellen, far from being fuel, was a weakness: there only for women to want – fleshy women. Fighting flesh – and its sins – Ellen had been battling with hunger for so long, it was barely recognisable. It came not just in the form of breakfast, lunch or a mid-morning snack but with bath-time and embarrassment and in the dead of night. Then, she would creep downstairs, crawling through bin-bags and dirt-caked tampon packets, in search of the elusive Flake, the hidden Caramel, the mocking Hob Nob.

But she could never eat publicly. Restaurants had become torture chambers to Ellen – places for people to watch her cut up meat, chew on potatoes and swallow olives. In restaurants and at dinner parties, Ellen watched and waited for friends and waiters to laugh, to burst into giggles as she worked her way through food minefields. Only at home, in the privacy of her kitchen, could she tear at chicken bones and cheese on toast, away from smiling, prying eyes, waiting for Ellen to show her teeth or – terrible – an appetite for food.

(Berkovsky: 'Still hasn't declared yet, has she Ellen?')

During the tube journey, Ellen listened, loudly, to an English-language programme on her personal stereo, learning how to accept an invitation to a party in Proper English.

'Lou's entourage . . . born, Peckham . . .' she mumbled, walking past cars parked against the flow of traffic. Ellen saw Lucy and Darren through the windows of the café; both fair-haired, jumpered, and broad. They looked dangerous together, alluring, like Shakespeare's twins in *Twelfth Night*. Neat in their seats, they painted a pretty picture. *Spoiled only by me*, thought Ellen, as she waved briefly through the glass.

'You have to go to the counter and order, I'm afraid,' Lucy apologised, as Ellen came into the café, catching a thread of her coat on the door and having to unhook herself.

'I thought I was fine for time,' Ellen said, puzzled. Her hair had been soaked to her head by the dribbly rain.

'We arranged to meet earlier,' said Lucy. 'As you had so much to do.'

Two waiters leaned against the staff-side of a glass cabinet, which housed big, black cakes, creamy puddings, croissants, ciabatta rolls and white bowls that were plump with sandwich fillings. Ellen, despising the choice, chose a cheese sandwich.

'With pickle?' asked the bored, brown waiter.

'No thanks.'

'With ham?'

'No. Just on its own.'

'With avocado?'

He forced her, finally, to accept black pepper and a slice of tomato. It was always the same with waiters. *Parmesan? Another roll? Would you like dressing with that, Madam?* The smirks spoke volumes. Resistance was futile. They would pile necessities on to Ellen's plate, forcing her to pick at more and more food, to play around with growing piles of salad, to pretend fullness as friends' food disappeared and her own plate filled out by comparison, developing to monstrous proportion.

She carried her plate – a strand of cress placed bitchily beside the sandwich – to Lucy and Darren. Despite the rain Lucy was wearing a tease of a sleeveless shift dress. She was sucking on a candy bead necklace, which hung around her neck, in every colour of the rainbow.

'Ellen, you know, we've decided that you're too young to get married,' said Lucy.

'And you know what *I* think,' said Darren. 'But when does Ellen ever listen to anyone? Least of all her own *brother*.'

'Oh, don't start, Darren,' said Ellen.

'Why Jeffrey, though?' asked Lucy. 'Why *him*?'

Jeffrey was Ellen's final choice. Over the years she had filtered out the wealthy bounders, the beggars, the poor lost souls, and the thieves. She had sifted through the rot of relationships. picking out the hard, cold, mean ones that had refused to settle down. Jeffrey had been left. Jeffrey Bell, who had a degree in Business and Administration, who supported Spurs with frightening regularity, who played squash each Saturday with his estate-agent friends – all called Jeremy.

Jeffrey Bell had a long lean body, which looked good in label wear. He had discussed the sterling crisis with Ellen. He had asked her to water the green shoots of an economic spring with him. They had talked about Aristide's refusal to endorse the agreement in Haiti; Major's meetings with James Molyneaux in Downing Street; Balladur's call for a three-tier Europe; anti-Semitism in the former Soviet Union. When Ellen had asked a former boyfriend what he felt about the holocaust, he had jumped up, thrust the compact disc of *Schindler's List* into her player, and said: 'Let's make love to this.'

Cruel, lazy men had, in the past, hurt Ellen. Men like Sam, who had 'borrowed' money from her to pay for his law studies. Men like Tony, who had juggled their lives, dating several women simultaneously. Men like Christian, who had taken Ellen

98

to pool parties in order to show off her swimsuited breasts to his friends.

Jeffrey Bell had been different. 'Will you come out with me?' he had asked Ellen. 'To a restaurant?'

The formal invitation out had surprised Ellen. In the past she had dated on assumptions. Men had assumed that, because they had snogged or fucked, Ellen was theirs, simply for the taking. But Jeffrey had taken her to see *Cats*. They had had an expensive Thai meal for two. He had asked for the right to be with her, to kiss her.

Jeffrey, her own Jeffrey Bell, had understood the significance of news stories. He had shown interest in Ellen's news database, set up to monitor significant historical events. His feet had, interestingly, grown out of the average shoe shop and she enjoyed their visits, made together, to specialist shops. Plus his mousy hair lighted on blond sometimes and, if you squeezed his right cheek hard, he developed a sweet dimple.

Ellen was engaged to be married to Jeffrey Bell, who had introduced her to her house in Harrow-on-the-Hill, as well as to his parents. He might not have been Ellen's intellectual equal, or have Ellen's earning potential. But Ellen liked to close chapters on relationships. She liked the idea of reaching conclusions, generally; of ticking the *Completed* box in her notebook.

'But it's not exactly *love* with Jeffrey, is it?' asked Ellen's brother.

'Darren, *don't*,' said Lucy, giggling.

Ellen Abrahams was twenty-nine, and had been in and out of love countless times. She had been in and out of men's dressing-gowns and men's bedrooms, borrowing their jeans, their homes and their toothbrushes, kissing their heads, their private parts and their mothers. Trying out numerous sexual positions, she had been through a frightening number of men and a good assortment of emotions, from rapture, through satisfaction, through frustration, to apathy.

Ellen was, by now, scared of the tangles of romance, the mess of emotional upheaval. Love had become an unpredictable chemical rush of seratonin, clashing with career paths and ironing hours, baking schedules and administrative urges. Now, she wanted just safety and the emotional investment in two pairs of elderly slippers, side by side, at the fire. She wanted Jeffrey, who understood monogamy and monogrammed hand-towels. Guileless Jeffrey, who would answer his telephone on a Sunday and talk, not of castles in the air, but of property prices in Harefield.

'If you're going to start slagging off Jeffrey,' she said, rising to leave.

'Oh no, Ellen, *stay*,' said Lucy, anxiously, biting off a sweet, pink bead. 'This isn't about Jeffrey,' she said, hesitating. 'It's just that . . . All we wanted to know is, how do you decide? I mean, I can never *decide*. How d'you know *Jeffrey* is Mr Right?'

Ellen felt the urge to say: 'What? Where? When? How Much? And Why?' which seemed, to her, as reasonable a list of questions for would-be lovers, as it was for journalists covering a breaking news story. To Ellen, Jeffrey Bell was: Jeffrey Bell, of Hendon (good), aged thirty (good), earning £32,000-ish (presentable); and Why? Well, see above. He didn't disrupt Ellen's life. He fitted in perfectly; the perfect male accessory to life in the television fast lane.

Ellen replied: 'You just know,' flossing her teeth with the strands of cress on her plate.

Ellen knew everything. She had made her choices, taking out a pension, home-contents insurance and Jeffrey Bell. She had taken him out of his real-estate office and he, in turn, had shown her around houses from Wembley Park to Willesden Green. Jeffrey had pointed out signs of damp, the cost of repair, subsidence, Jacuzzis, and south-facing gardens. He had grown confident in the company of this career-woman, asking her how she felt about kitchens, cooking facilities, knocked-through studies, working from home, and reception-room wallpaper.

Ellen had realised, while progressing further and further up the Metropolitan line in her search for a house, that Jeffrey knew far more about her than was professionally comfortable. But she had, surprisingly, allowed herself to be swept along. She had allowed him to tell her of damp, to take her out for that Thai meal and, later, to a chicken dinner, at a Jewish restaurant of her choice, so that when Ellen said of the house in Harrow-on-the-Hill: 'Yes, I like it. Yes, I'll take it,' Jeffrey Benjamin Bell felt that he should snatch Ellen Abrahams up, as quickly as he could, from a newly buoyant singles market.

'I know we haven't been together long,' he had said. 'But I have a proposition. I mean, I have a . . .'

'The answer is yes,' she had said, pre-empting his proposal. 'But I'll want a long engagement. At least a year.'

Neither of them had been tempted to write love poetry. Indeed, neither of them had been tempted to mention love. Those who had watched the house-buying, the proposal and the purchase of the diamond-encrusted engagement ring from Jeffrey's uncle, Malvern Bell, would have been disappointed. The romance between Ellen and Jeffrey wasn't exactly the love gamble of the year. But it was probably good for Britain's economy.

'Just tell us the truth,' said Lucy, spreading the usual number of penny sweets on the table before her. All of Ellen's friends loathed Jeffrey Bell. And that feeling was, of course, mutual. 'Are you getting married for the linen tablecloths and the cut-glass candle-holders?'

Ellen felt that this was as good a time as any for her to risk taking a bite from her flat cheese sandwich. 'No, it was the Le Creuset pans that did it for me.'

'Blue or orange?' asked Lucy, sucking on a sweet banana.

'Orange,' said Ellen, who had made up her mind some time ago.

Ellen and Darren Abrahams sat on the tube together. She reading the *New Scientist*, he chuckling at *Viz* magazine. Ellen noted down the name of a new chromosome, discovered that week, in her blue fact book.

'So, we're not going to talk about Mum at all, then. We'll just pretend she doesn't exist, OK?'

'What is there to talk about, Darren? They're looking after her in that place, aren't they?'

'You know, Ellen. I didn't *mind* finding the nursing home. When you were out filming . . . When you were out with Jeffrey . . . I didn't *mind* all that.'

'Good. Because I happen to have a very demanding job. Which is something you, a . . . *a broom-seller*, would never understand . . .'

Darren, who managed the family chain of hardware stores, persisted. 'Why you can't visit once in *months* is beyond me. Why you can't see her *once*, Ellen. Why you haven't talked to her about the wedding. God knows if you'll even invite her . . . When she talks of nothing else to me . . .'

'Please, Darren,' begged Ellen. 'Shut *up*.'

Northwick Park cut to Harrow-on-the-Hill and Ellen stood up to leave. 'You can't just ignore her,' hissed Darren. 'She won't go away, you know.'

'Leave me alone,' she said, as the tube doors snapped shut.

Chapter Eleven

Office life was fun, from the moment the machine spurted its cappuccino into her polystyrene cup to the moment Susan Lyttle waved goodbye to Kelly and Karen on reception and emerged, through double doors, to face the outside world.

Inside the office there was Clive, who flirted outrageously with Julie, who sat behind Susan. He threw pencil sharpeners at Julie, which whistled in flight above Susan's head. There was Peter, a homosexual, JJ, a wit, Bruce, a depressive, and Gary, who was clearly the office intellectual.

Then, of course, there was the elderly Sam Dutton, who was retiring that day. The firm was holding a drinks party for him in the pub across the road, during the lunch-hour. Susan had given the collection box a pound, which had gone towards buying him a lawnmower.

Susan had once heard a radio programme about dying office life. 'We're all freelances now,' a dull-eyed woman had said on one occasion, in the shoe shop in Southport. 'Are we bugger,' Aunt Cyn had said.

And yet those who talked of big social change had obviously not worked at Dutton's, which, on celluloid, would be black and white and grained all over. Dutton's worked on the premise that work went against everything the firm stood for. On weekdays, during office hours, one was always present and that was always enough.

'Sam Dutton is leaving', a beautifully printed card had said. 'Please come to his leaving party.' Susan, not owning anything in the way of business cards, mobile phones or modems, had placed the card on her kitchenette mantelpiece, behind the kettle, as a personal reminder that she was a working woman, playing hard.

Outside office hours, time passed slowly for Susan. She did not have a social life as such. She had taken to making frequent visits to the corner 7–11, ostensibly to shop, but really for the company. After all, her only true, outside work friend was Barbara Peabody, and Susan had left *her* behind in Southport.

In Southport, Barbara Peabody had been the height of glamour, having found – after school – a boyfriend (albeit married, and fifty) and a position as a *personal assistant* in Ainsdale. Having spent four years in Barbara's company (every Saturday and once during the week), Susan was an expert on Barbara Peabody's boyfriend's wife and Barbara Peabody's boss's wife, neither of whom either of them had ever met. When in company with Barbara, Susan had secretly read novels, placing them strategically in front of her, for contingency entertainment as well as for those times when Barbara – who suffered from a bowel disorder – needed to visit the toilet.

Barbara had represented herself to her friend as at one with the outside world. But the world she had shown Susan had been empty of romance. It had been a world without shopping trips for anything other than cleaning fluids or lightbulbs. It had been a world stitched together with A-line skirts and cinema trips on a Saturday night. Whereas, in London, no one said: 'Oh, Susan,' or snatched novels from her at the dinner table just as Susan had reached a cliffhanger.

She could lie on her bed for hours during the evening, reading. No one came in to tell her to 'get out and do something. A girl of your age, lying in your bedroom . . .' She could shop for tagliatelle, and packets of grated cheese, with money in her pocket. She could choose luxury blue rather than economy white toilet tissue. And she could spend Saturday afternoons in WH Smith, feeling the paper inside new, hardback novels.

'You coming to the do, Susan?' Julie had asked her that day. They had been in the ladies' together – Susan applying her Damson Pink and Julie patting almond face powder into large, open pores.

Julie was an English Rose, as defined by tabloid newspapers: *Do you want to be an English Rose? The English Rose look. Every inch an English Rose.* She looked like the picture inside papers, wrapping chips, of a face made muddy by stale, blotted print. Yet such beauty lasted two years at the most; and Julie had spent her pretty years behind cash tills and in wine bars, sipping white wine and soda, or lying on her back on the beach applying yellow-white sun-tan cream.

'Oh yes. I like him.'

It seemed to Susan as if the men in power were dropping like flies, leaving behind big, leather seats for younger men with tighter suits and brighter ties to fill. It was a pity, Susan thought, that it should happen just as she came out into the world. It was a pity, too, that, just as she had emerged, romance should die. Because, rather than at a museum, or on a mist-filled moor, she had become acquainted with her Angel beside the feeder on Dutton's second-floor photocopying machine.

'You know, I recognise you,' he had said to Susan, whose face had melted, with terror, into a mess of expression. 'Yes,' she had said, photocopying her hand in fright, and escaping the stud earring and the green eyes, which threw chips of black ice at her, as she ran along the corridor.

On another occasion, he had stood in front of her at a bus-stop. (Susan had been reading Trollope's *The Way We Live Now* and wondering when the seamier side of life might be introduced to *her*.) She had been startled to see the back of Angel's shirt, inked with small drops of wet sweat. 'Ohhh, it's the Angel,' Susan had thought, before he, a real smelling, thinking man, had turned to face her.

'Have you read any Marquez?' the Angel, generally known as Charles Pickford, had asked her. 'No, erm never,' Susan had said, as the words had spluttered, gloriously, eventually – and surprisingly – from her mouth.

'Well I think he's great. "If you have to go away again, at least try to remember how we were tonight," ' he had quoted. 'My hero.'

Susan had taken away these two encounters with him. Replacing her Angel fantasies with these meetings, Charles was there, purely for Susan's pleasure. Belonging to Susan, he was there simply for her to manipulate mentally, on dreamy, dark nights under the duvet.

'We don't fit in at Dutton's, do we?' he had said at the bus-stop. 'We're different. And just remember,' he had added, leaning close, 'you can't spin an egg on the prong of a fork.'

Susan was not used to being treated with exception. As an orphan, she was grateful for anything, from a book token on a birthday to a double helping of attention during dinner. She often felt as if, by rights, she should be somewhere else. Even Aunt Jane had said, when taking her into Seabank Road: 'Don't worry, my dear, we won't be *cramping your style*, as you young people say. And whatever we do, we won't try to take the place of your parents.'

Susan, however, wanted families. She wanted to disappear inside families of five in queues, for buses or for Southport's big dipper. She wanted the certainty of someone's affection. She wanted to have it there as a right, rather than on request.

Charles Pickford shone spotlights on Susan. When he was around, Susan felt physical. With other men she still felt blank inside clothes. But with Charles, she actually felt flesh, moving about under tops and skirts and jumping to the beat of hidden heart movement. Charles had found, in Susan, womanhood and a sexuality that curved, blushed and craved discovery. He had made clothes an embarrassment to her, there to accentuate crook and curve, form and outline.

'Fit bod, but looks as though your legs could do with a work-out,' Charles had said to her once, as he had followed her closely up an emergency staircase.

(After this, Susan had booked herself in for ten aerobics sessions at Finchley's Catholic church hall, and sat, as a 'guest onlooker', watching women point their inner-thigh muscles at images of the Virgin Mary, crotches parted to breaking point in tight, stretchy leotards.)

And yet: 'Suse, babe, do us some copies of this, would you?' That had been Charles Pickford, at the photocopier, leaning over her, making her body shiver with warmth. She had kept the words 'Suse, babe,' to think of later over baked beans, melting through white, buttery toast, deep inside the thread cracks that stroked her china plate.

'Susan not so Lyttle,' Charles had said, as she had walked in that morning. Nudging life along a bit, she had arrived at work early in the hope of watching his lips rolled up into two strips of wet pastry. She had hoped for those builder hands; the thick, chip fingers and the chopped, chapped palms; that broad chest, firm like a slab of butcher's-board beef; and the green, stalking eyes, seeking Susan out.

'Well, if you can look this good at seven in the morning,' he had said, sitting alone in the office. 'Your hair's grown, hasn't it? It used to be such a schoolgirl shape,' he had said. 'But now, you're a *woman*.'

For breakfast, Susan was eating two oranges, and had just sliced her second segment using a plastic café knife when, looking around, she saw Charles standing next to her desk, looking down into her lap.

'Bloody hell, do that *again*,' he said, his eyes like black-eyed beans.

'Oh no. What?' she panicked, startled and sucking out an orange segment.

'Oh, my good God. *That*,' he groaned, pointing at Susan's mouth. 'I have never, ever, seen anyone eat oranges in such a *sexy* way.'

Susan, of course, went on tearing, with her teeth, at the orange skin's insides, taking care to appear both sensuous and, naturally, slightly hungry at the same time. Because, despite everything, she had long believed herself inherently insatiable. Those long evenings spent upstairs, alone, in Seabank Road had fuelled the sort of *self*-complex that might just as well have turned her to psychopathy as to literature.

She was, however, a virgin. Aside from dying uncles and bloated second cousins, Susan had yet to be kissed properly, at the front of her face. Something she felt should have come as easily as a Catholic confirmation, or hairy underarms, had yet to take place, despite the contraceptive pamphlets in her GP's surgery, which had insinuated, quite categorically, that Susan would be fighting men off with feminism and Femidom as soon as she turned sexy, at sixteen.

But, at twenty-three, a man had begun to leave romantic notes on Susan's desk, in Charles Pickford's handwriting. *There are strings . . . in the human heart that had better not be vibrated.* Or: *For I am nothing, if not critical.* And Susan had taken these crumpled notes and had placed them in her box at home, beside well-worn photos of her adoring father and adored mother. She had folded them into four, and had sat on them her mother's thick gold brooch.

She knew Charles's notes by heart, their every word written down, and signed in that scrawling, left-handed way, which bounced letters backwards, bending them in the wrong direction. She loved the odd-shaped letters and the way he had of ignoring the cross of the T, or the loop of the Y. She found his notes on her desk, at the curve of her print ribbon; or inside her mug in the coffee room, folded to fit, flat, at the bottom.

Let me to thy bosom fly, a note had read this morning. *While the Tempest still is high*. Susan had found it clutched to the clasp of her stapler. She twirled her seat around, bravely finding words. 'What . . . What does this quote mean?' she had asked him.

'It loosely translates as: "Are you going to Sam Dutton's leaving do today?" '

Susan stared at her feet. 'Yes,' she had whispered, spotting stretch marks crumpling about her right ankle. 'I am.'

'D'you want me to show you where the pub is?' he had asked.

'Oh, please,' said Susan.

Now, of course, she was a muddle of nerves. The prospect, not only of a boyfriend, but of *Charles Pickford*, had sent her into a wash of panic. She wasn't at all certain that she was ready for a relationship. Susan had been brought up on a diet of literature, as well as the occasional sex-education pamphlet. Was that experience enough for *a situation?*

Mr Matlock's wife, Hilary, had telephoned three times to ask Susan to tell 'Hughie' to come home. 'Tell him it's about my temperature,' she had said to Susan. 'He'll understand.'

Hugh Matlock looked like a squatter, shrunken version of Bill Clinton. He had once been described as 'dashing'. But he had traded in his looks for Hilary Dutton, who soon gave up her job as a dental assistant for something more permanent, like charity functions and children.

'I am *not* going home,' Mr Matlock had said.'

Hilary had been a casualty of Empty Nest Syndrome ever since the Matlock children had left home. She mourned her lost children and their belongings, which she had built up alone, painstakingly and from catalogues. On the day they had left, she had felt burgled by her own children. She had searched for signs that they were ever there. She had found just a bear and a bar of chocolate. How she grieved for the toddler trucks, the school uniforms and the teenage tantrums about television. Unlike her friends, who became magistrates, or who cleaned the house, harder, Hilary decided to begin again, by having another baby. And Hugh, who was tired of rearing and roaring at blank, childish faces, regretted their decision to start another family.

'I'm sorry, Mrs Matlock, but Mr Matlock says that he's not going home,' Susan had said. 'Do me a favour, Susan,' Hilary had said, tearfully, on the third occasion. 'See whether the words *approaching menopause* change his bloody mind.'

Susan could not concentrate on Mr Matlock's affairs. She wanted time to recall Charles's words. Had he asked her out? Had his expression changed? Had she teased him with her segments of orange? Had she, perhaps, sucked on them too sexily? Had she, in the process of sucking, promised far more than she could possibly deliver? The flesh he had made her feel crawled with anticipation.

As Charles approached her desk, she realised that he was with another woman. Susan suspended herself for a moment, with one thought. 'I don't actually need him. I have a trust fund.' That was Susan Lyttle's thought, as her tiny, imaginary world subsided and then crashed about her desk.

'Susie, meet Hanna,' said Charles. 'Hanna. Susie.'

Up close, in the pub, Hanna Thames – Charles's 'old friend from Oxford' looked like a beautiful, black-haired, brown-skinned boy.

'Hanna thought she was meeting me for lunch,' Charles had said. 'But Hughie said I should show my face at Sam's thing.'

'Charles tells me you're always reading,' said Hanna, offering her a cigarette.

'Er, yes,' said Susan, taking the erect cigarette from Hanna's packet. (She had practiced at home and was now something of an inhalation expert.)

'So, have you read the new Amis?' asked Hanna.

'No, erm,' she said, her head swimming with whisky. (When Charles had offered Susan a drink, she could think only of Aunt Cyn's Saturday-night poison.)

'What about, *What A Carve Up*?'

'No, er, Eliot, Austen . . .' she said.

'Ah,' said Hanna, as if that explained a great deal. 'Five unmarried daughters, one or two eligible men, at least two balls and you'll be happy. Am I right?'

'Yes,' said Susan.

Susan wanted her own love scene. If her life story had been written by a Brontë, Mr Pickford would have made his move. But Charles, who was stroking a pretty secretary from the first floor, seemed unaware of Susan. He was aware only of the two slits at the side of the secretary's skirt which flapped apart to reveal pink legs as she drank.

The carpet in the pub merged, patterned, with the wall, as Susan drank. Men in rolled-up white sleeves loosened their ties. Susan, meanwhile, was on to her third glass of whisky. 'Are you sure you don't want anything with that?' Hanna had asked. Susan, misunderstanding, had opted for a packet of pork scratchings.

Hanna was dressed, as Aunt Cyn would put it, 'for the beach' in a tiny black mini-dress; her tanned legs bare. She was wearing orange trainers, the flaps hanging out repulsively, and a shoelace necklace of huge, black sunglasses. Her right shoulder was tattooed with an illegible word; its faded appeal outlined by a heart.

'Where did you get your dress?'

'Oh, this? Agnès b, I think.'

'Is she a friend of yours?' asked Susan.

'No, she's a *designer*,' she laughed, looking down at Susan's salmon-pink outfit, the blouse bow tied loosely at the cleavage 'Sounds as if you haven't discovered London properly yet. Shopping heavens like the King's Road, Covent Garden?'

Susan blushed, wondering whether it was possible, when drunk, to fall up and over the head of someone, landing embarrassedly in, say, Sam Dutton's lap, who was talking about the musical he would write in retirement.

'Better to love someone than not at all,' sang Sam, badly, at everybody. He had drunk five pints of Newcastle Brown Ale. 'I know I've not got a voice as such but, honest, if I'd been born a Rodgers or a Kander or a Hammerstein instead of a Dutton, I'd be minting it by now in musicals.'

Sam sang on, his voice drifting through Bruce who, Susan overheard, had been celibate for a year and four months (a year and five if one didn't count the grope with Julie in the stationery cupboard last year. Julie certainly did not). 'Without love, we're nothing . . .'

'Look, have this,' said Hanna, taking out a book from her bag. 'It's great. All about life for women in Harlem. Anyway, I know her. She's one of ours. You should try reading *some* from this century.'

'One of yours?' asked Susan, taking the book.

'I'm in publishing,' said Hanna. 'An editorial assistant at Davey Lot's.'

'You know the *author*? You meet authors?'

'Meet authors, make the tea, go to parties . . .'

Lunch-hour was over but, as a Dutton was leaving, Clive could compete with Hugh Matlock over beer consumption, Peter could argue with Gary about the age of consent and Julie could continue to flirt with all in the pub, from the barman to the fruit machine. The new lawnmower stood awkwardly beside Sam Dutton. Now that its jolly 'Sorry you're leaving' wrapping had been discarded, it seemed incongruous alongside empty beer glasses and squashed cigarette packets.

Susan had, meanwhile, been asked to a party. 'Charles is coming. Give me your telephone number,' Hanna had said, taking out the sort of full Filofax Susan would have photocopied and framed. *So this is it*, thought Susan. This was real life, as other people lived it, with office work and pub drinks and parties at the weekend.

'Is Charles your . . . ?'

'Lover?' laughed Hanna. 'No,' she said firmly. 'I'm more friendly with his flatmates, actually. Have you met Ken Painter?'

Charles had crept into Susan's life when she wasn't looking. He lodged there now, as a wispish thought or a hazy portrait. He had touched Susan's fantasies, washing them with his image. As he kissed Hanna goodbye, as he laughed with other women, or bought them lager tops, Susan watched, fascinated at his Adam's apple, as it swelled and collapsed on the stubble-papered throat. She gazed, infatuated, as the throat inflated and shrank with those man-sized gulps of Yorkshire bitter.

Susan sloped off, escaping the smoke, the sounds of other people and her own headache, for the stillness of her office machines. As she stood at the door to the office, Susan could see Sam Dutton – strangely small from a distance – leaving the pub. He was carrying the lawnmower with such care that it seemed, to her, as if it might break him.

'Any messages?' asked her boss, returning to the office, some hours later.

'There's something about the ribbon ceremony in Swindon. They're opening a Dutton's store there. Mr Dutton wants you to provide the person who'll cut the ribbon, Mr Matlock,' said Susan, putting away Hanna's book and busying herself with a pile of paperclips. 'He said: "as you're so well-connected".'

'He wants me to provide the personality? Damn him. Only because I suggested we might try and raise our profile a bit. Get someone a bit more important than Jimmy Ray Crockett or Boris Godfrey, that man from the *Consumers Digest*. Damn him. Damn them. I don't know anyone. Can't the marketing department handle this? What do *you* think, Susan?'

Susan Lyttle had travelled far. She was not the same girl as at Seabank Road; the one rolling golden potatoes across fat, flat china, which bumped into slabs of stringy beef and slices of burnt carrots, every Sunday.

Susan was now a secretary with a well-known retail company. She was a London secretary, a London party-going secretary, with a television, a mug tree, and enough certainty about her life to have bought a one-month travelcard.

'How about Lou Matherbay?' she whispered.

'Lou Ma . . . ?'

'The politician.'

'I know who *Lou Matherbay* is, Susan. But, would she . . . ?'

'Shall I ring her, Mr Matlock?'

Her boss nodded.

'Is this Lou Matherbay's office?' asked Susan.

'This is the Pluralists' Press Office,' sighed a woman's voice, losing patience.

'I am a secretary with Dutton's,' said Susan, scared. Her voice was disappearing again. 'I work for Hugh Matlock.'

'Not *the* Hugh Matlock?' laughed the lady on the line.

'Dutton's will be open . . . opening . . . Dutton's will be opening a store in Swindon in a few months' time. We would very much like Lou Matherbay to be the one to open it. We would like her to cut . . .'

'Sorry. Can I stop you there?' said the lady's voice, turning. 'I mean, first of all, this is completely outside my remit. And, you know, I doubt very much that Lou *Matherbay* will have time to . . .'

Susan's tongue mashed inside her mouth. 'Sorry to both . . . to bother . . .' The tears came. 'Oh no. I gave the impresh . . . I gave the impression that I knew her. Lou Matherbay. To my boss, I mean. I'll be sacked. Oh *God* . . . And she could have been the first one to *buy* something . . . I thought . . . I thought that you might have some influence . . .'

The lady's U-turn was astonishing. 'Look, I'll see what I can do,' said the voice. 'I suppose there might be some publicity in it. Just put it in writing and fax it through. To Myra Felt. *Of course* I have influence . . .'

Susan Lyttle, secretary extraordinaire, supreme Londoner, had simply to press down on a few of life's techno-buttons to achieve something astonishing in Britain's capital city. Without her, the Dutton's department store would be bereft of a ribbon-cutter; its Swindon store for ever closed, its ribbon for ever uncut.

Her mother's image came to her, as it had millions of times; an image rooted in certainties. Susan had a large collection of Mother images, sorting through fast, like a flipping photo album. She had a Ghost for each circumstance: cooking ('beat it fast, Susie'); looking through her cuttings collection ('Can *you* see a similarity, Susie?'); finding trampled lilacs ('Nothing but trouble') But this Ghost Picture was smiling, teeth spilling out of her mouth; hair as warm as tomato soup, spilling over her novel, replacing beautifully the cover shot of a young African-American. *Go girl*, it said to Susan, formerly of Southport.

Chapter Twelve

Myra's throat had collapsed with the cigarettes whose stubs she discovered in mugs of vodka and long dead plants or spilling out from pottery ashtrays. Her bedroom, she knew, looked like the jumble sales she frequented in big, draughty halls, their tables piled full of clothes and bric-a-brac.

It was nine o'clock – far too late to be late for work. She would have to be ill instead, indulgently forgetting about the newspaper which lay folded and starched, pushed through the door. It was the only fresh item in a room which smelt of a thousand students having sex.

The telephone rang, disturbing dust on the dressing-table. It was Sara Cinnamon.

'Just checking to see what time you're thinking of leaving, Myra. I told Larry that you'd be working from home, reading papers for mention of the Pluralists. And that if you left now you'd be in time for the morning meeting. Is that right?'

Myra agreed, slipping on plastic clogs. She could hear Sara sipping the white wine she always drank, emptying a bottle a day. The bottle was always placed in the far right-hand corner; a corner that others would reserve for, say, a pen-and-pencil tidy. Myra thought that this was common working practice, just as she had come to believe that Sara's Alice bands, which pushed back greasy strands of hair each day, were the height of classy working chic. Certainly, Sara's 'boys', as the MPs, including Lou Matherbay, were referred to, did not seem to think it peculiar.

Sara Cinnamon did not have a job title, a job description, or, it must be acknowledged, a job as such. For most of the day she sat at her desk, chatting, discussing *Hansard* and – now and then – selling a piece of gossip to a newspaper's diary column. When Myra asked her what she *did*, on one occasion, Sara had said: 'Oh, I just am', and on another occasion: 'Don't you worry about me. I have more than enough to do.'

Myra had talked to Larry Beat. 'Can I just ask you what Sara's role is in the office? I don't want to tread on her toes . . .' And the Chief Whip had said, before rushing off for a vote: 'Do you know, I don't know. She's been around for so long, I thought she was part of our Constitution.'

Myra Felt had been the Pluralists' press officer for over two months. She had one hundred business cards to prove it. Lou Matherbay had not yet taken Myra into her confidence. But Myra had, in fact, forgotten the impulse behind her career in Pluralism. As a party propagandist, she had become her own best punter, swallowing each party line as it was delivered.

Now she was as familiar to the Parliamentary policemen, standing guard at each entrance, as were the green, leather seats lining the lobbies, the corridors and the secret annexes, pocketed away behind streaming halls. She could pass former, present and future cabinet ministers in the Members' Lobby without staring at them, startled, with recognition. She could walk past Cecil Parkinson and David Mellor without blushing for their shame. She could walk into Ian Paisley's stomach, and hear it apologising, without fear.

She no longer laughed when people whipped each other, metaphorically, or when men, dressed in black-and-white frills, led the Speaker to the Chamber, as they banged, cabaret-style, on the floor with gold sticks. Hell, she could even get drunk in the House of Lords bar and creep back to spend the night, asleep, on the whips' office sofa.

In the dead of night and all day there were silences, slow steps and a feeling that legislation can take for ever to pass through the buildings of Parliament. But as the ten o'clock vote approached, the footsteps grew faster and the sounds harsher. The world outside closed its day and people across the United Kingdom shouted at spouses, watched the soaps, and fell over children, as this place rose from the dead, scattering shadows.

Myra thought, having found democracy, she wanted only to find the handle. Once the handle was found, she wanted only to turn it herself.

As to her position, she had been forced to confide in Marion. After all, she was now expected to do any *socialising* inside office hours. Friends had simply to be forgotten. Night-animal Marion was particularly difficult to fit in. And, although she could not keep to it, Myra had started something approaching a schedule. To Marion, she had couched her embarrassing position in phrases like 'overdraft', 'temporary' and 'secret' but, nonetheless, the phone conversation with her closest friend had been painful. 'So, this is it then, Myra. You've become a mute,' Marion had said. 'Just another one of *them*. Living in *their world*.'

The heady tube rush in the morning; the lunch gossip; the keyboard tapping; the Pluralist MPs dipping in and out of her office, opening strongly worded letters: Myra liked *their world*. *They* listened and bitched and lobbied and talked. They discussed questions, like the environment one. They asked whether it had been right for the United Nations to offer Saddam Hussein an oil-for-food deal. They asked who would win the forthcoming United States elections. *They* had all, but for Lou Matherbay, tested Myra's political round. Was she standing on their ground? Which way, with what strength wind, would she blow?

Myra had been lobbied on issues ranging from East–West relations, through freedom of information, to teabags in the office. She had been asked where she stood on office furniture and the nuclear question. The retiring party leader had taken her aside to ask for Myra's opinion on the deputy leader, Ray Hines. 'You mean on TV?' Myra had asked. 'Yes, if you like,' he had said. On another occasion, Sara Cinnamon had asked her what she thought of Lou Matherbay.

'Oh, I think she's very . . .'

'I mean as leader . . .'

'And not Ray or . . . ?'

'Well, let's face it Myra. Lou's more *marketable*.'

'She's more *radical*,' Myra had said. 'I'll give you that.'

Myra had thought that, with all her experience of work experience, she had become something of an expert on office politics. That was until, of course, she had entered political office.

Myra stretched into a lime-green top, which she had found behind a box full of stale Thornton chocolates, thinking about Patrick, the Irishman who had loved her for three weeks and with whom she was now in love. He had approached her that night, as Myra had been drinking vodka, with Kasha, Dill, and Marion, in the Pig and Whistle. He had tweaked her right buttock, saying: 'I'll know that bottom anywhere, Myra Felt.'

Patrick, who had shared some of Myra's schooldays, had bought her an Irish beer. She had commented on the Irish Question, of which she knew nothing, but seemed to have all the answers. And they had talked, until bedtime, about the potato famine, crisp flavours and the Bloody British. So that now, three weeks later, Myra Felt's thoughts were filled with Patrick, tanned Patrick, broad Patrick, with the black peat hair and the cracking dislocated Irish accent, as the impatient sounds of the top forty came on her radio.

The UK had slid to number fifteen in the world competitiveness league table before Ellen had had a chance to brush her teeth. 'Number fifteen, number fifteen, number fifteen,' she muttered, looking for her stack of green supermarket own-brand tooth-pastes. And, aloud, with a mouth full of toothpaste (while the presenter moved on to item number two on the radio): 'Slipping, fifteen, slipping.'

Beautifully scrubbed, Ellen negotiated London's Underground network, battling an elderly, farting lady for a seat and then surrendering it gracefully to a pregnant, smiling woman just before she needed to change lines. *North Korea today unleashed its strongest weapon in its war against South Korea*, she read, elbowing a ruddy, round man in the ribs as he tried to lean against the window.

The Russian leader, Boris Yeltsin, signed a ceasefire deal with the Chechen rebel leader, Zelimkhan Yandarbiyev. Ellen was sure he had died two weeks ago, glanced up at an advert for a pregnancy testing kit and saw a lady looking at her. *Months after they were seized at gunpoint during a trekking holiday, Indian officials cannot agree whether they are alive or dead.* The lady had splints on her leg, the result either of a skiing holiday or some tragedy. Ellen gave her the benefit of the doubt and smiled broadly in her direction. *'This whole thing is very mystifying,' a senior official said. 'We really don't know what to think.'*

Seven French monks in Algeria were believed to have had their throats cut last week. Three Rwandan Hutu extremists stood accused of mass murder. And an estimated 5,000 people were killed in government-sponsored violence in Haiti. Meanwhile, Ellen was eating a smoked salmon and cream cheese bagel, the cream cheese squeezing, like depilatory cream, hard out of the edges. As she pushed it back in, a slice of smoked salmon fell on to the fold of an Asian woman's sari. She didn't notice.

Ellen found herself in the lift ascending to the *FastNews* office with Dan Berkovsky, her editor. Despite their mutual admiration, they rose in shy silence. The ride seemed long, stopping as it did on every floor, expelling producers, VT editors, secretaries, the occasional vision mixer. On the third floor, they acquired a presenter, who kept looking upwards, towards the heavens, as if in thought. By the time the lift arrived at the sixth floor, Ellen realised that there was a mirrored ceiling above, and that the presenter was examining his reflection.

Ellen and Dan Berkovsky had arrived at their level. Ellen disappeared into the ladies', in order to touch up her revision of that day's news, and to avoid walking down the corridor with her editor. She felt vaguely strained around the stomach and stuffed into her mouth two of the paracetamols she always carried, gulping them down without water.

'Anything prepared for tonight's programme?' Ellen asked the deputy editor, Simon Nuttall. (Now that Elliot Banding had been forced to resign, he was the only one.) Nuttall sat in the special seat, twirling about and pressing computer buttons as if he were a pilot in flight. He didn't answer Ellen immediately, but she stood her ground, pulling at a strand on her jacket button, and – as Nuttall said: 'Seven-minute film from Israel. Empty programme otherwise. We'll need everybody' – Ellen's button dived to the floor.

Everyone pretended that all was right with the world; that buttons were still attached to jackets and that *FastNews* was going to be fine and dandy, filled at nine thirty-five with fresh, thoughtful slices of that day's news and features. Ellen made her way to her desk, logged on to the computer, checked the main diary for any important events that day, checked the politics diary for any significant political events of the week, and asked her colleagues, who sat like bears in the ring, if they had any ideas.

Oh, and they were all sweet now, rolling their ideas around the room, like candy floss, sharing the fluffy ones. 'Let's do something on Arthur leaving *EastEnders*. That's what everyone's talking about.' Or: 'Internet. Got to do this Internet story.' But, as soon as Nuttall said: 'Now,' and the meeting began, they would all, politely, apologetically and without dirtying their hands, tear each other loudly to pieces.

'We have seven minutes on Israel tonight,' Simon Nuttall said, starting the meeting. 'Masses of time to fill but, luckily, I have a small but beautifully formed team today.'

'Is that a stand-alone or will there be an interview off the back of the Israel film?' asked Blond Young Buck producer, hungry for blood (or *something*).

'No interview. There's nothing left to say. Unless anyone can think of anyone interesting?'

Of course, most producers could, even if they couldn't, but as Ellen had underlined so many names in newspapers, she was able, while others were saying: 'Hanan Ashrawi, Faisal Husseini, Amos Oz, Rana Kabbani', to draw in breath, roll her eyes around, as if with impatience, and wait for Nuttall to say: 'You think they're obvious, Ellen? Any ideas?'

Ellen leaned back in her chair. 'Well, how about Nabil Shaath, Ehud Olmert or someone like AB Yehoshua?' she asked, drawing a picture of a stick man with huge, red eyes, sitting in a cube.

Purely Decorative Producer and Young Buck Producer shot stares at Ellen, willing her to add someone improbable to her list, someone whose name they were familiar with. 'Sounds good,' said Nuttall, unwilling at this stage in the meeting to show ignorance. 'If we can get them, that is,' said Young Buck Producer, riding his chair like a horseman, with legs splayed either side. 'I'm not sure it'll be easy today, it being one of the Jewish festivals.' But YBP was on shaky ground here.

'It's not an important festival. There won't be a day off,' said Ellen, helpfully, to YBP. Purely Decorative Producer played pretty for the time being. Clever Ugly Producer looked thoughtful and brought up the various Israeli wars – Yom Kippur, the Six Day War, the War of Independence. Were there any precedents that *FastNews* could spin around, turn on heads, squash to bits and then take apart for those of an ordinary intelligence to consume? Young Buck shook his head. 'We did that last year,' he said. 'It's just not interesting any more.'

'Right. Ideas,' said Simon Nuttall fiercely, as Dan Berkovsky appeared at his shoulder, muttering and scratching parts of his body.

'We need ideas,' said Berkovsky. 'No one on this programme has any *ideas*,' he said, pointing at Ellen suddenly, as if the Messiah had returned, 'except Ellen Abrahams.'

Young Buck said: 'I think that we should do something about battered husbands. There's a good peg today with that Peterson court case and a lot of people feel that women are getting away with murder.' Purely Decorative and Churn Crap Out Constantly Producer nodded fiercely. 'Yeah, what with Sara Thornton and everything – battered wives – let's turn the issue on its head and look at its underbelly.'

'How would we do it, though?' asked Nuttall, who was jerking his pen off, clicking it down and up. 'What do you think, Malcolm?' he asked Clever Ugly Producer, who was tapping into the news wires. Clever Ugly leant his head to one side. Everyone waited. They all, apart from Young Buck and, possibly, Nuttall, wanted him to rubbish the idea. 'It can be done,' he said, finally.

'I don't know,' said another producer, Experience Without Promotion. 'I can see the issue, but not the story. Do we really want to jump on the back of the tabloids' agenda?'

'Don't mind,' said Nuttall, lightening up a bit. There was – at least – one idea to fill his programme. Ellen added a skirt to her stick man. She was anxious, lest someone else on the team might have the same ideas.

'OK, cut the crap, let's get on,' said Nuttall. 'I want ideas for a main item and ideas for a light item. Israel, hopefully, goes second. It's not strong enough to be a lead. So, *ideas*.'

'There's no news today,' wailed Churn Crap Out Constantly.

'There's no news full stop,' said Experience Without Promotion.

Purely Decorative suggested the on-going hostage crisis as the lead item and the anorexia issue as the third. 'There's two more psychologists jumping up and down,' she said. 'They're saying anorexics are getting younger and younger; that if we go on allowing them to read magazines and to refuse meals, *all* our children will be anorexic.'

'How young?' asked Experience Without Promotion. 'Toddlers counting calories on the abacus?'

'Babies insisting on low-fat milk?' asked Nuttall.

'Seriously,' said Purely Decorative.

'It sounds good,' said Churn Crap Out Constantly.

'Well, possibly,' said Nuttall, scribbling something in his book and circling the scribble. Later, he would add a question mark. Ellen drew a cloud around the cube, added a ponytail to the stick lady and, in red, gave her two big ears.

'We'll have to get some anorexics into the studio. Seven-year-olds, I'm talking about, just to sit there. Any older, and it's been done.'

'I can get them,' said Purely Decorative. 'There's some around, I know that,' she said, anxious to prevent the collapse of her beautiful idea. 'What about my idea of doing the hostages?' Decorative asked weakly.

'Well, I have to say,' said Young Buck. 'I've been put on a watch for that story before and the truth is, it doesn't move. There are never any new pictures – it's always just that still photograph. And a still isn't television – it's far too static. No one wants to watch a photograph for six minutes, and it's all we have.'

'But it's so *important*,' said Less Decorative Producer.

'There's no legs on the story,' said Clever Ugly.

'It's dull television,' said Quiet Ambition, quietly.

'We've done it before; read the book; seen the movie.' said Experience.

'Watched the TV programme, bought the T-shirt,' said Churn Crap Out.

'Eaten the ice-cream, peeled off the stickers,' said Quiet Ambition, laughing.

'And sold the lot back to the Americans,' said Experience, with satisfaction.

'Well, there's lots we can do in graphics,' said Nuttall. 'And plenty in reconstruction. There's no such thing as unimaginative TV, only unimaginative producers.' He scribbled, circled and questioned the circle. And then said, brightly: 'Ellen?'

'I think we should do Korea,' said Ellen, with the emphasis on *Korea*. 'Let's get ahead of the game: cover the brinkmanship, the political games that North Korea plays with South Korea. Maybe a two-minute profile of Kim Jong Il. The only thing we know about him is his hairstyle.'

'Good idea,' said Nuttall. 'Malcolm, what do you think?'

'Well, it would need something clever,' said Clever Ugly. 'It would make a good lead. If Ellen can find a North Korean to interview.'

Ellen enclosed her stick lady's cube in a box. In Ellen's history, possibly in the history of *FastNews*, perhaps in the history of television, there had never been a North Korean prepared to face questions on the box. 'Oh yes,' she said. 'Of course.'

Myra Felt was at her own morning meeting. The room contained Myra, one chief researcher, one plain researcher, one junior researcher, two MPs – Larry Beat and Billy Todd and Sara, who sat in the comer, Alice-banded, if not winsome. Each person took their turn to talk about their work for that day.

Chief researcher: 'I'm very much consolidating at the moment, as are my team.'

Plain researcher: 'Yes, consolidating as well. Generating ideas, bringing forward campaigns, thinking about the election.'

Junior researcher: 'The election is important, yes. We're all consolidating any gains made last time, looking to make new ones this time around.'

'Pass,' said Sara Cinnamon.

Larry Beat: 'Well, that sounds good. I wouldn't mind this meeting ending early, actually. I have to collect some Czechs from the airport.'

'Can't you have them sent?' asked Myra.

'I don't think that would be very politic, do you?'

Chief, plain and junior researchers: 'No, no, definitely not.'

'Only I was going to talk to you about a campaign. A press conference today, to start with a press conference.'

'Well, can anyone else get the Czechs for me?' asked Larry Beat, looking around hopefully.

'All this over a few lousy cheques,' muttered Myra, drawing a large childish house in her notebook, rounding off the windows with sad faces, and adding bars.

She had found just one story in the papers to interest her. The hostages in India, kept cooped up in Kashmir for so long. She had read just the top paragraph, determined to *do* something. She, Myra Felt, would push the issue into the mouths of Pluralists. There would be Early Day Motions, written questions, a campaign, a rally, demonstrations. There had, after all, to be some advantage in collaborating with the establishment. Looking, or so she hoped, like a Rosa Luxembourg or an Aung San Suu Chi – a female revolutionary with just the purest of political thoughts – Myra sat at the edge of her chair, talking hostages.

'I really want to do something,' she said. 'Here's something that the Pluralists can *really* call their own. Nobody's commented. We can do something here that might mean something.'

Larry Beat and Billy Todd exchanged glances. There was a near-obscene passion about Myra Felt. 'Calm down,' said Billy. 'Talk to Ray Hines about it. And if he wants to do something, fine.'

To talk hostages *properly*, Myra found Ray Hines in his tiny second-hand bookshop of an office, pushed high into the building; the ceiling sinking down at the centre, almost meeting the piles of paper and the pulpy, bent files, which gathered pace as they climbed up the wall. Ray was standing on a short, fat ladder, stretching for a piece of paper, its corner fluttering as it flirted within reach. 'Er, Ray?' said Myra, upsetting Mr Hines, as she so desperately wanted to call him, who, as he heard her, turned only the head, and that with ginger disdain.

'Yes?' he said and made his way down the steps, with such visible effort that Myra regretted, well, everything that had brought her into his room. 'I'm sorry to bother you,' she said, 'but . . .' Ray's telephone rang and he picked it up with almost palpable relief. As he talked (about mesh sizes and the Fishing Bill that was passing slowly through the House), Myra shrank, like Alice in Wonderland, into the chair, her skirt sticking, on and off, to the sweating leather.

Turning to Myra, Ray Hines suggested she read about Indian politics and the Kashmir Question if she wanted to campaign; that feelings were no good on their own. They had to be blended with some knowledge.

'But,' said Myra, 'the men are hostages *now*. What's going to happen to them while I'm reading textbooks and briefing papers?'

'You're a silly girl,' Ray said, gently, looking up at the mountain of papers he had climbed that morning, the bound books he had certainly read. 'If you knew anything about anything, you would know how little you knew.'

Myra couldn't bring herself to say anything. She left for the ever-empty Family Room in the House of Commons and there drafted a press release headline, about road rage. 'Robert Harvey is Angry,' she wrote. She would push it at lobby correspondents this afternoon. There had to be, at last, some mention of the Pluralists in tomorrow morning's papers.

Simon Nuttall's programme running order ran as follows: North Korea, Israel and Battered Men.

'If you can combine the battered-men issue with the men-and-feminism issue, that would be great,' Nuttall told Young Buck.

'We're getting some pictures of a feminist rally in France. If you can throw them into your film too, wonderful. And can you talk about the shifts in attitude towards men? The way men perceived themselves in the last century as compared to today. Oh, and try to include this MP having an affair, too. You'll have to read the wires – the story's just broken. I'm sure you can throw in a bit about men and sleaze in the House of Commons. He is a *man*, after all.

'And I want some figures – real figures, not attitudes – some statistics on, I don't know, the number of men committing suicide, that you can put into a graphic. I'll need a good discussion off the back of this. You'll need to set up all the arguments in the film. But I can only give you three minutes, I'm afraid. It's a tight programme today, too much news around.'

Ellen, Young Buck and Experience had been put in charge of producing the film on Men Today. But Ellen had to find a North

Korean as well, for the package on North Korea, which Clever and Quiet were producing. Decorative had to find a guest for the Middle East film.

'Can I have those telephone numbers of those people you were talking about?' Decorative asked Ellen. 'Those Middle Eastern contacts?'

Ellen flicked through her address book, shuffled the *Sun* and the *Mirror* around on her desk and said: 'God, sorry, they must be at home. Still, I'm sure they'll be easy to find.'

'Thank you,' said Decorative, bitterly. As a bitchy after-thought, she added, 'How's your 'Women In Power' film going, Ellen? Personally, I think it's unlikely that Matherbay would want to lead the Pluralists. But I don't think that matters. You can make a really nice, little film about all those sit-ins she started in the *seventies*.'

Ellen Abrahams phoned Myra Felt. 'Have you got any news on Lou Matherbay? Has she said anything yet?'

'Well, there's *Peyarth*,' said Myra, sorting out her accent into something approaching Ellen's. 'She might say something at the by-election.'

'Has she said so?'

'Well, no.'

'Does she confide in you at all? I mean, am I speaking to the wrong person? Is there anyone there that she *talks* to?'

'She talks to me,' said Myra. 'It's just that . . . Look, I've just arranged for Lou to open a store in September. Dutton's. It's in Swindon, away from London and all the hassles of Westminster, so she's bound to open up more. And she probably won't say anything until after the by-election in Peyarth, anyway, so why don't you come along. Talk to her then, before the opening.'

'But that's ages away. Oh God. Can't you do any better than that, Myra? I mean, I'll come to Swindon, but try and get something out of her before then. Don't you realise how impor-tant this is?'

'Yes,' said Myra Felt.

Chapter Thirteen

Ellen was on her way to South London to film a Mr Bob Holland, who had been battered by his wife. Young Buck had talked to him on the telephone. 'He sounds promising,' he said to Ellen. 'Get him to show you his bruises or whatever.'

En route, her mobile phone had rung three times. Each time, Young Buck's voice cracked through, making demands on Ellen.

Call Number One:

'I'll need you to film photographs of his wife, preferably, er, hitting him . . . He told me on the phone that he was terrified of women. Can you get him to say that to you? Look, this is turning into the bulk of the piece, this filming. You'll have to bring me back at least two minutes. Think of something arty.'

Call Number Two:

'Forget about the photos of his wife. Simon says there'll be problems with the lawyers . . . Can you get him to say that he thinks it's because of feminism? That would fit in nicely. Ask him if he knows anyone who's been battered for live.'

Call Number Three:

'Korea's falling down. We've been given three more minutes. It might even turn into a lead. Forget about asking him for a live guest. Simon wants just any old man from a men's organisation, not a battered man, particularly. See if you can get any figures from him. I haven't done the graphic yet. Make sure he says he's terrified of women. Without that, we're wasting our time. Oh, and be back in an hour. They're shouting about the North Korean interview.'

Bob Holland had been standing, smiling, at an open door as Ellen's car drew up outside. 'Tea's on the table,' he had shouted to an unmoved neighbourhood. And: 'Can I help?' to the cameraman and the soundman.

'I'm Ellen Abrahams,' she had called to Bob, unnecessarily, catching a tripod from a cynical cameraman and throwing smiles at a springing soundman. 'I'm from *FastNews*.'

Ellen looked around the shabby house, which smelt of cats and convenience food. 'Out you go, out you go,' she could hear Bob saying, and wondered, vaguely, as she picked up photographs and closed curtains, whether he was talking to his cats or her crew. You could never tell with men of a certain class.

She came down the stairs, almost tripping on a loose bit of carpet, and said brightly: 'OK, I've had a look around, Bob. I think we're going to have to move some furniture, though.'

Sound and Camera were sitting at the dining-room table with Bob, who had, indeed, prepared a large tea. Spread on a yellowing lace tablecloth, ironed with creases, were white plates of sliced ham; white-bread sandwiches, filled with egg mayonnaise; sponge cake and tarts; and packet chocolate rolls, unwrapped. 'We should start, you know,' said Ellen, as Camera poured himself a cup of tea from the brown teapot and Sound helped himself, with one hand, to a bakewell slice, and with the other, to a scoop of cheesy balls.

'Aren't you going to have any tea?' asked Bob. 'I made it specially.'

Ellen Abrahams knew charm; she had learned charm for all circles. She had trimmed it to fit all social groups, flattered it at the edge for the chattering classes, spotted it with cynicism for the influential and brought it down to earth for the disadvantaged. At work, she was a chameleon; it was her trade. Plumbers unblock toilets; producers merge with backgrounds, stand behind cameras, whisper to reporters, question continuity. It was her job to plonk herself in people's lives, like a long-running social affairs documentary.

'I'll just have a bit of bread,' she said to Bob, taking a bite out of some bread with what seemed to be honey, but turned out to be dripping. Ellen went to the bathroom, took the unswallowed piece of fat-coated bread from her mouth and squashed it down the sink. They had already been in Bob's house for fifteen minutes.

'Bob, is there a photograph of you and your wife that I can put behind you for the interview?' Ellen asked.

'Oh, yes, plenty,' said Bob and walked, with difficulty, to a chest of drawers.

'Has something happened to your leg, Bob?' asked Ellen, feigning concern, as Bob pulled the gold handle on the stiff wooden drawer. 'You poor thing.'

'It's when my wife pushed me down the stairs,' said Bob, smiling. 'Ah, here's the box. There's some lovely ones of Sheila. My wife.'

'You've got to get some set-up shots of Bob walking down the stairs,' Ellen said to Camera, quietly.

'Ready,' said Camera. He was all set up. 'Yes. Ready to go,' said Ellen. And, with different inflection: 'What did your wife do to you, Bob?'

'Well, we love each other, still. I love her and we love each other.' He paused. 'I'm not doing very well, am I?' he asked Ellen, looking into the camera.

'Whatever you do, Bob, don't look at the camera. First rule of television.' She looked at her watch. 'Now, don't worry, just answer my question. What did your wife do to you, Bob?'

'I love my wife. It was one of those things, I suppose, which happens in every marriage. She just pushed me, in an argument. I would have hit her back, but I was down the stairs.'

'I'll just go with that again, Bob. Don't think about the camera. Now, what did your wife do to you?'

'Well, we had a good marriage. Don't get me wrong. I love her, and I'd take her back tomorrow. She did hurt me then, I must admit that. But I'd take her back tomorrow.'

'Just one more time,' said Ellen. She wanted to ask him not to smile, which he was doing – to spite her, she thought. 'Repeat what you said on the phone to my colleague. Or tell me again what you were saying earlier, about how she hurt you, that you can't walk properly now...?'

Myra was taking press releases around the House of Commons press gallery. The corridor, dense with political correspondents, churned stuffy, bad air around her lungs. Male and female journalists, all in grey and burgundy, but cheerful, swooped like vultures on to her pile of press releases, which detailed a press conference about carbon dioxide. 'Well, these are good for trees,' said the man from the *Financial Times*, placing his press release back on to Myra's pile with distaste. 'In the long run,' said Myra, hopefully.

She felt like an air hostess as she went down the corridor, popping into the different newspaper rooms to offer up what she had that day. 'Carbon Dioxide and Sleaze,' she called out on entrance. 'Tea or Coffee?' she could have been saying. 'Beef or Chicken?'

'Oh good, Sleaze,' said the men in the regional-newspaper room, unsmiling. 'What are you saying on Kashmir?' asked the man from the *Independent,* who didn't know her name.

'Nothing at the moment,' Myra said, smiling, showing teeth.

'Typical,' he said, wiping his nose with the sleeve of his jacket. 'I'll take Carbon Dioxide then.'

'What are you Pluralists saying about beef again?' asked the mop-haired man from the *Guardian*, leaning far back in his chair and grabbing a comer of Myra's skirt.

'Why are you lot going so big on the environment?' asked the *Daily Express* man, short neck squashing into his open-shirted shoulders like a concertina. 'We're all doing adultery.'

'Can I take you out to lunch next week?' asked the toothy one from the *Glasgow Herald*. 'I've been ordered to do a series of backgrounders in the run-up to the Peyarth by-election. I want to know what you're doing about inner cities.'

'When's Matherbay goin' to declare herself, Myra?' asked a BBC reporter.

The *Daily Star* journalist beckoned Myra over to him. 'Any of your lot having affairs?' he asked her. 'I'll exchange anything you've got for a guaranteed two hundred words on carbon dioxide.'

'How you going to do in Peyarth?' asked the *Daily Telegraph* correspondent, Adam's apple racing up and down the neck, as she met him in the corridor. 'Oh, we'll be fighting to win, Rupert,' said Myra.

Fighting to win, she said to herself.

Watching Prime Minister's Questions from her seat in the press gallery, Myra felt frivolous, looking down on people of renown. She had one of the 'cheaper seats' upstairs, the proceedings obscured by two journalists from Welsh newspapers and the barrier beneath them.

When Myra had first entered the press gallery she had, as a matter of course, sat at the front in the middle. The seat had been just a box of popcorn short of perfect, but the *Daily Telegraph*'s Rupert and another gentleman had turfed her out, horrified.

'These are *Daily Telegraph* seats,' the dusty, elderly gentleman had said. 'They have always been *Daily Telegraph* seats. They will always be *Daily Telegraph* seats.' Myra had escaped and a man at the door had said: 'You were sitting in seats reserved for the *Daily Telegraph*. You can only sit there if you are with the *Daily Telegraph*.' His voice had echoed after Myra, chasing her downstairs.

As she emerged from Prime Minister's Questions, Larry Beat caught her. 'We want you to go to Peyarth,' he said. 'As you know, it's not all that hopeful a by-election.' He paused. 'But it'll just be for a few weeks – I'd imagine until the end of August – and Sara can understudy for you. Billy and I think you can do some good. And I'll be pretty involved in the campaign, so I'll be backwards and forwards. What do you think, Myra?'

'Wow, yes. OK. Yes,' said Myra – and then suddenly thought of Patrick and his thick Guinness voice. 'The people who write career advice and the people who write relationship advice should get together some time,' she thought. And, later: 'I'm too young to be settling down with a career. I want to climb up the ladder of love.'

'Er, Larry, about Lou,' Myra said.

'Lou?'

'Well, is she going to stand in the leadership contest or not? I keep trying to get hold of her but it's as if she's avoiding me. I mean, I've barely seen her since I started. And it's annoying, to be honest, because I have this woman from *FastNews* who's very persistent and . . . ?'

'And she wants to know about this phoney war between Ray and Lou? Well, that's something we're all wondering, actually. And your guess, Myra, is as good as mine. Although Sara seems to think she'll announce something after the by-election. There's actually something, Myra, that I wanted to ask *you*,' said Larry, switching tone. 'Sensitive, this. But how about investing in a few smart suits? Get rid of the student image? Maybe get your hair cut in Peyarth?'

'But what's wrong with *hair*?' Myra asked, horrified.

'Well, it's the image thing. You, out of anyone, would understand that. And, you know,' he said, his voice leaping to persuasion. 'I have, never, *ever* known a successful woman to have long hair. I mean, look at Mo Mowlam. Look at Sue Lawley.'

'Look at Lou Matherbay,' said Myra.

'Well, yes,' he said, sadly. 'But, you know, there's only one Lou Matherbay. And her hair isn't *long*. It's just *big*.'

And Myra nodded, touching her head. Her hair hid strength, like Samson's, giving out femininity, in place of places that nature forgot. For a woman as breastless as Myra, her hair was a sign of fertility, and proof of an essential womanliness. She used it, for God's sake, and not simply for the sake of sex. 'He doesn't realise,' thought Myra, as Larry left her. 'He doesn't realise it's a part of *me*.'

Ellen had surrendered her interview with Bob. Sound and Camera had tried to help. All three of them had worked hard at it. They had worked hard to squeeze information from him, to pulp out emotion. But as Ellen had frowned, Bob had smiled. He wasn't going to give her what she needed for the interview.

He was going to sit there, smiling, talking about women's rights and his strong marriage. He was going to ask her when the programme was on. He was going to tell her that he didn't watch *FastNews*, that he hadn't heard of *FastNews*. He watched *Direct Live*. At that point, Ellen might have started to wrench feeling from him, as one might from a lover. But there wasn't time. 'We'll stop there now,' she said. And to him: 'That was great. I think you've done this before, haven't you? What a star.'

The mobile phone rang. It was Young Buck. 'What have you got, Ellen? I need to know for the script. I've written: "I tried for years to stop her bashing me about, but she wouldn't stop. Sixties feminism has led to women treating men like rubbish (or whatever) etc." And that will lead me nicely into those pictures of the French march. Which, by the way, are fantastic. Ellen, are you there? Ellen, can you get him to say what I've written? Ellen?'

Ellen was asking: 'Did she leave any marks on your body, Bob? Any bruising?'

'Oh, I see what you mean,' he said, voluble now, off camera. 'What she did to me, you mean? No, my legs looked bad then, really bad. But they've healed up nicely now. I'm fine, love. Thanks for asking though. Not many people want to talk about it.'

Ellen thought about sitting him down for another try at the interview, but there wasn't the time. As Bob climbed the stairs, in pain, in order to be filmed walking down again, in pain, Ellen looked out of the window at his garden. In the middle of the lawn was a Wendy house, broken up and trampled. 'Get some shots of that through the window,' she said. 'It would make a great metaphor.'

Bob had to be filmed from all angles coming down the stairs. 'Sorry, Bob,' Ellen said, thinking about Young Buck and his so far all-but-empty film. 'But this is television. We don't have three cameras, you see, so we have to do each action three times.' Bob clutched at his leg and groaned, gently and pitifully.

'Did you get him doing that?' hissed Ellen at Camera. 'Look, can you do your job and I'll do mine?' Camera said, with venom, thinking about maintenance payments and his next filming trip to Liberia. Sound, in his own little headphoned world, took an egg mayonnaise sandwich out of his pocket, and munched, meaningfully.

'Sorry. I just can't do this any more,' said Bob, sitting on the top stair, his little smiling face now twisted in agony.

'OK then,' said Ellen. 'Don't you worry. That's it. We'll call it a day. Your furniture will be moved back to the living-room, and it'll be as if we were never here.'

Bob nodded, his grape face scrunching like a raisin. 'Yes, love.'

So they left him, waving, crumpled and crumbled at his doorstep. And as the production team drove away, Bob limped inside to set the video recorder for that evening's *FastNews* and to throw food into cats' bowls or greasy swing bins.

'He was a disaster,' Ellen was saying to Young Buck on the

mobile phone. 'Honestly, don't expect anything. He wasn't upset at all. He'd only hurt his *leg*, and he seemed to be still in love with his wife, for God's sake. I think we can squeeze one bit of synch out of him but *that's it*. I mean, I don't know who *found* the man but, whoever it was, they shouldn't be in TV.'

'Did you ask him what he thought about feminism?' asked Young Buck, who had found the man.

'You must be joking . . .'

'God, why not? This film's turning into a disaster. Everything's going mad here. They're desperate for your North Korean now. Simon's banking on it.'

'Well, I got a nice set-up with him, anyway, walking down the stairs. And some good cutaways – photos of him and his wife.'

'How many seconds can I squeeze out, synch-wise?'

'If anything, twenty seconds.'

'Well, are there some nice shots of his bruises?'

'He didn't have any bruises.'

'Well, why the hell did we do him then? What the hell *did* he have? Why didn't you ask him about feminism? I mean, do I have to do *everything*?'

Ellen pressed the tiny red 'off' button on the telephone.

Ellen's driver was asking her about beef. Should he eat it? Ellen said Definitely Not, asked him how much he earned, and whether he knew who was fashionable at *FastNews*. The driver stopped at a zebra crossing to allow a young mum, smiling at her child, to cross the road. For some reason, Ellen felt a stab of envy. 'Care for a Smartie?' asked the driver. 'It's only the red ones that contain beef gelatin, apparently.'

An open suitcase sat on Myra's bed. It was brown, hardening and softening in spots, bending like cardboard on the roof, where she had sat squeezing it shut at the clip. It might have been her grandmother's, but she had bought it in a charity shop for £4.99, and had taken it to Egypt, Morocco, India, South Africa, China and around most of Europe. And now it was going to Peyarth, to a by-election, with Myra, who was throwing unironed clothes indiscriminately from the wardrobe to the suitcase.

Packing for Peyarth, she decided, was a career issue. Patrick would be arriving soon, and she would look efficient, using her time effectively, to further her career. Myra looked around her room, and at the shut suitcase on her bed, the pillowslip, which read 'Night' (bereft without 'Good'). Her make-up tubes lay like dead soldiers on the dressing-table; foundation pot fallen, dribbling like paint; powder tin, cracked and erupting; lipsticks, standing to grubby attention at pencil point, or collapsed, bloody on the table. She went to sit by her suitcase, an earnest evacuee, hand around handle, patiently waiting for Patrick.

Ellen was telephoning potential North Koreans in Washington, Brussels, Bonn, London, Paris and South Korea. She had found a North Korean who had defected and was willing to speak against the regime. 'Do you want him, Simon?' she asked Nuttall.

'What does he say?'

'Well, he's defected and he's critical. He says it's like a backward China, that it won't last long, and that it still wants to push South . . .'

'We don't want a critic, Ellen. For God's sake.'

'Yes, yes, I know.'

'Do you want some help on this?' (Kiss of death – the big bail-out.)

'No,' said Ellen.

Ellen found South Koreans with North Korean roots and journalists who happened to be North Korean. She found North Korean ambassadors whose press officers couldn't speak English and North Korean diplomats who put the telephone down as soon as Ellen spoke. Finally, Ellen found a North Korean in Seattle, nowhere near a *FastNews* studio.

'Simon, I've found him.'

'God, at last. One person doing their job on this programme.'

'But it'll have to be a telephone interview. He's in Seattle, miles from a studio.'

'Well, get him to San Francisco. We might be able to do something from there. I don't want a phono on my programme.'

'He's not going to go to San Francisco. He says he lives near the Canadian border . . .'

'I can't talk, Ellen. I've got a *programme* to sort out. Just find a North Korean.'

'Ellen, phone for you,' said a production secretary, waving the telephone in the air.

'I'll only take it if he's from North Korea.'

'Well, he's not. He's . . .' Ellen pressed the top line on the telephone.

'Ellen, can you come down to the cutting room. I'm in 132.' It was Young Blond Buck.

'I have to find a North Korean.'

'Look, just come down, OK?'

Ellen Abrahams didn't have a stomach any more. Her intestines curled around her head, agonisingly. Her lower abdomen ached for food. Her arms withered near her shoulders. The legs she knew, she felt sure, were begging her, in their own fatty, breathless, way, to stop her running, to stop running up and down the stairs to cutting rooms, to the newsroom, to the studio. Her organs had stopped playing, sleeping as she ran. She dared her body to keep up with her mind, which raced around, which refused to eat, which slowed her down. She dared her body to keep up with her brain, but she just felt pain.

'You wanted me?' asked Ellen.

The picture editor, Steve, who started broad and tapered towards the legs, was lying on the floor. 'I can't do anything with it,' he said. He was lying down because this was the fifteenth hour of his sixteen-hour day. He worked sixteen-hour days, every day, to earn the money to pay for a permanent holiday, so that he could lie in the sun without his brown cardigan, and tan his hilly stomach. Originally he had accepted overtime so that he and his wife could buy a cottage in Wales and convert it into paradise. But the wife he hardly saw had left him for another woman, so now he would have to go it alone in paradise.

I can't do anything with that,' said Steve, pointing at Ellen's tapes. 'There's nothing there. There's sod all there.' He closed his eyes.

'He's appalling,' said Young Buck. 'I don't know what to do.'

'You can get twenty seconds out of him, can't you?'

Ellen was in a cutting room, ten thousand miles removed from reality. She was a hundred light years from life as the rest of the world knows it. The house in Harrow-on-the-Hill, the mother she had ignored for months, the fiancé, Lucy's new romance with her brother, Darren, the fading memories of her father, Helen's rekindled relationship with Solly. To Ellen now, sitting in this airless room, dug out below the ground, just for this purpose, this life she vaguely remembered as hers was ludicrous, and illusory.

Bob now existed only on tape, to be pushed forwards and backwards, to be refined and polished, edited to perfection. Bob was a man on television, a man without choice, to be called: 'Silly old bugger,' in his absence by Steve; to be shouted at by Young Buck: 'Why couldn't you say you were battered?' To be betrayed by Ellen, who had sat at his table, who had accepted his food, who had complimented him, who had called him *star*, who had, not for one minute, felt sorry.

'Honestly, I could have killed him,' she was saying now. 'Wasting our time like that. He wasn't battered at all. He was just a stupid little man, conning us all.'

Around them, men and women ran.

'Have you seen the pictures on the South African feed? Bloody brilliant. Bloody, but brilliant.'

'Can you get this translated?' I think it's Serbo-Croat.'

'Just pull some synch out of this interview, would you?'

'The tape's stuck in the machine.'

'Did you *see* that piece to camera? How does she think she can be a reporter?'

'No, I've been switched. I'm doing South Africa.'

Muddy coffee and soapy tea spilled out of tiny rationed polystyrene cups as producers ran with them. Reporters strolled, essentially in thought. At computers, six people corrected scripts. 'I'm not having you say that. You can't say that. It's racist. Oh, brilliant, brilliant. Put this . . .'

Purely Decorative popped her beautiful face around Steve's door. 'Simon said to say, can you cut it down, he hasn't as much room as he thought. And he says sorry.'

'Did you find your Middle East guest?' asked Ellen.

'God, eventually. Horrendous,' PD said, sucking on a cigarette. 'Ho-ren-duss. I'm not sure his English is very good. How's it going here? Alison's having a terrible job up there, trying to find two

136

people for the Men discussion. Everyone's agreeing. I think I'll just sit here for a second, or they'll ask me to help.'

'OK, I've used your cutaways to come up with this. But it's up to you,' Steve said, looking at Young Buck. He pushed 'play' on his machine.

Bob's image played. 'She did hurt me then, I must admit that. She just pushed me, in an argument. I would have hit her back, but I was down the stairs by then.'

'Yes, that's fine,' said Young Buck. 'I'll take that. It's short, but it's a cut. Yup. It'll do.'

It had all ended for Myra. Patrick sat away from her, at the dressing-table, twisting lipsticks. 'You're too sexual for me,' he was saying. 'Too all over the place. Emotionally, you're demanding. You have no drive. And, you know what bothers me the most? You smell like an ashtray.'

'But I love you,' Myra was telling Patrick. 'It had nothing to do with sex. I don't understand. We had sex. Yes. You said I was sexy. But . . .'

'Myra, Myra, Myra,' he said. 'You are one hell of a girl. But you're not for me.'

I *am* for him, thought Myra. I am for anyone.

She lay on her bed, with Patrick beside her, contemplating life without Patrick. The suitcase had been pushed to the floor, open, apart, clothes dangling outside. She wanted a new suitcase now, a career suitcase, hard and blue, with a clasp that stuck firm. She wanted suits, as Larry had suggested. She wanted a professional, tidy outline. She was sick of sticking out everywhere, like a sore thumb. She wanted to look capable. And Myra knew she could become capable. It was only a matter of buying the right products.

The mirror opposite them showed Myra pretty: long curls, big, grey eyes irredeemably red from tears, fashionably thin. Yet Patrick was leaving Myra. And of course she was crying. She did, after all, appear to lose boyfriends once a month, and painfully, like blood. Yes, she felt empty, of course she felt empty; there were Saturday nights to fill, with thousands of friends, that couldn't quite make up for Patrick.

*

Ellen, oh lovely Ellen, Ellen of Troy, had found a North Korean, in Geneva. 'Yes,' Mr Lee had said, finally, as she gave him a list of questions, which she would, in time, brief the presenter to ask. 'I will not answer questions about any nuclear bombs,' he had said.

'Fine,' said Ellen.

'I will not answer questions about South Korea.'

'Oh yes, fine,' said Ellen.

'I will not answer questions about the Americans.'

'But you'll be there? At the address I gave you, at twenty-two, twenty-five, your time? That's twenty-one, twenty-five our time?'

'I will want to say that North Korea wants peace.'

'Of course,' said Ellen.

Simon Nuttall was apologising, as he always did at the end of the day. 'Sorry, Team, but I'm dropping Men,' he said. 'We'll still have the Men discussion but not the film now. I'm going to lead on South Africa and I'll need you,' he said, pointing thoughtfully at Young Buck, who found the strength, as he had always done, to unfold himself and go fight. 'I'll just read the wires, Simon,' he said.

(Bob was checking his video recorder, crouching down, with the sock of pain in his leg rolling up to his hips and circling them. He had made himself a large cup of tea, leaving the bag to soak. It kept company with the plate of jam tarts, which he had bought, quickly, from the shop across the road that morning. 'I'm having guests,' he had informed Mrs Wong, who hadn't cared. 'They're from the television,' he had said, popping a bag of teddy-bear-shaped crisps into his basket. 'They're coming to film me.' 'Really?' Mrs Wong had asked. 'The *TV*?')

The familiar theme tune played in the gallery for the rehearsal of that evening's *FastNews*. 'Good evening,' said the presenter. 'In South Africa this evening, scores of people are looking . . .'

'Good evening,' said the presenter, for real. 'In South Africa this evening, scores of people are looking . . .' Ellen looked at the screen on the right, saying: 'Geneva', for her North Korean. 'Where's your North Korean chappie?' asked Dan Berkovsky, appearing beside her, jaws snapping, bottom heaving and hair falling out in pieces as he spoke.

'Er, he's coming,' said Ellen, who felt sick.

A man, a Korean, fuzzed into view, on the screen which had said Geneva. 'He's here,' said Ellen, to bodies in the gallery that weren't listening, but were, like Experience without Promotion, worrying about guests on the Men debate, now just a discussion without a film. Or the bodies were, like Clever Ugly, worrying about the film he had made about the problems facing North Korea, talking about the relationship Kim Jong Il had had with his father, Kim Il Sung. 'The content is there. But I'm worried about its aesthetic value,' he was telling Young Buck, who wasn't listening, as he was worrying about his South African film, exploring the problems facing South Africa and Nelson Mandela, which as it had been made quickly, didn't make any sense. He hoped it was making sense to Simon Nuttall, but the programme producer wasn't watching; he was worrying about Dan Berkovsky, and what he felt about his programme.

'Have you checked on your guests in hospitality?' Nuttall asked Experience. 'Make sure they say the right things. There's only the discussion now. It has to be good.'

Experience found her discussion guests in the hospitality room, bonding furiously. 'Hi, I'm Alison,' she said. 'We spoke on the phone and you disagreed about Men and it's important for a good discussion that you disagree on air as well,' she said, fainting down into a chair, and pouring herself some warm, white wine. Guest One turned to Guest Two and asked her if she minded him eating the last sandwich. 'Not at all,' said Guest Two.

(Myra Felt sat with her television twiddler, alone, at home, finding *FastNews* and sticking with that. 'Typical. They never have any Pluralists,' she thought, believing her own propaganda, which poured vitriolic from her mouth every morning on to editors or producers. 'Ray Hines would have been great on South Africa,' she said aloud, drunken with vodka. 'I'll complain tomorrow,' said Myra, as she smoked herself to tears.)

Ellen stood – her vital organs circling her body like clouds – as the presenter introduced her Korean.

'Do you have a nuclear bomb?'

'What?' the Korean said.

'Does North Korea have any nuclear weapons? Yes or No?'

Ellen's body dipped at the middle, the neck bone connected to the ankle bone. Another button popped off her jacket.

'You cannot say yes or no to such a question . . .'

'God, he's good, your Korean,' said Clever Ugly to Ellen. Ellen's organs returned, with grace, to her body, as she realised that he was saying all the appropriate things. 'Yeah,' she said. 'He's not bad.'

(Bob's mind wandered, away from world affairs and towards his wife. He wondered whether he should telephone her, to say that he was on television; a star. He could feel her pride, drowning him, drowning out the pain from his leg. But the organisation had told him to 'steer clear' and his sister had told him to 'keep away', so he took a bite of a jam tart instead, wiping gummy blackcurrant from his teeth and dropping crumbs around the settee.)

'And now. Men,' said the presenter, smiling, with cynicism. 'Are they or aren't they . . .' Guest One and Guest Two were being hooked with microphones, sticking out breast and chest, rolling bottoms around chairs, finding a position for legs, smiling and thoughtful and scared. Experience lazed against the wall in the *FastNews* gallery, her thick lips souring at the edges, her skin tinting grey under the lights.

'Well, I agree entirely with Jean,' said Guest One. 'Of course, men are scared, they're terrified.'

'They're panicking,' said Guest Two.

'Jean's right. Men are getting the raw deal . . .'

'The short straw.'

'The worst of all worlds.'

'And I agree with Boris. Women should be bearing the burden of responsibility for this.'

'Absolutely right.'

'The absolute burden.'

In the gallery, producers crunched their eyes, drank their tongues dry, held each other's jackets, dry-cleaned to fade. Dan Berkovsky marched between them, exclaiming wildly. 'Who got these two? They're agreeing. They're bloody agreeing!' Experience said that they hadn't agreed before, on the telephone. 'Wind it up, wind it up,' said Berkovsky to Nuttall.

(Bob blinked as the *FastNews* music played, lyrically, with the credits. His absence on the programme had left a tiny pit in his stomach, hungry for something. He brought the cup of tea to his mouth and the stewing bag fell forward, on to his closed, dry lips. Spitting it back into the cup, he let it down on to the table, knocking the pot. The tea showered the plate of jam tarts.)

'The programme tonight was rubbish,' said Dan Berkovsky.

'Absolutely awful,' Simon Nuttall was telling his small but beautifully formed team.

'The Middle East item looked late; the guest didn't speak English properly. The discussion about Men turned into some sort of hippie love-in. I'm going to have to hold an inquest about that, Alison. We just can't let it happen. South Africa was, of course, clear but I didn't understand what you were going on about, Malcolm, with your Korean film. Utter garbage. There was, however, one good thing about tonight's programme, and that was the North Korean. *What* good television. Ellen Abrahams, you are the only member of my team with any television talent.'

A clapped-out old Ellen Abrahams, redundant outside the *FastNews* office, made her way home. Clutching her jacket shut, Ellen, who had once been neat in shapely suits, now felt her body burst at the seams, breaking buttons.

Chapter Fourteen

In preparation for Hanna's party, Susan sat in a hard, striped towel, allowing the dye she had soaped into her hair to do its stuff, and smoking cigarette after cigarette. Products, lined up on her table, looking excited.

Susan was excited, as she stuck her head in the bath and showered her pampered head with the extension. Later, the woman in the mirror might argue that she had bleached her hair too blonde, but Susan would be pleased. And she would see only a reflection of the woman on the dye box, laughing. She had been shopping that day. She had had to buy accessories, for an anticipated lifestyle.

Out would go the mug tree and the tape rack. Susan had considered both items chic, before spotting them holding up a cardboard wall in a daytime soap opera set in Scotland. In would come a new Susan, bouncing – flying – like a magazine cover girl. An interesting Susan, a sexy pulp-fiction creature; a woman with built-in anti-perspirant and inconclusive features, with eyes that ran in pools around her face, and legs which went on like slim, golden batteries – for ever.

Susan shopped at Oxford Street and, as a woman possessed, grabbed at lime green, crimson pink and fluorescent yellow items; placing them in a basket, along with skinny, ribbed knickers and stretchy, silken bras. The cash register buzzed in time with the store music. Susan went next door, for more fun; for further armloads of casual and evening wear; for hangers of stiff, smart clothes and plastic bags, expensive with thick handles, or cheap with hand holes, that stretched, all but broken, with purchase upon purchase.

Then, Susan Lyttle caught up with machines. Machines which played music or wide-screen television programmes; video recorders and clock radios, with built-in electric toothbrushes and digital alarms. She bought seven gadgets, to be delivered the following week without fail. Only when the shops had run out of energy-saving devices did Susan Lyttle buy a long, scarlet skirt for Hanna's party. Susan chose the skirt because it gave her hips, and it gave her legs. It even attempted to give her a bottom.

Retail therapy had worked for Susan, but her old wardrobe could not cope with the summer collection. It rejected hangers dripping with clothes. It threw her peach-purple sequinned bra top and flower-stained mushroom-coloured tunic to the floor. Susan looked at her shopping, scared. She knew she could never wear any of it outdoors.

The household goods, bought to bring light into Susan's Finchley flat, looked cheap and garish next to the timeless landlord wallpaper and the dry brown carpet, padded flat by tenants. Yellow mugs and wire egg baskets looked fine on shop shelves, surrounded by other yellow mugs or wire egg baskets. Alone in Susan's flat they looked temporary, if not ludicrous.

'Oh well. I'll just have to live with them now,' she thought, attaching the diffuser to her hairdryer and blow-drying her hair, straight from Southport and into London society.

Ellen Abrahams had marinated her mushrooms, spiced her pears and crumbled her blackcurrants. She had herbed her bread, glazed her turnips and ironed her linen napkins. She had positioned her glass bowls beautifully on the table, filling them with quails' eggs and flat strips of smoked trout. She had choreographed her after-dinner mints to lie down, synchronised. She had chopped up her fruit to swim daintily in low-fat cream.

Ellen had cleaned away evidence of cooking from her kitchen. She had folded away traces of drying washing, hanging about her utility room. Her collection of potboiler novels was hidden behind hardback biographies at the back of her bookshelf. Any possible signs of house life had been cleaned, turned around, or discarded.

Except, of course, for Jeffrey Bell. He was reading an adult comic in her flowered-print armchair in the living-room. 'Jeffreey,' yelled Ellen, with panicked vowels. 'They're almost here. You can't read *that*. *Please . . .*'

'Let's have sex,' said Jeffrey, wrinkling Ellen's blouse as he grabbed at her elbow. He smelt of empty real estate.

'Here. Read this instead,' Ellen said, breathlessly, handing Jeffrey *The Economist*.

'I'm not reading this shit.'

'Just don't lose my place. I'm halfway through Asia,' Ellen said, spilling a bowl of cashew nuts on the floor. 'Oh my *God*. Oh my *God*, *God*. Oh, my . . .'

Ellen vacuumed the carpet clear of nuts, and wound the cable to create a perfect oval shape. A platter of brightly coloured sashimi glared at her from the table. Ellen tried it out at the table's centre, but it clashed with her trout. 'Jeffrey. *Please* don't lie on the couch. They're almost here.' Ellen tried the sashimi on the television, but it was tipped off by the vibrations of a political argument. 'Shit. Shit. Shit,' said Ellen, wiping her sashimi stains. 'I mean, it *has* to happen. It has to happen.' Jeffrey yawned and lay back with his eyes closed.

'Just calm down,' he said, through his nose.

Ellen moved the television to stand on some strands of raw fish, still floating on her carpet. She sniffed to check that the right sort of smells were rising from her toilet. She sprayed aftershave liberally over her fiancé.

'Please, Ellen. I'm still a guest in this house,' whined Jeffrey, who had stolen five squares of after-dinner mints and a quail's egg.

Ellen moved her mints about to create a feeling of living space on the platter. 'Don't take anything else. Those mints were *important*,' she said to her lover. 'And watch where you're putting that egg shell.'

At ten minutes to eight, Ellen spotted a hair in her bath. At five minutes to eight, she found several green political source books in her blue world travel section. At three minutes to eight, Ellen saw her Donna Summer album sitting at the front of her record collection. At two minutes to eight, she discovered a duvet cover which did not match her purple pillow slips. At one minute to eight, the doorbell rang.

'That *bitch* Elizabeth. She's always early,' said Ellen, almost crying with venom on to her pillow slip.

'I thought you *invited* them for eight,' said Jeffrey Bell, shouting from the living-room. He was behaving as if Ellen's house was not about to be invaded by three relative strangers, and one strange friend, all intent on having a good time at the expense of her aired, pressed cushions.

'Shut up. She might hear. She's supposed to be my friend. She could have the bloody decency to be late. Helloo, Elizabeth. How *lovely* to see you,' said Ellen Abrahams, opening the door.

Hanna's house was jumping with sounds borrowed from her older brother's best mate's boss. As Susan walked inside, holding a bottle of white wine in one hand and two packets of cigarettes in the other, she felt temporary, if not ludicrous. A woman was gyrating in the hallway to the sounds of the 'Lightning Seeds'. Susan tried to dance alongside her, without feeling like a foreign object, in a party where a woman sat in the corner of the living-room with her bare breasts exposed.

Ellen Abrahams and Jeffrey Bell sat at opposite ends of her king-sized pine table. Blond Young Buck producer and Mrs Young Buck sat to Ellen's right. Clever Ugly producer and Ellen's friend Elizabeth sat to the left.

'So what do *you* do?' Elizabeth asked Mrs Young Buck. 'Because we know that, apart from Jeffrey, everyone else here works in television.'

'Elizabeth has a chip on her shoulder,' said Jeffrey, sniffing Young Buck's bottle of wine. 'Mmm. Good wine. Anyone?'

Elizabeth heaved herself up. 'Don't be ridiculous. I mean, before anyone asks, yes, I was made redundant just recently. But I would recommend freelancing to *anyone*. It's so . . .'

'What do you, er, freelance in?' asked Clever Ugly, who seemed uglier and, indeed, cleverer outside of an office environment.

'I'm a fashion buyer,' said Elizabeth, elegant in Escada.

'When Elizabeth says freelancing, she means she shops. A *lot*,' said Jeffrey, to a look from Ellen which fried her fiancé to a burnt crisp. 'I'm sorry. That was a joke,' he added, looking sheepishly at his wife-to-be.

Ellen's clothes, although casual, were far from *comfortable*. The pain of her brown trousers, cutting, like a rubber knife, into her waist, was hidden from her guests, only by a long, designer jumper and a forced, delighted expression on her face.

'So, what do you do?' Ellen asked Mrs Young Buck, pouring professional charm over her guest, filling up her wine glass. 'I'm a doctor,' replied the small thin one, sniffing as she drank.

'Well, I'm pleased you're here then,' said Jeffrey. 'Because I have this knee injury, actually. When I was playing squash . . .'

'I don't suppose I can ask you about *joint* aches?' interrupted Elizabeth. Clever Ugly leaned forward, with his elbows on the table. 'Gosh. As everyone else is. I mean, I have these boils on my underarms. Found them quite by ch—'

'Shut *up* you lot! Poor you, you must get this every time. So what do you specialise in? Or are you in general practice?' asked Ellen, who felt genuinely unwell.

'No, I'm an oncology specialist. Cancer,' said Mrs Young Buck, bringing an unwelcome sense of mortality to Ellen's lively table.

Cries of: 'Wow' and 'Gosh' broke the four-second silence which followed. 'That must be depressing,' said Jeffrey and Elizabeth, at once. 'I've heard that treatments have advanced quite rapidly,' said Clever Ugly, who was eating an after-dinner mint, much too early. 'More marinated mushrooms?' Ellen asked Clever, weakly. 'Anyone?'

'It all sounds very *scientific*,' said Ellen to Mrs Young Buck. (She would not have welcomed Mrs Young Buck into her house if she had known about her important-sounding career.)

'Oh, well I'm doing a BA in medieval history in my spare time,' said Mrs Young Buck, airily. 'That just about satisfies my less *rational* side.'

'And then there's your exhibitions,' smiled Young Buck.

'Yes. I sculpt as well,' Mrs Young Buck said.

'Naked bodies,' laughed Young Buck. 'My wife really *understands* the naked body.'

Susan swarmed through the mass of people, in a bid for the bathroom. She passed bare, tanned legs, scents care of Givenchy, Chanel, Marlboro and marijuana, open-mouthed sets of teeth and tonsils, sounds of Britpop music, and polite bitching. She walked by English faces, strained post-sun. There was an overwhelming sense that something was about to happen, or that it had happened already.

Standing still was social suicide and Susan, very much on the move, heard chopped-up bits of conversations, leftovers from something deep and meaningful.

'Well, no, I haven't read *The Little Prince* but I have read *The Prince*.'

'He's a financial adviser, if you know what I mean.'

'Is that your biological sister?'

'I'm an *It* girl actually.'

'They should add two inches to the goals. That way, they'll score.'

'Not in *Burma*.'

'Su-Susan!' Hanna said, slurring drunkenly, and grabbing at her arm. 'Have you met Rhona?'

'No. Hi,' said Susan to Rhona, whose red-orange hair was cut to meet the exact shape of her head, and which stopped, as if in protest, as soon as the neck started.

'Now, *you* don't look like you're in the media,' she said, her sharp Scottish accent burning through Susan, who shone pink under the weak lighting.

'I'm a secretary,' said Susan, shyly.

'She's from Southport,' shouted Hanna, above the sounds of Liam Gallagher.

'Well, I'm from Edinburgh, but I don't crow about it,' Rhona said, breathing down through the nipped nose.

'What do *you* do?' asked Susan of Rhona, whose big ears flared out at an alarming angle.

'Oh, me, I'm writing a novel,' said Rhona.

'Really? But, that's just so . . . What's it about?' asked Susan Lyttle, impressed.

'It's about this woman, who's writing a novel,' said Rhona, a Jean Brodie well past her prime.

'So what do you *think*?' asked Ellen of Elizabeth, who had come in to the kitchen to offer support to Ellen, who was having trouble with her chocolate mousse.

'How *could* you? That's what I think.'

'But Malcolm's OK,' Ellen said, clutching her aching stomach with her only available hand. She noticed dry lines around her friend's mouth and thought: *You can't afford to be too picky.*

Elizabeth dipped her finger into Ellen's collapsing mousse. 'Ellen. You told me he was bright, and he is. You told me we have a lot in common, and we do. You told me that he speaks six languages, which is great. And that he's taller than I am, which helps. Oh, and that he's rich, which, yes, is wonderful. But you forgot to mention one little detail, didn't you?'

'Did I?' asked Ellen, dumping the dessert down her waste-disposal unit.

'You forgot to say, quite by chance, and I *completely* understand the oversight, that he's pig ugly. Didn't you? I mean, please Ellen, don't mention the fact that he looks as if he's auditioning for the main part in *Woody Allen, The Musical*.'

'Hello, girls,' said Clever Ugly, coming into the kitchen. Ellen and Elizabeth looked up guiltily. '*Hiii*,' said Ellen, over-compensating. 'Now, could you just take in the fruit salad, Malcolm?'

'Well, I thought I'd come and have a word with Elizabeth, actually. It's getting very heated in there. I think I started something when I brought up Proust's handling of the adjective,' he said, chuckling.

'Well, I'm going back inside,' said Elizabeth, picking up the fruit salad, as if it was a lifebelt.

Susan, nearing social-butterfly status as she flitted silently from one bore to the next at Hanna's party, could see Charles Pickford, simply surrounded by women, and yet looking at her, from the centre of the room.

'I was just explaining Megabytes,' said the man, blocking her view. 'You see, it's not computer operators that are interesting, so much as the computers themselves.' The man looked as if he had drunk far too much milk over the years. It had sallowed out his complexion and drained compassion from his eyes. 'Anyway, anyone who isn't hooked on to the Internet over the next couple of years will be . . .'

'Is this woman boring you?' asked Charles, who was sneering over Susan's right shoulder. 'No, we were just having . . .' said Milk-man, parting his thick, wet lips in surprise.

'Only, a bit of a social inadequate is Susie,' said Charles, nodding his head conspiratorially. 'Socially desperate,' he said, confidentially.

'I'll just go and fill up,' Milk-man said, raising his glass, bewildered.

'You do that, darling,' said Charles, whose face looked smooth under the dimmed light of the living-room. Little specks of green flickered like fairy lights in his eyes, which darted blackly inside Susan.

'Why did you do that?' she asked him, trying out cross, and settling for smitten. 'I don't *understand* . . .'

'I have this theory, you see,' he said, walking her slowly back to the wall. 'I have this theory that the uglies of this world should be kept apart, at all costs. Now, what would have happened had I – with my quite exceptional good looks – not intervened just then? The two of you would have flirted, outrageously, I'm sure of that. One of you would, at some point, have puckered up. You would probably have copulated. You might even have reproduced. And that's the point I'm trying to make. Because, out of one innocent little situation, you would have, quite unknowingly, created another ugly.'

'What an ugly situation,' said Susan, tilting her head and puckering up, as Charles Pickford had suggested was protocol. But he laughed at the sight. He laughed and he left her, standing by the wall, stared at by three accountants and a management consultant.

'Ah, *Thinking the Unthinkable: The Economic Counter-Revolution*,' said Clever Ugly, taking a book from Ellen's shelf, to expose Jackie Collins's *Hollywood Wives*.

'Oh, that's Jeffrey's,' said Ellen quickly. 'Yes, *Thinking the Unthinkable. Such* a good book. Shall we go on in then, Malcolm? Now. More coffee anyone?' asked Ellen as she entered the dining-room. Ellen felt sick at the thought of caffeine. Her stomach churned with rich food. An odd mouthful, stolen from each course, was the only nourishment Ellen had had all day. And now a couple of mushrooms sloshed about in globs of cream inside her.

Ellen's guests sprawled in their seats. Her linen napkins had been soiled and crumpled. The odd glazed turnip or spiced pear stuck to the table. Ellen picked off the rubbish, cleaning frantically. She hoped that the dirty tablecloth would be overlooked by Young Buck, who she had invited tonight to help her with her career in television.

'So, how's your Lou Matherbay profile going then, Ellen?' asked Clever Ugly.

'Yes. How *is* that?' asked Young Buck. 'I think I've got all I need on Benazir Bhutto. And I had a great filming trip out of it, to Pakistan.'

'There's no need to brag,' said Clever Ugly. 'Ellen, I believe, is going to Swindon soon. And I've been as far as *Westminster* for my study of Barbara Castle,' he said, facetiously.

'I didn't know you were doing some shooting with Lou Matherbay, Ellen,' said Elizabeth, finding the wrong expression. 'God, she used to be a heroine of mine. In my more *impressionable* years, of course.'

'That's the trouble with Lou Matherbay,' said Clever Ugly, picking out the herbs from Ellen's herbed bread. 'Her ideas are only appreciated by adolescents. I mean, why she went over to the *Pluralists*. Unless she *is* going to stand for the leadership, of course. She's been very quiet about that. I'll bet Ellen knows what's on her mind, am I right?'

'Oh yes,' said Ellen quickly. 'I mean, I know all I need to know about her. But Berkovsky won't let me do any filming with her, until she's said something. I'm going to Swindon to talk to her, not to . . .'

'You should have caught her in '78, Ellen,' said the avuncular Clever Ugly. 'That's when you'd have seen her being arrested, or staging mass protests. Not now. Since joining the Pluralists, it's as if she's disappeared. So much for the promised resurrection.'

'I think we should change the subject,' said Ellen, embarrassed, as her video recorder clicked, loudly, in the background. 'What are you taping?' asked Young Buck. 'Jeffrey likes *Casualty*,' Ellen said quietly. 'Now, *nobody's* going to refuse cheese and biscuits, are they?'

'I think I'll say no to the biscuits,' said Young Buck, patting his washboard stomach.

Toilet-roll innards littered the bathroom floor uselessly. Susan squashed a couple with her heels as she walked to the sink mirror. She stared at the cracked glass checking for signs of emotional embarrassment.

She looked strangely, drunkenly beautiful. In the bright bathroom, her face-bones had been high-lit. Because of her last minute use of the curling tongs, Susan's newly blonde hair hung in long curls around her head. Her lipstick had been patted off on to wine glasses and beer bottles, wiped on to cigarettes and the occasional cheek. She had been left with a little blusher, which hid her natural blush, and a sheen of ivory foundation, which checked any hint of sexual disappointment in her complexion. Pushing open the toilet door into the head of the queue's face and apologising distractedly, Susan walked into the party again. She wanted to see Charles.

'Oh yes, lovely. Real coffee,' said Clever Ugly, spilling the cup which Ellen had handed to him across the table. 'Sorry, Elizabeth,' he said, as a brown pool of coffee sunk into her Escada outfit. 'Hope it'll wash out.'

'Everything comes out in the wash,' said Jeffrey, looking at the back of his wife-to-be, who had gone to fetch her carpet-stain remover.

'Never mind. Never *mind*,' Elizabeth said. 'I'm in the business. I'll buy new. So, you were telling me whether you were *happy* in television.' She looked at Young Buck, hopefully.

'Ah, yes. Television,' said Young Buck, leaning back in his chair for full effect. 'The great equaliser.'

'The great *divider*,' said Clever Ugly. 'I think . . .'

'OK, Malcolm. Let's not go into that,' said Young Buck, who was keen to save the spotlight for himself. 'So, Elizabeth. Did you see my Pakistan film on *FastNews*?'

'Don't think I did actually,' said Elizabeth, taking the last piece of mature Cheddar. 'Oh, Ellen, this is wonderful. Is there any . . . ?'

'Well, you missed something there,' said Young Buck. 'That was my best work. The poverty really *worked* for me, do you know what I mean? I mean, I *made* it work for me. I pointed the camera at it – some lovely GVs – and I wasn't at all afraid. And this is something about me. I wasn't scared to shoot what I saw. *Most people . . .*'

'So how long have you been fashionable? I mean, in fashion,' Clever Ugly stupidly asked Elizabeth.

'Sorry, Malcolm. I'm just listening to . . .'

'Thank you, Elizabeth. Thank you,' Young Buck said. 'Now, I was saying. Most people are afraid to go in really close. But I love zooms. Close-ups are my thing, I suppose. Tarantino has his . . .'

Jeffrey Bell had gone to sleep. 'Wake up, Jeffrey,' said Ellen, who was starting to fall apart. And to everyone else: 'He works *really* long hours.'

'As an estate agent? Hardly,' said Elizabeth, as Jeffrey snorted and stirred.

'Oh, sorry, people,' he said, looking at his watch. 'Bloody hell. Is that the time?'

'Susan Lyttle. Back for more?' called out Charles but, as in novels, no one but Susan had heard him speak. He was with a circle of friends. The double doors had been opened to the garden patio and Charles was standing at the bottom of some steps, holding forth. Susan bravely joined them, sitting in the gods on the top step. Sound system echoes stretched out along the semi-suburban landscape.

'Charles Pickford, you're not right,' said one girl. 'The invisibility of Thomas Pynchon is far more marketable than the invisibility of JD Salinger.'

'Well, I disagree, Jackie. Susie, what d'you think?' asked Hanna, looking up.

Susan, her head drowning with diluted vodka, said: 'I think novelists *should* be invisible. I like imagining what they look like.'

Had she spoken? Had all her words come out in the right order, without pause? The voice sounded most unlike her own. It was a voice from this century, from this era; unashamedly '96. It could have come from any of the party girls; the comments theirs, as well as Susan's; the shyness shared. She watched them cloak themselves with words, wrapping one another with thoughts that Susan had, if only she dared to express them.

'All authors are,' said Susan, daring with drink. 'I mean, look at Jane Austen. She wasn't *attractive* . . .'

A girl, sitting on the grass, joined her in fuelling the controversy. 'Well, yes, you're right,' she said, straining at the seams of her dress. 'Modern writers are almost always ugly.'

Settling back, Susan marvelled, drunkenly, at the way she had started a casual conversation. She watched, with pleasure, as it grew into something more serious. Then slowly, the crowd began to have better things to do. Rather late in the day, these party people had discovered each other and mutual attraction, both physical and spiritual. As they paired off into twos and threes, edging away from the more public entertainment, Charles stood beside Susan, pouring bottles of beer on to the grass.

'You'll ruin it,' said Susan.

'It's beer. It's good for grass,' said Charles. 'It makes it grow hairy.'

'Well, it's a waste of beer,' said the last hanger-on, the last vestige of something more communal.

'It's piss anyway,' said Charles, looking at Susan's cream T-shirt and wanting, for what he thought was the first time, to take it off.

'Which is just what I need,' said the vestige, leaving Susan and Charles together, as far as Susan hoped, forever.

Charles was pouring beer on to Susan's skirt. 'Oh please don't,' said Susan, rubbing the spot vigorously.

'You're almost human when you're angry,' said Charles, rubbing at the wet patch with her.

'Why are you so nasty to me?' asked Susan, lighting a cigarette and trying out an accent that wasn't at *all* Southport.

'Well, you have this victim quality,' he said. 'I just love hitting people when they're down, particularly women.'

Susan looked up at him. 'I hope you don't mean that,' she said. 'That you're a sado-masochist.'

'I have metaphorical sado-masochistic tendencies, if you have to label everything,' said Charles, smelling strongly of expensive aftershave, pouring the smell over her, hugging her with it. 'But

153

I can see you're not into labels,' he said, looking at her skirt.

'This *is* a label,' said Susan.

'There you go again, getting angry. You're even more human now, you see. I'd almost forgotten the animal in you, although I'll bet it's still there, hidden in that sexy skirt you're wearing.'

Little leftover women approached Charles constantly, to ask after a stray joke or a friend who had left with a lover hours before. They refused to allow Charles to lie in peace, ten centimetres away from Susan. They refused to believe that a game of musical relations had been played away from them. They remained at the party, and they pretended to party.

Charles: 'What is it about you, Susan?'

Susan: 'I'm nothing special.'

Charles: 'There's something about you.'

Susan: 'There's nothing special.'

Charles: 'It's not your looks, and it's not your personality.'

Susan: 'Well, what's left?'

Charles: 'Well, whatever it is, it's bigger than I am.'

'Thank God they've gone,' said Jeffrey, closing Ellen's door on Clever Ugly. 'I've never met such boring people in my...'

'Well, they're more interesting than your friend *Jeremy*,' said Ellen, rushing to the toilet. 'Which Jeremy?' asked Jeffrey, picking at bits of cheese and chocolate from the table. '*All* of them,' screamed Ellen, puzzling over her recently acquired weak-bladder problem.

'So, are you coming to bed, Ellen? Or are you going to be *filming in Pakistan*?' her fiancé muttered darkly, picking up a newspaper from the rack.

'Do you always have to be so rude to my friends? I'm going to clear up,' said Ellen Abrahams, surveying her mess and feeling weak. She sank down into an armchair, overwhelmed by tiredness. 'Maybe tomorrow,' she said, closing her eyes.

'I'm worried about you, you know,' said Jeffrey quietly. 'You don't seem well any more. Is it the job, do you think? Or just the fact that you're always cleaning?'

'Well, that's hardly anything to be worried about, is it?' asked Ellen, opening her heavy eyes. 'It's not as if I snort heroin. I just like *order* in my life.'

'Something's wrong, that's all. You don't think it's that contra-ceptive pill, giving you trouble again?'

'No,' said Ellen, heaving herself up to switch on the midnight news. 'I stopped taking it.'

He lay, beautiful and asleep, beside Susan Lyttle. His eyes were shut together like a rat's; his pink eyelids close together and satisfied. A duvet shrouded his body delicately, like a toga. His chicken-bone arms poked out of the cover and the blades on his back sharpened to stillness, as if to remind Susan of his strength.

They had had sex. Susan had felt like a complicated biology diagram, with pink lines mapping out her body, as Charles had pulled at her, stretching her very veins.

Susan lay there for hours in his bed, urging on the digital alarm clock, which changed numbers like a quiz-show score-board, so that there could be an incident. The darkness outside slitted slyly in through the curtains, washing whiter as the numbers grew on the clock. Charles turned over at intervals, so that sometimes Susan could see his face and the fillings inside his straight upper teeth. He looked as if he was dead, although his teeth sucked in air, and his nostrils swelled slightly, because the bones in his face had rotted his skin grey, and his head had bent to break at the neck, backwards on to an escaping pillow.

Susan was intimate with every colourful object in Charles's room. The rug, striped with contrasting colours of strawberry ice-cream. The wardrobe, of walnut wood, skewered by hangers which draped, twisted, from the top, and hung through with scarves, like seaweed. The child's gum machine, cracked at the edges, which contained colourful ball-bearing sweets. The sink in the corner, its enamel bitten and chewed, toothpaste squeezing on to its rim and a can of soapy shaving mousse, spitting drops of foam. Susan realised, looking around his room, that she had bought too many things for her own room at home.

Although she was waiting for him to wake, when he did Susan was staring at the gum machine, while Charles looked at her. 'Hello, you,' he said, as if surprised to find Susan sitting there beside him.

Charles sat up with his back to the wall. 'I can't remember whether we did pillow-talk. Did we actually talk?' he asked, and Susan thought of things she could have said, but they were all the things she would have said yesterday. She shook her head.

'You are so beautiful,' he said. 'As much beauty as could die.' Susan swallowed. She could not cope with this. She was full to capacity with experience. 'A sex goddess in the mornings. But then, I'm not surprised, you're a very sexy woman,' he said, reaching out of bed, naked. He went towards the wardrobe and unhooked a dressing-gown which Susan wouldn't have suspected was there. 'It's always the quiet ones,' he said, knotting the weedy rope around his waist, and pushing his hands through his fair curls. 'They're uncontrollable, the quiet ones.'

Charles left the room and Susan rushed to get dressed in clothes she found pushed under the bed, finger-rubbing her teeth with hard white toothpaste and hooking the back of her clinging skirt, clasping her bra at the back, and dipping her feet into cold shoes. Her skirt had been soiled by the night. It looked cheap now. Not having been informed otherwise, she then sat on Charles's bed, fully clothed, waiting, probably, for the flowers to come, or the letters, or the little frilly gifts.

But she must have fallen asleep, because when she woke up Charles had left the flat, leaving behind two men, called Ken and Jerry, swearing blind that they had both slept with Susan at Glastonbury. 'Yes, I know,' said Susan, as Jerry told her that Charles had once sold a photograph to the *Sun*, and that, seven years ago, he had dated Lady Helen 'Melons' Windsor.

'I have to go,' Susan said, as Ken guided her to the door. In the hallway, they passed a gallery of large black-and-white photographs. Some of them caught a smiling Charles Pickford wrapped around women.

'Oh my God, is that me?' asked Susan of Ken, startled to see herself in the photographic gallery, half-lit to throw colour on to her filthy, fair curls, the clothes, the piping-thin arms.

'What?' asked Ken, leaning forwards to see the sole photograph of a woman on her own. 'Nah, I don't think so,' he said. Susan leaned closer, to read *As much beauty as could die* scrawled above her own half-image.

'He must have taken it when I wasn't . . .' She faltered, trying to remember everything. 'Maybe last night . . . I don't know when he took it,' she said. 'When do you think . . . ?'

'It was a bird called Myra,' said Ken, remembering. 'Mind you, I can see the resemblance.' He looked backwards and forwards, between the photograph and Susan. 'But that's Charles for you. Like me, he likes sexy blondes. He likes sexy blondes *a lot.*'

'Oh yes,' said Susan, mortified. She pretended to study the photo more closely. 'Oh yes, of course,' she said, laughing, staring, horrified at *As much beauty as could die.* 'I can't believe I was so *stupid.*'

Chapter Fifteen

A tropical cyclone and heavy rainfall hit southern India yesterday, killing at least 110 people. At least fifteen were feared dead when a wall collapsed on fans leaving a soccer stadium in the Zambian capital Lusaka.

Bulgaria's former king, Simeon II, ended a triumphant three-week tour of his country and flew back into exile, just as Myra Felt's train arrived at Peyarth, and Myra emerged, boss-eyed with interrupted sleep, to face a city big on a redundant textile industry. It was a blastingly hot afternoon. The heat was diving on to this sleepy, cold city, sending it sickly. Towering blocks of room upon room; men with muscles, piping thick, and women, with faces brutally sandpapered, all emasculated by the pouring sun. Myra sat under a large sign telling the world, stupidly, that it had arrived in Peyarth.

As if one didn't know, simply by sitting at Peyarth station, that one had descended to that place made famous by documentary and double-spreaded inner-city-focus features. That place where, predictably perhaps, people lived in poverty, picking at incomes. Old Peyarth, where, as one newspaper cutting put it: 'People laughed at lifestyles, reserving them for the rich and famous. Here holding down a living is enough,' said the article.

Myra, aware only of cuttings and constituency profiles which showed high figures for unemployment, high figures for those living below the poverty line, and high figures for crime, sat with her bottom fixed to her baggage, trying not to cry. She was waiting to be picked up by a Pluralist local bigwig, Cathy Tanning, who was, according to the gossip floating around Myra back home, 'one helluva bitch'; 'caustic as soda'; 'loved and loathed'; and, most terrifyingly, 'terrifying'.

'I'm not entirely sure I *like* the idea of you going to Peyarth,' her mother had said this morning, phoning Myra on the portable. 'Oh come on, Penny,' Myra's father had said, taking over their phone. 'Since when does *Myra* listen to *us*?'

She was exiled to a portable caravan by Cathy Tanning, whose clicking Welsh accent sliced her to small, even pieces during the car journey. 'You'll be much more comfortable there, we feel. Away from the local riff-raff. We know what you Londoners are like, you see. You like your comforts, don't you? You like to be the big bosses. We have all been working here for several weeks, you see. Since the beginning of July. Formed a *community*.'

The caravan, dumped in the back garden of the Pluralist campaign office, like so much rubbish, burned in the sun like a tin can, boiling Myra, who sat in there, sealed to a plastic chair. 'We'll let you get on with the press releases then, Myra. We know how you lot from London like to get through paper. There's a typewriter in there, somewhere. On the floor, I think.'

At the back of the caravan, underneath Pluralist banners, campaign posters, dehydrated bottles of burning water, and a cardboard box full of packets of soggy, flaking crisps, Myra found the typewriter. She plugged it into the wall, and sat in shocked silence as the caravan blew into darkness with an explosive clang. Bits of the caravan's interior fizzed in the darkness as Myra sat, freezing in the heat. Myra, who wanted to change the world, and if not that, then Peyarth, contemplated her next few weeks, clamped to this chair, without light, work or company.

Defrosting only slowly, and sucking on a cigarette, she decided to do nothing for now. Cathy Tanning, with her greying fruit-bowl hair, which once glowed with lots of natural colours, her thin, sleepy lips, and her figure, cut from the same cloth as thousands of determined women, with shield-like breasts and legs shaped like the barrels of a gun, was best avoided by women like Myra Felt.

'It has a habit of doing that,' said Cathy Tanning of the caravan, when she visited Myra with a chipped cup filled with dirty tea and pushed it through the window at her, tut-tutting, as if to a convict.

'It went black,' Myra said. 'There was an explosion.'

'Oh, yes,' said Cathy, who feared the pretty Myra, with her

make-up and her thick platform clogs, the blonde curls and the easily flowing cotton dress. Moving her back into the office with the rest of the Pluralist workers might be difficult. It might tempt the scrawny volunteer men to flirt with this capital woman, from London. 'It has a habit of doing that. You just need to wind this generator up, you see. It's very easy. You can do that, can't you?'

Cathy cranked up the machine, as if it was child's play. 'You can do it, too,' she said, as light steamed inside. 'Just wind it up, remember,' she said, leaving the caravan, and Myra looked at her tea, highlighted with a filmy mess, and at the typewriter, jumping with the sounds of the generator. She wondered at the way she attracted experiences, like a pile of shit did so many flies.

ONE MORE HEAVE, typed Myra, as a headline for her press release. *The Pluralists are set for victory in Peyarth, winning over the other parties with their combination of plain common sense and caring—*' As Myra typed *policies* the caravan bombed to darkness once more. It was turning black outside, too. Myra left her brown case sitting beside the typewriter table and went outside, in search of a telephone, despairing at the generator, and at Peyarth.

It seemed odd coming down here from Westminster, where people lunched and had meaningful conversations, to a place where shops displayed luxury toilet tissue as if it were a luxury. Myra crossed the road to avoid toothy, bullying dogs, strolling with, as if courting, their more feminine-looking boyish owners. The Rottweilers should have been put to sleep four years ago, Myra thought, as laid down in the legislation. They should not be free to stand outside telephone boxes, as one pit bull did with his owner, barring entrance to all those who had pulled themselves up, by the bootstraps, to the aspirant classes.

'Hello, this is Patrick. Sorry I can't be here right now to talk to you, whoever you may be, but do speak into my little machine and I'll return the call as soon as possible,' said Patrick's machine to Myra, who had telephoned to have his voice wash over her like a pint of Guinness; to remind her of home. 'Hello, this is Patrick. Sorry I can't be here right now to talk to you, whoever you may be, but do speak into my little machine and I'll return the call as soon as possible.'

Myra stood in the telephone box, with the old-fashioned telephone to her ear, half-delighted with the restorative voice which she had phoned four times to listen to, and half-scared of the pit bull, which had returned, without its owner, to stand guard outside the box.

'Marion, it's Myra.'

'*Myra*. Where are you?'

'I'm in Peyarth. For the Pluralists.'

Marion laughed. 'You wouldn't see me going to Peyarth for *anyone*,' she said. 'What the hell are you doing there? I've told you . . . I mean, if it's about paying rent for that dump you call a . . . Well, you don't need to bother 'cause Jasmine's moved out. She's gone on tour with *The Moving Horizons*. And you know, you're being talked about down here. Everyone's saying . . .' she said gently.

'*What* is everyone saying?' asked Marion's friend.

'They're saying: "Why don't we see Myra any more? What the *hell's* happened to Myra?" '

On her way out of the telephone booth, stained with urine and what, to Myra the optimist, was ketchup, she saw that the dog's owner was, in fact, standing at the other side of the booth, pressing his face up to the strips of glass, pugging his nose and thickening his lips in the process of pressing.

She walked away fast, only to feel an arm coming around her mouth, holding her. Biting down on the flesh closest to her teeth, as he felt inside her dress pocket for money or something more sinister, Myra heard a yell and, not knowing whether it was her own or his, she unlocked herself from him, with an energy she later wondered at, and ran down the road towards the campaign headquarters, and her caravan.

'Coming to meet our candidate, then, Myra? Coming to meet Tom Evans?' asked Cathy Tanning, who had poked her head around the caravan door, in an attempt to make her peace with the London girl who had been locked up for long enough. Myra was pushing down the letters on the electronic typewriter, forming words, and whole sentences, typing: *The Pluralists will introduce crime prevention measures, ranging from discussion groups for local drug addicts to longer truncheons for your local bobby on the beat.*

The London girl looked up, her pale face sticky with internment. She seemed shorter than Cathy had remembered her. She must have smoked at least one hundred cigarettes, judging by the ashtray which wormed with fag ends. Brown crisps were showing at the crown of her blonde hair.

'Well, are you coming? You'll be staying with Tom Evans, our candidate, and his wife. I don't think this caravan is quite the thing, do you? We'll have you in the office tomorrow, tucked up with the rest of us. We're quite a community, you know. And just remember, I'm always here, if you have any trouble with them old fools over the next week. Tend to resent Londoners, coming here telling them what to do, how to do it. Don't know why exactly.'

Myra, who was walking next to Cathy, with her brown case gaping at the edges, leaned slightly to the woman's shoulder. She had forgotten some time ago about violence, and her own fear of it. Taking risks over the years, and concluding, as she walked down alleyways, alone, in the little hours, past Camden's canal after club chucking-out time, that the streets were calm, had led her to complacency and a feeling that all that brutality, displayed on television news, was simply a con. It was a fiction bought by a media hungry for stories of muggings and beatings and buggery and rape.

If she had felt any anger, Myra would have told Cathy what had just happened; used it, perhaps, for Pluralist advancement or self-publicity. But Myra was terrified, aware now that the world wasn't arranged as neatly as she thought: on shelves, for her own consumption.

'Yeeesss,' said Tom Evans, the Pluralist candidate, as a man on the television humiliated himself in public and won a holiday for two in St Lucia. They were watching a game show: Myra and Tom and Mrs Tom, as Tom's remote control, forever pointing or pressing, ran out of political or news programmes. 'Now, that was worth watching,' said Tom, all vanity and low self-esteem, his ego and his neuroses taking over the sofa. 'A bit dirty though,' said Mrs Tom. 'There's *never* an excuse for bad language.'

'That'll be what the voters are watching,' said Tom, whose remaining strands of grey hair maypoled around the head. 'Forget *Direct Live, Channel Four News, FastNews*. It's the money they like. Forget Tony Millwauki and Zeinab Badawi; they won't be watching them. No, they'll be doing the lottery and trying to get to St Lucia. That's what they ask on the doorstep. Forget dog crap and—'

'Tom. Dirty,' said Mrs Tom.

' . . . and petty crime. They'll be asking me: "What are you going to do about the rollover jackpot?" That's what they'll want to know.'

'No excuse for language of any description,' Mrs Tom said, looking scared. 'Now. What will you want for your breakfast, Myra?' she asked.

'I can only manage coffee and cigarettes in the mornings,' laughed Myra.

'Well, that would explain your lovely figure then, won't it?' said Mrs Evans, her eyes pipping inside an apple face. 'I thought you were taking drugs.'

A strand of beef stuck through her front teeth, caught there during dinner, destroying the stereotype. 'Got something here, dear,' whispered Tom, touching his teeth with his fingers.

'Food?' asked Mrs Tom, coming up to her feet, alarmed.

Myra had entirely forgotten about home. She was sitting, instead, in a circular bath, decorated with golden taps and a silver shower. She was bathing in the largest bathroom she had ever seen, tiled in cream, with white bottled cosmetics and jars, inexplicably filled with coloured cotton-wool balls. Soft blue walls toned in gently with the creamy toilet, covered in lambs' wool, and surrounded with a round yard of fluff. The room was snug with new toothbrushes, still packeted, bristling to get out. Long, square towels hung, unnecessarily heated; ready to wrap a million squealing clean children, cosy and warm.

There was space to cartwheel in; to jump about like a child; to country-dance. There were products around the bath, sitting complacently, and yet so much a product of local Llandarren industry that even Myra, who owned almost everything, didn't know of them. So many glass bottles of pink liquid; fat, small tubs of pale cream; round jars of blue crystals; long, thin tubes of green oil. And Myra, who had poured and stirred and shaken the mess of merchandise into her bath, finally smelled as she wanted to look – like a clean, fresh meadow.

Then there was her bed. Layer upon layer of plumped-up cream blankets and flaked white sheets, like a slice of *millefeuille*, crisp at the edges. White lace had been flung over the top; six yellow feather pillows were piled high, like custard slices. Victorian dolls, sweet in yellow and white dresses, ribboned, with real hair, lay beside her, coquettish and preening. Pretty, clean Myra had been flung inside it all, her eyes shut tight, sleeping safely, as her evening's mugger bashed his boot, hard, into his best mate's face.

Chapter Sixteen

At the door stood Aunt Jane, knitted together in a tweed suit. It was her only fitting outfit for a day trip to the capital. She hugged her niece, standing back from her, to keep from soaking Susan's new image with blubbing tears.

Susan had not known properly, until then, how much love she had taken from her aunt. Aunt Jane looked so tiny and so fragile, squashed into that square, itchy suit which Susan knew gave her so much pride and irritation. The small crevices in her skin breathed open and shut, as Susan stood back from the hug, to show off her pink top and jeans, complete with second-hand patches and frayed shreds hanging around the ankle at her platform shoes.

'Oh, Susan,' she said. 'You look so *London*. Like a . . . Why are you still in your vest?' she asked, hesitating with the giant packet of cheesy snacks which she had brought to fill up her niece's cupboard (presumed empty). 'Shall I put this away? It's just small, but I know you like them. And you've gone so *thin*.'

'This isn't a *vest*, Aunt Jane,' said a scathing Susan. 'It's a *top*.'

'You mean, you wear it *out of the house*?' asked Aunt Jane, drawing herself up to look like an Oscar Wilde character.

'Well, yes,' said Susan, unhappily, dragging on a cigarette. 'Of course.'

'Has that man seen you dressed like this? Oh,' she said, disappointedly, opening a cupboard. A packet of pasta fell, full, on to her face. 'You have so much food.'

'What *man* are you talking about?'

'A man came out as I came in.'

'Oh, the *Yeti*. Upstairs.'

'So, you're happy to let men see you half-naked?'

'Fully, sometimes,' she said, smirking.

'Oh, my *God*, Susan.'

'I'm twenty-three, Aunt Jane. It's been known, you know.'
'Oh my God, *Susan*.'

Weeks after they had made love, Charles Pickford had left Susan, alone and empty beside the bones of workers, during regular office hours. He had left his vacant chair to swivel about, and his coffee mug, chipped and saying something saucy, to stand on the coffee-room counter. Susan had seen dust collecting on his desk, as days passed, as daylight dotted the blond wood pale.

Moments had come back to her, in little pools of warmth about her stomach. 'It's always the quiet ones,' she heard him say. 'As much beauty as could die.' She liked to think of him touching her, outside of the sex. At Hanna's party, his hand had come towards her own. Their fingers had touched, plausibly, and he had said: 'You're coming back with *me*, young lady.'

Susan had drained these vignettes of nuance and strained them with repetition. Over and over, the dialogue had been played. The strung-out scenes, hanging on their own, away from Julie's discussion with Bruce about rejection or Hugh's ovulation arguments with his wife – these moments were almost beautiful. Isolated, they hovered towards poetry.

Clive had seemed, at one point, to be asking her to the cinema, albeit clumsily and with one eye on Julie's thick lace camisole. Susan had been surprised, dimly aware that she had entered into some sort of dating game. By sleeping with Charles, she had, clearly, been accepted into some wider coupling community. But she had refused Clive, preferring to sit on her bed with her cigarettes and her little, remembered moments.

In his absence, Julie had said that Charles was ill. Bruce had said that Charles had left. JJ had said that Charles had been in the office all along, sitting in the stationery cupboard. Peter had said that Charles had been seen at a well-known homosexual haunt in Soho. Gary had said that Charles could be anywhere.

He certainly wasn't at home. Susan knew that much. She had located Charles's home telephone number, dialling it so often that British Telecom had suggested she list it as a priority cheap call, along with Seabank Road, Barbara Peabody, and her Auntie Emmie in Skegness. The answering-machine message had comforted Susan. She had taken Grandmother's Footsteps towards the voice: 'Charles, Ken and Jerry. After the beep please.' She had grown closer with each additional beep.

She imagined, on his return, that they would visit Homebase together, each and every Sunday afternoon, picking out items of garden furniture. They would grow into a family of five in queues for buses or for Southport's big dipper. She would have the certainty of someone's affection. She would have it there as a right, rather than on request. She would have it there daily, like literature and soap operas; lending her life the passion of high drama and the relief of light entertainment.

She would have Pickford babies, wrapped in white webbed blankets, Charles-scented. Agatha, she had thought. Agatha Pickford. Bramwell Pickford. Charles Pickford *Junior*. They would buy a house in Salford, soaked in ivy; Camphor Avenue, growing lilacs, tall and splendid. She would be a Pickford wife, entering Pickford girls for Miss Pears. But this time, she would win.

Susan pulled her aunt's hand to the sofa, which she had switched for Aunt Jane, in the nick of time, from a bed into a sofa. 'Look, Aunt Jane,' she said. 'I'm not a tart, I promise. You don't have to worry about me any more. D'you want a cup of tea?'

'I'll make it.'

'No,' she said. 'Let me make you tea for once, in my home. Let me entertain *you*.'

Jane Fry recalled, with a shudder, her visit to Margaret and Peter Lyttle's marital home. 'Don't you stir,' Margaret had said. 'You've dragged me up screaming and kicking. The least you can do is allow me to make you a cup of tea.' And, then, the blow: 'You are my *guest*,' she had said. Jane had never treated Susan, or Margaret, as a guest in her home. She had let them all seep into her life, taking it over, and giving it the illusion of fulfilment, as all the time they had prepared to leave. And then, once a year, she would be invited into their homes as a guest, as a stranger.

'Women, Susan, are like oranges,' Aunt Jane decided to say. 'The harder they are to peel, the sweeter the fruit inside.'

Surprisingly, Hanna Thames had telephoned. Susan had thought of the call as an offer of friendship, until Hanna had said: 'I'd watch out, Susan. Charles can be a right bastard.'

He's not a bastard. He's a cad, thought Susan, coughing up her cigarette smoke in globs of brownish-green. *And there's a difference.*

'Where's he disappeared to?' she had asked. 'He hasn't been at work.'

'He's been away walking in Wales. Just got back. Look, Susie, Ken says he's going out with someone else. He's *always* going out with someone else.'

'No,' she had said.

'Apparently, you left a lot of messages. Ken asked me to . . . Look, he's a bastard to women, Susie. Put it down to experience, or something. I know I did.'

'No,' she had whispered.

She hadn't believed Hanna until, a few day's later, reality hit. 'Susie-babe,' said a voice behind her office desk. 'I haven't seen you for ages.'

'Charles? Where have you been?' She wanted his hug-warm pale-blue jumper, worn through in private places. She wanted a feel or a sniff of the wool. She needed to feel him moving about inside it: his ribs, his skin, his muscle; to wrap herself in Charles, stroking his chest.

'Oh. Here and there. But I'm not going to be *here* any more,' he had said. 'I'm leaving Dutton's.'

'Why?' Oh why.

'I'm going into photography. Newspapers, you know.'

'I didn't know you took photographs,' she said, remembering the photograph in his hallway.

Charles: 'Ah, there's a lot you don't know about me, Susie.'

Susan: 'So, I won't see you again then?'

Charles: 'Well, no. I s'pose there's no reason to.'

For one moment, Susan thought she might collapse. Underneath the office desk, her legs were in chaos, her joints mashed up to flesh. She felt like a baby, falling slowly from a building.

'And that's all?' she asked, sadly.

'You know, Susie, *life*,' he said, his eyes laughing, 'is not like a Victorian novel. You'll find there's a lot more shagging going on.'

Susan's breath held throatily, trapped, audibly fighting. Inside all that jam of teeth and tongue she had so many words. She had read them, different voices, inside books. Loud, like *War and Peace*. Soft, like *The Glass Menagerie*. They were all useless, just as she needed words.

Jane Fry knew that she looked ridiculous, sitting on a sofa upholstered for young people. Sesame seeds rolled under her tights, like sand after a day spent at Southport's pleasure beach. Clutching at a clasp handbag, Aunt Jane knew that she must have looked very *Lancashire* to Susan, who was smoking a cigarette and seemed to have all but dropped her northern accent.

'You'll find, Susan, that men will only hurt you.'

'You can't wrap me in cotton wool.'

'I just don't want your life ruined.'

'Well, I don't want to end up . . .'

'Like me? Is that what you wanted to say? What would you rather? To end up hard, like Aunt Cyn?'

They sat for a while in silence. Susan busied herself with her new consumer durables. Jane fiddled with her buttons. '*Ecstacy*?' she asked, after a decent interval, reading the title of a psychedelic book which lay on Susan's sofa. 'So you don't even read nice books any more?'

Hanna and her friends had invited Susan to the theatre, to see a rather static one-man play. Charles's flatmate, Ken, had been there.

'I found that really moving. What did you reckon?' he asked her.

'I wasn't sure why he wore women's clothes.'

'You know you're right,' said Hanna. 'I wasn't sure what that symbolised either,' she said. 'Susie always sees the emperor naked.'

Hanna Thames had lived in unpronounceable places. She had

done unspeakable things to men. She had introduced Susan to a world in which people talked about the dangers of capitalism, while sipping cappuccino. Or discussed God, while downing Bloody Marys. Susan had been forced to buy an answering machine, simply to accommodate all of the friends she had made, through Hanna.

'Susie, it's Hanna here. D'you wanna come to the Café Latte? We're here for a while, then it's back to Silvio's.'

'Hi, it's Silvio. Remember me? I remember you. No, Hanna. I want for you to come round. Do me a favour, eh?'

'This is Hanna again. Sorry about Silvio. You working late or something? Derek says he owes you a coffee 'cause of that awful Taming of the Shrew last week. I mean, making it political like that! Anyway . . .'

In Hanna's world, Hamlet was a homosexual; Maggie Tulliver a makeshift martyr; and *1984* a Brave New World. Vladimir and Estragon had dreaded the arrival of Godot; Mr Biswas had dwelt in hell; and as for Portnoy, well, he had no complaints. In Hanna's world, Susan *had* to catch up with modern literature because, according to her, Dutton's was Dickensian; the classics irrelevant. Although Susan had been known to disagree with Hanna, what mattered were Susan's own opinions, teased out by Hanna herself as they discussed literature in bookshops, coffee bars, or in other people's houses.

'Hey, Susan. I just wanted to remind you about my poetry reading tonight. The more the merrier, as they say. Seriously, I'd love you to come if you've time.'

The idea of dissecting books, underlining them, basking in them, was a novel one. At Susan's school, books had been either educative or an embarrassment. She had tucked her novels inside *Smash Hits* and *Formative Physics*. At Seabank Road, literature was a private affair, an illicit pleasure, to be kept secret from society outside. 'Not at supper, Susan!' 'Not in a hotel, Susan!' 'Not in *the shop*, Susan!'

Yet, amongst Hanna's friends, literary discussion was positively encouraged. *The Trial, On The Road, The Moonstone*; they had all been lent to Susan. She had been invited to book readings. And, although she had been embarrassed to ask a question, she had, on one occasion, accepted Hanna's offer to join a Hampstead group outing, poking around Keats house, and exploring his private letters.

'I'm thinking of moving to Notting Hill. My friend Hanna says it—'

'Over my *dead* body,' said Jane Lyttle, putting on her Sabbath face. 'I'm not having you live there. Near riots and black people.'

'Actually, some of my best friends are black now. And it's OK if you die on me too, because I'm pretty bloody used to that,' screamed Susan. She had wanted all of Seabank Road's warmth to flood into her flat, lit pink with lightbulbs, with Aunt Jane.

'Aunt Jane. Aunt Jane. Aunt Jane,' Jane Fry was saying, in a sing-song, rocking in her chair, like a polite madwoman, obsessed with etiquette. 'We mustn't row, Susan. You just say, Aunt Jane. Aunt Jane . . .'

Susan had not had many arguments with her *nice* aunt. Aunt Cyn had usually been there to neuter Aunt Jane. She had set her sister off, with her own apparent wickedness, and had made Jane, in the process, appear almost harmless. But there, spread out thinly on her sofa was undiluted propriety, and Susan found her *good* aunt disturbing, without her *bad* aunt's obscene interruptions and wry asides.

'I'm sorry,' said Susan, who now wanted, above all, to wash her hair. 'I didn't mean it about dying. I shouldn't have mentioned death.'

'You poor child,' said Aunt Jane.

'No,' Susan said. 'I am *not* a poor child any more. I'm not poor. I'm fine. I mean, my parents died sixteen years ago. You can actually stop walking on egg-shells now. You can *all*—'

'Aunt *Jane*. *Please* Susan. Come on, with me. *Aunt Jane* . . .'

'I can't even remember what Mother looked like any more . . .'

'Aunt Jane. I'm not listening,' the old woman said, with her hands clasped like muffs to her ears. 'Aunt Jane.'

'And I'm OK. I think I'm happy.'

An incredibly hirsute man smeared a piece of toast with honey in his first floor flat in Finchley Central. Downstairs, his neighbour was having company. He heard, through the ceiling: 'I'm fine.'

'Well,' came an older, more northern, voice. 'You won't need me any more, will you?'

Chapter Seventeen

Ellen stood at the altar, beside a scrubbed-up groom. John pointed the camera at her. She swung around, as if full of energy. 'John, it would be nice, before the bride comes up the aisle, to get a point-of-view shot of the groom from where she would be standing.' Ellen stood firm in loose, canvas trousers and a generous jumper. 'From here.'

'I'm not in the way, am I?' asked the vicar, approaching to smile at the camera, forgetting his own God for a moment. That morning, he had polished his teeth. He had straightened his dog-collar. 'We'll need you, Reverend,' said John, pushing him a little to the left. 'We'll need you standing there.'

'Isn't this exciting?' said the vicar. 'There are so many I wouldn't mention in this diocese who are on television for this, who are on television for that. On television all the time. And I wonder: "How do they do that?" Because, you know . . .' He leaned towards Ellen. 'I'm happy to be on television at any time. At. Any. Time. You remember that.'

The groom looked bored. He would have preferred to be on a football pitch, in football strip, throwing lager over his mates. 'Now, can I explain anything else, Duane?' Ellen asked. Duane scratched the crotch of his slate-grey trousers. 'I need to 'ave a slash,' he said, straight to camera.

Deep inside Ellen's black flapping bag, a mobile phone rang. 'Yes?' she asked, as Duane looked greedily at her phone. It was Ellen's Senior Producer. 'How's it going?' he asked. 'Just wanted to remind you. My needs . . .' Ellen looked down at her round stomach, which seemed to expand as she spoke. It had grown too big for all her suits. 'It's fine, Crispin. Everything's going really well,' said Ellen.

Yesterday, Senior Producer had leaned against Ellen's desk. 'I need you,' he had said, his shirt-tails floating artistically around cotton trousers. 'Just to do a leeetle filming tomorrow, you know. It's for this damn divorce-law film that I've been asked to put together. Berkovsky says I can use one of you lot tomorrow, as I have to go to a wedding myself. Can't put it off, you know, bloody cousin getting married, piling up the invitations. It's like four fucking weddings and no damn funerals in my family. Could do with a few funerals. Save on the present bill!'

'Tomorrow?' Ellen had grumbled, plucking at a bra strap which was fitting too tightly. 'Only tomorrow's difficult. Any other time, but I'm going to be choosing my *own* wedding presents tomorrow; doing up a list. I'm getting married next month . . .'

Senior Producer had leaned closer to Ellen, yellowing teeth puffing clean, toothpaste breath into her face. 'Thing is, Ellen, I need someone talented, you know. I mean, someone who knows the difference between noddies and noodles, you know? Someone with a visual gene. Someone like you.'

'Well I'm flattered, of course,' said Ellen to the man who had won a TV Prime award for directing documentaries. 'But—'

'Thank you, Ellen. Thank *you*. It's just a bit of filming at a wedding. Shouldn't eat into your own wedding list too much, your Saturday. And, you know,' he said, walking away, and to more important people than Ellen, 'you're the *only* one I can really trust.'

He had half-sprinted across the room. In his path, a secretary stood, her beauty ostentatious in a room churning with the tragedy of news events. 'Damn you to hell,' Senior Producer had said, bumping into her. 'Don't you look where you're going? Don't you know how busy I am?'

'D'you want to do some bridesmaid interviews?' asked John, discovering her behind artificial gladioli. 'Only I've got all you'll need in here.' Ellen nodded weakly, following him. They passed vase after vase of plastic poppies.

'This isn't just a video. It's *television*, you know,' said the bride's mother, inside the ante-room. The child bridesmaids jumped about in lacy purple, their skin grey under pink lighting.

'D'you think I did the right thing?' Tina, the bride, asked, interrupting Ellen and John.

'Yes, of *course*,' said Ellen. 'Everyone feels nervous on their wedding day. Everyone has last-minute doubts.'

Dressed in sequined satin, Tina was as pretty as she would ever be. Cheap lace sprouted everywhere: on Tina's lap; purple around bridesmaids; floating, stained brown, from Tina's mother's hat. 'I didn't mean *Duane*,' laughed Tina. 'I meant the cameras. Letting you TV people in. God, I know *Duane's* right,' she roared.

Tina's father, puffed out with pride and best bitter, held on to his daughter. They were walking the aisle, against a camera and Ellen. 'I'm going all soft,' Ellen heard the father say, unsteady on his feet. 'I'll cry in a minute.' And Ellen, oddly, needed to cry too, fortunately stopping short of emotion. 'Don't start me off, Dad,' said Tina, tiny tears around her eyes. 'You'll crack me foundation.'

Ellen walked up the aisle behind Tina's bridesmaids. She imagined Darren beside her, reluctantly giving her away, as Frankie Bell stood under the canopy, fluffed out of course in unfashionable mink. Ellen made-believe neat, pretty bridesmaids lined up in lilac, and cold chicken served *à la* everything. She pictured cold faces drinking icy champagne, and Jeffrey watching her while she took the long walk. *Was Jeffrey right?*

The point was, she felt tired. She couldn't remember the last time she had seen a friend, let alone dusted her corners. Every day at work seemed longer, and Ellen more fragile. She couldn't focus her energies any more. Often, she didn't have any energy. Yet no one commented, so Ellen presumed that life was moving on, as per normal.

Duane married Tina, in front of a generous crowd. 'We love ya, T. Go for it,' yelled a grubby friend. 'I will,' said Tina, blinking through her contact lenses, as the camera closed in on her face. Tears started, on Mum, Best Friend, First Cousin and Nana Fee. 'I will,' said Duane.

'You'll get me spots if you go so close,' the bride said, as John edged closer. The crowd tittered. Ellen groaned. 'Can we just take that again, Reverend?' she demanded. 'It's *useless* if you say anything other than "I will", Tina. OK? Sorry, John. Sorry Reverend. Sorry, everyone,' she said, taking a background seat again.

Wedding guests queued at the reception, patient for the buffet, to pile paper plates high with dry smoked salmon, crackers and lump-drenched, home-made potato salad. Filling their glasses with cheap, bubbly wine, excited by the bustle, as plates bent double under food, while eyes wondered up at the hyperactive balloons, floating in nets above them all.

Meanwhile, Ellen asked for opinions. 'What do you think about a law to make divorce easier?' she asked the guests, wearily, as John stood beside her, pointing his camera at willing interviewees. 'Sorry to bother you,' she was saying. 'But can I ask you what you think about divorce?' 'Er, excuse me. I'm from *FastNews*. Can I just ask you a couple of qu—'

'Look, love, this is a wedding. Come and enjoy yourself,' said a man, confetti falling from his head and shoulders like dandruff. 'Oh *yes*,' thought Ellen, beaming at his back.

'What do you need?' John asked Ellen.

'I've got one person saying no,' she said. 'So I need someone to say that we should change the divorce laws, make them easier,' said Ellen.

'All righ'?' asked Duane, the groom, strutting towards them with his friends, all high on testosterone and the freely gushing sparkling wine.

'What do you think to divorce, Duane?' asked John. 'Only Ellen here is doing vox pops.'

Duane leered, along with his friends. 'She can do my vox pops any day,' he said. 'Nah. Trufe is, I think they should make divorce easier, y'know . . .'

Ellen looked at John, with relief. Like a strange sort of falling in love, she knew that Duane would make her film. 'I think they should make divorce easier, y'know, defini'ly,' said the groom, to camera. *Now* I can relax, thought Ellen, fiddling with a tape box.

On the dance floor, make-up ran and uncles attempted to cut a dash. Duane's friends jumped to the music with Tina, Marie, Chantelle, Debs and Lisa. And the guys called off the bet as to how long Duane and Tina's marriage would last, and, indeed, it looked now as if it would last for ever, or as long as the cake icing remained soft, white and pretty. Tina's sister forgot her envy and the fact that she was thirty-four. Carla forgot about the pre-cancerous cells in her cervix. And Della was happy, as Brett had danced with her daughter. Chantelle ate slab after slab of chocolate cake, delirious with cream. The camera caught their happiness, and asked them to repeat it, but this time for the camera.

Ellen smirked at the plastic bride, standing stiff, and the plastic groom, which had fallen down, landing softly on the icing. Her own wedding would, naturally, be a grander affair. More profiterole than sausage roll, she thought. More silk than satin. More style than sequin. More of everything, including the complaining.

'Do you wan' some food, love?' asked Tina's mother, her posh outfit wrinkling furiously. 'You look so pale.' Ellen looked up at Tina's mother. Her weathered face had dried out with skin complaints, a bored husband and problem children. Her grey hair had been dyed, half-heartedly, brown. Her legs sagged under the swish skirt. Her face, which was all compassion, willed Ellen to accept a slice of her buffet. *More of everything?* thought Ellen.

Ellen looked down at her stomach. It was unlike a successful woman's stomach. Her stomach was large and jolly, where Ellen wanted small and mean and she wanted Scotch eggs, a slice of pork pie, a tummy-full of cake and lemon meringue pie. She wanted to feel filled with food: with the smoked salmon water biscuits, the crisps of chocolate after-dinner mints, the strawberries, soaked in melted chocolate. She wanted Mum, boiling borscht in the kitchen, giving her something, anything, on a stick.

'Oh, no,' said Ellen, to Tina's mother. 'I'm fine. I always look like this. I'm not hungry at all,' she said, trying to laugh.

'Ha! Look at your cameraman,' laughed Tina's mother, pointing at John who was dancing with a blonde, on a table. His shirt edged out of his trousers. 'You should join in too,' she said, nudging Ellen. 'You never know. You migh' just enjoy yourself!'

'Ellie, you should join in. I said, join in. For once in a while, enjoy yourself. Because *tomorrow*, you might die,' screamed Miriam, party-loud in bright colours, spraying her voice everywhere, from Ellen's past into her present. 'Who wants to dance?' Mum would scream at weddings, pulling strangers from chairs. 'Don't be a wallflower, Ellie,' she would shout, dragging Ellen up to talk, to dance, to grin.

'Your mum's full of life,' fat, silly guests would tell Ellen. 'Life and soul of everything. Life itself, Miriam Abrahams.'

Ellen had forgotten how to relax. She made her exit, leaving John with the blonde. Offering grateful thanks to all inside, this particular producer was glad to hit the cool early-afternoon sun, divided now from Tina and Duane only by the double-glazed doors and, possibly, wealth.

'Let's burst those balloons,' she heard Tina say, through an open window.

'How long have you been waiting?' asked Jeffrey, inside a dark, double-breasted suit, white, thinly striped shirt and tie big and colourful. She had been sitting on the store's steps for a while, listening to Lou Matherbay on *Any Questions* on her personal stereo. 'I've only just arrived,' said Ellen, kissing Jeffrey and marking his face with Almost Cherry. 'I came straight from the wedding.'

The couple sat in the bridal-list department, next to other couples. A pastel lady offered Jeffrey a wedding list with her compliments, assuming, wrongly, that he was in charge. It was an empty sheet of paper, aside from the headline, *Jeffrey With Ellen*.

'Where shall we start?' asked Ellen. 'The top floor,' replied Jeffrey, pressing buttons on his mobile telephone. 'Always start at the top. You can see what a place has, if you start high up.'

Downstairs, in Fragile Glass, Jeffrey tried again. 'So, when will you allow me to meet your mum?' he asked. She seemed to lose her balance, avoiding a frail decanter.

'They shouldn't put cut glass on display,' muttered Ellen. 'We could easily have knocked that over.'

'Wow, this is great,' he said, stopping beside a china figurine. 'No thanks, love,' he added, to a lady handing out broken bits of cookie.

'It's *expensive*,' said Ellen, touching the price tag, desperate for a crumb of cookie.

'Yes, it's the top end of the market, definitely,' said Jeffrey. 'But remember,' he added. 'We're effectively cash buyers. It makes a huge difference.'

'I don't see how,' said Ellen, looking hungrily at a display of plastic fruit.

'So, I embarrass you, is that it?' he asked, as Ellen sank past shoppers, all messily moving about, thinking of tactile, un-tutored people, dancing at a wedding, hugging. 'What do you do?' she had asked Tina. 'I'm a temp, daytimes. Just get married at night,' giggled the bride. Ellen had laughed, as if she found that funny. 'Yes, but what d'you want to do with your *life?* I mean, will you always just temp?' 'I'll have babies, soon as I can,' Tina had said. 'Then I can give up my job, which is crap. It'll be great.'

Ellen pictured Tina with triplets, sitting in a nice little council house, with nothing more pressing on her mind than a full Hoover bag, joining a health club, drinking cranberry juice on the top floor of Harvey Nichols, holidaying in a glossy pull-out part of Wales, sleeping, occasionally, *free* of . . .

'Ellen, *careful*,' said Jeffrey, as Ellen walked into a child. He apologised to the child's mother. 'So what d'you say? Can I meet your mum?'

'Do we have to talk about that here? People are *listening*, for God's sake. Anyway, don't you think I've got enough on my mind? The films have to be in by October, if I want a *chance* of a TV Prime award. I mean, I'll be on my honeymoon then, and I haven't even *started* my . . .'

Jeffrey juggled a couple of wooden apples. '*Our* honeymoon. Anyway, there's always some excuse, isn't there? Awards aren't important. You never want to talk about what matters.'

He led Ellen towards Electrical Items. 'It's getting ridiculous, anyway,' he said loudly, to make himself heard. 'They all ask me: "What do you think of your future mother-in-law? Have you met her yet?" I wouldn't mind, but Mother's met her and *I* haven't. Mother says she's quite a woman. Quite a handful, but quite a woman. I mean, I'd quite like to meet her . . .'

'Tell them she's *sick*,' said Ellen, panicking. 'Tell them she's *dead*. Tell them . . . You know, I used to get calls at work,' she said, as if to prove a point.

A glamour-girl stood in front of them, looking at the cost of a Facial Steam Machine. She picked the machine up, carefully checking its posterior. 'I don't know why they've got beauty aids in Kitchenware,' muttered Ellen, furiously. 'They don't know *how* to arrange shelves here.'

Jeffrey reached for a liquidiser inside a bargain bucket. 'It's best to jump in with a deal like this,' he said. 'May not be up for grabs in a week.' He stood, poised with his pencil to note down the number of the item for the list. 'Can't we at least invite her to the wedding, Ellie?'

'For God's sake,' she muttered. 'Don't call me that. You weren't around when she . . . Way before Dad died. I mean, that's ten years ago . . . She'd bath in *Diet Coke*. I'd find her eating next door's flowers . . . And we don't *need* an electric mixer.'

Ellen raised her voice above the heavy-duty shoppers. She was furious at the rush of post-recession bargain-hunters; the hard core of a down-sized workforce, desperate to consume as much as possible in the shortest possible time. 'It doesn't matter what we need *now*,' said Jeffrey, clutching the body of an electric mixer. 'We've got ample storage space, remember. And, anyway, it's not about needing things; it's about investment. In our future . . .'

'Which can go down as well as up, remember,' said Ellen, drily.

'I just think we should do the right thing,' he said. 'That's all. We should . . .'

Ellen replaced the liquidiser, her calm restored. 'I just want a simple wedding, Jeffrey,' she said. 'Is that too much to ask? I mean, I don't want it ruined by Mum. I don't want it ruined, full stop. I want it *perfect*. Without fuss.'

'You win,' sighed the perfect man, without fuss.

Chapter Eighteen

'No music then?' asked Tracy, surrendering scissors to a plastic tray. 'No music then, Janet?' she screamed, her accent on the Welsh.

'Had enough of the news, me,' Tracy informed her client, scissoring again. 'It's so *depressing*. It's as if they *want* to upset people. Make them miserable. This for something special, then? For a holiday or something?'

Returning Tutsis wept, to see their homes destroyed . . .

'What's wrong?' asked Tracy, chopping curls as Myra wept. 'Janet,' she yelled, through an open door, at her junior. 'You know, I've never had a client cry before. Not in twelve years of hairdressing. And I haven't even *done* anything yet. Janet, what happened to the music? Morbid, isn't it, Myra? Janet, bring some tissues, will you?'

Children watched, as their parents were butchered to death. Using machetes . . .

Myra's hair floated, like snowflakes, to the floor. 'Bring us some tissues, Janet. For heaven's sake. Poor love,' said Tracy, patting the pitiful Myra. 'Not too happy are you? You'll see it when it's finished. I can promise you that,' she said. 'Like him, do you?' Radio Four had been replaced with George Michael. Out of the back salon he now sang.

'Oh dear,' said Janet the Junior, waving a broom. 'Always happens, doesn' it? It's the length, you see. As it's cut off, they cry,' she said, dancing on an unswept carpet of other people's red, brown, blonde hair. And as fat Janet jigged about, the door opened to reveal a monstrous machine-like pram – huge, hideous and dragging a mother in its wake, a mother yelling: 'All right, Tracy? All right, Janet?' into the salon. The woman was awash with children. They dripped from her, like pearls in Peyarth.

In the mirror, Myra saw everything. 'I'll want every one of

them cut,' said the woman, pushing her little treasures at Tracy. 'Can't see their eyes no more.'

'Do you want a cigarette?' Janet asked Myra, lighting one up for herself.

'No. I've given up,' admitted Myra, needing nicotine.

'What did you want to do that for?' asked Tracy, astonished. (Stub-it-out proselytism had bypassed the Peyarth proletariat.)

'Always for men, isn't it?' asked Janet, breathing in. 'That's what I think,' she said, shaking a dead match. 'Always for men.'

Three weeks ago, a beautiful man had walked into Myra's life. Shining brightly, he had white-blond hair and what appeared, at first glance, to be a golden body but what was, in retrospect, a cream linen suit. He had walked in, sitting beside Myra, who had fallen in love as never before that month. 'Dominic, meet Myra. Myra, meet Dominic,' Tom Evans had said. 'My son.'

He stood, beautifully smart in his linen suit, amongst the swine of journalists, local and national, as they swilled press-conference tea, sloping around in shabby, stained suits. 'I'd rather you didn't smoke, actually,' said Dom. 'I'm scared of dying, see. It's the cancer.'

'Why do you think you've got a cat-flap's chance in hell of winning this by-election when your own poll says you're on twenty per cent?' a notoriously sharp journalist asked the Pluralist panellist, Mr Tom Evans.

'I'm a local candidate, who understands local issues . . .'

'You're not local,' said the journalist from the *Peyarth Chronicle*, who wanted a job on the *Guardian*, and to prove himself capable to the bored *Guardian* correspondent who sat beside him, and who himself wanted promotion as the *Guardian*'s political editor. 'You live in Llandarren.'

'But I was born in Peyarth,' said Tom, with passion. 'My family are from Peyarth, I played in the Peyarth park, I have a business in Peyarth . . .'

'What do you say to twenty per cent?' asked Sharp Journalist.

'That was a leaked poll. It had nothing to do with us,' said Brian, the campaign manager, who didn't speak much in private, and had never been known to speak publicly before.

'Well, where was it leaked from then? The local bloody

toilet?' asked Sharp Journalist, losing his rag. He wanted to be a foreign correspondent, ducking spears in Zaire, not sitting here, beside unfresh suits; political bores the lot of them, talking swings and shifts and tactical voting, in the same way football bores in the Pen and Anchor discussed tactics, trends and positioning.

'I'll tell you why we'll be fighting to win Peyarth,' said Larry Beat, smooth and tanned next to Tom and Brian. 'We'll be fighting to win because we *believe* in this city. This city is not a loser, it is not inherently weak. It has been failed by its politicians, failed by old parties corrupted by power and corrupted by their own vested interests. It is *they* who have dragged Peyarth down,' Larry said, infectiously, with intonation all over the place.

'So, you're gonna win this seat are you, Larry?' asked Sharp.

'We're not dreamers. We come from a low base. In the last election we didn't do well. We did badly in the local elections. But we have something that the other three parties don't have, and that's stamina. We have a new logo, new colours, a new symbol. We symbolise something new. Isn't that something Lou Matherbay recognised? And I'm going to do something now that a politician never does and that is to promise you something. I shall stick my neck out here and say: *We will surprise you all.* Thank you, gentlemen . . .'

'But are you going to win? Yes or no?' asked Sharp, desperately.

'Thank you, gentlemen,' said Larry, as Myra circled her finger at the back to wind up the press conference, and journalists hung around her, as at discos, to ask her what the team were planning for that day, whether they could do some filming with Larry, Tom or the campaign poodle, Constitutional Reform.

The next day, Dominic Evans had asked her out.

'Why have it cut, if it upsets you?' the other client asked Myra, inside Tracy's Trims. One child stuck to her hips with the aid of a life-sized blackcurrant lollipop; another hung, sagging, from her breasts. A third clambered on to a stool, to stare at Myra.

'Always for men, that's what I think,' said Janet. 'Everything for *men*.'

Myra looked at her lopsided reflection. (One half of her head still hung with curls.) 'Actually no,' she said. 'Not this time.'

'Nice suit, Myra,' Larry Beat had said, leaning across to whisper at his press officer.

'Scrubs up well, doesn't she?' Dominic Evans had added, lazing an arm around Myra.

'Well, *I'm* taking her more seriously,' joked Tom Evans, Pluralist candidate for Peyarth. 'Seriously,' he added, to Myra.

The campaign proper had begun. There was a campaign bus, painted carnival-style in Pluralist colours. But Myra was still at the streetwalking stage, grabbing at people, holding on to their arms, willing them to stop, sticking stickers – *Be Singular, Vote Pluralist* – on to their chests and their private papers. This was unmixed politics. The enemy was the electorate, walking around Myra with their support for other parties; with their Don't Knows and their Don't Cares. And all Myra wanted was for them to belong to her team, waving her colours, learning her lines and chanting her party's anthem. She did not want to party in Peyarth. She did not want to shop in Peyarth.

Peyarth's concrete shopping mall, kept out of the chain-store loop, sold everything by bulk, from shampoo, through biscuits, to tins of soup. Nappies were sold in baby-boom boxes of two hundred. Food was advertised as if in famine conditions. *Two bags potatoes, get one free.* All the clothes came in one, economy-large size.

'Any ciabattas?' Myra had asked at a Peyarth café. A pinnied woman, behind the counter, had looked behind her at a box of Kit Kats and a tray of crispy bread rolls. 'We've got cappuccino,' she had said. 'If that's what you mean.'

Consumers, to Peyarth-dwellers, were part of a capitalist conspiracy. With shop-owners, there was a natural suspicion of Switch cards, an inflexibility over Access and an apprehension about cheque books. Bank-notes were held dangerously close to the light. Products kept their shelf-life long after sell-by dates had passed. And, far from promoting certain brands, Peyarth shops would not stock popular lines, faking ignorance of McVities Chocolate Boasters, Kellogg's Cornflakes and Quaker's Harvest Crunch bars.

'Can I have the morning off?' Myra had asked Larry Beat. 'I need to go to Llandarren,' she said. 'I need to buy clothes.' Larry had looked down at Myra's dog-eared, collared, ribbed top; her black, flared hipsters. 'I'll give you two hours,' he had said. 'Come back looking smart.'

Out of her London mould, Myra was unrecognisable. Beaming in a new blue suit, scented with Samsara perfume and herbal cigarettes, Myra had bought blouses and some of the lowest denier tights in Llandarren. This time she had shopped for quality, finding spike-heeled shoes and thermal underwear. In London, Myra had suffered compulsive disorder. In Llandarren, she kept a shoe rack.

'So, what is it you do, then?' asked Tracy, lopping off the last of Myra's curls.

'You up for the by-election?' asked Janet, hovering about with hairspray.

'I'm here,' Myra said, 'for the Pluralist Party.'

Myra had canvassed for votes like a door-to-door saleswoman. In a strange Pluralist initiation rite, Brian had asked her to 'do over' the worst housing estate in Britain.

Grey tower blocks hung around the estate, as if with nothing better to do, their walls coloured with graffiti, their windows smeared with net curtains. Women stood around the doors, dresses clunk-clicked at the waist with seatbelt-like contraptions.

Sounds rose from each block. 'Fuck off. Hey, dildo. Fuck off. Sod off. You cunt-bastard.'

Myra, who hadn't been told, marched prettily into the estate arena, her Pluralist hat firmly on, clutching at lists and cheap pens threatening to leak at any time. Wearing one of six new suits, which itched around the labelled collar, Myra cut a comic figure. Her black slim court shoes stuck inside the cracking pavement at intervals as she walked, and the thin, almost-black tights slithered at her thighs. Pushing open the glass door to the first block, releasing a strong scent of urine, she heard a man say, at some distance: 'What the fucking hell, in fuck's name, is that?'

Many entrances to flats, inside the blocks Myra visited, did not have doors. They suffered gaping holes, like a tooth's painful cavities. She did not know whether to walk in, presenting herself: 'Sorry to bother you. I'm a Pluralist. Are you?', or whether to wait there until the owner appeared, bare-chested and unmoved by the presence of a stranger, standing in the spot where, in conventional society, there would have been a door, blocking out the world.

Only when she found a proper entrance to a proper flat did Myra ring a bell, which hung off the door, rudely exposing wires. A woman answered it. She was carrying a packet of Battenburg cake, which reminded Myra of school, and of her own hunger. Because Myra was often hungry now. She had begun to taste food, eating plates of the stuff at Mrs Evans'. She had become discriminatory with her pizza toppings, daring with her desserts in restaurants, finishing whole mouthfuls. 'Sorry to bother you, but I'm here on behalf of the Pluralists. Which way are you planning to vote?'

The woman said: 'I don't know yet. I haven't decided.'

'Well, hopefully I can persuade you to vote Pluralist,' said Myra, enthusiastically. 'We will provide decent housing for all those needing it,' she continued, gazing through the body of the woman she generously considered in her early thirties.

'Are you saying there's something wrong with my flat?' asked the woman sharply, whose mother, unlike Myra's, hadn't weaned her on mashed swede and carrots, whose mother hadn't learned about attachment disorders, and whose mother hadn't, unlike Myra's, bought her the latest in child-educational and learning-facility packs. 'Are you trying to patronise me?'

'No,' said Myra, as the door slammed closed and the doorbell sprang forward at her, like a cuckoo from a clock.

At another entrance, Myra asked: 'Can I just ask you, er, are you a Pluralist?'

'Am I a what? Turn that bloody music down, Euan.'

'Do you think that you might consider voting *Pluralist* in the by-election?'

The man, in pale brown canvas shorts with the top button undone to allow the hirsute, overgrown belly to breathe freely, laughed loud and long, as if he had been waiting for this opportunity to let rip for most of his adult years. Myra allowed him to laugh, and a female to join him, as she moved away to the neighbouring cavity.

'Yes?' asked a woman at the door to her flat. It was the first flat that smelled good; of meat casseroles and floor polish. 'I'm here on behalf of the Pluralist Party, to find out which way you're planning to vote,' said Myra, who wanted to wrap her arms around this woman. She wanted to hug her, and to call her Mom, in an American accent.

But the woman was expecting her own child to visit, after a five-year gap in relations. Her flat normally stank of cats and tinned sausages, but she had cleaned as far as the kitchen, for this reunion with her son and his wife, whom she had called 'a conniving little hooker' more than half a decade ago. 'I'm not sure I can help you, you know,' she said, looking oddly at Myra. The woman's twin brother had died ten years ago, from a stroke, and still she carried around the guilt. 'I'm not strictly political.'

'But are you going to vote Pluralist?'

'No, I always vote Conservative.'

Bashing her foot into the bar of a child's rusty swing, Myra walked over to a block called Mount Pleasant, which appeared to be anything but. 'Will you be voting Pluralist?' she asked some newlyweds, who had just had a baby and a minor win on the National Lottery. 'Oh yes,' they said, as they had said to all-comers.

'Will you be voting Pluralist?' Myra asked an obese woman who puffed past her on the stairs.

'Will you get the lift working?' she asked, rhetorically. It was Joan Clark, the woman who had been likened to Jayne Mansfield in her day; who had inspired people to love and envy. The same Joan Clark, who now inspired people to watch what they ate.

Myra emerged from forgotten flats to face a built-down darkness, unlit by street lamps or motorists, unlike London's darkness. Brian had said he would wait for her in his Volvo around the corner. Indeed, he had dropped her off, as if for her first ever mixed-sex party. 'Don't be late,' he had said. And, for the first time ever, she wasn't.

'So, will you be voting Pluralist?' asked Myra of Tracy, from Tracy's Trims. Frankly, Myra felt it was the least the stylist could do, as she had just ruined Myra's appearance.

'Oh, I just go for looks me, don' I, Janet? Whoever's the best looking. I always say that.'

'She's a flirting voter,' joked Janet.

The campaign for election buzzed on endlessly. Tom Evans had grown out of Tom Evans The Peyarth Newsagent, and had become Tom Evans The Future Member of Parliament. Little men and women sat around him in summer anoraks, filling up envelopes with campaign literature and querying procedure (although never policy) in a manner normally reserved for driving examiners and nightclub doormen.

They had fallen, *en masse*, in love with Tom Evans and every visiting Pluralist MP. It was as if Tom was the lead singer in a band of politicians and they were adolescents all over again, despite their mostly forty- or fifty-something ages. They all had crushes and pimply spots that grew huge with the nightly send for pizzas and curries as they sat licking envelopes and bits of lamb korma from their pale lips, waiting for something to happen.

Tom Evans would stand, taller now, with the visiting MPs in the corner, talking politics and pizza, while the MPs, who recognised the Tom Evanses of this world as their bread and butter, patronised him and threw crumbs of charm to the party foot soldiers, creating a collective nervous tug on kagouls and little temporary smiles on pale faces.

Myra felt the same way she had felt when she was a child, whenever her parents, usually at home, had gone abroad. Myra and her sisters had stayed with one laughing grandmother or another. And as Myra's mother or father reclaimed their daughters, Myra would wonder to which world she belonged: that of Grandma, smelling of motorway service stations, and littered with compilation love albums and china collectors' items, or that of her parents, safely department-store scented, who brought up their children according to the diagrams.

She was hesitant with her own MPs. It was as if Myra had been sent to learn provincial before she was accepted back, folded in, as part of the capital. Events like the European football championship, flash floods in Oman and the Radovan Karadzic resignation in Bosnia were all very much a part of London, and irrelevant here in Peyarth, where most people wanted only for England to lose the football cup, for the estates to be cleared of crime and poverty, and for dog turds to be removed from those wealthier suburbs pushing away towards Llandarren.

'Will you want your hair coloured?' asked Tracy.

'It's gone very *dark*,' said Janet, who was chopping off a child's fringe. 'Always happens if you cut it short. Goes back to the roots, you see.' And Myra felt her new, short curls.

'Of course, if you dye it any more, it will be ever so dry,' said Tracy, who was more comfortable doing trims.

'Men like it natural anyway,' interrupted Janet. 'That's what I think,' she said. 'At the end of the day, they prefer the original hair.'

Myra had, yet again, been forcibly ejected from a relationship. But, this time, she had tried out dignity. 'That's fine, Dom,' she had said. 'Long-distance romances don't work. That's a fact.' He had popped his big blues semi-sympathetically, glazing them with tears.

But he was beautiful, and so he was lazy. Dignity had not worked, so Myra tried misery. She doused her own eyes with watery tears, just covering her own smaller grey-blues, leaving the dark pupils alone to simmer. But, in a lesson still not learned, Myra's misery quickly boiled over into melodrama. Mistaking his expression for compassion, Myra quoted lines from emotional pieces in magazines, as if they were her own. Although Dominic Evans believed that the lines *were* her own, they only underlined his impression of her. Myra Felt was unusual. And Dominic did not want unusual. He wanted the usual Llandarren girls: the ones who poured wine over other female heads as an expression of emotional disappointment.

Even then, he did not want them for long. Had Myra been aware of the fact that Dominic was the most desired date across both Peyarth and Llandarren, she would almost certainly not have tried all one hundred of the One Hundred Different Ways To Hang On To A Man At All Costs. Now on to sexual provocation, she practised the proud seductress, pointlessly pouting her skinny lips; skilfully lighting herbal cigarettes as her bony bottom sashayed, without her, around the room.

She wished it was protocol for ditched women to have one last-ditch attempt at enticement, displaying all their points of attraction at once. She would then have tap-danced, played 'Memories' on the piano. She would have shown him a yellowing newspaper cutting of herself in the background as Peter O'Toole sat with Jeffrey Bernard outside a pub in Soho. But as it was not protocol, Myra Felt sat in the campaign HQ's back room. There, people made instant coffee or grey tea. There was always only a drop of milk left in the torn cartons and the sugar was wet and lumpy. She sat opposite Dom at the little green-topped table, stirring an empty Pluralist mug with a teaspoon, clinking the inside, as if they were breakfasting communally and politely at a small guest house, speaking inaudibly, like a couple of forty years' standing with nothing left to say. Behind the couple-no-more, in the campaign office, a crowd of humble people sat around the table licking and folding, folding and licking.

When the crowd of faces was broken into little delicate pieces, there was Fred, who talked of by-elections as a buff would talk of opera, endlessly and with a boxful of precedents. There was Pamela, who believed in the Pluralists in the same way some women have faith in religion – all a bit messily spiritual, but there were those lovely cake competitions that one couldn't quite do without.

There was Victor, who still believed that he was a Pluralist despite the latent Darwinism and the membership card for the Campaign For The Reintroduction Of Capital Punishment. There was Lydia, who asked people not to mind her as she tore open envelopes already licked, and unfolded literature already folded, in an effort to produce something pretty and neat, like herself. And Tony, whose wife had just died of multiple sclerosis, but who didn't want to waste time grieving. Young 'Glasses' Katie, whose friends filled up their spare time at discos, while she filled up her curriculum vitae. Middle-aged 'Orange' Katie, who always wore tangerine and knew a great deal about torna-does. And Trevor, who telephoned talk-radio programmes, simply to talk.

Leading the team into oblivion, Cathy and Brian would

occasionally appear out of the important side office, carrying a smell of influence and chocolate biscuits. Small maps stretched around the walls of this office, and a large one hung like a cloth over the centre table – the chief toy in the war-games played by Brian, Cathy, Billy Todd, Tom Evans and Larry Beat. Pointing, with pencils, at chunks of council wards, and carving up profiles of constituency pieces, the campaign cabinet could decide where best to target their efforts and resources.

This office played host to Westminster politicians – MPs who were once mere men and women. They had been sent to London by men and women such as Brian and Cathy or Tony and Pamela. And now they were blown up like balloons, and tied with the most fragile of strings to their constituencies, drifting far and away from people like Lydia and Glasses Katie and Victor. Their office had flowers in a vase on the side. Their office had a fridge-full of cartoned skimmed milk, and a cafetière and a kettle. Their office had a green glass bowl, filled with fresh, heaped brown sugar.

Steam drifted from the kettle's spout, and Myra, in vain, tried to stem the tide of rejection. Cathy Tanning appeared at the door, cloudy amidst the steam, summoning Myra to the war room. The young woman followed her, theatrically through the mist, bringing the curtain down on Dominic's relationship and Dominic's entertainment for at least the next few hours. But Dominic was bored of the drama, and he would bow out of this by-election tomorrow, just as Myra would wake to a feeble stomach and decide to throw her energies back at Dominic, in one last-gasp attempt at intimacy.

A mirror was held up to Myra's head. Tracy moved it about, showing Myra at every angle. 'Don't bother,' Myra said, irritably. 'Really, I don't need . . .' she said, finally losing patience. In London, Myra had searched for herself in passing shop windows, tube-carriage glass and in the eyes of compact discs. But in Peyarth there was no time to reflect on her reflection 'I've got to go,' said Myra Felt. 'The by-election's tomorrow. I was given *one hour* to get my hair cut.'

'Well, all I'm saying is that we can't let this go, not without doing something,' Billy Todd had said, eating a tortilla chip messily.

'I'm not saying we should let it *go*, exactly,' said Larry Beat. 'I'm just saying that it should look as if it's another party that's not letting it *go*.'

'The latest poll returns are terrible,' said Brian, who always blossomed in by-elections, coming out of his cardigan for the course of the campaign.

'Myra, what do you think?' asked Cathy Tanning, who could have been an MP, were it not for her lack of charm and her numerous, demanding children.

'What do I think?' asked Myra, eating tortilla chips whole.

It had been brought to Pluralist attention that Gareth Holt, the leading opposition candidate in the Peyarth by-election, liked to dress up in women's clothes. When he wasn't playing rugby, or manhandling his wife, lifting weights or washing the truck, he was spending his time rolling sheer almond tights up his hairy legs. He was buttoning up bright dresses over a flat bush of chest hair, and he was slipping, sadly, into shocking-pink shoes. While other men cried at the cinema, hugged their crying children or were creative in the kitchen, Gareth compulsively cross-dressed, craving the feeling of eye-shadow, shortie skirts, and shiny pastel blouses.

Over the past three weeks, Gareth Holt had dressed up for Britain, never mind his party, wearing shorts and a rugby shirt for one photo call, dressing in stripes for a press conference or two: quiet ones on his suit, loud ones on his tie. To watch some heart surgery at the hospital, he had worn a white coat and mask. To visit a nightclub, he had worn an open-necked white shirt. For a quiet day in the countryside with the cameras and his wife, there was the big ribbed pullover. For other occasions, there was the sports gear, city gear, casual wear, smart suits, a miner's outfit, a track suit, and a monkey's mask for the play-group photograph, which had appeared with the headline: 'You can't make a monkey out of him.'

But, as Myra knew, they *would* make a monkey out of Gareth Holt, if the news came out about any cross-dressing in *private*. The public and the press would destroy him, in fact. The Pluralist Party itself would prepare a press release saying: 'The

Pluralists despair at the rough treatment Gareth Holt has received at the hands of an illiberal press, bent on the destruction of this candidate's reputation.' This press release would be put in the files, rather than sent to the press. It would be whispered about. It would be talked about in policy meetings and argued about amongst MPs, rather than pushed down the throat of popular opinion at a public already sick at Gareth Holt's indiscretion. The Pluralists would play it down. They would allow others to party on the moral high ground; to be seen to profit politically as Gareth was ground down. And, secretly, the Pluralists would profit in every which way.

'Yes. I'd like to know what Myra thinks . . .' Larry Beat had said. 'If we're ever to give her the *more senior* title of Communications Director, Myra should have more to say.'

Billy Todd looked at her, his mouth soiled with tsatsiki, offering excuses as he wiped the mess up with a serviette. 'These tortilla dips drip all over the place. Yes,' he said. 'I suppose Myra *is* in the best position to decide . . .'

Myra had said: 'What do I think?' just the once, but it had stayed there as a question to all of them sitting in this room, feeding their faces.

She had, of course, made up her mind as soon as the swirl of the campaign began in Peyarth. The carnival atmosphere had crashed any niggling doubts about the party. She had been swept along in the procession of press conferences and opportunities, canvassing and campaigning, partying and politicking. She wanted Tom Evans to win. She wanted to bring him back to Westminster with her as a souvenir of the great times they had had together, knocking on doors in the dripping summer rain.

('Hello there. Tom Evans here. I'd be glad of your vote next week.' 'And I'd be glad of a bloody win on the lottery, but it won't happen, will it?')

Myra Felt had made her decision. She had spent time with Tom Evans. They had visited schools together to look at rows and rows of Bunsen burners flickering up to plain pubescent faces as the camera lights shone more kindly on their own faces, already grown. They had been to state-of-the-art factories together and estate projects, all the while playing their campaign song, and offering ribbons and stickers and posters in exchange for votes and in place of practical assistance.

(The *Daily Telegraph*: 'Still going to win this seat, Myra?' Myra: 'Too close to call, Rupert. Too close to call.')

Looking down at her green linen lap, Myra said gently: 'I think I can trust Paul from the *Peyarth Chronicle*. I'll leak it to him.'

'Nooo,' gasped Myra Felt, rubbing at sticky, blackcurrant patches. The salon child had leaked lollipop on to Myra's suit. 'Oh *no*,' she said furiously, at the child's mother. Myra no longer had time for pleasantries. 'Why didn't you *watch* him?' she asked, panic-stricken and scraping her skirt. She had been shorn of her strength. 'I can't get it out,' she said, pathetically, to all in the salon.

'She's right, you know,' said Janet. 'That stain's permanent.'

Chapter Nineteen

Myra Felt believed that the world could be divided into those people who divided up the world and those people who didn't.

Susan Lyttle believed that the world could be divided into those people who had read *Breaking the Barricades*, and those people who hadn't.

Fed up with fiction, Susan had read much of Lou Matherbay's *Breaking the Barricades* on the train journey between London and Swindon. The penultimate chapter had, it seemed, been written simply for Susan. *'Families are an outdated concept. We are all forced to believe in parents as all-important. The truth is that most people can find Mother-love almost anywhere: connecting, often, more closely with relative strangers than with birth mothers or fathers. Learning to—'*

'I wouldn't read that rubbish,' Hugh Matlock had said, sitting next to Susan on the train. 'I'm happy for *Ms* Matherbay to open the Swindon branch, but there the story ends. She's not a woman I admire,' her portable employer had said, sipping polystyrene tea. 'But as you do, Susan, perhaps you'd like to meet her at the station? Wait for her train? I told Marketing *I'd* look after her. But, it's a bit tricky. There's things I need to discuss with Mr Dutton. The family as a concept, eh?' he had said, reading over Susan's head. 'I wish mine had stayed that way.

That morning, Hilary Matlock had stuck a digital glass stick in her mouth yet again. 'I thought you'd taken your temperature today,' Hugh had said, reading a sports magazine.

'I'm not sure it was right,' Hilary mumbled incoherently. 'I might have had a hot flush.'

'Are you coming to watch Lou open up in Swindon?' asked Hugh, fast-flipping the magazine pages to find a speed-car article.

'I can't. Damn. 98.8,' read Hilary from the digital display. 'I suppose that's normal,' she said sadly, picking up a book on sympto-thermal reproductive methods. 'Oh Hugh, I don't have time for things like that any more. *No.*'

A young woman stood with Lou Matherbay on the station platform. *Lou Matherbay*, busily signing autographs for the indifferent. Susan stood, immobilised.

'Why is she so important to you?' Hanna had asked.

'She looks like my mother.'

'Oh.'

'Not that that *makes* her my mother, of course,' Susan had said. 'But it'll be interesting to see if Mother was right. I mean, if they are as alike as she thought.'

'I see,' said Hanna, who didn't.

'So, what d'you think I should wear?' Susan asked, flicking through Hanna's wardrobe. 'Can I borrow this?' She pulled out an old end-of-summer dress. 'I want her to think I'm interesting. Where's it from?'

'Oxfam,' said Hanna. 'By the way, Ken was asking after you last night. I was at Rudy's thing – you should have come – and he said—'

'*Oxfam?*' Susan said. 'I'm not wearing dead people's clothes.'

'Well, I reckon that's what you should wear. Mauve suits you. It's a mature colour. Wear it with your DMs, introduce yourself properly, talk a lot, and she'll be *impressed.*'

'Hello. I'm Susan.'

'Susan?' asked Lou Matherbay, confused; her skin like tracing paper, close-up.

'Susan Lyttle,' she said, remembering herself. 'I'm from Dutton's . . .'

'Ah,' said Lou. 'So you're the one who'll be looking after me, are you?'

You, thought Susan, *should be looking after me.*

Myra Felt looked closely at the Dutton's girl; at the grubby blonde curls and the urchin-skin, melted hot over cheekbones. She looked like an extra in *Les Miserables* or *Annie*, smelling precociously of cigarettes. She looked as if she was about to tap dance, or to walk the streets.

'I'm sure I *know* you,' said Myra, finding the hob-nailed boots familiar; the blonde curls; the unironed dress. 'Did you by any chance go to school in Ruislip?' asked Myra.

'No, I grew up in Southport,' said the girl, irritatingly pretty. 'And, yes, you look familiar too. I mean, I know the name Myra.'

'Myra? Is that you? Wow. I barely recognised you.'

'Charles Pickford! What have you got to do with this by-election?'

'Mmm, can I have a piece?' he had said, staring at Myra's Dairy Milk. 'I like the suit.' He had watched, as she unwrapped chocolate. 'And the hair. Secretly brunette . . . You *are* looking good. And well done. The Pluralists deserved to win, I reckon.'

Last week, she had stood in the town hall, against party banners saying *Come The Evolution*, among Pluralist cheers. covered in the attention of reporters and Charles Pickford.

'I'm here for the *Sketch*. Official photographer,' said Charles.

'I thought you worked for Dutton's. I'd hoped to see you at the Swindon opening, actually. I'm going with Lou,' she had said, breaking off a chunk of chocolate for Charles. 'This, by the way, is a ciggie substitute. I'm eating so much *chocolate* now. I will die late,' Myra had said, melodramatically. 'But unbelievably fat.'

'Well, you were too skinny before. You've actually got cheeks now,' he had said, grinning. 'No, a lot's happened recently. I sold some pictures of Gareth Holt to the *Sketch*, you see. You must have seen them. Down to luck, really. I was out climbing, in Wales, with Ken and Jerry, when that transvestite story came out. Near Llandarren. And I thought, why not? Got the only shots of him in a dress . . .'

'If Gareth Holt hadn't cross-dressed, Myra, would the Pluralists still have won?' interrupted Paul from the *Peyarth Chronicle*. (He had secured a job interview with the *Guardian*'s news editor and hoped to escape Peyarth before winter.)

'Your man enjoying his dead man's shoes, Myra?' asked the man from the *Sun*. 'Or, should I say ladies' *stilettos*?'

'Up to your old tricks were you, you Pluralists?' Sharp Journalist had asked, breathing curry fumes over Myra.

'I'm sorry?' asked Myra, bloated with pride and a large pre-election dinner.

'Just wondered how the *Peyarth Chronicle* knew about Holt's dressing-up box,' he said. 'Wouldn't have come from you lot, would it?'

'No, it *wouldn't*,' said Larry Beat, coming up from behind. 'We won Peyarth because we're in tune with the times. Tom Evans won this by-election because he's in tune with what people want from politicians. They're *fed up* with sleaze. They want honest, down-to-earth—'

'Write it on a postcard, Larry,' interrupted Sharp, lazily. 'Wish you were here, on the moral high ground. Oh, look who's appeared at last. Now that's the man we all *really* want to talk to,' he said, running after Gareth Holt.

The losing candidate stood alone, covered in an irritation of reporters.

'How does it feel to lose your party's tenth most winnable seat, Mr Holt?' Sharp asked, running ahead of the rest of the press pack.

'Well, despite coming in a very fair second, I am, naturally enough, very disappointed,' said Gareth Holt, whose wife and life had collapsed from the shock. 'I had hoped to win this seat . . .'

'In a dress, Mr Holt?' asked the man from the *Sun*.

'What about your wife, Mr Holt?' asked Sharp.

'Have you lost your job, Mr Holt?' asked Paul.

Praise had come from on high. 'We've all been very impressed with the way you handled things here,' Larry Beat had informed Myra. 'And we've decided to give you more influence. Greater seniority. Sara's put out a press release already, announcing your new title. From now on, you'll be the party's *Communications Director*.'

'Well done again,' Charles had whispered. 'I heard that. You're pretty important now, aren't you, Myra? You know,' he said, leaning close. 'I've missed you. I really have. How about coming back with me tonight? I've moved out of that dump I shared with Ken and Jerry.'

'I don't do things like that any more,' said Myra.

'No, you don't understand,' he said. 'I mean it seriously. Us. Together. It would work now, I think. You're different. I'm sure I'm different. It was just bad timing. And somehow . . . I've missed you . . . I think, Myra . . . What I'm trying to say is, you're the one for me.'

I am *not* for him, Myra had thought. I am for *me*.

'You know, a woman's whole history is the history of her affections,' Charles had said, taking her hand.

'What *are* you going on about?'

'She is a woman, therefore to be won.'

'Oh, for God's sake, Charles. They're just quotes,' said Myra, brushing his hand away. 'They don't mean anything.'

'So, are we going for that cup of tea?' asked Lou Matherbay. 'Only I'm *parched*.'

Myra looked at her watch. 'Well, we're supposed to be meeting that *FastNews* woman. She'll only scream at me, if we're not here. I mean, she can be an incredible bitch.'

The incredible bitch from *FastNews* knelt, as if in prayer, at one of Swindon's station toilets. Ellen's stomach felt torn apart. But this was a natural force; not a nausea brought on by two fingers tucked inside her throat, pressed down in the neck, hard and harder. 'Oh *God*,' she gurgled, wiping fresh sick from her hair. Something had happened to Ellen's insides.

Something had happened to Ellen's hair. In the past few weeks, it had taken on a life of its own, the curls growing at an alarming rate. Something had happened to Ellen's house. It crawled with empty chocolate wrappers. Business sections of Sunday newspapers piled up on sinks. Toothpaste lay, unlidded and slightly squeezed, on beds. Teaspoons travelled, dirty and hard, to table-tops far from the kitchen. Squeezy ketchup bottles wept tomato sauce everywhere.

The dirty-linen basket had caved in. Weaving out of the basket, straw twisted and relented under the weight of Ellen's washing. Skirt hems, which Ellen hadn't known she had, fell down, as if by accident. An ironing box, polished wood and waiting, piling, inside the airing cupboard, had packed tight with mature clothes. Whenever Ellen fell behind with life, her laundry boxes collapsed. Some people suffered skin complaints under pressure; she developed dried-on stains spreading, like acne, around her clothes.

Something, too, had happened to Ellen's hormones. In the

past few weeks, she had not known whether she was man, woman or adrenal clinic. For the first time in ten years she had cried, disturbing Jeffrey. '*Ellen*,' he had shouted, shaking his fiancée. 'PUK defences are crumbling in Koi Sanjag,' she had screamed, tears streaming down her face. 'Ellen, please wake up,' he had said, trying to find a face inside all those brown curls. 'What's *happened?*'

She had sat up, suddenly. 'Oh my God,' yelled Ellen Abrahams. 'Jeffrey. Which countries surround Saudi Arabia?'

One August night, Jeffrey had found Ellen downstairs, cleaning bottles of cleaning fluid. 'Come to bed,' he had said. 'Whatever it is can wait until morning.' Ellen had muttered, half-awake: 'My home's being invaded. Limescale . . .' It had climbed up her pipes. It had sucked down her plugholes. It had lain dormant down Ellen's drains.

Frankie Bell had visited, to discuss photographs for the wedding. 'So this is where my son lives now?' she had asked. 'I never see him at home. Oh *Ellen*,' she had said, wading through newspaper cuttings. 'This room looks like a guinea-pig cage.' *Economist*s mounted, unread, in Ellen's rack.

'They're my *ideas*,' Ellen had said, scooping up the newspaper scraps.

'Poor Ellen. She's been working sixteen-hour days *every* day. This is her first day off for weeks,' Jeffrey had said, bringing in messy plates heaving with spaghetti bolognese.

'I don't want any of that,' Ellen had said.

'Good idea,' whispered Frankie, patting her future daughter-in-law's large stomach. 'You want to go easy on *the food*.'

'Lou, I'm so sorry I'm late. I *never* am. It's just the train . . .' said Ellen.

'I don't think we've properly met, have we?' asked Lou.

'It's Ellen Abrahams, Lou. I was telling you . . . Anyway,' said Myra, 'I'm glad you came.' She had all the force of a Communications Director. 'Shall we go across to the hotel?'

Ellen glanced at Myra. 'You've changed your image, haven't you?' she said, wanting Myra to feel her pain. 'I mean, you look so *clean*,' she added, hoping to hurt.

'Well, it's been such a long time since we met,' said Myra,

who didn't envy Ellen. (She had clearly let herself go.)

The station hotel smelt of puddings, musty with long traditions of people having to spend time in Swindon. In the lounge, a lazy stew of voices stirred, as Lou Matherbay walked in, pursued by three women. Reheating sounds, the MP inspected the tea menu, pinned to a wall. 'Mmm,' she said, as people, polite with hotel manners, pretended interest in anyone other than her. 'They're still doing a full tea.'

Myra pulled out a file from a bag, padded with newspapers. 'Now, Ellen,' she said. 'I've got all the facts you asked for. So . . . ?'

Stuffy smells stifled childish sounds, like Susan's laughter. Hotels unnerved her. The elderly wallpaper inhibited all inside. Hotel walls, easily shocked, had, in the past, amplified Aunt Jane's shame. On days out, from Southport to the South of France, Susan had often offended indigenous hotel culture with her adult literature, scuffed shoes and crumbling, jam-bloody scones. 'Put that book away,' Aunt Cyn had said, ritually. 'This,' Aunt Jane had said, regularly awed, 'is a *hotel*.'

'Put that file away, Myra. This,' said Lou Matherbay, 'is *tea-time*.'

Lou had led Susan to expect her face inanimate. She had led Susan to expect it still, like the photographs; not blinking, life-like. Susan had been led to expect a sixties *Watch With Mother* face. She had expected the strength of Mother-love. She had expected a faint, forgotten, treasured face, thick with smooth skin; not this loose-leaf, lined, paper woman, long since out of print. She had expected an extraordinary woman; a beautiful, youthful woman, recognising in Susan something extraordinary too.

'Work comes second to *cakes*,' this middle-aged woman said, breathing commonplace air. 'Are there any cakes?' asked Lou.

'Someone will be round with a trolley in a minute,' said the waitress. 'My mum loves you, by the way. Says you changed her life.'

A girl, dressed in a doilie, wheeled in a cake trolley. Lou said: 'We're having the full, standard tea. What do you say, Ellen, to one of those last two apple turnovers?' She patted Ellen conspiratorially, on the arm. 'Shall we live dangerously?'

Terrified by the trolley, piled high with fat, creamy cakes, Ellen froze. She hadn't bargained for a tea that was greater than the sum of hot water and a bag. If Ellen had known they would make her eat cake, she would have suggested dinner instead. Because, with a meal, at least the kilocalories came incognito, and without the floods of cream. 'Er, fine,' she said, avoiding a scene.

'Does anyone smoke?' Susan asked, trying to look comfortable and in place.

'Only passively now,' said Myra firmly.

'Everything I *do* is passive now,' said Lou Matherbay. 'Shall I play Mother?' she asked as tea was brought out, inside all manner of elegant pots. 'Yes,' said the young women, out of synch.

'Now. Ellen. This film you're making . . . ?' asked Lou.

'Women of Achievement,' said Ellen, feeling sick rise. 'Women in Power.'

'I saw one of those programmes,' said Susan. 'The Madonna one? Hanna and I thought . . .'

'Well, I'm not sure it's me *at all*,' interrupted Lou.

'Of course it is,' said Myra.

'Actually,' said Lou, taking apart her turnover, to get at the apple. 'I have a confession to make.'

'What's that?' asked Myra.

'Just that I *could* have been wasting your time.'

Susan felt as if she was paralysed, in a dream. She was invisible to this woman, vaguely like her mother – certainly, it was as if she had stolen certain features sitting beside her, alive. 'Be Mother,' she found herself thinking, staring at the orange hair. '*Mother*,' she thought, loudly. 'It's me, *Susan*.'

'Why do you say that?' Ellen asked Lou, panicking. 'Don't tell me you're not standing for the leadership, after all you . . .'

'Well, actually, I never *said* I was going to stand. And it's more than that, anyway,' she said. 'I'm actually going to be announcing my *retirement* soon.'

'I'm *sorry*?' said Myra.

'*No*,' said Ellen.

'So it's pointless pursuing me. For your film, I mean.'

'Yes, it is, isn't it?' said Ellen.

'Well, I think,' said Susan, who was interrupted again.

'How can you retire now?' asked Myra, angrily. 'When in a month you could be . . . When you could be our *leader*?'

She was not Susan's mother who was, of course, dead. This woman, collected by Mother in boxes, had, all along, been a fake. She had insinuated herself into all their lives, passed on from Mother to Susan, who had inherited her along with a love for pineapple chunks, a vague Catholicism, and a share in a Southport shoe shop. Mother, thought Susan, might just as well have collected cookware. Or crockery.

Lou Matherbay was as ordinary as her aunts. 'I mean, her obsession with cakes made me want to laugh,' Susan planned to tell Hanna. 'It was as if I was back in Seabank Road.' She wanted, however, to cry. Who will keep Mother alive, thought Susan, if not Lou Matherbay?

'I just wish you'd told me before,' said Ellen. 'I've done so much *work*.'

'I didn't know before, my dear,' said Lou. 'I think it was the by-election that made me realise.'

'You *can't* retire,' continued Myra, glancing, horrified, at Ellen's chest, which was of saucy seaside postcard proportions. 'That would just leave Ray. And he's useless. I mean, he has no *ideas*. He *never* sees the big picture. He just gets caught up in tiny little details, like proportional representation. Everything's *academic* with Ray. I don't think he's ever *campaigned* in his life. Actually got his hands dirty . . .'

'Now, now, Myra,' said Lou. 'I think that Raymond will do very well for the Pluralists. He's just what the party needs. I mean, he pretended blind to all that business in Peyarth, with Gareth Holt. Just ignored it. Which was the right thing to do, of course. Whereas I would have got very angry in my day. Barged in, trying to change the way things have been done for *ever* . . .'

'You don't understand, Lou,' said Myra, with mock patience. She had forgotten that Ellen was there. 'Holt was . . . Well, you weren't there. Look, that business with Gareth Holt was *inevitable*,' she said, losing all of her mock patience, as she imagined Holt wearing women's clothes, hard shoes, sad clown's make-up. She rubbed at her own red lipstick, bloodying her hands.

'Myra, my dear, his life was *ruined*. But, you know, that isn't the reason I—'

'What was *inevitable* about Gareth Holt? The fact that he was a transvestite?' asked Ellen, confused. (She couldn't keep up with a teatime conversation. It was no wonder she had lost all thread of events in Sulaymanyiah.)

'We *won*,' said Myra, ducking Susan's cigarette smoke. '*That* was inevitable. And with more MPs, we can *do* more.'

'What exactly can we do, Myra?' asked Lou, smiling, eating a spoonful of sticky apple.

'Well, we can do all the things you've talked about over the years. Finally, we can . . . Well, if only the means of capitalism could be given away,' Myra said lamely. 'Not exploited.'

Lou Matherbay laughed, long and derisively. 'Didn't some German chap with a beard say the same thing?' she asked.

Ellen pictured Purely Decorative Producer picking up her TV Prime award. 'I couldn't have done this without all the help of Dan Berkovsky, and the *FastNews* team,' she would say. 'And last but not least, thank you, Margaret Thatcher . . .' She would see Ellen, on her way out. 'Ah, Ellen,' she would say. 'Whatever became of Lou Matherbay? Come to think of it, Ellen, who *is* Lou Matherbay?'

Silence came, hovering about them. Empty of these strong women's sounds, the lounge jumped with tiny mosquito voices, anxiously clicking. The waiting staff took on more significance, bringing beef smells with them, fresh from The Carvery. Myra feigned interest in a young woman at a table nearby. *Save the Hard Rock Café*, her T-shirt said. 'Why bother?' thought Myra. 'It's just a commercial enterprise.'

'Do you want anything else?' asked a waitress, standing by with a pad.

'I don't think so,' said Myra, looking at her watch. 'We'll miss the ceremony, at this rate.'

Sickness rose and fell in Ellen's throat. 'Oh *God*,' she thought.

'Calm down, girls,' said Lou Matherbay, finishing her pastry. 'We've time for another *cake* at least.'

'In *Breaking the Barricades*, you said,' Myra started to argue. She had ordered a custard slice and was counting calories for the first time.

'Oh *don't, please,*' said Lou, laughing lightly. 'What I said was hardly ground-breaking, Myra, even at the time. Yet people constantly quote my words back at me. All that adolescent *babble*. When even my Private Member's Bill—'

'Exactly,' said Myra, as if winning a point. 'Your Private Member's Bill. I mean, women would still be having back-street abortions if it wasn't for you.'

'Yes,' said Lou, lightly. 'All about to be repealed with the Amendment Bill. So, it'll be back to the back streets for women, won't it? What a pity.' The waitress tentatively picked up a cake, with pliers. 'Wipe away some of the creamy stuff, would you?' asked Lou. 'Only I don't have the strength to do it myself.'

'You should eat the rest of your cake, Ellen,' said the MP, turning away from Myra.

'I don't *want* the rest,' said Ellen, moving the remains of one apple turnover and one cream cone around her plate. 'I'm *full,*' she said.

Ellen had spent months chasing after the MP, only to be told, over tea, that, effectively, her career was over. Why had she ever suggested filming Lou Matherbay? There was never going to be a comeback. She had disappeared from all the news bulletins, just as she had in the early eighties (after getting it all wrong about the Falklands War in '82.)

Lately, Ellen had been getting things wrong. She had lost all sense of news information values. In the context of an inter-national news agenda, for example, a bomb in the capital of Taiwan could rate lower than a flood in rural Bangladesh. Her perspective on global events had warped; events in black Africa coming closer to home than, for example, a fire on the London Underground. Should Harriet Harman take precedence over Edwina Currie in a news running order? Where did Barbara Cartland come in relation to, say, Shirley Bassey? Who was more important – Larry Beat or Ross Perot?

'What's *full* got to do with it?' asked Lou, surprised. 'I always liked that part of pregnancy the most,' she said. 'The eating for *two.*'

Myra stared at Ellen, amazed. 'You're pregnant?' she asked her.

'No, of course . . .' The moment froze. *Of course I'm*

pregnant, thought Ellen. A round, hard stomach. It was a baby, inside Ellen Abrahams. The worst place it could find to grow. 'Yes,' she said, suddenly understanding almost everything. '*Obviously.*'

'Come to think of it,' said Myra, who had never considered motherhood. 'You don't look well at *all*.'

Ellen sat cold, with something growing inside her. She would get rid of it. She would purge her stomach. It was unnatural, poisonous even. She would have to be cleaned out; scoured, with wire wool.

'She's not *ill*, Myra,' said Lou. 'She's pregnant. I was very sick during both of my pregnancies. But it's nothing to get excited about. You're feeling nothing *new*, Ellen,' she said, signalling the waitress. 'The oldest sickness since time.' Ellen Abrahams, hard golden girl, shining bright, tasted metal. She pressed her hijacked stomach. It felt like rubber, rounding like a bouncing, airtight ball. 'Can we have the bill please?' asked Lou.

'Have you finished?' the waitress asked Ellen. She took the confused movement to be a yes, tipping Myra's nibbled slice on to Ellen's filthy plate, smeared with sticky apple, flakes of pastry and wipes of cream. 'Lovely,' said Lou Matherbay, passing up her own dish, eaten clean, to be stacked. '*This* is how I plan to spend my retirement,' she said, turning to her three companions. 'Tea. The odd novel. And cake after cake after cake.'

Chapter Twenty

Susan Lyttle sat on the London–Southport coach, reading *Less Than Zero* as two children played Car Numberplates in the two-seater across the aisle. If the coach arrived on schedule at Southport Station, Susan would find her aunts at the bridge table, playing kalooki against Barbara Peabody's grandmother, Cora. Then Susan would win twenty pounds from Aunt Cyn, in one of several of their bets about her life in London.

'I bet we'll never see you in Southport again,' Aunt Cyn had said today, on the telephone. 'I bet you a fiver you will,' Susan had said. 'Too easy money,' said Aunt Cyn. 'Now that you've got a boyfriend, I don't think you'll find Southport *quite* so attractive.' 'Bet you twenty,' Susan had said, in a precisely manicured accent. She sounded London itself.

He had sandy, stiff hair, bristling like a blusher brush, and tiny, pale blue eyes, threaded with cotton-white eyelashes. His skin was sandy-pale too, like Hucklebury Finn's, and sugared generously with brown and white freckles. Sleeping, he looked sweetly soft. As he breathed, he had inflated the duvet around his stomach, rhythmically, and Susan had lain there, that morning, mesmerised by a man's life, in her bed.

She was supremely, dreadfully, pitifully in love with him. As his muscles twitched, so did Susan. He inhaled; she hugged her delicate knees to her sticky-out ribs. He breathed out; she sighed.

On Friday evening, at Silvio's party, she had danced, for the first time entwined, with Ken. And yesterday, she had spotted Ken's face all over London, not Charles Pickford's. Then she had seen him genuinely, seriously, near the Tesco cheese counter, soaked in a winter coat, beer in basket, saying: 'Susan!'; taking her out, promising dinner. 'Don't worry. I'm not like Charles,' he had said. 'He has no idea how to treat women.'

'I can't stay long,' Ken had said, on waking.

'But it's Sunday,' said Susan, beginning to beg. 'Can't we have breakfast?'

She had bagels, ready to toast. She had the smell of home-baked bread, bought yesterday in a bakery just off Ladbroke Grove, a bakery selling bread in all manner of foreign shapes and textures. She had the smell of independent living; the scent of dirty laundry and cosmetics for one; the stink of a feminine bachelor pad, chosen by choice in jar upon jar of pulses, pennies and thirsty flowers.

She had muddy blonde hair, unnaturally, if permanently, curly. She had long hair, straying past her shoulders, halfway to those narrow hips. She had night-blue eyes, chosen from a colour chart at the opticians during Contact Lens Happy Hour. She had white-with-a-hint-of-cigarette-ash skin.

She had a man, lying, alive, in her bed. 'Look. I bought this yesterday,' said Susan, coming into the bedroom. 'You just put the bagel in here,' she said. 'And you slice . . .'

Ken looked around Susan's bedroom, at her conspicuous, near-brazen consumption. 'Your new job must pay well,' he said, smelling burning bagels. 'I thought publishing paid lousy, but your standard of living seems to have gone up.

'I earn hardly anything. Actually, I was left money,' said Susan. 'By my mother and father. They died . . .'

'I'm sorry,' said Ken. 'Charles didn't tell me. That must have been hard.'

Susan felt the tears, stopping them in the nick of time. She was determined to impress on Ken not her inane sensibility but her innate sense. Because, this time, Susan hoped that at last she had found her literary hero: the man who would save her from standing still. She wanted Ken, who was polite and clean-shaven, to be her Edward Ferrers, her Mr Knightley, her Fitzwilliam Darcy. She wanted him to spend the night with her, and every night after that, stopping off at DIY stores, on his way to a suitably tragic literary end.

Scraping the bagel's burnt bits, Susan called through from the kitchen: 'Oh no, I'm not. It doesn't make me . . . All I'm saying is that without the money I couldn't have afforded *this*.' (Her tone implied that she had been offered the chance of a lifetime's supply of parenting but had opted instead for the cash.)

'And I love living off Portobello,' Susan had said. 'As Hanna says, there's always something happening.'

Inside the coach, pink people sat, on their way to Southport, reading primary-coloured novels or elementary newspapers, as motorways rushed past coach windows. Drips of drab conversation would, every so often, overreach the cries of children, and Susan saw the commonplace everywhere, and felt very cosmopolitan and very worldly, in a Hanna Thames kind of way.

Hanna had helped Susan to fill up her electronic address book with fairy-tale names like Snowy Lucas and Ginger Smithson.
    'Snowy? Is that what you were christened?' Susan had asked him.
    'I think it's got more to do with what I put up my nose,' he had said, confusingly.
    'Real name John,' whispered Hanna. 'It's the cocaine.'
    'He's a *drug addict*?'
    'Well, no,' said Hanna. 'He's not an *addict*. But I reckon that's rich coming from you who, when we first met, drank her whisky neat.'
    When Hanna had been promoted, she had put Susan's name forward as the woman to replace her at Davey Lot's.
    'They're too lazy to interview for my replacement. And you've met Jackie anyway, haven't you?'
    'Yes, at your party. But I don't have any experience as an editorial assistant,' said Susan.
    'You're motivated, aren't you?'
    'Yes, but . . .'
    'Well, that's all that matters. Jackie started off as a secretary. I'd say she'd understand you but she's become hard as nails.'

Lord Street seemed smaller from the coach window; cheaper. In Susan's absence, Aunt Jane – the greatest ambassador Southport had known – had painted the town beautiful, filling Susan's imagination, on the telephone, with its every advantage: meteorological ('The sea air's better than Florida's'); anthropological ('Just a different class of people in Southport, that's all'); or, for the tourist, all-round superiority ('Find me entertainment like *that* in the south of France!').

Fairy-lights blushed along, hanging from trees, lighting Lord Street. Susan stared at the uneven pavement; the dingy shops; the Lilliputian adverts, promising forthcoming attractions. She felt ashamed of herself, as if, due to Susan's neglect, Lord Street had shrunk, withered away, growing old like her aunts, like Aunt Jane and finally like Aunt Cyn.

On her last, and first, visit to Susan's flat in Finchley, Aunt Cyn had at last looked her age. Her beauty had all but disappeared, let down gently with the memory of it. She had looked lost, surprised to find herself standing in Susan's London flat. She had looked with envy at Susan's exposed midriff and youthful, pig-skinned stomach. Finally, she had looked for a place to sit, wrinkling down, dressed to the hilt in layers of winter clothes and wrapped in elderly jewellery: monster rings, thick gold bracelets, a throttling choker, clucking.

'You can't live here,' she had said, polluting Susan's Finchley flat with stale eau de parfum, wafted in from a different era. 'It smells *terrible*,' she said, sinking deeper into Susan's sofa. 'It smells . . . *semi-detached*. If only I'd known, I wouldn't have let you live here,' said Aunt Cyn.

'Well, I was saying to Aunt Jane,' said Susan, 'I'd rather move to Notting Hill.'

'But this is *Victor Loning* we're talking about, Susan,' continued Aunt Cyn, bewildered, as if the name *Victor*, in association with *Loning*, had always been London's last words in rented accommodation. 'Victor always had *taste*, particularly in his women,' said Cynthia. 'So, when he said he'd found somewhere for you, I thought I could trust him. He's let me down,' she said. *Again*, she thought.

'It's OK,' said Susan, flicking cigarette ash into a soapdish. 'Well, you've got some new things of course,' Aunt Cyn said, staring at Susan's wide-screen television. 'But that doesn't make up for the fact. I should have come to *see* it, I suppose . . .'

They sat there, aunt and niece, for minutes, before Aunt Cyn said: 'Now, Susan, I don't suppose I could have a cup of tea, could I? Or does this place not stretch to hot drinks?' Susan switched the kettle on, narrowing her eyes, as her aunt kicked one of her Booker prize-winners out of the way. 'And then, perhaps we can discuss the *real* reason for my visit.'

'What's the *real* reason?'

'Well, I wanted to talk to you about the shoe shop,' she said. 'Your aunt and I can't manage it any more.'

'I'm not going back to Southport,' said Susan, emphatically.

'I'm not sure *Southport* would *accept* you back,' Aunt Cyn said, as the kettle clicked off, ejaculating steam. 'Now that you're at that in-between age. Not fifteen,' she drawled. 'And not fifty.'

'We'll be selling the big house, too . . .' said Aunt Cyn.

'Seabank Road?'

'What do we need with all that space? Anyway, when it's all done and dusted, what I'm saying is, you won't be badly off. I suggest, Susan, that you spend your money *properly*. Not on those tops. You're not *developed* enough for them,' she said, raising an eyebrow at Susan's cut-off T-shirt. 'And not on unnecessary electrical items, either,' she added, finding the flex for a steam iron under her skirt.

Susan handed her aunt a cup of hot water, drowned in sour milk.

Aunt Cyn pulled at her gold choker, as if to breathe. 'I want you to rent a nice flat, with proper rooms and clean carpets. Ugh. Do I get any tea in this? Start dressing like a lady, not like some dirty boy.'

'What do you want me to do?' asked Susan, snatching back the cup, spilling the tea. '*Dress* like you do? *Act* like you?'

'Well, what's the alternative? D'you want to end up like Aunt Jane? Without a man to your name, watching life pass you by?'

Seabank Road was empty. Susan realised, searching the rooms, that she had not heard the house without sound. In the living-room, the fire was out, all doors closed. Cats, of course, clawed silently at the window. Curtains mimed life, moving in the draughty cold, but Susan wasn't taken in, not for a minute. It all smelled shut up, like a lady's bottom drawer, lined with old wallpaper.

She went upstairs to Aunt Cyn's room. Susan had once wanted it, with its memories of life as it had surely happened, with its confused rota of young men; its comings and goings in multifaceted, foreign places with names unheard of since. She had once wanted life as Aunt Cyn had lived it; its streets paved with lovers, its sky lightbulb-pink, its grass Rizla-rolled. But in a pathetic attempt at metaphor, just two of the lightbulbs remained screwed in around the mirror.

'Who's there?' called a fragile voice.

'Aunt Jane! It's me . . . Susan.'

'Susan,' said Aunt Jane, squeezing all life out of Susan with a hug. 'We thought it was burglars. Oh my goodness,' she said, releasing Susan, to look at her. 'I'm still shocked by the change in you. You don't look like Susan *at all*.'

Aunt Cyn smiled uncomfortably, as if about to break wind. 'Jane. What do *we* know? We've never had a publisher in the family. I knew that reading would come in handy. Now I was never clever. I was beautiful, so I had no use of clever. Where's my purse, Jane? I owe Susan twenty pounds,' she said, looking wildly around. 'She has *finally* won one of my bets.'

'Cyn, do you *have* to bet Susan's life away?' said Aunt Jane, leading them into the living-room, switching on lights. 'How long will you be here, darling?' she asked her niece. 'I do wish you weren't living in that riot place.'

'I can only stay a couple of days,' said Susan. 'I've got to get back.'

'For Charles, is that?' asked Cyn.

'Ken, Aunt Cyn. Not *Charles*. Ken Painter,' she said proudly.

'I thought it was *Colin*,' Jane said primly, going down on all fours to light the fire.

'Oh, you're behind the times, Jane,' said Cynthia, as Susan lit a cigarette. 'It's Ken now. *Next* week it'll be Colin. And then back to Charles.'

'Where were you just now?' asked Susan, breathing in smoke. 'I thought I'd find Cora Peabody here,' she said. 'Have you stopped playing kalooki on Sundays?'

'Of course we still play *kalooki*, Susan,' said Jane, shocked at the inference. 'Poor Cora,' she said, shaking her head, removing her head scarf. 'Barbara's brought scandal to the Peabodys. Why she had to pick a married man . . .'

'This is a special Sunday,' said Aunt Cyn, coughing at Susan's cigarette. 'Put that out, Susan. *Please*. The house is officially sold. And today, we've been the special guests of a unique retirement village, with exclusive views—'

'You've sold the house?' asked Susan, sadly. There was a six-second silence, for contemplation. 'I didn't think that would really happen. I can't imagine other people living here. What will happen to my things?'

'Your things?'

'My bed and the cats?'

'Well, we can take them with us to the retirement village,' said Aunt Cyn. 'I didn't know that you'd *left* anything here.'

'So, what is a retirement village?' asked Susan wearily.

'*Designed on a theory of space and light*,' read Aunt Jane, from a pamphlet. Susan sat on the wobbly bridge table. '*In Dudcot retirement village, home is just a helping hand away from round-the-clock care.*'

Cynthia took the pamphlet from her sister. 'Let me read that rubbish,' she said, finding her glasses and fiddling them on. 'Now, let's see what they say.

'*Dudcot retirement village, close to the heart of Southport, yet far enough away*,' she read. 'What's that supposed to mean? *Dudcot retirement village. The Last Word In Growing Old Gracefully*. Well, Susan? What do you say? Does it sounds as if it's *us*?' She raised her eyebrows theatrically, as Susan stood up, towering above her aunts. 'You know, in London I'm known as . . . I'm now . . . My name's Susie,' the tall girl said, her eyes elsewhere.

Myra Felt threw out everything, from multicoloured tights to moulding food. She threw away pamphlets and banners, and badges, and rosettes. She dumped batteries that had been dead for years. She chucked fluorescent clothes and tube tickets, stained Chinese teabags and folding, tearing text-books. If there was a corner, she would clean it; if there was a drawer, she would dust it; and if there was a mark, she would scrub it. She found loose ends indiscriminately, and tied them up, all the time eating calories and listening to the news on the television.

Myra Felt was twenty-six, and in need of an ordered life, to keep her from insanity or flavoured facial washes; special offer promotions; temporary, thoughtless men; Cartier cigarettes; and empty shoe boxes, stuffed with unnecessary letters, all mentioning love.

If she didn't start underlining newspapers or making lists, she would be useless to anyone, because ill-considered opinions on an Independent Nuclear Deterrent or Terylene nappies wouldn't buy her votes in next May's elections, where Myra was a prospective councillor, or a lifetime with her lover, Jack Temple, whose only caveat to a promise of commitment was Myra's sloppy drawers, packed with junk.

So she sat on the tube, underlining *The Economist* and ignoring her man, occasionally looking up to glare at the thin lady opposite, whose metabolic rate was exceeding the maximum speed limit, breaking down food as she spoke. 'My boyfriend,' thought Myra, looking at the man sitting beside her, 'has lost his looks to time.' She surprised herself by using words, even thoughtfully, that were better written down. He had lost some hair, certainly (the lunatic fringe had disappeared), and an elasticity in the skin. He had lost, surely, some height, as well as the cardboard stomach. And, although he was confident one day of rediscovering the *stomach* – underneath folding fat, or inside a fully-equipped private gym – Myra had been disappointed to detect, as they met at a Pluralist conference, an unhealthy cynicism even in *Jack*, who had been the one, all those years ago, in 1991, to introduce her to politics. Jack Temple, who, according to Marion, had led Myra astray to a life of active participation; in demonstrations, marches and *society*.

'Why are you here?' she had asked. 'I thought you, out of anyone, would be New Labour.'

'When really I'm just old and tired,' he had quipped. 'No, I'm not a Pluralist. I'm a lobbyist. Rockform Tactics. We're small but *important* . . .'

Since Myra had had a short-lived romance with Jack Temple at university, he had developed a sense of humour. Or was it a sense of irony? Either way, he now had a dry wit, which followed Myra around as she sold Pluralism to the press, behind the scenes, at conferences. She was conscious of Jack listening to her talk as if she was a press officer – in bullet points.

'The reason Lou Matherbay resigned is because:

– She never even hinted at wanting to be leader.
– She had reached her career's natural end.
– She will eventually go up to the House of Lords as a Pluralist.
– She recognised Ray Hines as the party's obvious leader.'

'You didn't used to like explanations,' Jack had said, shadowing her.

'What did I like then?' asked Myra.

'Well, I suppose just about everything else.'

Myra remembered Jack as he had been, persuading her into politics; persuading her of the need to campaign. And she had marvelled, too, at the change in herself; from the type that screamed, just seven months ago, at demonstrations, to the type that screamed at television editors, when they wouldn't give Pluralists a proper place in their running orders.

Myra, inevitably, remembered her university lifestyle, when there had been too many people calling themselves friends, or calling her up, or just popping round. Even post-university she had had too many friends for too few chairs in her flat. But now, her two-seater sofas, bought by Flatmate to fill up with Myra's friends, were empty. 'I'm sick of them sitting on my rug, spilling food.'

Had Myra dropped her overflow friends, or had her overflow friends dropped Myra? Either way, she had grown familiar with the machine which would unnecessarily inform her: 'You have *no* messages.' She had grown familiar with a painfully empty, rented flat; there just for Myra when she returned home, after working late at the House. Even Flatmate was absent, constantly with a Boyfriend Up North.

Friends such as Kasha or Steve, Jenny or Rob, had all disappeared into other people's squats or on youth-hostel world tours, leaving behind useless telephone numbers in Myra's old address book that she didn't know whether to transfer. Since her trip to Peyarth, Myra hadn't even seen Marion. They had talked to each other's answering machines, for a while. Which had been a form of friendship.

She couldn't possibly contact, or be contacted by, any former friends in political campaigns. Now that Myra was absolutely a Pluralist – even accepting nomination as the party's prospective council candidate – she wasn't able to continue that type of 'single-issue' friendship, formed just for the duration of one's belief.

Inside work, she liked the company of Sara Cinnamon, chewing the fat of politics with her, over sandwiches and endlessly emptied red wine bottles. She had begun to drink with Larry Beat and Billy Todd, too, blurring the line between the personal and the political. This despite the fact that Myra had, at one time, found it difficult to talk to men at any length when they were beyond the age of sexual corruption.

But Myra, in age at least, was beginning to catch up with her parents. And, now that they all knew the value of money, Myra was beginning to spend more time with Roger and Penny. Well, there was more to chat about. Myra reasoned, what was to separate her mother and father from her other friends: Larry, Sara and Billy? They would have fitted in at any one of Myra's planned dinner parties.

And it was all reason enough for Myra not to decline Jack Temple, when he invited her back to his hotel bedroom. Because, although not as attractive a proposition as seven years earlier, Myra had reached a stage in life where she was bound to accept. Because it was not just Jack Temple who had piled on the years, or the pounds. Myra was not as skinny, or as pretty. She would not look good in a flowered, poppied field with the light shining just so, never mind a ladies' leotard, hugging every nook and cranny. She could only locate a couple of nooks now, and would have been hard pressed to find a cranny. Myra's one enduring, beautiful feature – a great pair of eyes – she counted as two, hoping that Jack did as well, as he gazed at her inside his hotel room.

Inside his room, this time, he had given her a pamphlet, not about politics, but about his own lobbying organisation, boasting success. And this time, she had not wanted to spend the night, but had made her excuses and left. In his London room, another time, she had slept with him, deciding that Jack Temple – despite having lost the body which lived up to the name – was, nonetheless, a better bet than nights spent at supermarket checkouts saying *Eight Items Or Less*, which might just as well have said *Cooking For One*.

So that now they sat on the tube, she reading *The Economist*, he looking up flats in the *Evening Standard* for the two of them to share. 'Brixton's cheap,' he said, scribbling furiously in the margin. 'If you like riots,' Myra said, drily.

'Myra,' said a familiar voice.

'Marion.'

'How are you?'

'God, I wouldn't have recognised you. You look so different now.'

'I haven't talked to you for so long! Not since . . .'

'Beginning of August. When I'd just arrived in Peyarth,' said Myra helpfully. She would have preferred to have been the one standing up. 'God, that seems ages ago. Since *that* election, I've been busy with another one, of course. Ray Hines' leadership campaign.'

'I'm sorry?' asked Marion. She had not been aware of Ray Hines or, indeed, of any leadership election. *Vox populi est vox diaboli*, thought Myra. *There's never an excuse for ignorance.*

'Forgive Myra,' said Jack possessively. 'She thinks the world revolves around the Pluralists. I've tried to tell her how unnecessary they are.'

Marion looked from Myra to Jack, registering the renewed relationship. 'It's Jack Temple, isn't it?'

'Yes, do I . . . ?'

'No, you won't remember me.'

'I'm sorry I haven't been in touch. But I've been so busy. Did you know, I've decided to stand for election, as a councillor?' bragged Myra. 'And then, who knows? They're talking about finding me a parliamentary seat, to nurture *properly . . .*'

'No, I didn't,' said Marion. 'Did you know about Grog's record deal?'

'No, I didn't,' said Myra.

There was a painful gap in the conversation. Jack felt it, filling it. 'What do you think to Highgate?' he asked Marion. 'We're trying to decide where to live.' He unfolded a pocket tube map, as if it would signpost their dream location.

'I don't think Highgate's the most interesting of places,' Marion said, evaluating Myra's long black tailored coat and her face that looked pinched in the wrong places. 'Well, *I* wouldn't like to live there,' Marion added quickly, staring at Myra's just-varnished nails. 'I prefer a place with more life. With stuff going on.'

'You know, I don't have time for *stuff*, any more,' said Myra. When she wasn't at a strategy meeting or in a policy group, she was on a planning committee, or dry-cleaning her clothes. When she wasn't having on-the-record chats with 'real people', she was having off-the-record chats with journalists. In her spare time, she was turning straight to the *Time In* section of the listings magazine *Time Out,* ignoring the clubs, the theatre and the comedy altogether. Despite the occasional professional dinner party, Myra was spending her time reading TV listings, highlighting the documentaries, and filling and emptying the dishwasher.

'My stop,' said Marion, relieved. 'I'll give you a ring,' she said, lying.

'Yeah. I'll call you,' said Myra, lying.

'I *do* remember her,' said Jack, as Marion vanished into crowds at King's Cross. 'She was that dirty one, always just back from some drugs 'n' music fest. Is that right?'

'Yeah. So what's the cheapest area?' Myra asked him, having reached the end of this week's *Economist.*

'Cheap and meaningful. Cheap and meaningful,' he muttered, scanning the tube map. 'How about Wimbledon?' he asked, circling a large chunk of the district line.

'But it's at the end of the line,' said Myra.

'Miles from all that *smog*.'

'Miles from *work*.'

'Well let's compromise then. I like Battersea.'

'And I don't.'

The train stopped, to gorge on commuters. 'How about here? Euston?' he asked. "It's *expensive*,' she said.

'I bet you'll be glad to leave Camden,' said Jack, as they emerged to face station pushers, offering them drugs, homelessness magazines, joss sticks, candles and confectionery. 'It's so bloody urban.'

'It *has* changed,' agreed Myra, treading on a sleeping junkie.

'For fuck's sake, FUCK OFF,' the junkie screamed, wrapping half of himself in the *Daily Telegraph*.

'It's the end of an era,' said Myra.

Its organs were fully functioning, that much was certain. Ellen recalled the sickness, the screaming crowd of baby faces. Her coffee had spilled over, staining her dungarees as the announcement came. It had panicked her; she had wiped up the mess, the pool of black coffee, and in the panic she hadn't listened out for her name, her name on the GP's waiting list, called out that Tuesday. Oh, Ellen had expected it all right; she had been aware of her test at home; its thin blue line, along with Lou Matherbay's assurance and Jeffrey Bell's confirmation that, yes, she must be pregnant. But then, Ellen Abrahams had to think about so many things. It was too much to expect her to know that there was a baby inside her, one inside the other, as if Ellen was a Russian doll.

Thick, disinfected sounds garbled their way from the adjacent hall through to the room where Ellen sat, her baby swallowing amniotic fluid, her growing uterus displacing other organs. As her image of the GP's waiting room went blank, Ellen picked up her *A-Z of Babies' Names*, considering the names Fidelia, Prudence and Candice Connaught, as black leggings swelled around the bump. She liked the long names, the ones littered with consonants, the ones she remembered from her ante-natal conversations with Aurelie, who was fat with anticipated twins, in her class. They had all been weighed up and thought about in the bath and with her fiancé, where decision upon decision was made, and fact read up on, as Ellen and Jeffrey ran out of time.

Ellen Abrahams had facts at her fingertips: information on chorionic villus sampling, foetoscopy, and amniocentesis; lists of pelvic-floor exercises and pre-eclampsia indications; pre-natal advice centres and protein tests; columns of drugs, dietary advice, and disposable nappies; tables of hospital care, health visitors and homoeopathic remedies. She knew everything, or thought she did, that icy afternoon in October 1996, as white colours shone light from the walls, and a Jamaican care assistant, Rosa Riley, stiff inside a striped uniform, interrupted her thoughts to ask if Ellen was ready to see her mum, as she had just woken up and was excited at the prospect of a reunion with her daughter.

She led Ellen out of the nursing-home lounge and into the

maze of carpeted halls, shaken and vacuumed with smells, reminiscent of airspray heather and elderly urine. They walked along, these two tall women, passing door after identical grey door. The care assistant cooled the heated corridors with her breezy Jamaican accent, while Ellen's small voice limped along, with comments about the cold snap and the bottled-milk scare.

'Your mum's our youngest resident,' said Rosa, who had found Miriam's door, complete with name-plate, just in case they all should forget. 'And the most *popular.*' And, as they walked through the grey door, Ellen's stomach jumped to the tune of her baby, fluttering about like butterflies.

A pale imitation of Mum faced Ellen, as Rosa asked them if they would like coffee. To the right of Miriam, on a table, sat a jug of water, ready to fill two glasses. Ellen could hear Mum's wriggling voice, throughout her childhood. 'Barry! I am *not* drinking water. I'm *not*. You know I hate it neat.'

'No, thank you,' said Ellen. She was tempted towards a trestle table, towards shameless piles of potboiler novels and Life In The Royal Family hardbacks, full as they were of sex and short, easy-to-swallow sentences.

'You shouldn't read such *rubbish*,' Ellen said, for want of a more appropriate opening to their conversation, as Rosa left them to it. She picked up one of the hardbacks, flicking through and finding glossy photographs of the Prince and the Princess of Wales. '*Despite the press rumours,*' one of the captions read, '*one only has to look at Charles and Diana to see that they are, and always will be, very much in love.*'

'It's my Ellie,' said Ellen's mum at last, fixing her eyes on her daughter. 'Let me look at my daughter. And at the baby bump,' she said in a voice reminiscent of Miriam Abrahams, columnist with the *Kenton Gazette*. Her right hand went up to her mouth. 'Well, whaddoyouknow? You're *big.*'

The words, mashed up and yelled like that, concerned Ellen. She rested her hands on her stomach. '*Unless care is taken,*' thought Ellen, overwhelmed by the number of pregnancy-care books she had consumed, '*the presence of loud, female relations may result in miscarriage.*'

'Do you have to shout?' she asked, sitting on Mum's bed with a book on her lap, open at a photograph of a very pregnant

Princess. 'I want my baby to hear nice things in the womb . . .'

'Well, *you* heard me, didn't you? Oh, Ellie, did I ever tell you how you looked when you came out? Barry and I both agreed. Like a *rat,* we said.'

'Oh, please don't start all that again,' said Ellen, looking around the room for entertainment. She itched to open the mini-fridge.

'So, why haven't you come before?' asked Mum, as Ellen opened the mini-fridge.

'I haven't had time,' said Ellen, finding it empty. She had prepared herself for this question, indeed for every possible question. After all, the last time Ellen had seen Mum, she had screamed: 'Friedl, is that you? I thought you'd died in the camps.'

Miriam beckoned Ellen, gesturing wildly. 'Ellie, be careful. They poison the food here,' she whispered loudly, through fat fingers. 'I even had to throw it out the window. Go and find it if you want. Have it checked. Only don't tell anyone here. Or they'll get me in other ways.'

'Oh, not that again,' said Ellen. 'I poisoned you. Darren poisoned you. Then *Safeway's* poisoned you.'

'I *knew* you wouldn't believe me,' interrupted Miriam, stretching all sense from her vowels. She crossed her arms, harrumphing, like a sulking child. 'I knew you wouldn't,' she screamed.

'I said don't shout,' said Ellen, losing it; trying to remember her relaxation techniques. '*Visualising a peaceful, relaxing scene may help you relax,*' she muttered, thinking of her house in Harrow-on-the-Hill; clean and packed with old friends.

Jeffrey had returned home yesterday with three types of buggy brochure. He had found the couch full. Helen, Elizabeth and Lucy sat with a lisping Bridie, eating apple pie on the three-seater. Ellen was on the floor, with her own plate of pie, reading *The National Childbirth Trust Book of Pregnancy, Birth and Parenthood.* Between forkfuls of apple, the sofa girls were competing over the lengths to which their men would go to hurt their respective women.

'Well, I don't see how you can compare what Darren did to Solly's treatment of me generally!'

'Excuse *me*, but I think being told you're just not up to it by your man is pretty awful actually. I mean *sorry*, Ellen. I know I'm going out with your brother but . . .'

'At least you can afford to live on what your father gives you,' said Bridie. 'I have to rely on handouts from Tom all the time. I mean, he always wants to eat out and I just can't afford to.'

'You know, you can all fall back on your families. But I need to rely on Darren for *everything*.'

'I think it's worse to be told you're not up to it, than being dumped after *two weeks*. I thought Brian . . .'

'Ellen, I don't think you should be sitting on the floor,' said Jeffrey, who had come in on Elizabeth's lament. 'How can you read through this racket anyway, Ellie?' he asked Ellen, who was still consuming facts about motherhood, and apple pie.

'Please, don't *call* me that,' said Ellen.

'I just can't believe that Brian and I are *over*,' said Elizabeth, ignoring Jeffrey, who was loudly helping himself to the pie on the table.

'Well, at least it hasn't been long,' Helen said. 'Solly's been dumping me, on and off, for *years* . . .'

'Oh, for God's sake,' groaned Jeffrey. The apple pie ate all the room on his plate, greedily spilling over the sides for space. 'Pur-lease. Ellen's told me I've got to try and get on with you all but, you know, I'm actually living here now. It's my home and I can't cope with it being taken over every five minutes, by women and their *anxieties*. Ellen, I've been thinking,' Jeffrey had said, picking apple from his teeth. 'Any chance we can call it Jeremy?'

'Boy or girl, Jeremy it *isn't*,' said Ellen. 'My child is *not* going to grow up into a social stereotype.'

'What are you going to call it then?' Ellen's mum asked, pulling at strands of wire-wool hair.

'That's for *me* to decide,' said Ellen, lying on the stiff bed. 'Don't start interfering. Or I won't visit you again.'

'So, there's not going to be a wedding now?'

'Oh yes, you'd love *that*,' snapped Ellen. 'That would really suit you. Drawing attention to yourself. Look at my daughter! Four months pregnant, walking up the aisle. That would be *just* your style. Over the top, as ever.'

'So, there's not going to be a wedding now?'

'You just *said* that. For God's sake.'

'You know, I'll tell you who won't like that. Frankie Bell. She won't like that at all, Frankie won't. Will she? You know what we called her in Kenton? Tight Knickers,' she yelled. 'Tight-Arsed Knickers. That's what we called her.' She was tearful with laughter.

Shut up,' hissed Ellen. 'You're disturbing *everyone* . . .'

'Tight Drawers. We called her that. Honest to God. Tight Knickers. Frankie Bell. Honest,' she said, sobering quickly. 'Ellie,' she asked, 'have you come to take me home?'

In the space of a month, Frankie Bell had gone through a year's soap opera's worth of emotions, from fury, through disappointment, through grief, to pleasure. She was now the perfect granny-to-be; insisting that Ellen eat for a family of five; changing Hoover bags in Harrow-on-the-Hill; and rifling through loft boxes for Jeffrey's baby things.

'I can't wait for you to see what I've found,' she had said yesterday on the phone. 'Plimsolls labelled *Left* and *Right*. He had them when he was five years old. Because he had no sense of direction *at all*.'

When she had heard the news, Frankie had raised her voice. 'I can't bel . . . No, you can't . . . What will happen with the wedding? It's in two weeks! Everything's booked! I *knew* something would go wrong with you. I confirmed the band yesterday. Oh, I should have known, coming out of Miriam, that you'd be . . . This is going to be as bad as the Glickenstein scandal. This is going to be as bad as . . .' She could not think of as great a matching scandal. '*Ber*nie' she had wailed. '*Bernie*. Come here. I *need* you . . .'

Eventually, however, Frankie had come to terms with the fact that she wasn't going to have her dream wedding. Then, she had become excited at the prospect of a baby Bell; another Jeffrey, writ small. She had filled up Ellen's house with cots and prams and posh, quilted baby outfits, saying: 'Don't stretch like that. You mustn't eat cheese. It's bad for the baby. Look after your body, Ellen. There's a baby in there, not a pound of *bananas*.'

'Mummy, I can't move in with Ellen. What would the community say?' Jeffrey had said.

'Who cares?' argued Frankie, cooing over Ellen's stomach. 'I don't mind *what* anyone says. You should move in with Ellen. You're a man now. There are consequences to your actions.'

So Jeffrey Bell had moved his belongings from Hendon to Ellen's Harrow-on-the-Hill house. His brown pyjamas clashed with her purple duvet. His CDs – Imagination and Fat Larry's Band – stood at the front of Ellen's collection. His grey suits battled with hers inside the wardrobe. His Mickey Mouse clock had woken Ellen up with its huge head, ticking alarmingly in time with monstrous, swaying arms.

Ellen wanted to be alone, to lie on her bed, learning about colostrum and lanugo and alpha-foeto protein. She wanted to be alone with the feeling of bubbles, gently popping inside. She wanted to buy Jeffrey out of his share in the baby. She wanted to own it completely, to have and to hold. Living in Ellen, it seemed to give her life.

Now that she had come to terms with being pregnant, she had had to tell Jeffrey. That Monday, he had been in Ellen's study, surfing the Internet. 'Ellen, you should hear this about Slobodan Milosevic.'

'I have something to tell you,' his fiancée had said, shaking her test stick at the door and praying for one of the blue lines to vanish.

'This is *so funny*,' said Jeffrey. 'Listen to this.'

'I'm pregnant,' she had said, feeling as if she was playing a part in a popular, prime-time telemovie on cable.

'I take it back. It's absolutely *hilarious*.'

'You're going to be a father, Jeffrey. I'm having a baby.'

She had left the room, leaving him to tap her computer keyboard. She had heard him tap, slowing down as seconds passed. Eventually, the tapping had stopped and Jeffrey had appeared at her bedroom door.

'Is it definite?' he had asked.

'Almost. But I've got an appointment at the clinic tomorrow. Then, I'll be told for sure.'

'I've been thinking,' he had said. 'Now that you say... Well, lucky I persuaded you to go for the three bedrooms. "You never know," I said, when you were looking. Do you remember, I said that? You wanted that maisonette, next to Northwick

Park Hospital, and I said: "No, wait a minute . . ." '

'No,' mumbled Ellen, turning over on to her stomach, to squash the foetus flat.

Later, Jeffrey had woken her up with a plate of vegetarian sausages. 'I think you should eat,' he had said, putting the plate next to her nose, on the bed. 'Ugh. No, *please*,' said Ellen.

'I want you to look after yourself.'

'I'm sorry about the wedding,' she had mumbled.

'Well, I'll talk to Mother,' Jeffrey had said, kneeling beside her bed. 'We may not have to postpone it. I mean, we'll do what everyone wants. Except . . . Ellen, I want you to give up *FastNews*.' He had stroked her hair.

'I *can't*,' said Ellen, looking at Jeffrey. How could she give up a career at *FastNews*, now that the most important film of her career hadn't even been made? She imagined herself at home, looking after a baby, with nothing more pressing on her mind than a full Hoover bag, joining a health club, drinking cranberry juice on the top floor of Harvey Nichols, holidaying in a brochure pull-out part of Wales, sleeping, occasionally, *free* of everything nastily competitive, like TV Prime awards. She would put the baby in for competitions. Maybe it could do some child modelling? Or, if it grew into an actress, or a dancer, or an award-winning film director? 'Unless you really think . . . ?'

He had lain down beside her, loving her. 'I *do* think. I really *do* think.'

'Well, I'll think about it.' She had loved him, kissing him, saying suddenly: 'Maybe I'll put all my energies into this baby. Bring up the *perfect* child . . .'

Her expression had terrified him.

'So, when do I meet your young man?' Miriam asked, pressing a red buzzer.

'Why are you pushing that button? What do you want?'

'I want to meet this Jeffrey, Ellie. Is that so much to ask?' She pressed urgently.

'Don't. Press. That.'

'Darren says he's wet as a weekend in Manchester.' She laughed. 'But I think he'll be *dishy*.'

'I doubt Darren said that. I doubt very much . . .' She tried to move Miriam's hand. 'Leave that alone. D'you want someone to come in?'

'You never liked *people*,' she shouted, keeping her finger firmly on the button. 'Why do you always hate people?'

'*Please*.' Their hands wrestled for a while. 'Stop it. Oh, I see. You're going to say something about me. Am I right? That I'm the *worst* daughter? God knows what you've said already.'

'I just want to meet Frankie Bell's son,' she said, her accent controlled. 'The son of Tight Knickers,' she said dramatically. 'I just want to see him for five minutes, OK?'

Rosa came in. 'What did you want then, Mirry-um?' she asked. 'Sounded urgent.' Ellen shot looks at her mother.

'It's Ellen here,' Mum said, raising dying dog eyes as Ellen glared. 'My daughter wants *coffee*,' she said at last. 'Milk, no sugar.'

'I'll bring you some chocolate cake too,' she said. 'For Mirry-um, my favourite.'

'I tell you. You want to talk about babies? That girl's got them coming out of her ears,' Miriam said, as Rosa left.

'She can probably *hear* you,' said Ellen.

'So, do I get to meet him?' asked Miriam. 'I can come to your house, for supper?'

'Don't push it, Mum. I'll bring Jeffrey here.'

Miriam sat on the chair, picking up a telephone directory. 'You know, I can ring whoever I want. There's no stopping me. Do you want to ring someone, Ellie?'

'No,' said Ellen. 'Put that away. When the house money runs out . . .'

'No, you don't understand,' she said. 'I don't *pay*. Everything comes free, because of my *money*, from the hardware shops. Do you want to watch the TV?'

'No, I don't.'

'I always watch you, you know. Darren tells me when you're on,' she said. ' "That's my daughter," I say.'

'Try and talk *quietly*,' Ellen said. 'I don't even work there any more.'

There was silence.

'So, d'you really watch *FastNews?*' asked Ellen.

'Of course. I watch it every night. It's a real party in here.

You should see me. "That's Ellie. That's my daughter," I say. I mean, they're all old here. Some are mad, even. "The Loopy lot," I call 'em. But we all cheer when your name comes up. Look, Ellie, do you want to take the TV? Take it. You can have it, you know. Really, I don't need it.'

'So, what do you think of the programme?'

'Well, I don't like *all* of it. I don't watch the news,' she shouted. 'No one watches the news, do they?' she asked, as Rosa brought in coffee for two, on unsteady feet. 'But I watch the rest. I watch your name come up at the end.'

She had cancelled her newspapers. She had walked to Ranjit Singh's newsagent, for something to do. The tiny shop, unimaginatively described as *Newsagent. Proprietor: Ranjit Singh,* stood unkempt, like a newly arrived immigrant in between old established shops selling bread, furniture, meat and flowers. 'Hello, Ranjit,' Ellen had said, still taking pride in their acquaintance. 'But, what is this?' asked Ranjit, smiling broadly, with brilliantly white teeth. 'It is not Sunday today.'

'I'm here,' said Ellen Abrahams, steeling herself for Ranjit's disappointment, 'to cancel all the newspapers. All my magazines. Everything.'

Ranjit Singh pulled his ledger towards him. 'You will be moving away?' he had asked. 'You will be taking the news in another place? This girl is a journalist,' Ranjit had said, by way of explanation, to a woman buying chocolate. 'A clever girl. Gets all the news from my shop.'

Ellen read a headline on the cover of a woman's magazine. *How To Have Sex Without Really Trying.*

'She used to read them all,' said Ranjit sadly. '*The Economist,* the *Spectator* and the *New Statesman,* the *New Yorker* – after all that trouble to get it in – *Time, Newsweek,* that *African News Digest . . .*'

'Yes, I know,' said Ellen.

'Every Sunday paper, the *Bookseller, Harpers . . .* She wants to see everything, this girl.'

'Well, I'm afraid I don't need them now.'

'But it doesn't have to be all or nothing, does it?' he had asked. 'Will you be wanting to cancel it *all*?'

'You don't have to give up TV,' Ellen's editor, Dan Berkovsky,

227

had informed her. 'It doesn't have to be all or nothing, Ellen.'

She had interrupted him watching a training video, *Violence on Television: An Editor's Worst Nightmare*. Berkovsky had listened to her resignation speech, with half an eye on a rather dramatic Bosnian shoot-out.

Through the glass wall of the editor's office, Ellen had watched Dark Young Buck screaming 'Yeee-eesss', sweeping his hands through wholesome, mahogany hair. 'Got him,' he had told the *FastNews* room, standing up, legs primitively apart, chest expanding, as if he had scored a try on the rugby pitch. Gentlemen, in their natural habitat, had glanced up at Dark Young Buck, with pride. He was one of theirs: ruddy cheeks, the result of centuries of good eating, and a neck that swallowed his chin as he talked.

'Who have you got then, Tark?' Blond Young Buck had asked, passing through the office on his way to promotion. 'Only the next but one Russian President's aide,' said Dark Young Buck. 'Alexander Lebed?' asked Blond. 'The very same,' said Dark. And, in quieter voice: 'Lebed's aide.' 'Yeee-esss,' said Blond, and Ellen and Dan Berkovsky had watched them, through the glass, clapping hands in the air, like black ghetto kings in New York, excluding women the world over.

Inside the glass walls, Berkovsky had tried sarcasm on Ellen. 'As far as I can make out, you're only having *a baby*,' he had said. 'Not a nervous breakdown. And, you know, these days Ellen, women do *have* careers with their babies.'

'I know,' said Ellen. 'But I want to do it properly.'

'Well, is there anything I can say to change your mind?' Berkovsky had asked, leaning back in his swivel chair, hands behind his head, revealing dried-on sweat patches on his under-arms. 'Because, you know, you are the *one producer* on my team that could have made it.'

Made it where? thought Ellen. She had long ago drifted away to life outside newsrooms, frozen screen people and neat slices of sound.

'It's not because of your Matherbay film that wasn't, is it?' he had asked. 'I mean, I think Malcolm will win the award for *FastNews* anyway. So you don't have to worry about *that*.'

'I'm just sorry she didn't stand as leader in the end.'

'Yeah, it did rather change things,' her editor had said. 'I mean, *nobody's* interested in her now, are they?

'Now, this is *supreme*,' said Miriam, enjoying a slice of chocolate cake. 'I love this. They don't poison the cake here,' she said. 'They do poison the potatoes. But they don't bother with this.'

'Oh, what a *surprise*. They only poison the food *you* don't like.'

'Taste this, Ellie,' said Miriam, leaning over Ellen. 'Go on, taste it. It's only chocolate cake.' Her breath smelt of institutional food.

'I don't want any. Stop forcing food down me all the time.'

'I know you like chocolate,' she said, taking her hand. 'I understand you. I mean, I'm your mum, remember.'

You'll never understand me, thought Ellen.

She wouldn't visit her mother again. This would be the last time. After all, she was soon to have the responsibility of her own child.

'You can see the change in her,' said Rosa Riley, leading Ellen out, through corridors. 'She'd be fine at home now, we think.'

'Oh, she's much better off here,' said Ellen. 'You're all doing *such* a good job with her *here*.'

'Well, here we are then,' said Rosa, as they reached the exit. 'Thank you for coming. Mirry-um says you're a television presenter. So it can't be easy.'

'Not at all,' said Ellen. 'Thank *you*.'

Rosa thought how lucky Ellen was to have such a glamorous job in television. To bring up her four, she had had to give up nursing. For many years, she had been stuck with the smell of dirty nappies, the sounds of toddlers, and launderette washing machines. No doubt, this Ellen would get some nanny in to do her dirty work, while she got on with life, rushing about, meeting people. How happy Rosa had been, to return to work. Now, having adult conversations, feeling a sense of purpose, she realised what it was like to be alive.

'How much longer?' asked Rosa, smiling and pointing.

'About five months.'

'You looking forward to being a mum?'

'I can't wait,' said Ellen. 'It'll be wonderful.'

In truth, Ellen was bored at home. There hadn't been any lunches at Harvey Nichols with friends. ('How can I, Ellen? I'm *working*.') There hadn't been any new clothes. ('With you not working, how can we afford *holidays*?') If the house was always clean, there was nothing left for her to clean. And she knew everything there was to know about motherhood. (There was only a limited amount of information out there.) *Still*, she thought, walking away from Rosa, *as soon as the baby's born, I'll feel more in control.*

'Well, I have four,' Rosa yelled. 'And let me tell you, enjoy your freedom now.'

But the pregnant woman caught just one word. 'Thank you,' she shouted.

Only five more months, thought Ellen. *And then I'm free . . .*